## What Others are Saying About *The*

"*The Ghost Box* is a triumph of unfettered creativity. Ancient relics, paranormal happenings, and epic schemes—this one has them all. Fans of shows like *Warehouse 13* and The *X-Files* will love it."

—Kerry Nietz, award-winning author of *Amish Vampires in Space*

"In *The Ghost Box*, Mike Duran brings us the very best of contemporary supernatural noir. Every genre trope is given its due, and then spun on its head. The tragic back stories, the haunted protagonist (in more ways than one), and the eccentric gatekeeper staving off Armageddon. The wry wit of the narrative keeps the reader smiling even through the grim ironies of the plot, as if the horrors of Lovecraft were being described by Raymond Chandler. Not afraid to call its own bluff, *Ghost Box* makes the incredible credible as it introduces us to concepts that feel as though they just might exist in some arcane corner of the world. Terror and glory abound as the reader alternates between goose bumps, laughter, and tears. I, for one, am very much looking forward to the next Reagan Moon adventure."

—Robert Mullin, Author of *Bid the Gods Arise*

"*The Ghost Box* has all the things that make Mike Duran's writing so good: unique characters, evil from another realm, and atmospheric description. Duran does a great job capturing the right voice for an urban fantasy, and kept me turning pages with smooth pacing and action that built steadily throughout the story."

—Kat Heckenbach, author of the *Toch Island Chronicles*

"A love for genre fiction runs strong through this novel, as well as a fascination for the weird and the offbeat. And yet Mike Duran makes it all work and keeps the pages turning while his protagonist falls ever deeper down the rabbit hole. You've got a struggling investigative journalist, arcane relics, a labyrinthine plot, a clever variation on the femme fatale, and an evil so great that it takes your breath away. This novel is audacious, brash, free-wheeling, and utterly fearless. It's also straight-up fun. I had a blast getting to know Reagan Moon and can't wait for him to save the world again."

—Johne Cook, former editor, *Ray Gun Revival*

"A Koontz-ian supernatural thriller, with a dash of *Warehouse 13* and *Max Payne*. Thoroughly enjoyed *The Ghost Box*. A wry, easy voice rides deep and dark currents. Don't read this with the lights out."

—Patrick Todoroff, author of *Running Black*

"With echoes of Jim Butcher, *The Ghost Box* by Mike Duran is urban fantasy at its brainiest. Hardboiled tabloid reporter, Reagan Moon, gets caught up in a supernatural roller coaster when he discovers a dark, steamy side of Los Angeles where psychics are murdered and mysterious billionaires vie for Moon's services. *Ghost Busters* meets *The Dresden Files* in this page-turner."

–Merrie Destefano, author of *Afterlife: The Resurrection Chronicles* and *Feast: Harvest of Dreams*

*About the Author*

MIKE DURAN is a novelist, blogger, and speaker, whose short stories, essays, and commentary have appeared in *Relief Journal*, *Relevant Online*, *Rue Morgue* magazine, *Zombies!* magazine, and other print and digital outlets. He is the author of the supernatural thriller *THE RESURRECTION* (Realms 2011), which was a finalist in the 2011 INSPY awards, an e-book fantasy novella entitled *WINTERLAND* (Oct. 2011), *THE TELLING* (Realms May 2012), and *SUBTERRANEA* (Blue Crescent Press Oct. 2012). Mike contributes monthly commentary at *Novel Rocket*, one of Writer's Digest 101 Most Helpful Websites for Writers. Mike is an ordained minister and lives with his wife and four grown children in Southern California. Mike's novels explore the boundaries of belief, the fragile tether between science and superstition, the depths of despair and the reaches of faith. You can learn more about Mike Duran, his writing projects, cultural commentary, and arcane interests, at www.mikeduran.com.

# THE GHOST BOX

MIKE DURAN

Mike Duran
THE GHOST BOX
A Reagan Moon Novel


Published by Blue Crescent Press
ISBN 978-0-9909077-1-8

*Acknowledgements*

Many thanks to my writing partners Merrie, Becky, Rachel and Paul; to beta readers of *The Ghost Box*, Melody, Mirtika, Kat, Jay, and Merrie; to my faithful blog readers and social media friends for their interest, support, and encouragement in my writing projects. Huge thanks to my literary agent, Rachelle, for her wisdom and professionalism. Thanks to Jill Domschot for her editorial prowess and to Kirk DouPonce for his fantastic cover design. My wife, Lisa, our 4 children and their families, for their ongoing love and laughter. Zoe, who despite eating my iPod, I still miss. And to my readers, for growing with me. Thank you!

# CHAPTER 1

IF I REALLY HAD MAGICAL POWERS, that's the day I should have used them.

It was February the 18th and the moment I saw Blondie waiting at my apartment door, I remembered the date. The number 18 has always been significant for me. I said *significant*, not lucky. I don't believe in luck, especially now that Ellie's gone. Nevertheless, that number seems to pop up in the oddest places. Like the car accident that put me into a two-week coma. It happened on Highway 18. I received fifty-four stitches (that's 18, thrice) across the back of my right shoulder after escaping from organ traffickers at their Malibu Canyon ranch. Then there's my apartment number, which Blondie was standing and looking at.

Despite what you may be thinking, Blondie was not some curvaceous Marilyn Monroe look-alike. In fact, Blondie wasn't even a *she*. He looked like a Swede, tanned complexion, chiseled features, large blue eyes, and hair so blonde it was almost white. And he was built like a defensive lineman.

"You Moon?" he said. "Reagan Moon?"

Yep. Swedish.

I shot him a suspicious glance before I hunched forward with my hands on my thighs, still panting from my morning run. I'd started jogging again and was up to five miles a day. Trust me, I'm no health freak. Running was a diversion, kept my mind off the bad stuff. When running got old, I'd go back to video games.

Or drinking. But for now, Ellie would've liked knowing I hadn't turned into a hermit.

"Who are you?" I asked, in between breaths.

"My boss has a job for you."

That got my attention. I straightened, unzipped the pocket of my sweat jacket, and removed my keys. "Did Arlette send you?"

"No. Felix Klammer."

I stopped with the key midway into the lock.

"Felix Klammer?" I said. Then I smirked. "Right."

I unlocked the door and pocketed the keys. But he just stood there, unflustered. So I called his bluff. "*The* Felix Klammer?"

"Yes."

"Of Volden Megacorps?"

Blondie squinted. "Mister Klammer and Mister Volden are no longer associates."

"Right."

Seems I did hear about the tycoons having a rift of sorts. When you go messing around with the dead, rifts are inevitable. "And he has a job for *me*?" At this point, I was beyond trying to mask my surprise.

"Yes."

I pushed the door open and stood there, giving myself a moment to ponder the arrival of this stranger.

Klammer was iconic in his anonymity. He'd fallen off the societal radar after a decorated venture into the neurosciences, surfacing, at least in rumor, to join forces with Soren Volden, perhaps the world's wealthiest occultist. Volden made Aleister Crowley look like the sorcerer's apprentice. Supposedly, Klammer had joined Volden in developing a new line of brain prosthetics. When the research drifted into the metaphysical, apparently Klammer split, returning to the more docile field of brain science.

So what would a gazillionaire genius like Felix Klammer want with a two-bit reporter from a tabloid paranormal magazine, like me?

I invited Blondie in. There was no sign of nerves or agitation in his demeanor. If this was some sort of stunt, he didn't show it. The mess didn't seem to bother him. Nor did the odd assembly of arcana I'd collected through my reportage over the years. Ellie used to joke that my place looked more like an obscure pawn shop than a bachelor's apartment. Curios and crime scene leftovers. Miscellany from Hollywood Babylon's ghoulish underbelly. Blondie stood appearing semi-interested, his hands folded politely at his waist. He wore a gold ring the size of a Buick. Did they even make pistol grips big enough for hands his size? But with hands that large, who would even need a pistol?

I removed my keys and set them on the roll top desk next to a small stuffed alligator head. A voodoo priestess had given it to me. Reminder of my stint in Louisiana. Supposedly, the gator teeth, if pulverized, would provide a protective spell when sprinkled in someone's shoe. I'd never tried it or bought into that backwater hokum. I just love the memorabilia. Hey, some guys collect football jerseys or beer steins. Me? I collect urban legends.

I dabbed sweat from my brow with the sleeve of my sweat jacket. "So what kind of job are we talking about?"

Blondie stared dully. "Look, I just extend the invitation. That's all."

I leveled my gaze at him. "So how do I know you even work for the guy? This isn't some kind of... Hey, you're not one of those Bloodline creeps, are you? Because the court issued a restraining order against you folks. You're aware of that, right?"

He looked slightly perturbed. "If you're not interested, I'll tell Mister Klammer."

He paused, and then moved toward the door.

Well, apparently I wasn't being shaken down. It wouldn't have been the first time. So if this gig was optional, what did I have to lose to follow it through? Especially if Felix Klammer was really on the other end.

As he reached for the door handle, I said, "Hold up."

He turned.

"Okay," I said. "I'm interested."

"Good. I will take you there."

I looked down at my sweat-drenched shirt. "Now?"

"Yes."

"And we're going where?"

"Not far. Twenty minutes."

"Uh, okay. Well, give me a sec."

Blondie shifted his weight.

"Thanks," I said, unzipping my sweat jacket the rest of the way, and hurrying into the bedroom.

Was this really happening? If so, opportunity had literally come knocking for me. And being that I was down to tuna and ramen in the pantry—and that one of the wealthiest men on the planet was offering me a job—how could this *not* be a godsend?

I removed my shirt, rummaged nervously about on the chest of drawers, found the cologne, and swabbed a healthy dose about my upper body. In my world, cologne and sweatpants were always a good combo. I retrieved a print shirt from a pile at the foot of my bed. An old Cure shirt with a sullen Robert Smith faded into black. Perfect. I slipped it on.

*Felix Klammer*. Arlette would eat her heart out. Or fire me on the spot. Moonlighting was fine. I'd done my share of parking lot security to make ends meet and, provided it didn't take away from my responsibilities at the Blue Crescent, would continue. But if it came down to working for Felix Klammer or the Crescent, the choice was easy. Bye-bye BC. Still, I couldn't fathom what someone of Klammer's stature could want with me. My only real expertise was paranormal trivia, which I couldn't imagine the mogul being bereft of. Either way, Arlette would understand. I hoped.

Before leaving, I instinctively snatched my camera bag and slung it over my shoulder. When I emerged, Blondie extended his hand, stopping me in my tracks. Then he reached toward me and slipped one finger under my camera bag, lifting it off my shoulder.

"My apologies. Mr. Klammer requests no photos."

"Well, then..." I shrugged and set the bag on the desk, next to the alligator head. "No photos it is."

It'd been a while since I'd had a *real* story. Something other than vampire lounges and Chinatown's fabled underground city. Sure, some of our readers liked that stuff. Can you blame them? The world was crazy. People were disillusioned with the vaunted claims of science, the pledges of windbag politicians. We'd been promised utopia: a better world, new frontiers, green energy, peace on earth and good will toward men. Blah, blah, blah. The twenty-first century delivered nothing but political scandals, economic collapse, pandemics, and global unrest. So why not look to the stars? Or to the shamans?

However, chasing down cryptids and paranormal phenomenon was becoming a drag for me.

Yeah, it'd been a while since I'd had a *real* story. Whether the one I was embarking on was a real story, had yet to be seen.

We left my apartment and I was thinking about the number 18 as we descended the steps. There were 12 steps. I'd counted them many times. Descending 12 steps on the 18th left six remaining.

And I knew enough about numerology to know that the number six was a harbinger of very bad things.

# CHAPTER 2

I ASSUME MANY ROLES. Private investigator, schlock journalist, general nuisance. And I make a mean Mexican omelet. Yet if billionaire brain researcher Felix Klammer had indeed summoned me, I doubted it was for my services as a chef.

A well-polished, cream-colored sedan was parked around the corner from my apartment. Our encounter had been nonthreatening enough that when Blondie opened the back door for me, I had few qualms about entering. Either his bodyguard was very professional, or Klammer had mistaken me for royalty. However, starting a conversation with the Swede seemed unlikely, so I settled in and studied our route.

We swept south of downtown Los Angeles, under the Santa Monica freeway. Los Angeles had its share of slums. One could pass from the ritzy to the run-down in a matter of blocks. And we'd crossed one such line. Highrises gave way to low-rent housing, dilapidated warehouses, and vacant storefronts. The area turned seedy and I began to have second thoughts. Here I was being chauffeured by someone I didn't know to meet someone I wasn't sure existed. At least the handle on the interior of the door appeared operable in the event I had to leap from the vehicle.

As he drove, Blondie put a hands-free device in his ear and mumbled cropped, incoherent sentences to someone on the other end. He turned down a side street, and then into an alley. Poorly constructed, post World War II, tenement-style buildings rose on either side, blocking the morning sun. Along with being a brain researcher, perhaps Felix Klammer was also a slumlord.

I thought for a moment about the pistol on the underside of my nightstand back home and how much better I'd feel with it tucked under my shirt. I'm hardly a cowboy, much less an expert on firearms. The pistol was purchased hastily after a run-in with some hayseeds who'd threatened to pickle my gizzards to satisfy a swamp witch. Not being sold on Magic 101, I concluded that the next best thing to a counter-hex was a gun. The moonshiners never got my gizzards, nor did I ever meet the crone. No thanks to the gun. But I'd kept it just the same and, frankly, wished I had it now. Hell, ground gator teeth in my shoe might even suffice.

We parked in the alley. Before I had a chance to grab the handle, Blondie exited the car and opened the door for me. I stepped out and studied the surrounding buildings. The windows on the ground level all had security bars. Crude murals and spray-painted monikers splashed the walls with incongruent swaths of color. It reeked of sewage and urine.

"You sure we got the right place?" I said.

But Blondie had started toward a battered wrought-iron security door with a hole where the handle used to be. He proceeded up a darkened stairwell. I remained at the entry, watching him, counting out the steps. There were nine of them. Ugh. The number nine had a florid history. Jesus was crucified on the ninth hour. Freemasons considered the numeral a symbol of human immortality and it also represented the Trinity, as in three-times-three. Which left me wondering where this stairway actually led.

Blondie stopped at the landing above and turned, silhouetted against a bare bulb. Waiting for me. It smelled like someone was harvesting mold in there. Dank and deathly, malaria just waiting to happen. Muffled voices sounded somewhere deep inside the building, and I could detect the tang of *lerium* mingled with the must. The drug had ripped through the city like a tsunami through a sandcastle. It started as part of the *nootropics* craze, a smart drug used by hard-charging professionals to give them a mental edge, boost memory retention, see the matrix. You know, the types of things that make someone a real dick to be around. But something changed. Word on the street was that the higher end clients used it to develop powers of the psychic variety. *Neuros,* they called them. A class of brainiacs who made the Powers That Be look like used car salesmen. Those were the higher end clients. The lower end ones? Well, they ended up in padded cells with brain rot.

"Here?" I stared up at the Swede standing in the stairwell. "You sure about this?"

"Yes."

I'd done plenty of questionable jobs in the past. What was one more? Worse came to worse, I could still run like hell. I hurried up the steps.

A narrow hallway with yellowed wallpaper stretched before us. Rat turds speckled the worn carpet. Not exactly the type of place you'd expect to find the filthy stinking rich. Blondie opened the third door on the left and stepped back. I moved closer and leaned in for a quick peek. Dreary light shone through a drawn blind, but the room looked empty. No furniture. Blank walls.

I turned to Blondie who motioned me to enter.

What was going on here? Suddenly, things weren't feeling right.

Blondie could tell I was having second thoughts, so he brushed past me with a slight grunt, and led the way. I entered and stood tentatively, scanning the place, giving my eyes time to adjust. Blondie closed the door after me and then walked toward a darkened corner, where he stopped and stared into the shadows. That's when I noticed a single leather chair with a table beside it. I froze when I realized someone was sitting there.

"Thank you for coming, Mr. Moon," the person in the chair wheezed. It wasn't the wheezing of a fat man, but of someone with emphysema. Or a deformity.

"Uh, my pleasure," I said, hoping I didn't sound as nervous as I was.

"You have studied hauntings, I hear."

"Hauntings?" I cleared my throat. "Yep. That's me. Poltergeists. Orbs. Ecto-mist. Shapeshifters. Garden variety apparitions. I've done it all."

Apparently, the flippancy in my tone surprised him. He paused for a moment. But the next words out of his mouth surprised *me*.

"So do you *believe*?"

"Excuse me?" I said.

He repositioned himself in the chair. As he did, I glimpsed a box or angular device covering his head. *What the hell?*

"Hauntings, Mr. Moon. Do you believe in hauntings?"

Well, this was pretty uncomfortable. As a reporter for the Blue Crescent, believing in hauntings was par for the course. Sure, I was their resident skeptic. But if I said *no* to his offer, I might be out of this job. If I said *yes*, I'd be lying. If Ellie'd taught me anything it was to speak the truth and let the cow chips fall where they may.

"Let me put it this way," I said. "I have a lot of doubts."

"Does Arlette know about your... *unbelief*?"

Arlette? *How did he—?* Apparently, Mr. Klammer had done some homework on me. I suppose I shouldn't have been surprised. You don't get as big as Klammer without a few background checks on hired hands. I studied the figure, trying to determine what sort of contraption was on this guy's dome. It looked like a crudely welded crab pot with Frankenstein bolts. What kind of freak show was I talking to?

"Arlette doesn't care," I said. "She just wants a story on her desk by deadline. And it's not quite unbelief. More like *skepticism*. There's too many quacks and fanatics to be a real believer. You know?"

The man sat, his breath rattling in his chest.

"Look," I said. "I just freelance for the Crescent. It wasn't a career objective or anything. I sort of stumbled into the job. It pays the bills. At least, it used to."

"Mr. Moon," he finally said with a twinge of frustration in his tone. "What I am requesting of you will involve a high degree of risk and a significant amount of, shall we say, *belief*."

Risk? I glanced at Blondie, but he remained placid, hands clasped at his waist. I was sure he could crush my skull with those paws.

I scratched the back of my neck. "Pardon me, but before I go stepping in something I can't get off my shoe, can I make sure who I'm dealing with here?"

"My apologies," the man rasped. "I am, as you've been told, Felix Klammer. However, if you require proof..." He nodded toward Blondie, who removed an envelope from inside his coat pocket. "Five thousand dollars cash."

I almost choked.

My inclination to play hard-to-get suddenly evaporated. *Five thousand bucks!* That was two months' rent and a shopping spree at the 99 cent store. I turned my hungry gaze away from the envelope, brushed my hands along my thighs, and said, "So what kind of risk are we talking about?"

Klammer nodded to Blondie who produced a scroll of paper from inside his jacket and passed it to me.

"What do you know about this, Mr. Moon?" Klammer asked.

It was lightweight, inexpensive paper, with ragged edges. I unrolled it and immediately recognized the image.

"It's Anubis," I said, somewhat surprised that he'd ask. I mean, everyone knew who Anubis was. "The Egyptian god of the dead, the mummy king. The drawing is crude, but yeah—head of a jackal, body of a man. He presided over the embalming process, or something. Supposedly helped souls get across to the other side. Or back again. You didn't know this?"

"Then you haven't noticed?"

"Noticed what?"

"Runes, collages, posters—all around town. Images of the Egyptian god of the dead."

"Is that so weird?" I scrolled the paper and handed it back to

Blondie. "Look. This is L.A. Maybe an Anubian cult is forming or something. I don't know. Egyptian Goths are making a comeback. Wouldn't surprise me. Pardon me, but..." I squinted at him. "This is what you wanted me for?"

"In part."

"Well, my knowledge of Egyptology needs brushing up. Last time I researched it, the Tutankhamen exhibit was at the Getty. That was a couple years back. A bunch of nuts tried to reenact some sort of purity ritual and ended up getting thrown in jail for public indecency and defacement of private property. So much for 'purity,' huh?"

He didn't seem amused.

"Anyway," I continued. "So what kind of risk are we talking about?"

"I also want you to visit a medium. A clairvoyant."

This time, I couldn't contain myself. I snorted. "That's it?"

"And speak to Ellie Wells."

I went cold. Then I got pissed. "Is this some kind of a joke?"

Blondie took a step to the side, angling slightly toward me.

Klammer said, "I don't joke, Mr. Moon."

"Necromancy's against my religion."

"Good. Mine too."

I stared at him. My fists were clenched. Who was this crackpot? Was somebody playing a joke on me? Was this payback for something I'd written, someone wanting to watch me squirm? Either way, the 5,000 dollars suddenly didn't seem worth it.

"Ellie's dead," I said flatly.

"According to *you* she's dead." Felix Klammer did not move.

I peered at the dark figure. I was quick on my feet, but this had taken them right out from under me. Now, most assuredly, I could make out the device over the man's head, an angular cage with hewn bolts, draped in front with a square cut of velvety fabric.

"Okay. What the hell's going on here?" I glanced between the two men, and then leveled my gaze at Klammer. "You guys better explain yourselves."

"It's quite simple, Mr. Moon. Ellie's spirit lives on. Just like mine will, like yours will. We are here on assignment. To learn and grow. And resist the darkness. I believe she explained this to you, no?"

He let the question dangle there, as if he knew how many debates Ellie and I'd had about the subject. She'd been as convinced of the afterlife as I was about the law of gravity. How did Klammer know so much about her? About us?

"Mr. Moon," he said. "I want you to investigate your girlfriend's murder."

"Murder? Okay. That's it." I stepped toward him. "Ellie wasn't murdered. It was an accident. A freak accident. And is it any of your business?"

Blondie tucked the envelope back into his pocket and officially assumed a defensive posture, chest open, arms poised at his sides. Hands twitching for a piece of me.

Klammer said, "Do you believe everything you're told, Mr. Moon?"

"Why would someone want to kill Ellie? Huh? She didn't have enemies. Besides, I had no reason to doubt the police. They investigated, said it was an accident. Bastion Sails paid. They admitted culpability. Case closed. My girlfriend's gone, my life's ruined, and I'm stuck in a dead-end job investigating astrologers and vampire crypts." I peered at him through the musty dark. "What do you know, Klammer?"

He sat for a moment, and then he relaxed. "I'm not sure. Not yet. Which is why I need your help. You are a man around town, with some knowledge of the city's occult underbelly."

Well, he had that right.

Klammer continued. "I have reason to believe it was no accident that took Ellie Wells and those twelve other people. Thirteen people—an auspicious number, wouldn't you say? They were intentionally taken and their bodies are being harvested."

"What?"

"*Harvested*. Against their wishes, I should add."

I licked my lips, doing my utmost to keep from bashing this freak in his metal grill. Nevertheless, his suggestion that Ellie was alive, even if it was in some invisible limbo, had wriggled into my brain and awakened something I'd worked very hard to suppress—hope.

"There is someone who may be able to contact her spirit," he said, almost reverently.

"This is a joke."

"If contact is possible, Ellie Wells can help us—both of us."

"A very bad joke."

"And you, in turn, can help her."

God, what I wouldn't give to help her. She was the one who'd always helped me; talked me down from the ledge after Germaine split, always cracking my gloomy cynicism with her playful wit. She had a way of looking into me, past my flimsy persona into a part of me that was fearful of human touch. She was convinced that I'd be great—just like my father was convinced—that fortune, or something bigger, shone on me. If I could only dig myself out from this self-imposed malaise. Ellie always said I'd make a great believer. And deep down inside, I knew she was right.

Yeah, I was still broken up about her.

"If that *was* murder, shouldn't we go to the police?" I asked.

"Eventually, yes."

"Why not now?"

"We don't know enough. To be more precise, *you* don't know enough."

"Sounds awfully cryptic."

"Doesn't it, though."

My pulse was thudding in my ears. "And how do *you* know about all this? Were you in on it or something?"

He chuckled, the first real sign of emotion from the hooded mystery man. "If I was, why would I invite you here to implicate myself?"

*Damn.* I gnawed the inside of my lip.

"And the Anubis cult," I said. "What about that?"

"It will come out in the mix. Just keep your eyes open." He watched me mulling things over. "Mr. Moon. I understand your reluctance. She was the one good thing that had happened to you since—"

"Ever."

"Exactly. The tragedy has left you embittered and even more agnostic than before. And just when Ellie had you tilting toward the light. Trust me, we all have our own demons." He gestured to the strange device on his head.

Ellie was dead, nothing could change that. But this was the first time since the accident that the suggestion of a crime had been floated. How could I have missed that? If Ellie was alive, in some weird way, if her spirit lived on in some other place, and she needed help, I had to try. Even if it went against everything I *didn't* believe.

Besides, I've never met a medium I couldn't figure out.

"Okay," I conceded. "What do you want me to do?"

"In Lincoln Heights there is a seer. A medicine man of sorts. You must pay him a visit."

"Lincoln Heights? Not exactly the mecca of mediums."

"His name is Gollo. He practices folk medicine. He's not advertised, but is well known amongst the locals. And... by *others*."

"And when I get there, I'm supposed to—what?"

"Tell him you wish to attempt contact with a deceased loved one. That should be enough."

"How original." I shook my head at the absurdity of it all. "And the risk involved?"

He paused, and then leaned forward as if telling me a secret. "Whenever you're dealing with the disembodied, Mr. Moon, there is risk."

The way he said it gave the impression he knew what he was talking about.

So many questions. So much pain. I felt like someone had

ripped open my chest only to discover a dark, rotting cavity. Nevertheless, my silence was my surrender.

Klammer motioned to Blondie, who stepped to the door, opened it, and stood waiting for me.

"Gollo," Klammer repeated. "Find him." Then he settled back in his chair. "We will be in touch, Mr. Moon."

I mumbled assent, left awkwardly. What could I say? I'd been flattened by a baby grand piano from the 12th floor. Or was it the 13th?

The security door clanged behind us. Blondie pulled the envelope from his coat again and extended it to me.

I stared at it. "I'm only taking this because I need to eat." Then I snatched it from him. "And because psychics have gotten way too expensive."

# CHAPTER 3

PEOPLE ARE LIKE GERMS, ONLY BIGGER.

That bit of wisdom has proven true, for the most part. Humans are little more than highly evolved bacteria, leeches on a rotting ball of clay. It's depressing, I know. It's also probably the reason I kept my defenses up and preferred video games to singles bars. But you'd be mistaken to interpret this as me being unsociable. I'm just cynical about our species, that's all.

Which is one reason I was a little reluctant to go digging around in the past.

But murder? How could you *not* go digging around? Especially if your girlfriend was on the receiving end? Allegedly.

I paced my bedroom, stopping every other turn to stare at the envelope lying at the foot of my bed. I'd already counted the money. It was all there, just like he'd said. Five thousand dollars cash in 100 dollar bills. Which was convenient. I couldn't see having to break a grand to pay a psychic.

I kept pacing and reflected on the details of my encounter with Felix Klammer, the bizarre box-headed billionaire.

*According to you she's dead.*

No, not according to *me,* Felix old buddy. According to the police report and the company spokespersons and the newspaper and...

*Ellie's spirit lives on. Just like mine will, like yours will.*

Germs, that's all we are. No one *lives on.* We're simply parasites on a planet spinning toward extinction under the dying embers of a burned-out sun.

Okay, Ellie would scold me for thinking that way. And deep down inside, I hoped to hell it wasn't true.

*If contact is possible, Ellie Wells can help us—both of us. And you, in turn, can help her.*

Dammit!

I stopped pacing.

In the corner of my bedroom stood a lamppost—not a real lamppost, of course—a Styrofoam and chicken wire prop made to look like a late 19th century gas lamp. I turned toward it. It had been used once on a movie set several blocks from my apartment. There are very few real cobblestone streets in Los Angeles. One of them was located nearby and attracts certain movie producers. This particular piece was part of a proposed TV miniseries about Jack the Ripper. Interestingly enough, the project was abandoned after a human foot was found on the set. Investigators surmised that someone was attempting to copycat the London serial killer. Neither the owner of the foot nor the perpetrator was ever uncovered. So either someone is hopping around town on one foot or decomposing in a landfill. In L.A., either was possible.

After the horrible event, a crew had returned to dismantle the set and, for whatever reason, abandoned the lamppost. So I helped myself. As I said, I like to collect bizarre memorabilia. It reminds me of how screwy this world is, which for some odd reason, keeps me sane. The lamppost wouldn't fit under my El Camino's fiberglass shell, so I hoisted it over my shoulder and carried it home. Getting it up the stairs was a scene.

At the base of the lamp is a spring-loaded trapdoor that opens into a two-foot-by-two-foot compartment. Dumbbells or sandbags had been inserted here to weight the lamp while on set, and then removed so that the lamp could be transported back to studio storage. I have very little of actual worth, but what I do have, I've stashed here. It's inconspicuous. I mean, who would think of looking in the base of a fake lamppost for valuables? Then again, who would have a fake 19th century gas lamppost in their bedroom?

I went to the lamppost, opened the hatch, wrestled out a metal artillery box, and popped the lid open. My father gave the box to me after his return from Iraq. He was shot and killed in the States shortly after that, a random holdup outside our house that left me and my mother alone for good. I witnessed everything. Allegedly. The event had traumatized me, leaving a gaping hole in my memory bank. I remembered only bits and pieces: him telling me to run, him strafing the opposite direction, drawing the gunfire away from me. But the one who pulled the trigger was just a shadow in my brain. A shadow who had haunted every day of my life since. I was seven or eight at the time. They'd found me sitting next to his body, dazed. Amnesiac. Fifteen-plus years later, and I was still a mess.

I'm not sure what was worse, knowing I'd witnessed my father's murder and not being able to remember anything, or having watched the girl of my dreams be snatched away. *Sucks to be you, Moon.*

I rummaged past my father's medal of valor, my social security card, and an eye patch. Letters from Ellie were bundled together. They smelled like basil. Near the bottom was a full-page newspaper clipping folded into an uneven wedge.

Before I opened it, I glanced at the envelope of money on my bed.

Was it worth it? And was I really ready for this?

I carefully unfolded the paper. I was hoping it would jog my memory, maybe reveal some overlooked detail. But the truth was I knew it would do nothing but bring me pain.

The story had made the front page. Ellie was working for Windsum at the time, a leading developer of alternative energy. She'd been equally convinced of the resilience of the human spirit and an impending apocalypse. Talk about cognitive dissonance. *History's a blank slate.* That's what she used to say. *We can always change things.* Well, she changed me. Who knows where I'd be if she hadn't died?

Or was she really murdered?

I unfolded the paper and read the headline for the one-thousandth time: 13 *Die in Bastion Sails Accident.*

Murder. How was this possible?

Then the subheading: *Irradiation chamber mistakenly activated; party vaporized in freak accident.*

I let the paper slip from my fingers and drop to the floor. I wasn't ready for this.

I stared at the envelope of money.

They'd been researching fusion fuels, trying to make dependence upon fossil fuels irrelevant. It was the Holy Grail of energy research. Unlimited sustainable energy. And then their reactor went bonkers. According to a Bastion Sails spokesperson, the deaths were instantaneous. The victims did not suffer, thankfully. Their molecules were simply disassembled. Painless, as I understand. The company claimed immediate responsibility, paying for the memorial service and a hefty settlement to Ellie's deadbeat mom. That was a shame. I mean, all that money going to a lousy drunk.

I retrieved the newspaper, refolded it, and dropped it back in the ammo box.

*Their bodies are being harvested.*

Harvested. What in the hell did that mean? I'd researched a lot of things in my day—invisibility, OBEs, grave robbery, just to name a few. However, now that my dead girlfriend was in the mix, I was suddenly getting cold feet.

I went to the bed, removed three 100 dollar bills from the envelope, put the remainder in the ammo box, and returned the box to safekeeping. I got out of my jogging sweats, changed into some jeans, and stuffed the money into the front pocket.

As I exited my apartment, I stopped with my hand on the light switch and stared at the picture of Ellie that was on the roll top desk. She'd taken it on the Santa Monica pier, pulled me into herself and extended the camera. I was laughing—one of those rare times—and so was she. In the background, the angle of the blue Pacific against her golden hair was as close to real magic as I'd ever seen.

God, I missed her.

*Believe big.* She always said that. *Who you are isn't all you can be.*

I switched the light off.

Earlier, I'd managed to find a parking spot out front. I unlocked my El Camino. It's a '66, vintage. But the black paint job has faded to gray and the cheesy hot rod flames to drab orange. Don't let that fool you—the Cammy's engine was a beast. The sun had warmed the car considerably. It was beginning to smell like my hamper in there. I removed a wad of clothes and tossed them through the hatch into the back. Then I brushed off my hands and looked east.

Somewhere out there, a medium named Gollo was waiting for me. Strangely enough, I hoped he had a hotline to my dead girlfriend.

# CHAPTER 4

AS LONG AS I COULD REMEMBER, I'd been fascinated by the paranormal, by the unexplained. The Loch Ness monster, shape shifters, psychic healers, things like that. I suppose when you're a kid, you believe in them because you don't know better. Because they speak to mystery. Science hasn't explained it away and religion hasn't sterilized it yet. Sometime after my father's murder, that's when I lost faith. *He* didn't lose faith. No sir. He was the toughest man I'd ever known. He'd tell me war stories—not just about the ones he fought in. Those were only shadows of bigger wars, good and evil in a cosmic cage fight. We were all part of it, he'd say. I'd sit spellbound and never once would I doubt him, even when he talked about werethings or subhumans.

Or the *Imperia.*

And how one day, I'd be part of that mystical coalition. One day, I'd leave my mark.

Now it all seemed so far away, like so much make-believe. I was a paranormal reporter, for God's sake, living in a one-bedroom apartment barely making ends meet. I was as far away from being a part of something great as pond scum was from being human. I buried those dreams along with my father. Perhaps my continued fascination with the paranormal and the unexplained was a chink in my armor. I'd be better off as a dog groomer or a fry chef. Maybe I stayed in this business secretly hoping that one day, it would prove true. To validate my father, to reawaken some childish hope. But it was never proven true.

The chasm it left inside me made the Mariana Trench look like a puddle.

I'm not sure why I was thinking about my father as I drove to Lincoln Heights. Perhaps it was that gnawing sense that, one of these days, I'd get a chance to fight in one of those great wars. Be the good guy. And prove him true. Prove myself worthy. Which only made his memory all the more painful.

I got off the Golden State Freeway heading east on N. Broadway.

East L.A. is considered a historical area of the city. But other than some of my favorite Mexican restaurants, I've never found much of historical interest here. Lincoln Heights is part of that mix. Perched on bluffs above the Los Angeles River, it was once home to some of the city's wealthiest residents. Now it's little more than a barrio.

Realizing I should probably break a bill, I found a small market just off the freeway. I purchased a bottle of water and a bag of pretzels there, put them on the counter and, next to them, a one hundred dollar bill.

The cashier, a hunchbacked old man, shook his head. "Naw. That's too big."

Before I had a chance to press him, he snatched the bill and snapped it lengthwise, studying it in the overhead light.

I glanced over my shoulder and, sure enough, the other customer, a *vato* in khakis and a wife-beater, was in the bread aisle watching us. *Great!* The last thing I wanted to do was broadcast my stash. Flashing 100 dollar bills in this neighborhood was like chumming for sharks with a side of beef.

The register clanged open and the cashier riffled through currency.

I cleared my throat and leaned over the counter hoping the punk in the bread aisle wasn't listening. "Gollo. I'm looking for a man named Gollo, do you—?"

"He ain't in business no more," he grumbled. Then he finished sorting the bills and slid the change across the counter, without bothering to count it out for me.

"He moved?" I asked.

"He ain't in business, I said."

I took the money and stuffed it in my jeans. "Then he's still around. Can you tell me where he lives?"

The man finally looked at me. "The fountains by Saint Michael's. Okay?" He shoved the cash register door in for emphasis.

I straightened.

Wow. Have a good day to you, too.

I left the store, stopped out front to open the water bottle, and took a swig. As I did, I stared back up the street. Meat markets and liquor stores were every other block, not a single residence without security windows. So what would a medium be doing in the hood?

Other than a refurbished laptop, my cell phone had remained my singular tether to technology. I did a GPS search for Saint Michael's and found it was four blocks away. I tossed the bag of pretzels on the seat and drove there. The butterflies in my gut had turned to buzzards, eating my innards. Except for the occasional murals and security bars, it was a rather quaint neighborhood. Some chickens wandered in a front yard as an elderly Mexican woman watered her flowerpots. In the distance, the LA skyscrapers could be seen behind a growing ridge of orange smog.

I approached the Catholic Church, a small, ornate Spanish-style building wedged into the neighborhood. I slowed, cruising down the street looking for 'the fountains' and any other possible signs of the psychic Gollo.

The one thing about driving a faded '66 El Camino with bleached hotrod flames is that you don't look completely out of place in the average low income neighborhood. Cruising Rodeo Drive was another story. I studied the houses, trying to appear incurious as I did so. But what would the house of a psychic actually look like? And if Gollo was no longer in business, maybe any evidence of his business had gone with him.

I spotted a large marble fountain peeking between rambling Bird of Paradise in front of a tiny white house. I nearly skidded to a stop in the middle of the street. *Sheesh.* You'd think I was on the way to my own execution.

I found a spot a little ways down, turned off the ignition, and sat for a moment. I'd interviewed enough mediums to know they were just a bunch of smooth-talking shysters who preyed on brokenhearted widows and starry-eyed believers. Why should Gollo be any different? It was the possibility that this guy *was* different, that he could actually contact my dead girlfriend, that was making my brain itch.

Rap music rumbled somewhere. I locked the car and briskly followed the sidewalk to a white wooden gate. Palm trees and overgrown exotic vines shrouded the house in cool shadow. Who knew Shangri-La was this close to downtown L.A.? I looked past the fountain to a small porch. A screen door was open and the garbled sounds of a television emerged. Could this be it? There was only one way to find out.

I glanced over my shoulder to see if I was being watched. Then I unlatched the gate and entered. A banana tree laden with small green fruit overhung the walkway. I ducked under it and stepped onto the porch. A cockatiel trilled from its cage nearby, scaring the wits out of me. Studio laughter rose and an electronic buzzer sounded notifying me that a game show was playing on the tube inside. But I couldn't see anyone through the screen.

I took a deep breath and knocked on the door.

Muttered expletives. Sofa springs squeaked and a shuffle of footsteps approached. A heavyset middle-aged Hispanic woman looked through the screen.

"Yeah?" she said, pulling her spaghetti strap back up over her shoulder. She had half the Black Forest hanging out of her armpits.

"I'm looking for Gollo."

"What for?"

"Uh. I'm with the newspaper."

"Yeah?" She straightened. "Which one?"

I could see the crater she'd left in the sofa she extricated herself from. The couch was surrounded by soda cans, snack wrappers, and an overfull ashtray. I guess living with a medium did not significantly raise one's fitness IQ.

"I'm with the Blue Crescent."

"Never heard of it. So whaddya want?"

"I'm, uh... someone gave me a referral."

She stared at me.

"Look," I said, "it'll just be a minute, and then—"

"Dad!" she barked. "Dad, someone from the newspaper's here!"

Then she shuffled back to her spot and dropped into the couch. Sirens blared from the TV as someone hit the jackpot on the program she was watching. However, this female Attila seemed more interested in giving me the evil eye.

An unshaven old man with tinted wire-rim glasses and an LA Dodgers baseball cap shuffled around the corner. He looked in my direction, hurriedly finished chewing something, and dabbed his lips on the sleeve of his worn flannel.

"From the newspaper?" He nodded vigorously. "*Muy bueno!* See?" He spread his arms. "They come again."

"Da-a-d!"

He motioned dismissively toward the woman on the couch. Then he shuffled to the door and hunched forward, peering through what I could now see were grimy lenses. Just outside the periphery of his glasses I could make out tattoos, old school ink and needle markings surrounding the orbits of each eye.

"Mr. Gollo?" I queried.

"Just Gollo." He brushed his hand through the air. "Gollo. No *Mister*."

"Okay. I'd, um..." I glanced at the woman on the sofa. "I'd like a session with you."

"He doesn't do that anymore!" the woman snapped.

"Ay! You shush!" Gollo came closer to the screen and lowered his voice. "She is worried. About the neighbors. Eh, *los jóvenes*. The drugs come hard here, *señor*," he said. "*Drogas de los demonios*. It possesses them. Makes them *loco*."

Lerium. I nodded.

"You know then?" he said. "The spirits also know." Gollo pointed, one at a time, at the houses across the street. His voice was now hushed, as if he were revealing a great mystery. "*El Diablo*. The devil comes for them."

Of course, the devil was coming for them. Either in the form of a police officer or a coroner. He was coming all right. Barreling down on all of us like a runaway semi with a cargo of nukes.

"So!" He straightened, blinking hard behind the dirty lenses. "The newspaper. You come with questions, *sí?*"

"Yeah. I'm with the Blue Crescent," I said, extracting a business card from my wallet. "We're doing a feature on local mediums and I was wondering..."

"He doesn't do that!" The woman shouted. "I already told you!" Then she snatched a cigarette from the end table, lit it, and muttered to herself.

Gollo nudged the screen door open and fumbled for the card. I slipped it into his palm. He backed away from the door and pressed the card between his hands as if he were praying. I've never known my business card to emit spiritual signals. But apparently this old man was searching for one. The cockatiel skittered nervously along its perch. After a long moment, Gollo nodded, unclasped his hands and slipped out the screen door.

"Da-a-ad," Ms. Amazonia whined from the sofa.

"Ay!" He shook his head as I helped him down the steps. Then he looped his arm in mine and pointed. "This way. Out back."

He steered me along the side of the house to a flagstone path. Despite his foggy glasses, he seemed to navigate his way just fine around the garden. The backyard was lush, manicured. A forest of bamboo bordered the property. A tiny shack surrounded by massive philodendrons sat in the far corner like something out of an islands getaway magazine. Nice setup. We followed the path. Gollo held my business card in one hand and with the other, patted my hand as we went.

"My daughter. She is afraid, you know? Many are afraid now."

"Afraid of...? I'm sorry. The drug dealers?"

He tilted his head to see me from under the bill of his ball cap. "*El mundo de los espíritus.* The Other Side. The, eh, world of the spirits. They are active now. Very... restless. They come to torment, bring messages. Of warning. Yes. Warnings, *señor*. And signs. All around. In the water. In the air. Something is coming. A great... *manifestación*. This is what you come for, no? To learn of the *manifestación*."

"Well, um... sort of. I guess."

He squeezed my arm and led me on.

There are two basic scams when it comes to psychics—curse removal and spell casting. Both of them usually require psychic junkies in order to work; individuals who are so heartbroken or so damned gullible that they will keep coming back and dispensing cash and information. From there, it's usually just a series of educated guesses on the part of the psychic. Hey, people just want to believe. No matter how much it costs them. Just last year a famous celebrity got swindled out of 10s of 1000s of dollars by a high-priced medium in Burbank who promised contact with her dead daughter. The Crescent conveniently downplayed the incident. Fraudulent psychics wouldn't look good for our business. But I had to admit, Gollo did not fit the classic conman profile. If the old man was out to make a buck, he wasn't following protocol.

We crossed a small bridge. It stretched over a koi pond and two fountains gurgled on each side. Tranquil. Inviting.

"The water is good for the spirits." Gollo said. "It calms the restless ones."

"Great," I forced an uncomfortable laugh. "I wouldn't want restless spirits around."

A bead curtain stretched across the doorway. Seashells were nailed above the entry forming an arch, christened at its apex by a large scallop. I was sure this had some significance but had no idea what it was.

Gollo parted the curtain with a brush of his hand. As I passed, brass wind chimes nearby tinkled in serenade. Real creepy like. Any minute the kid from The Sixth Sense would show up and admonish me for my unbelief. Man, I was losing it.

Unlike many séance quarters, the shack was sparse. Little room for bells and whistles. Or pyrotechnics. It reeked of incense and candle wax. A religious shrine erected around a picture of Christ occupied a prominent place. The picture made me feel strangely guilty. Did we have to do this with him looking?

Two plain wooden chairs with wicker seats sat in the middle of the room, a dark wood table resting in between them. Gollo shuffled to the nearest chair, turned, and motioned me to the other.

"Come, my friend," he said. "Let us see what awaits. *Aquí.*"

I sat down. He sat across from me and coddled my business card, patting it gently between his wrinkled hands. On the table in front of me were several recognizable pieces of occult paraphernalia. A brass bell, some scarves, a goblet. But one item in particular caught my attention. A long thin piece of dark, polished wood. A wand with an ornate metal handle, perhaps twelve inches long. I couldn't tell if the old man used it for spells or self defense.

He settled in, drew a deep breath. "Tell me now what you seek. A story for the newspaper. Or something else. A loved one, no?"

This was going too fast. I needed to breathe. Gather my wits.

"Yeah," I said. "A loved one. Or, I mean—both."

He nodded and set my business card on the table in front of him. Then he removed his baseball cap and hung it on the arm of his chair. He brushed his thinning gray hair back and then his hand fumbled forward until he touched the handle of the bell. Lifting it, he rang the bell. Three bright strikes.

Three.

Then he returned it to its place. "*Señor.*" He gestured to the other items on the table.

"What?"

"Something else. You must choose."

Huh? What was this, a game of chance? I surveyed the items. Did it matter which one I chose? Of course not. It was just part of his schtick. At least, that's what I was hoping to convince myself. I reluctantly chose the wand. I held it up and lightly twirled it, smiling dumbly as I did.

"Ahhh." He nodded vigorously.

I returned the wand to the table. Gollo made the sign of the cross. Then he leaned across the table and extended his hands for me.

I hated this part. Even as a nonbeliever. It felt too much like... complicity. Like a pact. It was the Faustian bargain, the crossroads, where I was about to sell my soul to the devil. Oh well, he wasn't getting much. I drew a deep breath. Then I scooted to the edge of my seat, reached across the table, and took the old man's hands. His grip was strong, like that of a guy who worked long hours in the garden or snapped the necks of chickens. He closed his eyes.

*Ellie's spirit lives on. Just like mine will, like yours will.*

I shook the thought off. I couldn't let my emotions get the best of me. *Focus, Moon. Focus!*

Like most psychics, Gollo appeared to be seeking a trance state. Eyes closed. Breathing steady. Deep. Muttering occasionally under his breath. But he had no idea what I wanted. What was he contacting? What manner of information was I seeking? He'd hardly asked any questions or queried for info. We were way off script.

Outside, the wind chimes tinkled. A breeze disturbed the bead curtain and, as it did, Gollo tilted his head, listening.

I shifted nervously in my chair. The residue of incense was so strong my eyes burned.

He rocked forward until he found some psychic rhythm. The chair creaked, counting out his hypnotic groove.

I tried to gently let go of his hands, at least to wipe my eyes, but he maintained his grip.

Then he stopped rocking.

"Hello?" Gollo said to no one. "Hello? *Bienvenido.*"

That's when I noticed a cat peeking around the doorway. A silver tabby. Feral looking. Its eyes sparkled as it stared at me. As much as I love animals, I consider cats to be the spawns of hell. Needless to say, being scrutinized by this particular feline was not a good sign. Not a good sign at all.

I tore my gaze away from Hellcat. Didn't Gollo need to ask me a few more questions? He couldn't have gathered many details from our brief encounter. I swallowed hard.

Gollo's brow furrowed in concentration. His lips parted slightly. Something was ticking inside that wrinkled melon.

I leaned forward, watching the old man. Anticipating.

Suddenly, it dawned on me how absurd this must look. Guy loses his girlfriend and less than a year later is leaning across a table holding hands with a medium in hopes of contacting her. My God, what a sucker I was.

*People are like germs*, I reminded myself. We live, we die. We return to the Nothing from which we came. We—

Gollo abruptly let go, jolting me from my thoughts. He settled back into his chair, his hands clasped before him. And just sat there.

*If contact is possible, Ellie Wells can help us—both of us. And you, in turn, can help her.*

No. No. No.

Fear seemed to lodge in my throat. A dread anticipation spiked me to the chair. He was a fake. He *had* to be a fake.

His eyes were closed, his features placid. Then his mouth began to move in soft spasms, twitching.

"*R-Reyo,*" Gollo moaned. "*Reyo. S-se enc... encuentra. Sí, entiendo.*"

I only knew fragments of Spanish, just enough to order meals and bargain with vendors. It was part of his act. It had to be.

The space where the cat had been was empty now, filled only by the gentle rustling of the bead curtain. I turned back to the old man who was rocking back and forth again, faster this time, eyes darting under his lids.

"*Rayo, en p-peligro.*"

He was panting now, almost hyperventilating. Sweat glistened on his forehead.

Then Gollo stopped rocking and went rigid. "*Peligro!*"

And he said something that drained the blood from my head.

"Ray!" Gollo blurted in near perfect English. "Ray!"

How did he—? It couldn't be.

*Ellie was the only one who called me Ray.*

"You're in d-danger, Ray." Gollo was shaking now, trembling to the point of convulsions. His glasses slipped from his nose and fell to the floor. I could see the tattoo in full now. Bluish green dots surrounding each eye. "He's c-coming for m-me. Ray, he's coming! You have to s-stop him. Please!"

I sprang from my chair so abruptly that it went clattering across the floor and slammed into the wall. My knees struck the table sending the bell somersaulting through the air, ringing as it went. The whites of the old man's eyes quivered as he convulsed. Spittle drooled from one corner of his lips. Then he grew still before slumping in his chair. His head lolled at his chest as if he were unconscious.

I gaped in disbelief. What the hell had just happened? Should I call an ambulance? Although, running seemed like a better response. Nevertheless, my eyes remained fixed on Gollo.

*Whenever you're dealing with the disembodied, Mr. Moon, there is risk.*

Yeah, but this was unlike anything I'd ever seen.

And much more personal.

*How did he know to call me Ray?*

My heart officially stopped when I realized that Gollo was awake and looking in my direction. He appeared exhausted, but his voice was calm again. His glasses lay at his feet. He blinked hard, his gauzy eyes seemed to be trying to locate me. Then his gaze steadied. His voice was placid. "The *Tau*. They said you need it. Celeste. Rapha. Orphana. The Elder Ones. They said you need the Tau. You must protect it, Ray. *Sí?* Protect it. Do not let it go."

I nodded dumbly.

Then Gollo reached toward me. His hand fumbled the air for my touch. I went to him and reached out. He gripped my hand in both of his and squeezed.

"Run, *señor*," he said, without emotion. Then he began panting. Trembling. Convulsing. His eyes grew wide, the veins in his temple swelled, and then he shouted, "Ray—ruuuunnnnnn!"

And I did.

# CHAPTER 5

I TOOK THE STAIRS TWO AT A TIME. When I turned the corner, Arlette was waiting at my apartment door, wide-eyed.

It was the 18th, remember? Things happen in bunches.

"What the—" She stumbled out of my way.

I pushed past her and fumbled to unlock my door. I'd made record time from Gollo's, running a stoplight and nearly flattening a pedestrian along the way. I was as confused as the Invisible Man in a house of mirrors.

"I've been trying to get hold of you," Arlette said from behind me. "Moon! What'n the hell's going on with you?"

I managed to unlock the door, slipped inside leaving Arlette in the hallway, and slid the dead bolt into place. I slumped with my back against the door, panting.

All I could think about was the old man's milky eyes the size of golf balls as he shouted my name.

"Hey!" Arlette called from the hallway. She thumped on the door. "Hey! You all right? Moon? What's goin' on with you?"

*He's coming for me. Ray, he's coming. You have to stop him. Please!*

This couldn't be happening. And if it was, there had to be an explanation other than the ones I'd already ruled out. How could a seer in Lincoln Heights know so much about me? *Ray*—how could he know she called me that? Had Klammer set me up, fed the old man information about me? About *us*? But why? Even if he had, no one knew about the Tau. That was strictly between Ellie and me. At least, as far as I knew.

*Thump. Thump. Thump.*

"Moon! Hey! What're you tryin' to do?"

If Arlette kept that up, the entire floor would be looking. I unbolted the door and opened it.

"Shhh!" I yanked her in. "Get in here and shut up."

Arlette huffed and jerked her arm free of my grip.

I closed the door and bolted it again. Then I turned to face her.

"What's wrong with you?" she said.

Arlette is a good ten inches shorter than I am, but she can breathe fire. Trust me. In her power pantssuit and bob cut, she looked as far away from the managing editor of a tabloid-style paranormal magazine as the First Lady did from Elvira. Despite her coiffed appearance, Arlette could be Godzilla in heels. The Blue Crescent was just a stepping-stone for her, a necessary rung on a ladder to somewhere better. *Anywhere* better. We had that in common. But unlike me, she put some credence in things that go bump in the night.

She glared up at me and then her features softened. "You look like you've seen a ghost."

"Yeah? Well maybe I have."

I hurried past her into my bedroom. Arlette has been to my apartment twice, but never in my bedroom. Our relationship is strictly professional. Okay, maybe borderline *friendly*. She'd helped me through a number of fairly personal messes and I felt reasonably comfortable speaking frankly to her. Divulging semi-sensitive stuff.

"What's gotten into you?" she said, stopping in the doorway. Then she curdled her nose. "It stinks in here."

"I think there's an old tuna sandwich somewhere."

"That's disgusting." She folded her arms and watched me. "Is it the Bloodline? Is that why you're acting like this? Because they received a court order to stay away from you."

"It's not the Bloodline."

I went to the lamppost, opened it, and drew out the artillery box.

"What is *that*?" she said.

"Just some mementos." I rummaged through the box.

"No," Arlette said. "*That*." She pointed to the lamppost.

"Oh. Something I picked up from a film set."

She shook her head. "Maybe you can find a matching horse and buggy for the living room."

I ignored her and kept leafing through the ammo box, flinging things aside, until I reached the bottom. The Tau lay there, just where I'd left it the day before Ellie died.

*They said you need it, Ray. You need the Tau.*

I reached in, dug it out, and held it up, studying it in the light.

"What's that?" Arlette crossed the room and stood next to me.

"I'm not sure," I said.

"A cross. An *old* cross."

I nodded.

The light from the window caught the corner of the Tau, sending slight refractions of color across the ceiling. Ellie had given it to me the day before she died. She said it was special—I remembered that. She said I should keep it in a safe place, but had offered no qualifiers. At the time, I hadn't thought anything of it. Ellie believed so many things were special, mostly things everyone takes for granted. She died so suddenly, it sort of got lost in the shuffle.

Arlette leaned closer—I could smell her perfume, the same almond-like scent she always wore—and studied the icon. "Is it stone? Or ceramic?"

"I don't know. Neither." I turned it over and back in my hands. "Too light to be stone. But really hard. Some type of wood maybe. Or bone."

"Where'd it come from?"

"Ellie gave it to me. I don't know where she got it. She knew a lot of people, you know, had a lot of oddball shops she visited. Venice Beach, connections in London. She loved crosses. Crucifixes. Things like that. Had a collection. Her mother sold it after she died. But don't let me get started about her mother."

I laid the cross flat on my outstretched palm, as if it were weighted in a balance.

"She was always looking for the perfect cross," I said. "She called this one a Tau."

"A *what?*"

"A Tau. It's fashioned after the Greek letter. Apparently, it's got all kinds of different meanings. The Egyptians used it. The Franciscan monks. Eventually it was adopted by the Church as a symbol of the cross of Christ."

Arlette straightened. "So *that's* why you almost ran me over in the hallway?"

But I was too busy examining the strange item. A worn leather strap dangled from the Tau and served as its chain. The cross was probably the length of my hand, much bigger and more conspicuous than any type of jewelry a normal person would voluntarily wear. Inlaid with tiny stones or aggregate, subtle carvings notched the arms, lithe shapes of angels or saints. A small symbol stamped the back, two feathery wings, separated, set parallel to each other, along with what appeared to be Latin letters, nearly illegible.

How would Ellie have acquired something like this? It looked like it belonged in the Natural History Museum, not in an artillery box inside a Styrofoam lamppost.

I shook my head. And I was supposed to guard this? Why? Or maybe a better question was—from whom?

*They said you need it, Ray. Celeste. Rapha. Orphana. The Elder Ones. They said you need the Tau. You must protect it, Ray.*

I stared at the thing for a while, turning it over and back, trying to decipher its significance. Finally, Arlette cleared her throat.

"I haven't forgotten about you," I said.

"I was beginning to wonder."

"Okay." I lowered the Tau. "I'm sorry. I *am* acting weird."

"Glad you noticed." Then her shoulders straightened and she said proudly, "You're not going to believe what happened."

"Try me."

"A representative of Volden Megacorps came to the office."

I looked up at her, incredulous.

"Hello?" Arlette brushed her hand before her face. "Anybody out there?"

"What'd you say?"

"You heard me—Volden Megacorps. Just a couple of hours ago. A celebrity wannabe-type. Tanned, big smile. And he requested you, specifically."

My mind, or what was left of it, was reeling.

Something was happening, there was no denying it. Something big and weird and totally outside the boundaries of my belief system. All that stuff about multiverses and parallel planes must be true—*because I'd just stumbled into one.* Klammer. Gollo. The Tau. And now Volden. Either someone was playing an elaborate joke on me or I needed to rethink my position about fate and chance.

Arlette peered at me. "You look like you've seen another ghost."

"Volden? You're kidding."

"Why would I be kidding? We've been trying to get a pipeline to VM forever. This could be it! Hey, you wanted more work. Well, I guess this is your chance."

"Yeah," I muttered. "I guess."

"Maybe they want a feature, a charity giveaway or somethin'. Who knows? Does it matter? Spiraplex is on the brink of opening. It'll get international attention when it does. This could be the break we've been looking for. *Volden Megacorps,*" she said dreamily. Then her tone grew stern. "Just, please—don't screw it up."

"What about Ashton?"

"What about him?"

"It's his story."

Arlette looked away, coolly. "Maybe that's gonna change."

I shook my head. "But why me? And why now?"

"Why *not* now. And who cares? They saw one of your pieces and liked it. I dunno."

"Right. Next you're gonna tell me I've been nominated for a Pulitzer."

"Why the hesitation all of a sudden? You wanted a big story, and this might be it."

I thought about that and conceded warily. "You're right—this might be it."

Arlette folded her arms and tapped the toe of her shoe. "And I hope you're not gonna wear that."

The dark surface of the Tau sparkled. Perhaps it had been doused with pixie dust. *Hmm.* No better way to protect this oddball relic than to keep it on me.

"I'm a loner, Arlette. A rebel."

"Whatever."

I parted the leather strap and slipped the crucifix over my head. The Tau fell into place, nestled perfectly over my breastbone. At my heart.

Like it was meant to be there.

# CHAPTER 6

BEFORE ARLETTE LEFT my apartment, she handed me the business card of the rep from Volden Megacorps, and then a laminated Press Pass with a bar code.

"You'll need this to get in," she said. "And do me a favor—mind your manners. Okay?"

My encounter with the old seer had knocked me into Oz. I mumbled something as she left and remained staring at the card as if it contained a hidden message.

It was on high quality stock, dolled up with flowing script and the unmistakable Volden Megacorps logo—an over-lapping *V* and *M* which formed a unique triangulation of color at its center.

*Selwyn Brook*

*Community Liaison & Communications*

*Volden Megacorps*

*ut astrum per mens*

It was Latin, "To the stars, through the mind." Very Volden.

I turned the card over and back.

First, Klammer and now Volden. This was no coincidence. But why me? And why now?

I'd done enough research to know that the information on these two men was scant, endlessly tainted by the network matrix. Exotic tales about Black Masses and extraterrestrial visitations were just parts of the florid conjecture about their brief partnership. The truth, though less sensational, was nevertheless florid. Soren Volden had moved to the City of Angels a decade ago, leaving a self-created technological dynasty in Berlin for a new stomping ground. He fit right in with Hollywood's spa and astrology crowd. The Tinseltown moguls loved Volden and his mash-up of science and spirituality. Klammer had joined forces somewhere along the way and Spiraplex was born, a pleasure center in downtown Los Angeles employing the latest in nanotechnology and AI/human interface. Supposedly, they'd developed a way to tap into one's subconscious and conjure dream states in living color. The result was something called the *Dreamchamber*. According to those in the know, it was the next "big thing." Along the lines of the printing press or penicillin. *That* big. A device that would vault humanity into the technological stratosphere. But along the way, the two men's relationship turned. Rumor was that when Klammer learned of Volden's occult ties, he split. Apparently, he didn't like ectoplasm in his corn flakes. Now, after ten years, Klammer and Volden had become adversaries, Spiraplex was nearing completion, and VM would surely usher in the next stage of human evolution. And the Dreamchamber technology was still just a rumor.

So what use could two billionaires have with me? And what, if anything, did Ellie have to do with them?

I caught myself touching the Tau as it rested against my skin.

A knock sounded at my apartment door.

My heart nearly leapt out of my throat. I spun toward the door in an instinctive crouch. Between Klammer's warning about *risk* and Gollo's ghastly shouting, I was teetering on the edge. Had Arlette returned? Or maybe the ghost of Ellie was hot on my trail. No. This was something else.

I stared at the door as if, by doing so, I might summon the power of X-ray vision. Instead, I opted for something more practical. I tiptoed back into my bedroom, went to the nightstand, and knelt down. My pistol was underneath, wedged in the crook of the joints. It was loaded. I felt around and yanked it free, rose, and crept to the door, releasing the safety as I did.

I'd never actually fired the pistol. In general, I don't like guns. But if I had to unload some lead into someone, I'd convinced myself I could do so.

Okay. Maybe I was delusional.

A faint slit of light shone through the bottom of the door. A shadow was there. It couldn't be the mailman. Too late in the day. I lowered the pistol to my side, slightly behind me, and let it dangle there in my hand. I listened. No whispers. No heavy breathing. So I inhaled deeply and with my opposite hand, flung the door open.

"Oh my!"

Gloria Richardson teetered in the hallway, gripping her handbag to her chest. I thought for sure the plump 65-year-old widow would have a heart attack on the spot.

"Mrs. Richardson!" I fumbled the pistol behind me and managed to stuff it into the back of my pants.

"My lands! Mr. Moon, are you trying to scare me to death?" She fanned herself, huffing and sputtering in melodramatic fashion.

"I'm so sorry. I, um, I—"

"You've been busy," she snapped, "that's what you've been." She continued fanning herself and snorting in comedic fluster.

I reached out to steady her. "Maybe you should sit down."

She slapped my hand away. "I'll be fine." Then her eyes narrowed and her nose scrunched like an oversized chipmunk. "You're on one of your school projects again, aren't you? People coming and going. All kinds of ruckus. Really, Mr. Moon, it's hard to *not* notice."

Mrs. Gloria Richardson believed I was attending a local college to finish my degree in photojournalism. I'm not a serial liar by any stretch. Yet I'd needed an excuse for lugging camera equipment around at odd hours and bringing bizarre memorabilia home. If she learned that I worked for the Blue Crescent, I could only imagine the type of interrogation that would ensue. You see, Gloria Richardson is our neighborhood busybody. So I'd played it safe and fudged the facts. In a way, I guess, I *was* trying to graduate to something bigger and better. However, going back to school was as far from my personal goals as was becoming vice chair for the local herpetology board.

"Yep, another school project." I laughed nervously, making sure the pistol was securely in place in my pants. "They just keep on coming."

"I thought so." Then her features softened and she leaned in closer. "And the lady who just left your apartment...?" Her eye sparkled with the prospects of some juicy tidbit of info.

I straightened and issued a wry smile. "So how can I help you, Mrs. Richardson?"

"Yes, I—" She stepped back and casually brushed at her sweater. "I'll be out of town a few days. I'm leaving this afternoon, and was wondering if you can look in on Chelsea."

*Ugh.* I hated cats. The proof that there was ultimate good and evil in the world is dogs and cats, in that order.

"Cat-sit?" I scratched my head. "Well..."

"Remember, she likes two meals a day—a big breakfast, and then a small dinner, more like a snack. She's on a bit of a diet, that little porker." She giggled.

Before I had a chance to refuse, Mrs. Richardson reached into her handbag and passed me the key to her apartment.

I suppose I should be happy that the woman considers me responsible enough to baby-sit her prized Persian. As much as I am a hardened cynic and a non-cat lover, I have not lost respect for the elderly. Or animals in general. Although, with everything else going on, the timing for this couldn't be worse.

What could I say? I took the key.

"Thank you, dearie." She patted my hand. "Chelsea will *love* seeing you again."

I smiled politely. Who was she kidding? That feline she-devil probably wanted to claw my eyes out and use them as pigeon bait.

"The food is on the refrigerator," she said. "Same place. And just ignore the leaky faucet. Gretchen is sending a plumber. So you might watch for him. I'll be back home Tuesday."

I watched Mrs. Richardson meander back to her apartment, carefully scanning the hallway as she went, eyes and ears on the alert for neighborly misconduct.

Great! Now on top of revisiting my girlfriend's death, seeing psychics, contacting a representative of Volden Megacorps, and protecting some oddball relic, I had to play caretaker for a cat.

Perfect fit for an already jacked-up day.

# CHAPTER 7

I SET MRS. RICHARDSON'S apartment key on the kitchen counter next to Selwyn Brook's business card and the Press Pass. Then I removed my pistol from my pants, reset the safety, and laid it next to them.

Where did I go from here?

I was still trying to wrap my brain around the incident at Gollo's. Part of me wanted to go back and quiz him, shake the old man by the collar and demand he tell me the truth. How did he know Ellie called me Ray? How did he know about the Tau? How did Klammer even know to send me there? And what the hell was that stuff about the Elder Ones? It went against everything I wanted to believe. Psychics were fakes. Except this guy... The convulsions, the terror in his features. Hell, he didn't even give me a chance to pay him! He'd told me to run and I knew I had to comply.

But what was I running from?

I stared at the four items on the kitchen counter, massaging my knuckles as I mulled my predicament.

In the back of my mind, there was always the possibility that this stuff was real. It's not something I like to admit. After all, journalists are supposed to be indifferent. Which put me in direct conflict with the aims of the Blue Crescent. Embellishment and sensationalism was the Crescent's stock in trade. How could one write about lycanthropes and leprechauns without being tongue in cheek? Nevertheless, on rare occasions I would run into stories that just didn't fit, didn't have a reasonable explanation. I filed those away in the back of my brain. That file seemed to be growing. And this story was turning into one of those.

Klammer had paid me well to investigate the events surrounding Ellie's death. I'd taken the money, so I had to follow through... even if it led me somewhere I didn't want to go. Despite Arlette's obvious enthusiasm for the VM lead, I decided Selwyn Brook would have to wait.

The Downtown Police Precinct was within walking distance from my apartment. I went to pay Jimmy Pastorelli a visit.

Any chance I had to walk, as opposed to drive, I took it. The Cammy's 396 big block engine was a gas-guzzler, so besides avoiding parking hassles, walking also saved me a few bucks. And in a way, I enjoyed it. It freed my head. More than once, I worked out an angle on a story or came up with a punchy headline during a long walk. So you'd be mistaken if you thought my enjoyment of walking was purely recreational. Or cost-saving. Of course, in Los Angeles, being on foot in the wrong place could be bad for your health. But since I'd taken up jogging again, I knew what streets to avoid. Either way, I like to walk. And when things get really serious, I talk to myself as I walk.

On this trip, however, I kept my mouth shut and just listened. Maybe I was hoping Ellie would show up and fill in the details of this mess. Okay, not so much.

The Precinct is an old, single level building. It has a mosaic mural out front that, on occasion, is tagged by daring street kids who leave their monikers and piss on the walls before getting shooed off by the desk officer. As I prepared to enter, a collage of ads and posters brought me to an immediate halt.

The image of Anubis—the same style as the one Klammer had shown me—was hanging there, tacked in place with a wad of blue gum.

What the hell? I stepped closer and studied the image. It appeared to have been mass-produced, something the local anarchists would crank out in their basement. But there was no insignia or website to direct me. Someone had scrawled the words *They Live!* on the print. A chill coursed my spine, sending the hair on the back of my neck bristling. I looked behind me, but no one was there. Should there be? All this talk about murder and mediums had spooked me. Gollo's warning had taken root in my subconscious and was strangling any rationality I had remaining. *Get a grip, Moon!*

I returned my gaze to the poster. Anubis, Lord of the Hallowed Land, the necropolis. The figure was black, draped in Egyptian garb, and stood holding a staff bearing the symbol of the Ankh. I stared, squinting in thought. What was going on? And why would Klammer be so concerned about this? Did he believe Egyptian gods were infiltrating the city or something? More likely, another Cult of Isis had risen among the post-punk crowd and was threatening to go mainstream. Which meant, in no time, we'd be seeing Anubis tattoos, figurines, and specialty Tees sporting the image of the death god. Oh joy. I pondered the poster for a minute, and then shook my head.

Before entering the police station, I stopped, reached up, and touched the Tau underneath my shirt. I had no idea what kind of material this was made of. There was only one way to find out if it would trigger the metal detectors. I pushed the doors open and passed through without incident. Well, at least I wasn't wearing a bomb.

The officer at the counter looked up from some paperwork and rolled his eyes. I get this response often and never take it personal. Reporters, in general, are nuisances to the cops. Being that I reported on fringe science and hobgoblins, I was even more loathed.

"Jimmy in?" I asked.

The officer pursed his lips and buzzed me in.

"Thanks," I said.

He returned to his paperwork without compensating my gesture.

I passed behind the swinging door to the office of Jimmy Pastorelli. Jimmy is a gnome of a man with oversized glasses and a balding head. He secretly read the Crescent. A lot of folks did. As much as people want to blow off the paranormal, part of us simply cannot peel our eyes away. Jimmy's interest was a little different. Several years ago, he'd been assigned to investigate a series of ritualistic murders, uncovering what he believed was a network of high-end occultists, real Satanic power brokers. Suspects were never named and Jimmy's findings were buried. Just like the body parts they'd left behind. The event turned Jimmy Pastorelli into a fount of conspiratorial logic, a fledgling believer in the paranormal. It also provided me leads and insider info that his compatriots at the station wouldn't dream of offering. After that, he was assigned to head the Special Investigations unit. In a city this size, this weird, you get lots of "special" crime. And with Neuros making inroads into the upper strata of the arts and sciences, the paranormal was experiencing a good old fashioned revival. Jimmy joked that he'd been drawn into the paranormal. I'm sure he was ribbed for affiliating with kooks like me. But to his credit, he didn't seem to care.

Jimmy leaned on his desk with his arms folded, looking at an odd contraption. It sat in the corner of his office and appeared to be an old jukebox force-fitted with a tube-style television screen. A jumble of electrical wires surrounded the device and fuses protruded from its sides. Jimmy glanced over his shoulder as I entered. "Kolchak!"

"Hey, Jimmy."

He pushed off from the desk and shook my hand. "So what's new on the psychic hotline?"

"Hm. Let's see. How about hooded billionaires and Mexican mediums."

Jimmy furrowed his brow in feigned fascination. "Sounds interesting."

"And poltergeists. Mustn't forget the poltergeists."

"Now you got my attention. But I'm all outta silver bullets, so don't ask."

I snapped my fingers in mock disappointment. "Oh, well. Silver bullets don't work on poltergeists or else I'd take a box."

Jimmy laughed.

"So," I gestured to the device he'd been studying. "Did you confiscate that from a mad scientist or are you trying to build the world's most elaborate short wave radio?"

"Heh. The former." He turned back to the contraption and folded his arms again. "Mad scientist all the way."

"So..." I stepped closer, examining the contraption. "What is it?"

Jimmy glanced at me. "You don't know?"

"Should I?"

"A ghost box," he said flatly. "Or something like that."

"You mean, those corny transistor radios that ghost hunters use to talk to the dead?"

"You got it, Kolchak. An electronic device used to contact the other side."

"Charming."

"Ain't it." Jimmy nodded. "There's all kinds of variations, I guess. From the commercial to the strictly homemade. This is on the more upscale end, as you can see. Basically, they're designed to produce random voltage." He pointed out several electrical coils twining from the back of the device. "That generates raw audio, which is then fed into an echo chamber and recorded." Jimmy then motioned to the large drum at the base of the ghostly jukebox. "It creates a vacuum, white noise, you could say."

"Which spirits use to transmit their messages."

"Correct."

"As if the airwaves aren't cluttered enough."

"Only this one was, apparently, designed to take things one step further."

"Lemme guess—*televise* the visitor."

"Correct again." Jimmy tapped the glass of the TV screen. "Hey, you're good at this. Ever think about a position in the Special Investigations unit?"

"Never."

"Did you know Thomas Edison was working on one of these at his death?"

"You don't say. And what about this one?"

"Yeah, well." Jimmy's expression sobered. "He was no Edison. The architect of this one is chilling in the morgue right now. Or what's left of him. Walked straight into traffic, ranting about the end of the world or something. Sorry son of a bitch. Got hit twice. Splattered his brains across two lanes of freeway. At the moment, they're calling it a suicide. Lerium related, most likely. But after searching the guy's place, he was knee deep in weirdness. Magic circles. Talismans. Spell books. Guy seemed convinced that someone was trying to get in touch with him. Started building this ghost box, apparently, as a last resort. Drove him cuckoo. You know what's even weirder?"

"I can't imagine."

"It's not the only one we've confiscated."

"There's more of these out there?"

Jimmy nodded. "Got about a half dozen of these in the tank. None as nice as this baby. But it's like, I dunno, folks are suddenly itching to talk to ghosts."

Jimmy stared in thought. I kept my trap shut while he did.

Finally he said, "It's weird, Reagan. You've probably noticed it, in your line of work and all. But it seems like something's going round, you know? The whole city. Folks are sorta drawing a breath and waitin' for the shit to hit the fan. Especially the wingnuts. Astrologers. Fortunetellers. Every day now we're getting reports of someone flipping out, some occultist hitting the wall, whacking out, and taking someone with him. It's weird. Reports to the SI unit have easily doubled in the last month. Doubled. And then you find contraptions like that," he jabbed his thumb toward the ghost box, "and have to wonder if things aren't a lot bigger and more crazy than you ever imagined."

Jimmy stared at the ghost box for a while longer, shook his

head, then wandered back around his desk and plopped into the chair. He leaned back, thoughtful. Then he snapped out of it and began twiddling his thumbs. "But you didn't come to hear me ramble on about a new conspiracy, did you? So what can I do you for?"

"Right." I leaned forward and spread my hands atop his desk. Lowering my voice, I said, "The Bastion Sails accident."

Jimmy frowned. "Please, Reagan, don't go there."

"Trust me, I don't want to."

"Then let's not." He sat up and shuffled paperwork on his desk.

I sighed. "Jimmy, somethin's come up. I need to pick your brain."

"You don't need to do this to yourself."

I wished he was right. "Just humor me, please?"

Jimmy shrugged. "Okay. It's your sanity."

I said, "What was the conclusion of that investigation? You know, the official cause of the accident?"

He sat up, looking angry now. "We've been through this, Reagan."

We had. My God, we had been through this to the point of complete burnout.

Seeing I was resolute, he shook his head. "The irradiation chamber was mistakenly actuated. That's it. Human error. It was like some massive particle accelerator in there, they said, hotter than the ninth circle of hell. All 13 folks were vaporized, catapulted into the fourth state of matter. The room became a flippin' plasma chamber, for shit sake. Bastion Sails admitted full responsibility. I'm not sure what else you wanna know."

I peered at him.

"Look," Jimmy said. "I realize this's gotta be tough. But it's been almost a year."

"Eleven months, seven days, to be exact."

His demeanor passed from one of concern to pity. Man, I must sound like a sentimental schmuck.

Still, I pressed him. "And forensics had nothing to work with, is that right?"

"Nothing. Not unless they'd had some way to detect biological molecules. But even then, what good is there in cataloging the molecules of your girlfriend?"

An awkward moment passed.

"Sorry," Jimmy finally said. "That was pretty tasteless."

"Any log or record? Video of the event?"

"None. It was all a big mix-up. They weren't following protocol—which they admitted. They were probably too enamored with introducing their baby to the world. It's not the first time technology's gone awry, and it won't be the last."

"And there was nothing suspicious to anyone?"

"Suspicious?" His eyes narrowed. "Okay, Moon, where're you going with this?"

I felt like a fool. But with what I'd just seen, I had to go for it. "Jimmy, who's to say they weren't murdered?"

Jimmy stared at me, his eyes slowly hardening. Now we were playing ball. "There was no reason for it—no motive, no evidence to the contrary. Why would murder even be suspected? This isn't one of your wacky stories, is it?"

"Not yet."

"Listen. Bastion Sails is all over the map. They've been experimenting with alternate energy for the longest. All kinds of whacky stuff—radiant energy, fractionation, electromagnetic bullshit. You know. Besides, what purpose would there be in killing thirteen random observers, huh?"

"I dunno. Were they random? Besides, if no one ever saw the bodies, and if the event was never recorded or documented, what evidence do you have that they *weren't* murdered? Hell, for all I know, they may still be alive."

"Okay. That's it." Jimmy pushed himself away from his desk and rose to his feet. "Now I know this is one of your stories."

"There was nothing to bury, Jimmy! We lowered an empty box into the ground for God's sake. No one saw anything. They just disappeared."

"Particle accelerators have that effect, ya know?"

"Yeah? Well who's to say there wasn't foul play involved? Especially if the possibility of murder was never looked into."

He stared dully at me. Then Jimmy walked over and put his hand on my shoulder. "Look, Reagan. It's been a year."

I pursed my lips in annoyance, mostly annoyed at his unwillingness to get on board with my new project.

"I sympathize with you," he said. "Ellie was cool. But this is... this is nuts. You gotta get on with your life, man. Take up a hobby. Write a book. Stop lettin' all this Weird Science shit twist you up. You're letting those whackjobs at the Crescent get to you, ya know that?"

"I thought you believed in conspiracies?"

He seemed to ponder that for a moment. "You're right. Just not *this* one. Besides, they admitted culpability and paid up. I don't know how much VM paid to the victims, but I'm assuming it was a boatload."

I stepped back and looked at him. "What'd you say?"

"I said they admitted culpability and paid up."

"No, about Volden Megacorps?"

"They're majority owners of Bastion Sails' electromagnetic division. You know that."

I stared off into space. "You're right."

"Volden's got his fingers in everything. Cryogenics, sea sieves, cellular reanimation."

"Now that you say that, I do recall VM cutting a check to Ellie's mother..." The pistons of my brain were firing on all cylinders now. "Thanks, Jimmy. You've been a huge help." I hurried toward the door.

"Really? So what'd I say?"

"Just do me a favor. Take a closer look at that accident, will ya?"

"Okay. But if you're messin' with Volden, you're messin' with the big boys." He meandered back to his desk, talking as he went.

"Just in case you haven't noticed, Spiraplex is a big deal. A *very* big deal. One-third of the force is tied up at that Taj Majal of his as we speak. Protests. Public disturbances. It's like the biggest porch light in the world got turned on and all the bugs in the city came out. There's more weirdos per capita in that block than a ComiCon convention. Not to mention, we've got dignitaries from around the world flying in here just to see it. To bow down and kiss the ring of Soren Volden." He plopped into his chair. "All that to say, VM is not the type of outfit you wanna pick a fight with."

I just stared at him, without concession.

Jimmy Pastorelli leaned back in his chair. "Better watch your back, Reagan."

# CHAPTER 8

WHEN I LEFT THE PRECINCT, Ellie was on my brain. How could she *not* be? Her memory had been resurrected by circumstances beyond my control. And now, like a ghost, she was beckoning me to follow. Her golden hair. Her laugh. Her whimsy. Why not follow? She always said she didn't belong, that this present world was just a training ground for the next. Yet Ellie Wells had brought me more into the present world than anyone ever had.

"There's a reason why you haven't died," Ellie used to say. "All those close calls and escapes—it's not just a coincidence, Ray. Something big's in the works for you."

Like I needed to hear that again.

I practically jogged back from the Precinct. Klammer knew more than he was saying. He had to. Hell, for all I knew, he might've been *involved* in the Bastion Sails accident himself.

I hurried past a cluster of pedestrians, bumping a kid who cursed at my lack of courtesy. My car was parked around the corner from my apartment. I started to get in and stopped. Something about the way this was unfolding gave me no choice. I hurried upstairs and retrieved my gun, wedging it into the back of my jeans. The way things were going, I might need it.

I drove south, retracing Blondie's route to Klammer's meeting place. The chances that Klammer was still there were slim. But I had to try.

Several cars were parked in the alley. It seemed even more intimidating without Blondie leading the way. The sun had arced its way west, leaving the alley in cool shadow. I parked the Cammy and headed to the apartment. As I climbed the stairs, I did not bother counting them again, or calculating any potential numerological anomalies. The door was unlocked and the apartment was empty. Figured. I went from room to room, just to make sure. Empty. The only evidence that they'd been there was the lone chair and table. I approached, studying the furniture for anything—an ash, a droplet of liquid, a strip of cloth, a signature carved in the wood—anything that could aid my fevered inquiry. There was nothing.

I stepped back and stood in the middle of the room, watching a cockroach skitter along the floorboard.

He said he would be in touch. And men of Klammer's stature got in touch when and where they chose. But now I needed to know. I needed to know what he knew about Ellie. I needed to know why he sent me to Gollo.

Although everything inside me screamed against it, there was only one thing left to do.

I left the apartments en route to Lincoln Heights. The old Mexican seer was my only connection to Klammer. To Volden.

To the Other Side.

When I arrived there, I parked across the street three houses down, and turned off the car. I stared at the tropical environs that surrounded Gollo's place. The cogs of my brain were doing double-time. The last thing the old man had implored me to do was to run. But where to? And from what? If Gollo had really gotten in touch with Ellie's spirit, or if he knew something he wasn't saying, then I had to dig it out of him.

Or her.

I left the car and stood on the sidewalk, brushing down the back of my shirt to insure the pistol wasn't showing. But if it was supposed to bring me confidence, something wasn't working.

A radio played somewhere. Oldies. Two men cruised by, riding low in a metal-flaked red Impala. They wore sunglasses and looked at me as if I'd just fallen off the ugly truck. They turned the corner. I waited and then hurried across the street, leaving Mick Jagger to serenade the homies. I opened the gate, and slipped onto the property.

I could hear the television through the screen door. Matilda the Hun was probably still plastered to the couch. Rather than suffer her interrogation again, I opted to follow a hunch and do a little investigation of my own. I hurried around the house, down the walkway to Gollo's cabana out back, hoping to God that noisy cockatiel didn't let loose as I passed. It was a decision I'd sorely regret.

The sun had dipped far enough as to leave the place in late afternoon shadow. Birds rustled in the palms beside the seer's hut. Perhaps he was here, servicing another customer. Or maybe he was still pondering our encounter. *Fat chance.* Then again, perhaps there was some tidbit of information I could dig up to connect the dots. Either way, I had to try.

The water fountain tinkled out its melody. Calming the troubled spirits, hopefully. But something seemed different about the place. I stopped halfway into the property. My mind was on another frequency, my motions measured. I stared at the entry to the room, fixated.

He was in there. I knew he was in there.

I crept forward. Everything seemed to unfold in slow motion. The bead curtain gently stirred. Something glinted in the doorway— dark, narrow.

This wasn't right.

God, this wasn't right.

Red flags unfurled inside me. A fire alarm clanging in my noodle. I wanted to remove my pistol. But sneaking around in someone's backyard in Lincoln Heights with a drawn handgun was asking for trouble. Besides, no firearm in the world could protect me from what I sensed was awaiting me.

I crept closer, over the bridge, onto the porch. The wind chimes jangled softly behind me. That's when I noticed the wand, lying on the porch. Glistening. What was it doing here? I bent down and reached toward it. Then stopped.

It was wet.

With blood.

I was standing amidst faint spatters. Droplets of blood dotted the entryway, a crimson colorwash.

A surge of panic tore through me. As I straightened, through the bead curtain I glimpsed something lying across the floor.

The hackles on my neck rose.

*Run, señor.*

I pressed through the curtain. Gollo lay sprawled beside his chair. His flannel was half off, twisted precariously around his body. The wire rim glasses lay crushed at his side. His body was punctured by multiple bloody wounds. Deep red perforations marred his flesh, soaking his flannel in dark crimson. Arterial blood had sprayed the place, making the walls look like a demented abstract. Even the picture of Christ had been spattered. Gollo's head was turned toward me, his tattoo in full display—blue markings that encircled both eyes like some demented clown. Even worse, both eyeballs had been punctured and were seeping white gauzy liquid mixed with blood.

*Ray—ruuuunnnnnn!*

I slowly backed away from the cabana. The last thing I saw was my business card still lying on the table.

I stood on the porch, too stunned to move, unsure where to go or what to do. Who would do such a thing? And why? Good Lord—what was I being sucked into? Someone had followed me. They had to have. Gollo didn't even have time to collect my card and leave after our session. Unless he had another visitor. But why the old man? He seemed harmless enough. I needed to call the cops. Or an ambulance. Did the woman up front even know? Hell, maybe she'd done it!

I was hyperventilating.

As I staggered across the bridge, grappling with my precarious options, the garble of a radio sounded somewhere out front and I jolted to a stop.

"Ohhhh, shit!"

I tiptoed across the path and peeked from behind a palm. Out in the street, through the foliage, I could see a police car.

I ducked back into the yard.

Maybe someone had seen me sneaking around in the back yard and reported a prowler. But this was the Heights. LAPD was probably a fixture here. Maybe they'd pulled a car over or were just checking some plates. They probably weren't even coming in here. If I just waited it out, they'd be gone before I knew it.

Yet the way things were going today, I doubted it.

*Ray—ruuuunnnnnn!*

I found myself drifting toward the bamboo hedges, my mind darting through potential alibis. I had no reason to murder the old man, so why should I run? I was doing a piece on local psychics, just like I'd told his daughter. But that was earlier in the day. She didn't even know I was back here. And now I'd returned, trespassing. Even if things panned out, I could be looking at jail time for wielding a loaded unlicensed gun. At least, a hefty fine.

*Nice going, Moon.*

My gaze flashed around the tiny jungle. I heard voices and more radio garble. I slunk into the bamboo. A small chain link fence bordered the property. I glanced over the fence. Other than a barren garden overrun with weeds and children's toys scattering the dry ground, the neighbor's backyard was empty. And quite accessible. I could slip out of here with no problem. Which I did. I leapt the fence, without giving myself time to parse the particulars.

I've jumped a lot of fences in my day, but never to run away from the cops. Or flee a crime scene. As far as I knew, my getaway was clean. But being this was the 18th, I guessed the fun was just beginning.

# CHAPTER 9

I WAS THINKING ABOUT Mrs. Richardson's cat while I ran. Don't ask me why. Anal retentiveness doesn't vanish just because you're running from the cops.

I scaled another fence, landed in some garden tools, and dogs began yapping somewhere.

I should've just stayed there, told them I'd found the old man like that. And what else? That a mysterious tycoon with a cage over his head had sent me there? That a psychic who couldn't possibly have known my nickname told me to run away? Or that my dead girlfriend just might be trying to get in touch with me? The only consolation was that even if the police did track me down, I had no motive for killing a medium.

Unless he'd told me something I didn't want to hear.

I kept running, skirting a clothesline draped with bras and bandanas. I caught a whiff of lerium as I followed a row of hedges. Quietly opening a gate, I poked my head from behind some bushes. I was four houses down. A second cop car was pulling up in front of Gollo's. *Dammit!* This was no traffic stop. I inhaled deeply, nonchalantly hit the sidewalk, and walked the opposite direction. Further down, once I was out of view of the cops, I crossed the street, found an alley, and started back the opposite direction, back toward the Cammy. I didn't run, though I was sweating now more from panic than exertion. Circling the block, I emerged down a small side street and peered from behind a parked ice cream truck. The Cammy was twenty feet away, waiting for me.

Another police car had arrived. Great! This was officially breaking news. Crime scene tape was being unfurled and Gollo's daughter was standing out front, inconsolable, sobbing, and throwing wild haymakers at the officers. Neighbors huddled on their porches in whispered conversation. I took advantage of the commotion by heading to my car and getting in. I fired up the Cammy, turned around in a driveway, and headed the other way.

Just like I'd never been there.

The city lights had begun to shimmer against the twilight sky. It was quitting time and the streets were packed. When you live in L.A., traffic is a normal part of your life. Whether it's detours, accidents, or just plain gridlock, you try not to sweat it. I was not a Type A driver by any means. But tonight I found myself wringing the wheel and cursing the traffic. It was road rage squared.

I dabbed sweat off my forehead and glanced at myself in the rearview mirror.

"You're screwed, you know that?"

I instinctively drove to my apartment, stopped in a loading zone, and just sat there with the motor rumbling, staring up at my window. Why had I even come here? I checked my cell phone. I was trembling so bad I needed both hands to steady the phone. There were no texts, just a message from Cyrus Moench, a neo-Nazi who'd been bending my ear for the last six months wanting a piece on his white supremacist group and their prepping for a superior race. I deleted the voicemail without listening. Arlette had not called, though I knew she'd be prodding me for an update about the VM rep. There were no other messages, no missed calls. I looked up from the phone and studied the apartments. Investigations, like the wheels of justice, turn slowly. And maybe I could cut an investigation off at the pass.

I put the Cammy in gear and drove straight to The Blue Crescent.

The symbol of the crescent moon was used by every other wannabe occultist or New Ager in town. To some it symbolized death, to others eternal life. Why our crescent was 'blue' was beyond me. Although, on occasion, one of the staff would use the expression, 'Once in a blue *crescent* moon.' Either way, it's not what you'd call a major publication. However, its rabid readership has made it a bit of a cult attraction. Every month, without fail, someone stumbled into our offices with a cape and a Hungarian accent asking to be interviewed. For this reason, we removed the sign out front. Now the only evidence of our location was the fading stenciled letters across the brick and a photocopy of a flying saucer with the words, 'We Believe' in block font pasted to the plate glass window. It's a long narrow complex, just off Hollywood Blvd, wedged between a dry cleaners and a business that offered 24 hour VIP tours of the stars' homes. Why anyone would want to see Spielberg's mansion at 2:30 A.M. is beyond me. Behind the facility is an enclosed bullpen where we stage shots, take photos, and deliver the print version of the mag. Arlette swears they once  had the remains of a space alien out there, before some stray cats dragged it away.

I turned into the alley. Arlette's car was parked there. Thank God. I parked behind Ashton's Ninja bike, got out, looked both directions, and hurriedly tucked the pistol under the driver's seat. Then I went to the back door and pumped the buzzer. My hands were still trembling, the adrenaline surging through my body like an injection of lightning. A halogen lamp winked to life overhead.

As I waited, exhaustion welled up and draped me like a hungry python. I slumped against the building. Images of Gollo's blood-spattered walls and his shrill, inhuman warning reverberated inside me. El diablo was coming all right. But it was the old man he'd been coming for.

The view hatch slid open in the door and I stepped back in order to be seen. An eyeball glistened and then Neville's ratty mop swept by. The hatch slid back, the door was unbolted, and he let me in.

"Dude, you're missing all the action!"

"You wanna bet?" I said.

Neville closed and bolted the door behind me. "Did Arlette tell you?" Before I could answer, he continued, "Some guy from VM came in. *Volden Megacorps, dude!* Do you believe it? All spiffed up—Italian suit, porcelain teeth. Looked like a game show host, or somethin'. Just walked in and asked for Reagan Moon. *Reagan Moon.* Dude. We were all just staring."

"Yeah, she told me."

Neville was our print and distribution guy with one foot in the web design department. He'd missed his calling as a Ronnie James Dio impersonator—tight black clothing, leather studs, and hair that deserved endangered species status from PETA.

"So Ashton knows," I said.

"He knows." Neville rolled his eyes. Yeah. No one much cared for Ashton.

"We got another one!" someone yelled down the hallway. It was Penny, our emo technician and expert on all things undead.

Garbled radio transmission sounded from inside her office and she leaned back in to listen.

"Got what?" I asked.

"As soon as Mr. Italian Suit left," Neville said, "they started popping up. First an astrologer in Echo Park. Then a psychic."

Now he had my attention.

Penny stuck her head back out. "Another one! Lincoln Heights. Sounds like some local fortune teller."

"Another what?" I said, not really wanting to know.

"See? I told you." Neville playfully socked my arm. "It's the fifth murder of the day!"

I mouthed the word *fifth.*

"Echo Park," Penny said, half-listening to the scanner in her office. "An astrologer. This afternoon, Koreatown, a medium's throat was slit with a ceremonial blade. West Hollywood, another medium. Then Vernon. A psychic. Strangled."

"It's Richard Ramirez, I tell ya!" Neville proclaimed, almost gleeful. "The Night Stalker. He's comin' back for vengeance. Dude!"

Arlette passed between offices, stopped, and stood with her hands on her hips, watching us.

"Back in the land of the living?" she said to me, seeping sarcasm.

"We have to talk."

"You're right," she said.

Penny and Neville glanced at each other and hustled back into their cubicles. Arlette had that effect on people. Then Arlette marched into her office with me in tow. Ashton swiveled in his chair as we passed, wagging his finger at me. It wasn't the first time Arlette had spanked me, and Ashton enjoyed every lashing. I gave him the finger and kept going.

Other than a few B-movie posters and a rather extensive, but ragged, actual library on the paranormal, the Crescent is just like any other newspaper outfit. Bland. Noisy. Cluttered. The way some folks talked, you'd think we'd have pentagrams and sacrificial altars strewn about the place. Not so. We just happen to collect the weird news. Other than that, we're just your average run-of-the-mill journalists. Sort of.

Arlette's office is abnormally neat. For me, any penchant for neatness is an abnormality. However, it matched her coiffed persona. Had you not known Arlette was the senior editor of the city's leading paranormal mag, you'd have mistaken her for a lawyer or a European power broker. She was slick. But I knew her soft spots.

Arlette sat down, swiveled sideways, and crossed her legs. This signaled we were about to talk. She spread her left hand on the desk and strummed her fingers. She used to do that, I thought, because of the sound her wedding ring made clicking on the desk. Like a timer, counting down the minutes to your departure. But she didn't have a wedding ring any longer. So the action did not seem to have the same effect.

She motioned me to sit, but I remained standing.

"I take it you haven't followed through on our contact." Her voice was tight. She was annoyed with me.

"Contact?" I searched my scattered mind. "Oh, yeah! I mean, no."

She squinted at me and shook her head slowly. "What is wrong with you today, Moon?"

I drew my hands through my hair. "Listen. You've helped me out of a lot of tight spots."

"Don't remind me."

"Well, I'm in a tight spot."

Arlette stopped strumming her fingers. She could tell when I wasn't joking.

"You didn't try to sneak back into the Hollywood crypt again, did you?"

"Worse." I swallowed hard. "I think I just stumbled on one of those murders."

"Huh? You mean *those* murders?" She pointed toward the hallway.

"Yeah."

"Time out. How do you *stumble* onto a murder?"

"Give me a minute."

I started pacing, and she watched me. Back and forth. Back and forth. Finally, I said, "His name was Gollo. He was stabbed. I left my business card there. And prints. All over the place."

Arlette sat stunned. "Okay. You've got some explaining to do."

I stopped pacing. "You have to trust me on this, boss. I can't reveal my sources. In fact, I'm not sure *I* even know them."

Arlette uncrossed her legs and swiveled to face me. Her eyes were tight, moving from suspicion to cold concern. "Just tell me one thing—you didn't murder anyone, did you?"

I hesitated just long enough for her to know I was angry at the assertion.

"Okay," she said. "I just needed to make sure. So what do you want me to do?"

"I'm not sure." I started pacing again.

"Well that's no help." She watched me. "So why'd you leave a crime scene?"

"I didn't! I mean, I didn't know it was a crime scene when I got there. I was scared. It happened so fast. The police showed up, I was where I shouldn't be and I made a quick exit. Plus I had a gun on me."

"A gun! You were seeing a psychic, Moon. *A psychic.* Why'd you need a gun?"

"I'd been tipped off. God, I should have known. Someone told me to be ready, that there was risk involved. I don't know..."

She was gawking. "Can this get any more weird?"

"They used a wand to kill the guy."

"Huh? You mean they zapped him like Harry Potter?"

"Not funny."

"Well, what?"

"They stabbed him. Multiple times. Blood everywhere. It wasn't a pretty sight. Please, just give me the benefit of the doubt, will you?"

"A wand..." she said incredulously, letting her gaze roam. "That's a first. Well, who was it? And why were you there?"

"He was just a medium. Some old man on the east side of town. I was sent there to investigate another possible murder earlier in the day. That's where I was coming from when you saw me at my apartment. But that was *before* the murder. *His* murder."

"Okay. I'm confused. You went there a *second* time?"

I nodded.

"Why?" she asked.

"It's a long story." I stopped. "Arlette, I think someone may be trying to frame me."

She stared. "You don't look well."

"I'm not well!"

"Frame you? Why?"

"I don't know."

She settled back in her chair. "Are you sure you're all right?"

"No, I'm not all right! This's been a *very* bad day."

She peered at me, and then her posture relaxed. "I'm sorry."

I could see Arlette thinking. She pushed back in her chair, gnawing her lip. Then she straightened. "I'll vouch for you, Moon. That's what you want, isn't it? You were doing some research for an upcoming piece." She shrugged. "A piece on local mediums. Nothing unusual."

"Right."

"But they can still charge you with fleeing a crime scene, you know?"

"It wasn't a crime scene when I got there the first time. And no one saw me there the second time. At least, no one that I know of."

She peered at me and started strumming her fingers on the desk again.

"It's good enough for now," I said. "Thanks."

"You just better not drag us down," she said coldly. "D'you hear me?"

I nodded. "So what the hell's going on here, Arlette? Why would someone be killing occultists in Los Angeles?"

"I dunno." She became thoughtful. "Maybe it's a signal from the other side. You know, someone doesn't want us to hear something."

I peered at her.

"Look," she said. "We get a leg up on this story and it could be huge. And seeing that you've already got a leg up on the story..."

"*Me?*"

"I know just the person who can help us."

I stared at her. "Not Matisse."

"He likes you, Moon."

"He's crazy."

"That's probably why he likes you."

She was right. If anyone could connect the murder of a bunch of psychics and astrologers, at least float some wild guesses, it was Matisse. The Mad Spaniard. I pressed my fists to my forehead.

"What's wrong?" she asked.

"Oh, nothing. I just think I'm losing my mind, that's all."

"You're just now realizing this?"

"And the guy from VM? What should I do about him?"

She straightened some items on her desk. "You can multitask, can't you?"

I groaned.

Maybe Arlette was right. It was a signal from the other side; someone was trying to send us a message. Send *me* a message. Of course, I'd already heard that message. *Run, Ray!* So maybe that was the message someone didn't want me to hear. Problem was, now I was running straight into trouble.

# CHAPTER 10

BY THE TIME I REACHED the Asylum, evening had descended upon the 18th of February. Fingers of clouds were drifting from the west, blotting out the faint starlight. Weather was on the way. Something dark and fierce, if my gut was to be trusted.

To the north, spotlights swept the sky. It had been like this well on a year in anticipation for the opening of Spiraplex. It was like a circus downtown these days. Arlette had put Ashton on the story but, frankly, I tended to ignore Ashton's pieces. His journalistic chops were undisputed. But it was the incessant one-upmanship that made the guy a pain in the ass. Getting the Spiraplex story was just another feather in his cap. And another dig at me. For that reason, I'd remained relatively low-key about the Spiraplex affair and our reportage of the approaching event. My bad. It was appearing like some of that info could come in handy. Meanwhile, the crowds had continued to grow around Spiraplex. The streets surrounding Volden's architectural wonder were constantly congested with junkies of obscura and fans of the mogul's intrepid experimentations. Anticipation for the grand opening was reaching a fevered pitch. Which is one reason why I found it hard to believe that someone as public and powerful as Soren Volden could be even remotely implicit in the Bastion Sails murder. Men of his stature did not dirty their hands in such affairs. Then again, men of his stature had all the resources necessary to keep any charges from sticking.

I stood outside the Cammy, closed the door, and looked down the alley that led to the Asylum.

The Asylum is not what you think. There's no straightjackets or sinister doctors there. It is not surrounded by gangly trees and ancient gates, nor patrolled by scarred, salivating Rottweilers. Although it probably should be. It was located south of Little Tokyo in the Warehouse District, blocks of industrial sites and factories. The Los Angeles River cordoned the property. The stink of pond scum and grease hung in the air.

Who would suspect that some of the world's most important religious artifacts were housed here?

I hurried through the alley between warehouses. It opened into a loading dock. A single vapor lamp cast a drab yellow sheen across a rotted platform. A freight elevator was situated next to a padlocked roll-up door. Someone had spray-painted neon green biohazard signs across the walls and stenciled the Obey logo. To my surprise, three Anubis posters were pasted side-by-side nearby, along with the words *They Live!* in bleeding black spray paint. A security camera perched high above was aimed in my direction.

I approached the speaker box next to the freight elevator and punched the button. A buzz sounded faintly down below.

I stepped back and looked up at the camera, but the speaker box remained dead.

After a minute, I punched the button again, knowing that my chances of catching Matisse were slim. The Mad Spaniard was probably off on one of his expeditions. Either that or he was sleeping off a hangover. Still there was no answer.

Horizontal metal doors were clamped shut across the elevator. Dappled in rust and old paint, they looked like something out of a Siberian bunker. I grabbed the handle and tried to hoist it open, but the doors were immovable. A mounted keyhole was located on one side. It could possibly be picked, if I had such skills. Then again, this fortress appeared impenetrable. Keyhole included.

I punched the speaker button one final time and then turned in frustration to leave.

The speaker crackled, startling me.

"Who're you?" a voice sounded.

A female voice.

This caught me off guard. Matisse was not married. He joked that his years as a Jesuit had rewired his circuitry. But maybe his need for female companionship had finally caught up to him.

I cleared my throat. "Reagan Moon. I'm a reporter with the Blue Crescent. I'd like to—"

The intercom clicked off.

I stood rather dumbfounded. Who was this woman? And where was Matisse? He was never one to turn me down. Discussing occultism and quasi-religious mumbo-jumbo was right in his wheelhouse. Which is why he liked me. It also gave me an idea.

I punched the button again and held it, just to make sure she knew I was serious. The radio crackled again.

"Matisse's busy," the female voice said. "Sorry. He doesn't have time for reporters."

"Wait!" I stepped back into full view of the camera, reached into my shirt and removed the Tau. It dangled in front me, hanging from my fist. "Tell him I found something."

I remained there with the Tau extended, peering at the video camera.

Finally the elevator buzzer sounded.

I knew it. Matisse could not resist a new mystery. I quickly returned the Tau to its place, tucked it under my shirt, and yanked the door up. The freight elevator doors clanged open like a massive metallic jaw. A large cross welded from mismatched parts of corrugated metal hung on the back wall of the elevator. Supposedly, the perimeter of this facility was blessed with holy water once a month. Matisse covered all of his bases. I stepped over a thick line of salt into the elevator. If I'd been a revenant, I would have been incinerated on the spot. But metal crosses and salt barriers have no such effect on plain humans. Even bad ones like me.

I closed the door, hit the switch, the elevator jolted and began its descent. I took a second to try to gather my wits. Images of Gollo's corpse riffled through my brain like a slideshow from a *Día de Los Muertos* carnival. I knew this was more than just some psycho copping revenge for a bad tarot reading. It had to be. Like Jimmy had said—something was brewing.

The elevator lurched to a stop. I hoisted the door open. Its metallic clang thrummed through the vast, spottily lit warehouse that stretched before me. I stepped out and my footsteps echoed across the concrete.

Scanners were erected on each side of the door and video cameras at multiple angles. The TSA would have been impressed. Around the corner, out of sight, Matisse kept a flamethrower and a javelin that he called the *Finger of God*. Just in case something undead made it this far without getting fried. Bays lined the cavernous facility, three tiers high, stacked with wooden crates and statuary. Exotic smells of wax and herbs commingled with the scent of propane. Matisse said they'd designed the place for a nuclear shelter during the Cold War, a potential hideaway for Cal Tech nerds, military brass, and scum politicians. Just the types of people you'd want surviving to kick-start civilization. Supposedly, the entire facility was encased in lead. And everyone knew that lead thwarted psychic attacks.

A squat, single level structure near the elevator cast a long beam of light across the dull concrete floor. Matisse called this his command post. He was fond of considering his mission militaristic. I approached the small structure, ducked under several hanging rosaries and camouflage netting, and poked my head inside. It smelled of wolfsbane. Maps of the city were tacked cockeyed on the walls, marked with odd inscriptions and notations. A partial bottle of wine sat on a table alongside a laptop, some flash drives, the latest edition of the Blue Crescent, and several Styrofoam trays of Chinese leftovers. However, Matisse's swivel chair was empty. I glanced at the surveillance screens overhead, including the one that I'd just been watched on. No sign of movement anywhere.

"Matisse!" I called. "Hey! It's Moon! You here?"

I walked into the command post, through the front room and into the hallway, glancing between two other rooms. In one, a large vault rose between a nonsense of books and scrolls, volumes strewn across sagging cases and bulging in boxes. Ceramic bowls laden with herbs, along with test tubes, and grinding stones, cluttered the shelves. Melted candles and glass jars with odd spongy specimens gave the room all the charm of a medieval laboratory. The other room consisted of living quarters: A couch, TV, refrigerator, microwave, and unmade bed. At the end of the hall was a bathroom and a moldy tile shower.

There was no one here.

I turned to leave, to head into the bays in search of the Mad Spaniard, but stopped in my tracks. A girl, slight of build with shoulder-length silver-white hair, stood in the doorway. She was without shoes. A mischievous twinkle danced in her eyes.

"Um, I'm looking for Matisse."

"Of course you are!" she giggled.

She couldn't have been drinking age. Pixie-ish features and spunk to match. She wore faded jean knickers and a black print shirt with pink skulls randomly dappled across it. Heavy eyeliner with sparkles. Tinkerbell turned Goth. She stood there chomping gum, bouncing on her toes, waiting for me to make the next move.

"Did you..." I began. "Who are you?"

She giggled again, a mirthful adolescence pinching her features in impish delight. "Oh, that depends."

"Really."

"Uh-huh!"

"Depends on what?"

She pressed a finger to her lips in feigned contemplation. "On what's needed, I guess."

I squinted at her.

"Or my mood," she continued. "Could depend on my mood. Maybe. I dunno. It's weird. I try not to think about it."

I wasn't sure if I should play this straight or put her over my knee and spank her.

"So, do you have a name?" I said, allowing just enough annoyance to seep into my tone.

"Of course! Everybody's got a name."

She kept bouncing on her toes.

Finally, I said, "So... what's yours?"

"That depends."

Okay, a spanking it was. I folded my arms and sighed.

She scowled. "You're angry."

"No. Actually I enjoy being toyed with."

"My mother named me after an insect."

"Oh yeah? Lemme guess—*Stink Bug*."

"That's mean."

"Exactly."

"No. This insect is nocturnal. They cannibalize each other when they're really hungry. And in Thailand—"

Suddenly she looked over her shoulder. "Oops!" she exclaimed, and then darted into the warehouse shouting over her shoulder, "Goodbye!"

"Hey!" I hurried after her, knocking some boxes over as I went. "Hey!"

She disappeared down a shadowy side aisle, her footsteps pattering into silence, swallowed by the vast structure.

I stood staring that direction.

What the hell had Matisse been doing down here? He sometimes spoke of others—traders, profs, archeologists. Even mercenaries. But other than Mace, world traveler renowned, I'd never encountered anyone else down here. Which made this barefoot pixie's presence all the more unusual.

And that was why I tore after her.

The bay she'd gone down was lined with statuary. Moldering casts of demons and altars stained from God-knew-what crowded the way. She was already nearing the end of the bay. Damn. This kid was fast. I put my head down and did my best Silver Surfer imitation, ziz-zagging past wadded Tyvek suits and tottering pallets of stone deities. By the time I reached the end of the bay, she was long gone. I glanced down the intersecting aisles, but there was no sign of her.

I stood for a moment, pondering my encounter with the waif, when my attention was drawn to a wedge of light closing behind a door in the opposite bay. I hurried that direction, this time yelling as I went just to let her know, or anyone else within range, that I was serious and needed some assistance.

It was a greenhouse, the kind a wannabe survivalist could buy from Popular Mechanics and assemble in their garage in preparation for societal collapse. Dull plastic sheeting draped a PVC framed lean-to with a rickety door on one side. Perhaps fifteen feet long. Artificial light glowed through steamy plastic panels.

I slowed and approached cautiously, staring at the door, fully expecting Tinkerbell to burst out in song and dance.

"Hey," I called. I could see no movement inside the greenhouse. "Hey. You in there? I'm looking for Matisse."

A pungent smell struck me. Licorice. Laced with ammonia or a similar chemical. I reached the door and stood there.

"I'm looking for Matisse. Hey, you in there?"

I didn't recall Matisse ever mentioning a greenhouse in the Asylum. It wasn't necessarily a surprise. In fact, considering the other items in his collection, this was rather tame. Yet somehow I knew he wasn't growing alfalfa sprouts and raspberries either.

I yanked the door open.

The girl was nowhere to be found.

Inside the greenhouse stretched a single aisle. On one side, the slanted side of the lean-to, sat plastic grower's pots holding starter seedlings. On the opposite side of the aisle, were the adult plants.

A warm aromatic fog surrounded me. Loam and licorice. The smell was even more pronounced now. Almost intoxicating. But underlying the vegetative richness was a sharp chemical smell. I scanned the area for the source of the smell. Near a leaky drip system sat several unmarked plastic jugs, beakers, and heavy duty rubber gloves.

What kind of operation was this?

I stepped further in so as to inspect the plants. I'm no botanist, but these were unlike anything I'd ever seen. The adults rose four to five feet high, single stalks, from which blossomed an umbrella of delicate branches, tendrils almost. At the end of each of these branches unfurled four broad leaves, fig-like, and inside these leaves clung translucent petals curling inwards to form a saucer. At this diaphanous center emerged a single cone, a velvety rust-colored cap.

I found myself staring at this wonder. Perhaps Matisse was collecting new plant species along with his pagan antiquities. Somehow, I didn't think so.

An engine started and began puttering somewhere in one of the bays. I quickly snapped off a loose strand of plastic from a greenhouse panel and then plucked a flower from the closest plant. Folding it into the plastic, I shoved the wad into my back pocket. Then I hurried out of the greenhouse.

The sound of the engine rose and I ran in that direction. I emerged near the command center, scanning the warehouse. A forklift skidded from one of the aisles, corrected, and barreled toward me, forks rattling as it approached.

What the hell was going on? Maybe Miss Manners had snatched the keys and was out for a joy ride.

I strafed toward the command center, eyes fixed on the advancing vehicle. The driver changed direction as I moved, headed straight at me. That's when I changed gears into full-on sprint. When I reached the building I skidded to a stop, turned, and stood poised. The forklift had picked up speed, its overhead lights bearing down on me. If this was a game of chicken, I had the most to lose by not flinching. It barreled forward, engine full-tilt. At the last second, I lunged out of the way. I somersaulted, but landed awkwardly and collapsed into a heap against the command center. I spun around on my ass as Matisse leaned out of the forklift, waving wildly. He braked, turned sharply, and skidded to a stop. Three more yards and I'd have joined Ellie and Gollo in the afterlife.

"Mr. Moon!" He spread his arms wide. "Ha-ha!"

"Are you nuts?" I shook my head. Then I pushed myself off the floor and brushed off my pants. "One day you're going to roll that thing and die down here. You realize that, right? Sheesh! Then no one will ever know about your mission."

His features quickly sobered. "I don't want them to. The Asylum's better left unknown. Leave the world to beauty. Things like these deserve to be hidden. Forever. Besides, it's armed to blow."

"As in..."

"*Ka-boom.* You never noticed?" He pointed at several clusters of metallic drums, banded together and situated at various locations about the floor. "They don't contain holy water, Mr. Moon. One flip of a switch and *whoosh,* this place will be a lake of fire. An inferno. All evidence of the Asylum, and probably half the block, gone."

"You've really thought this out, huh?"

"Yes." Then he reached out and we shook hands. "It is good to see you, my friend. C'mon Get in." He patted the other seat on the forklift. "I have something to show you."

I was eager to share the news about the murdered mediums and probe Matisse as to why someone would be killing occultists. Having learned about VM and their role in Ellie's death, I was also interested in Matisse's take on a possible connection between the two. Nevertheless, it would have to wait. The Mad Spaniard would not be denied. I went around the vehicle and climbed into the bucket seat.

Matisse wore his hair long, but it was thin, balding on top. He kept it pulled back into a tight ponytail. The style seemed to accentuate his strong features and penetrating eyes. He was a tanned, robust fellow, and wore long-sleeved shirts which he kept rolled up, exposing thick forearms. He often maintained a beard and now was halfway into a full one.

I hoisted myself up onto the forklift into the seat next to him. But before I had time to ask him about the girl, he said, "Hang on!"

I gripped the crossbeam as we peeled away in a plume of petrol and burnt rubber.

"Just got in from Bolivia!" He shouted, glancing at me as we tore through the warehouse. Liquor was on his breath. "Lucky for you. Kanya would've never let you in. She has strict orders."

"Who is she?" I asked.

"What?" He leaned in closer to me, swerved, and quickly corrected.

"Careful!" I yelled, tightening my grip on the vehicle. "Kanya! Who is she?"

He nodded and smiled. "Later. I have something else to show you."

Matisse's eyes glinted with his familiar madness. Most people who claim to be on a mission from God possess such madness. But few of them were as persuasive as the Mad Spaniard. Nor did they have a warehouse full of occult antiquities to back up their assertion. Believing in a New World Order was child's play for Matisse. Of course there *were* conspiracies. But according to him, something much bigger and more sinister was occurring. This wasn't just some Bilderbergian scheme to control the global economy; it was the Last Great War for the Soul of Man. Armageddon ultra. Perhaps even more crazy, however, was Matisse's conviction that he could thwart such an event and slow the spread of evil on earth by collecting and housing powerful occult relics. It was now his own personal mission, one he'd left the Jesuit order to pursue. The result was the Asylum—a holding tank for innumerable exotic pagan memorabilia. And, perhaps, the strangest museum on planet earth.

Over the last decade, the warehouse had become a virtual Pandora's Box of concrete and rebar. Some of the most infamous items were catalogued here: books from Hitler's lost library, two rods of power supposedly used by Pharaoh's magicians to battle Moses, and a massive collection of Mayan sacrificial blades. Talismans, amulets, shrunken heads, charms from around the world—the Asylum contained it all. National Geographic would have a field day down here. As would city inspectors. Matisse was probably in more violations of city codes than a liquor factory during the Prohibition.

Yet Arlette and I were vowed to secrecy about Matisse and his mission. He was the ultimate *Unnamed Source.* And when you have a source like this, you never ever give it up.

We whizzed past an aisle of sarcophaguses and skidded into the last bay. Matisse turned off the ignition and sat motionless. I cautiously let go of the forklift crossbar.

He slapped his thighs. "C'mon, my boy!" Matisse leapt off the forklift. "You'll like this, I promise. But no pictures. Understood?"

"Of course."

I followed him into the dimly lit bay. Crates rose on both sides of us. Traces of oils and incense laced the air. A large Plexiglas box sat on a pallet in the middle of the aisle. Inside was a single dark object.

"I didn't care for that last piece of yours," Matisse said as we walked.

"On the expedition for Noah's Ark?"

"You were wrong about the Nephilim, Mr. Moon. They were *not* extraterrestrials."

I shrugged. "I said they were *possibly* of extraterrestrial origin. That's true, isn't it?"

"Not exactly."

"Well, angels aren't *terrestrials*, are they?"

He stopped and turned to me. "Is the Holy Bible really something you want to toy with, young man?"

"Listen, Matisse. You can go on record whenever you want. I told you that. Front page. Cover story. It's all yours. My boss will be more than happy to make you the feature. You can quote chapter and verse, if you like. Just don't get too preachy. But set the record straight, by all means. Tell the whole world what's going on here." I slipped my cell phone out of my pants pocket and held it up. "It's one speed dial away. We can set it up right now."

His eyes moved through various shades of thought. Finally, he said, "You're mocking me, aren't you?"

"Absolutely not!"

"And reveal myself?" He brushed his hand dismissively through the air. "The Asylum remains a mystery!"

He turned and continued on his march. We approached the Plexiglas box.

"Is that a head?" I said, peering at an oval mummified object with dark empty sockets.

"Only half of one. But that's not what I want you to see. Over here."

He led me around the case to a long narrow empty crate full of straw-like packing material. Laying next to it appeared to be a pole or a totem. It was broken into three sections and lay end to end, stretched across the floor on plush burgundy cloth. I approached and studied the object. It was much narrower at the top—at least, what I assumed was its top—so narrow in fact that its tip seemed no thicker than my wrist, and was crowned with a gangly six-pronged star. A hexagram. *Solomon's Seal. Double Triangle. Shield of David.* It went by many names. Some even considered it the Mark of the Beast. It was one of the most universal occult symbols in the world. This one was perhaps the width of a man's reach. Its surface was pitted and several of the star's arms were bent at uneven angles. This thing had been around the block a few times. The pole it crowned was worn, yet fanciful Cuneiform-type carvings shone through. Symbols and scrawls and curlicues. I wasn't an expert, but this thing looked ancient. The totem did not appear to be made of wood, however, for it sparkled with a metallic, reddish-orange tarnish. Copper perhaps. A flagpole, I assumed. Maybe some sort of pagan mast. Assembled, it stretched eighteen or twenty feet long. I hunched forward, peering at the strange inscriptions.

"It's the final piece." Matisse walked around and stood across from me, staring at the strange object. "Mace and his men tracked it to South America. Bolivia, of all places. Heading downriver on a trawler. Probably being shipped to a port city. Some rogue merchant hoping to cash in on a relic, no doubt. They'd no idea what they had."

I inched closer, bending down to study the object. "Well, what did they have?"

"Ever heard of Babel?"

I straightened. "As in the *Tower of Babel?*"

He nodded.

I stared at him. That's how it was with Matisse. It took everything you had to keep from laughing in his face.

I cast a wry smile. "I take back what I said about a cover spread. You're too far gone."

"You don't believe me."

"Babel's a myth," I said. "Just like Noah's Ark. The Garden of Eden. It's a story to keep the faithful... entertained. This can't be from that. It never existed."

"You're sure about that?" He meandered around the perimeter of the pole, eyeing me like some large cat would a dying gazelle.

"Well, I mean... c'mon, Matisse."

He kept strolling, sizing me up.

"What?" I objected.

"You intrigue me, Mr. Moon. On the one hand, you come here asking questions, seeking answers. You traffic in the arcane, in mythologies and legends. On the other hand, you dismiss it, mock it, maintain the posture of a skeptic." He fixed his gaze upon me. "Do I detect some conflict?"

Apparently, the cracks were starting to show. "Okay. Well, it might as well be a myth. Archeology can't corroborate it."

"Oh? And this?"

"How should I know? It's a TV antenna for ancient astronauts maybe."

He yanked up his pant legs, knelt down, and pointed to some symbols along the object. "The epigraphy is indisputable. Common to the ziggurats of Southern Mesopotamia. They believed the pyramids were the gateway through which their god passed, from heaven to earth. Look. These inscriptions. Sumerian. Positively. *Anu,* it reads, *the heavenly one.* Greatest of all their deities. They sought to appease Anu, they sacrificed to him. This was the crowning achievement, to adorn the pinnacle of their edifice. And the metallurgy—early Bronze Age. The piece matches similar finds of that era, Mr. Moon, like those of *Tell Khaiber* near *Ur*. No. There is little doubt. This is genuine—*auténtico*!"

He settled back on his haunches. His voice became hushed with intrigue. "How many years has it been? Since I was a young man I've followed it. A starry-eyed fool back then. But sincere! At first, it was only rumors. Whispers about the mythical spire and its rediscovery.

"They called it the *Star of Anu*," he said. "It was to crown their achievement, to sit at the summit of the tower. Draw down the sky fire. A lightning rod for the gods. Not to divert electricity as a normal lightning rod does. No. This rod was meant to capture it! Create a generator of preternatural power. If they would have been successful, Babel would have ruled the world. Empowered by Nature. Governed by Man. Possessed by the gods."

His eyes narrowed, as if he were pondering the implications of such a scenario.

"And then we received word," he continued. "Proof of the discovery, of the first piece. A tribal warlord on the Pakistani border. How he acquired it, we can't say. Traders? An expedition of his own? Impossible to know. It was enough just to wrest the relic from his clutches. He was being worshiped as a god by his people, and using this to summon... *deities*. Gorgons, apparently. We intervened—God be praised—but lost a man in the effort. Such are the hazards of the Holy War."

He hung his head. Then he brushed his fingertips off on his slacks and stood.

"It is a ladder to the gods of fire, Mr. Moon. *A conductor*."

I peered at him. Incredulity and wonder were playing tug-o-war inside me. If this was true, it could be one of the greatest finds in modern history. But how in the hell could this be true? I stepped closer to the pole, as if proximity would upend my skepticism.

He watched me studying the relic.

"Fascinating, yes? According to legend," Matisse said, his voice now hushed with intrigue, "when God damned the builders of Babel and confused their languages, this rod broke into three pieces and was carried by the angels to opposite ends of the earth where they were hidden. It was said that when all the sections were reunited, great power would be summoned. Babylon would be reconvened. It lay undisturbed for centuries. But Evil has reawakened. The Star of Anu was sought out. It's only by God's grace and his holy angels that we have acquired it. And trust me—there are those who will kill just to have this. For those who wield such a charm could command immense evil. And now the final piece has been found." Then he stepped back and spread his arms. "Behold! The lightning rod from the Tower of Babel."

I stared, enraptured by the tale. Finally, I said, "This would make a great headline, you know?"

He scowled. "Absolutely not! This can never be written about, young man. None of this can! It will remain here in the Asylum where it can do no harm. And when the time is right, when the Consummation comes, it will be destroyed. Along with the rest of it." Matisse swept his hand through the air. "Only then will the world find peace."

He bent over, took the edges of the velvet cloth, and walked around the rod, covering it as he went. He rose and brushed off his hands.

"Now," Matisse said. "Show me what you've brought."

His tale had been so fantastic I'd temporarily forgotten why I was even there. I reached up, prepared to remove the Tau from under my shirt. Then I lowered my hand. "First, answer me some questions."

He raised an eyebrow. "Bargaining, are we?"

"Just making sure I get what I need."

He nodded. "As you wish."

"So why would someone be murdering mediums across the city?"

Matisse furrowed his brow. "Doing what?"

"Killing psychics. You know, clairvoyants. Why would someone want to kill them?"

He seemed a bit dazed. "You're sure?"

"Well, yeah."

"How many?"

"In the last twenty-four hours, at least five. That we know of. Maybe more. But why?"

The blood seemed to drain from his face.

Matisse hurried back to the forklift, leapt in, and shouted over his shoulder. "Hurry up. Get in!"

# CHAPTER 11

I KNEW MATISSE WAS A RECKLESS DRIVER, but not *this* reckless. We raced through the aisles of the Asylum on the forklift, dodging crates and statues along the way. We sped into the open and barreled toward the command post. I braced for impact. Matisse turned the forklift sharply and it skidded sideways, upsetting a stack of pallets before coming to rest in front of the building. He leapt off and hurried into the room, jabbering something about ghost waves and paranormal dislocations. I remained there, making sure I wasn't going to drop from a heart attack on the spot. When that possibility passed, I got off and followed him shakily. Who knew what madness the Spaniard had for me now.

I ducked under the rosary and netting hanging in the doorway. Matisse bent over the table, heaved aside a stack of books, pulled the laptop to himself, and flipped it open.

"How many?" he said.

"Of what?"

"Victims!" Sweat was gathering on his brow. "Murder victims!"

"Four. No, five. At least, that we know of. Why? What's wrong?"

He rapidly typed into the laptop.

"And where were they?"

"The dead? Uh..." Other than Gollo, I couldn't remember what Penny had said.

Matisse slammed his fist on the table, sending chow mien scraps flying and nearly toppling the wine bottle. He appeared manic. "The locations, Moon! Where did the murders take place?"

"I'm thinking! Hold on." I ran my fingers through my hair. "Lincoln Heights was one. Echo Park. Vernon, West Hollywood, and... and..." I snapped my fingers. "Koreatown. Yeah."

He typed on his laptop as I spoke. When he was finished, he straightened and stared at the screen. Then he hurried to one of the maps on the wall. You'd have thought he was planning the assault on Normandy Beach. There was a whiteboard and a topo map of the L.A. basin, now strewn with pins and illegible jotting. Taking a red pen, he marked five points on the map. Then he turned to me with a raised eyebrow.

"What?" I asked.

He capped the marker and stepped back from the map.

"What?" I repeated.

"My God." He set the marker down, went to his chair, and dropped into it. Matisse slumped forward. "It's beginning."

"What? What's beginning?"

"It has to be. There's no other explanation."

"Okay. What're talking about?"

"He calls it *the Gleaning*," someone said from the doorway.

I spun about, startled by the voice.

"Or something like that." A girl stood there. Another girl. Not the barefoot one who couldn't decide her name. This one was twenty-something. Straight, ink-black hair, pulled back with a clip to one side. She wore thrift store hand-me-downs like some artsy Bohemian, tight-fitting leggings, and expensive looking boots. Totally mismatched.

I shook my head, signaling my bewilderment.

"The Gleaning is the prelude to the End," she said, walking into the room. "The Singularity. Armageddon. The Apocalypse. Whatever they call it now."

She approached, glanced at Matisse, and scowled.

"He gets like that," she said. Then she returned her attention to me. "Supposedly, the Gleaning's a forerunner to everything. A series of supernormal upheavals—ghost currents, psychic eddies. That sorta stuff. He's been charting it for a long time. Way before I showed up. It's supposed to happen simultaneously all over the earth. Kind of a signal that things are winding down."

She stopped across from me and folded her arms. "Or a sign that something really big is about to happen."

Her voice was husky. She held my gaze for a moment, and then her eyes flicked away.

"Something big," Matisse said tiredly, with a hint of sarcasm. He sloshed wine into a used soda cup and gulped it down. "Really big. Earth shattering, in fact."

She wrinkled her nose at him and then said to me, "I gave you a hard time. Sorry about that. I was just being cautious. My father's been a little careless lately."

"Careless?" Matisse snarled. "Careless? No, Kanya. The Good Lord watches over us!"

"Yeah," she countered. "Just keep telling yourself that."

"Your father?" I looked at Matisse with arched eyebrows.

"It's a long story, Mr. Moon."

"And the other girl?" I asked reluctantly. "The barefoot one. Is *she* your daughter too?"

Matisse mopped sweat from his forehead with the sleeve of his shirt. "As I said, it's a long story." Then he poured another cup of wine.

"Her name's Cricket," said the girl. "She kind of does her own thing. Shows up whenever she wants. Usually at the wrong time. Which makes her a royal nuisance."

There was a note of frustration in her tone, not at me, but at Cricket.

Either way, I wanted to ask Matisse what he'd been doing. Did his Jesuit brothers know about this? About his *daughters*? We'd had so many conversations about the religious order he once belonged to and this never came up. He talked about vows and rituals, ecstatic visions, and then censure. But he never talked about daughters.

I probably would have tried to construct a timeline in my brain, but I was too busy trying not to stare at the girl. She was beautiful—beautiful in the same way a Bengal tiger might be. Her eyes were almond-shaped, suggesting a mixed Asian ancestry. She looked nothing like the other girl. So if they were sisters I doubted they had the same mother. She wore the slightest bit of eyeliner, just enough to accent rich hazel eyes. Her shoulders were somewhat wide, her frame compact, not at all dainty; she walked with confidence, supremely erect posture, as if she'd been raised by a drill sergeant. There was much more to this chick than tight leggings, killer thighs, and poor taste in fashion.

I collected myself enough to say, "Matisse never told me he had a daughter."

"I haven't told you a lot of things, Mr. Moon." Matisse swirled the second cup of wine before finishing it in one great gulp.

"I'm Kanya." She extended her hand. "But friends call me Kay."

"I'm, uh, Reagan Moon."

We shook hands. She issued a polite smile, but behind her eyes was more than a hint of suspicion. I could tell she wanted to ask me about my interest in Matisse and how I'd been granted access to the Asylum, but she stopped short. Then she turned, walked to Matisse, and put her hand on his back to console him. She moved with a certain grace, if not precision. Either Kanya moonlighted as a ballerina or a dominatrix. We'd met each other for all of two minutes and I knew this was one woman I didn't want to screw with.

I returned my attention to the maps.

"So..." I eased my way back into it. "What does all that stuff have to do with murdered psychics?"

"Really, Mr. Moon," Matisse said. "You're the paranormal reporter."

At this, Kanya turned to me. I could feel my face flush with embarrassment. Being introduced as a paranormal reporter is not at the top of the list of ways to make a good first impression. People like me are only slightly above politicians and arsonists on society's favorability meter.

Matisse rose from the chair and shuffled to the maps. "Clusters of Invisibles have been gathering." He tapped several spots on the map. "Random. More than the usual psychic disturbances, mind you. Many of them growing in intensity—wraiths, manes, incubi. We recently identified a Shezmu, a demonic executioner, prowling about Grand Central Market, of all places. Unusual to these parts, to say the least. No. These are not your customary spirits, Mr. Moon."

He stretched out his arms, his tone becoming sermonic. "We're at the threshold of an epoch. The signs are everywhere. Genetics, nanotechnology, robotics, and now spiritism. A toxic mix! Coalescing into a great event—"He slapped his hands together, simulating an explosion. "A great manifestation! The prelude to the end."

"Hey." I gaped at Matisse. "That's what the old man called it."

"What old man?"

"The psychic. 'A great *manifestación.*' He said there was this disturbance in the Force, or something. Said he could sense it. That something bad was brewing."

"Yes. Others sense it. The Gleaning."

"I don't know. After that, somebody murdered him."

"God have mercy." Matisse looked upward and crossed himself.

"Lincoln Heights," I said. "That's where he lived."

Matisse picked up the marker again, uncapped it, and tapped one of the dots. "Right here." Then he tapped the other four dots before connecting them, forming a crude circle. "Not a surprise it would come to this. The spirits have been gathering for the last few weeks. Congregating. We've watched them. But why now? Have they been summoned by someone or something? Awoken? I have my suspicions. But they're all very much alive." He issued a heavy sigh. "Such a gathering was inevitable. Alas, one can only hold back the spread of evil so long. Secret knowledge. The dark arts. Technological hubris. We're too curious for our own good, Mr. Moon." He wagged the marker at me accusatorily. "We were bound to awaken something. And now—" He traced the red markings again. "The noose is tightening."

"Yeah? Tightening around what, though?" I asked. "And why would someone want to kill clairvoyants?"

"Good question." He capped the marker and tossed it aside. Then he shuffled back to his chair and plopped into it.

I glanced at Kanya, who watched him and shrugged in response.

That was Matisse. He took his mission way too seriously.

"Hmm," I said. "Let me see. Maybe someone just hates psychics out there. You know, they got some bad info, something they didn't want to hear, and they snapped. Now it's payback."

"No." Matisse shook his head. "Too easy. This is more than just an angry client."

"Okay." I imagined another scenario. "So it's just your basic crime spree. Someone needed some money. Psychics and fortune-tellers, these people have cash on hand. They're usually open for business, there's no security to speak of. Someone could walk in without suspicion and rob them blind."

Matisse barely looked up from his sulking. "Robbing is one thing. Murder is another."

He was right. If money was the motive, why murder the lot of them? Kanya and I stared at the map.

Finally she said, "Maybe they knew something."

Matisse looked up.

"They knew something," Kanya continued. "You said the old man had sensed a manifestation, right?"

I nodded.

"Well," she said, "maybe these other ones did too. They were in touch with something. All of them. They knew something was happening. They sensed the Gleaning, too. Something's about to happen and they knew it."

The life seemed to return to Matisse's eyes. He was engaged again. "They were in touch with something. Of course! Something that someone wants... *suppressed*. Some information from the other side that they don't want getting out. A warning perhaps. Why else would you murder mediums? They're just the messengers. Ha-ha!" He sprang out of his seat, stomped to Kanya, took her head in his thick hands, and kissed her on the forehead.

Arlette had said the same thing. *Maybe it's a signal from the other side. You know, someone doesn't want us to hear something.* I found myself touching the spot where the Tau rested underneath my shirt and slowly withdrew my hand.

I cleared my throat. "You're suggesting that someone is murdering mediums because they know something's coming. Some psychic tsunami is rolling into town and these folks have the heads-up. Is that it?" I looked at Matisse, forcing myself to sound unconvinced. "And someone, some mystery man, is offing these folks because they don't want anyone to know that they know. They want to keep this... this Gleaning under wraps. Is that right?" I shook my head, feigning skepticism. "I don't know, Matisse. Sounds pretty farfetched."

Matisse folded his arms and glowered, while Kanya just looked on calmly, her chin tilted in faint defiance.

God, I must sound like an ass. The encounter with Gollo had sent me for a loop and I was leaking gas everywhere.

"What?" I said defensively. "I mean, how can you actually know any of this anyway? Ghost currents and pools of psychic energy. Demonic executioners prowling around Grand Central Market. You guys talk like you've actually seen them. No offense, Matisse. But this sounds pretty out there."

A cold, awkward silence passed. Arlette would not approve of me returning without some kind of spin to this story. Truth is, I was being a jerk and Matisse would send me home empty-handed. I couldn't blame him. I wasn't about to make something up to placate Arlette. I may be a stubborn jackass, but I'm not a liar. Nevertheless, if I was really after the truth about Ellie, alienating the mad Spaniard would not get me any closer. I needed Matisse's help and playing the Devil's advocate was not going to help me get it.

Finally, Kanya said, "And you're a paranormal reporter?" The question full of snark.

"It was either that or be a pizza delivery guy."

"Then I think you missed your calling."

*Hey!* I was about to counter when Matisse grinned, clapped his hands together, and wrung them mischievously.

"You're getting good at your game of cat and mouse, young man."

"Well, if—"

"No!" Matisse held up his hand to silence me. "No, Mr. Moon. You can't straddle the line on this one. Playing the middle may be good if you're running for mayor. But when it comes to the supernatural, the middle is a dangerous place to be."

"I'm a reporter, Matisse. For God's sake. I'm supposed to be objective."

"Objective?" He laughed mockingly. "Indeed. But being objective doesn't mean you can simply dismiss the evidence that's available. And I have a warehouse full of it!" He swept his hand through the air, motioning to the floor of the Asylum. "Have you seen the Devil Doll in B-2? Probably not. I keep her in a special place. Under lock and key. She is known to possess the simple-minded, to cause them to do the unspeakable. Would you care to see her? Or the Goddess of Death, a limestone statue that causes death and sickness to all who touch her. Shall I introduce the two of you? I've dibbuk boxes, a mummified werewolf's claw, Nuremburg Maidens, and a golem torso. Surely you can find something to be *objective* about."

"I never said there isn't weird stuff out there. But you're talking about *ghost currents*. At least I can *see* a Devil Doll. But how do you see a ghost current or a demon? Without more evidence, I can't be objective about something like that." I shrugged in appeal. "Sorry. I'll need to see it to believe it."

Matisse seemed to wilt a little after seeing my resolve. He glanced at Kanya who was busy scrutinizing me.

"Look," I said, trying to make amends. "The Crescent would be a great place for a story like this. Seriously. We could play it up, you know? Maybe go into detail about ghost currents, their history or something. We could mention the Gleaning, talk about various theories about the end of the world. Apocalyptic stuff is always huge with our readers. We wouldn't compromise your info, that's not what I'm saying. We'd just... allude to it. Maybe we could conjecture about areas of the city where psychic tide pools have formed, provide maps where the greatest density of ghost currents have gathered. Yeah. It would make a great spread, Matisse. What do you say?"

I folded my arms and smiled proudly.

Matisse and Kanya looked on dully, almost ashamed, as if I'd made a fool of myself and didn't know it.

*You'd make a great believer, Ray.* That's what Ellie had said. She was the perpetual optimist. Too much Pollyanna and not enough Doubting Thomas. She didn't know what it was like to have all these promises made about you, all this hope, only to end up being very much average. Maybe that's why I loved her so much—she'd never let me off the hook. *Ellie's spirit lives on. Just like mine will, like yours will.* Of course her spirit lives on, Mr. Klammer! People as good and kind as Ellie Wells don't just become cosmic dust and vanish forever. Unlike us germs, they live on. Somewhere.

I felt a little vulnerable standing there being scrutinized and tapped the toe of my sneaker anxiously.

Matisse and Kanya could sense my conflict. They knew I was hiding something. Then they looked at each other, as if weighing some grand option.

"Show it to him," Kanya finally said.

"We can't," Matisse said firmly.

"Show him the Curtain, Father."

"Absolutely not!" He threw up his hands. "He wouldn't be able to handle it! Look at him."

I wasn't sure exactly what he meant, but it left me feeling slightly offended.

Kanya approached Matisse. There was a note of tenderness in

her tone. "Others need to know, Father. We can't do this alone anymore. Too many others know." Then she looked over her shoulder at me and said crisply, "Besides, it might do him some good."

Her gaze lingered. "And I have a hunch about him."

Just what I needed. Some chick I'd never met having hunches about me.

"Rival's Curtain," Matisse said to himself. Then he straightened and turned to me, a newfound jubilance in his eyes.

"What?" I said. "What're you guys talking about?"

"You'll see." Matisse motioned for us to follow as he went down the hallway.

Until that day, there were few things I'd ever seen that I couldn't explain. But the way Kanya and Matisse carried themselves, the way they glanced at me and moved in such a circumspect manner, I got the feeling I was about to encounter another something that wouldn't fit nicely into my universe.

Nervous? Yeah, I was nervous.

Matisse turned into the first room, the one with the books and scrolls. It smelled of must and mold in there. He went to the vault. It looked like something out of an old Universal Studios gangster movie. Any minute G-men would come blasting their way in and shake us down. Matisse hoisted up his pant legs, knelt down before the vault, and tumbled the dial. When he finished, he stood and heaved the door open with a grunt. It ground to a standstill and he hunched forward to peer inside the dusty crypt.

I took a step toward the vault, unable to stifle my intrigue, tilting forward to catch a glimpse of its treasures.

A wooden cigar box. A skull with scrimshaw inscriptions and a dagger embedded in it. Some capped vials with brown liquid along with several hypodermic needles. Matisse pushed aside a stack of scrolls and removed an object wrapped in oilcloth. Then he stood and parted the folds. I leaned closer to see. It appeared to be an old pair of aviator goggles. Leather with tarnished brass buckles and fittings which looked to have been roughly stitched to hold two misshapen translucent lenses of unusual material.

"Rival's Curtain," Matisse said.

I hesitated. Then I stepped closer, studying the goggles.

"Crystalline lenses," Matisse said, pointing to what appeared two oval shards of solid amber, a cloudy mineral substance, inset in the goggles. "Unearthed somewhere outside Ankara. Centuries old. Rival's Curtain has taken different forms through the ages. Headdresses. Seer stones. Tribal healers were said to use the lenses to diagnose sickness and disease in a patient. Or to see demons that had attached themselves. It was guarded by a Coptic cult and passed down for generations before the group's untimely demise.

"This version appeared during the Victorian era. Apparently, the lenses had fallen into the possession of a collector whose fraternity fancied its alliance with ascended masters. He had them crafted, rather crudely as you can see, into these industrial frames. The glasses were a novelty at first. Those wealthy enough could pay for a glimpse into the spirit world, visit with departed loved ones. Etcetera. But intrigue gave way to madness. And then murder. And Rival's Curtain passed out of memory."

Matisse casually turned the goggles over and back, pondering them intently. They looked like something out of a Steampunk's wet dream. Leather, brass, unprofessional stitchwork. And those funky lenses.

"The glass was forged from the other world," he said. "A material substance produced from the immaterial. An ectoplasmic phenomenon, they say, that provided a literal portal into the world of spirit. Kings sought Rival's Curtain, rulers killed for the glass shards. The one who possessed the lenses, supposedly, could peer into the great beyond." Matisse leaned in and practically whispered the words, "Rival's Curtain allows one to see the Invisibles."

Kanya had stepped to his side, her eyes drawn tight. They both stared at me.

I would normally laugh at such an absurd proposition. But not that day. Something else—whether their tone of voice, the strange appearance of these goggles, or the prolific reminder of the number 18—kept me nailed me to the floor.

"You wanted to know about the Gleaning," Kanya said. "Well, that's how we know. We've seen them ourselves, the ghost currents. You don't believe us?" She gestured to the glasses. "Then put 'em on yourself."

I just stared.

"There is an invisible world all around us, Mr. Moon." Matisse smiled wryly. "Flora and fauna beyond your wildest imaginations."

I swayed forward and caught myself.

"That's nonsense." I cleared my throat. "I mean, come on, Matisse. How much wine have you drunk?"

"What'd Huxley say?" Matisse mused. "If the doors of perception are cleansed? Well, this is even better. Ha! Why cleanse the perception when you can open the eyes?"

He extended the goggles to me. "Go ahead, Mr. Moon. If you're so sure, what's to fear?"

It seemed as though everything converged right there. My stubborn unbelief. The sense of hope that had been awakened by Klammer's promise about Ellie and the afterlife. My unwillingness to admit the mystery that was all around me. Now I had something physical in my hot little hands that promised to do such a thing.

"Go ahead." He jabbed Rival's Curtain toward me. "Objectivity, young man. Objectivity!"

Matisse might as well have been asking me if I wanted the blue pill or the red pill. And after everything that'd gone down, I couldn't resist.

I took Rival's Curtain.

The specs were unusually heavy for their size. The frame was made of old leather. Nicks and scars marred the surface. The amber lenses had been inserted into the sockets, noticeably forced and pressed into place with brass fittings. I angled the goggles so as to study the lenses. The weight of the piece seemed to rest there, in this unusual material. It was much thicker than a normal lens and appeared uneven, wavy, as if it had been melted, poured, and pressed in some crude mold. This was not a professional production.

"Go on." Kanya brushed a strand of hair from her face. "Try it."

Her eyes sparkled with anticipation. If not joy. Ellie used to do that, sort of shimmer. Like she couldn't wait for me to bump into something that upended my worldview. She was always eager for me to investigate something that might blast away my cynicism.

I didn't need time to think about it. I didn't want to think about it. Besides, what should I be afraid of? They were just glasses. I swallowed and quickly pulled on Rival's Curtain.

Matisse muttered something, but I was concentrating on what I was seeing. A golden luster draped my field of view, as if someone had drawn the shades on an obnoxiously bright room, cloaking it in auroral dusk. The goggles fit snugly, almost to the point of being tight at the temples. I adjusted them and raised my gaze to my companions. Matisse and Kanya were watching me with utmost attention. I could tell it was them from their proximity, not their appearance. For through Rival's Curtain the two were just warm honey-glow silhouettes. Just humanoid shapes. Their physical features were not distinct. For a moment, I wondered if these weren't some wacky offshoot of the augmented-reality mapping glasses the government had been trying to push. But these weren't augmented-reality glasses. There was no digital ticker reporting longitude, latitude, air temperature, and the nearest Starbucks. Through Rival's Curtain, everything was obscure, shadowy, like I was peering through a gauzy veil.

Only this veil seemed to illumine colors.

The more I looked at the room, the more I detected colors. Of a wide spectrum. The spines of books blushing red and gold, almost with a low-level pulsation. Here and there, I noticed fractals of light, a strange efflorescence emanating from various objects. A medallion on Matisse's desk shone crimson and a jar on a nearby shelf fluttered as if filled with fireflies. Neon splotches dappled the safe, as if ultraviolet liquid had been splashed there. And the longer I looked, the more deeper layers of color seemed to bloom.

"Well?" Matisse said expectantly. "Do you see anything?"

I didn't answer right away. Partly because I thought it was some kind of trickery. Then I inhaled deeply and said, "I'm not sure."

I blinked hard and reopened my eyes, determined not to be so easily suckered in. Yet the colors seemed to sharpen. All around me. Particulate and atomic, melding into rivulets in the atmosphere. Golds. Greens. Rainbow droplets blanketing the room like dew. Now there was no mistaking it. It was everywhere. I was seeing more than just another spectrum of light.

This was another level of *seeing*.

I gaped. Is this what happened to people before they went completely mad? Yet how could I deny what was right in front of me?

While the room retained its shadowy density, swatches of light and pale elegiac tendrils seemed to unfold everywhere. The very molecular fabric of the room seemed to undulate in response to my witness. It was like an undersea garden blossoming before me. It had been there all along. I just couldn't see it.

I leaned forward, now captivated by my growing perception.

"What is it?" Kanya asked. "You see something, don't you?"

Matisse shushed her.

It was an exercise in perspective. The veil that draped my field of vision had no exact locality. It was not a literal veil, but a space. *The space I occupied.* I slowly turned around. Between blocks of shadow, glowing nooks of light shone, seemingly aroused by my curiosity. It was the Observer Effect, the term used in physics to describe how some things apparently react to being seen. Supposedly, certain particles will actually change when looked at. Well, this place was changing. The very atmosphere was transforming as I looked at it. The colors awakened as I turned. Multicolored runes, sigils were everywhere. As if someone had carved a signpost into this space, stamped our spatial locale with an invisible marker. A document bore luminous fingerprints and next to it, something that looked like a vase was bleeding neon slime.

It was a video gamer's ultimate fantasy. But this wasn't a *virtual* reality—it was reality!

I laughed aloud—laughing in complete disbelief as much as borderline euphoria. We were standing in the middle of some freakish inter-dimensional diorama.

That's when I noticed someone leaning against the table next to Kanya. Someone oddly glowing and very much unlike us.

I staggered back and gasped.

"Moon!" Matisse shouted. His thick shadowy figure lumbered toward me. "What is it?"

I extended my hands to stop him, steadied myself, and continued to peer at the visitor. The person leaned rather nonchalantly against the table, apparently oblivious to us. His body had a slight glow, a glossy burnished quality, like an airbrushed trapeze artist from a Cirque du Soleil show who'd gotten caught in a parallel plane. Kanya and Matisse were completely unaware of him. He had curly, short-cropped hair, wore an awl in his ear, and his clothes were plain: a long sleeve pullover shirt and linen-like pants with a drawstring. He was barefoot.

I might have said something. I don't know. He leaned back, inspecting his nails, seemingly ignorant to my amazement.

"Someone's here," I managed to whisper.

When I did, the burnished man turned and looked me square in the eyes.

# CHAPTER 12

MY FATHER OFTEN TOLD ME about the day he died. No, this was before he was actually murdered. He'd died twice. I'm not sure if that makes you special or cursed. Either way, he never came back from the second death. But this one, the first one, confirmed his beliefs. And a few other things. It was his first tour of duty in Iraq. You must understand, my father never told stories just for dramatics. But this one, the way he told it, always left me spellbound. It also left him teary-eyed.

Just outside Baghdad their unit was drawn down by gunmen into a sheep run, a corridor laden within IEDs. The first explosion shredded their truck, killed the driver, and blistered the rest of them with shrapnel. The next one killed two more of his men. The unit was ambushed, forced to use the burning wreckage for cover. They managed to survive for over an hour before a rescue unit arrived. Along with serious shrapnel wounds, my father had been shot during the firefight. That's where he got the Purple Heart. They'd applied a makeshift tourniquet made out of a flour sack they found in the alley. But before they could properly treat him, my father expired.

The medics couldn't say how long he'd actually been dead. Give them credit, they had good reason to stop trying, but didn't. He came to in the back of a truck on the dusty streets of Baghdad. But it's what happened in the interim that really seemed to mark him.

Unlike those who flat-line and return with stories about a tunnel of light, he said he met someone from the Imperia. That's the first time he'd ever heard of the celestial coalition. But his life would forever change because of it.

He met a very tall man he called a giant, dressed like one of those Grecian philosophers in robes and sandals. There was a gallery of onlookers content to watch my father and this Aristotelian giant as they strolled through lush gardens containing glowing flora and singing streams. There were people my father knew seated in the gallery. His sister, who'd died before I was born, was there. And a soldier friend he'd lost in combat. He even said his first dog was there.

And what did this strange man from the Imperia tell him? Just that it wasn't his time. That my father had something to finish first, some great task. That the Imperia was watching, that they were counting on him. Was the man an angel? Was there really some ancient order keeping an eye on us? Or was it all some grand hallucination? Whatever it was, when my father reached that point in the story, his eyes would get all watery and he'd wrap his arm around my shoulder and pull me into himself.

And I knew that to mean that I was one of the reasons he had come back.

Staring through the amber lens of Rival's Curtain, into an ethereal in-between place in a subterranean warehouse in the heart of Los Angeles, completely astonished by what appeared a golden man, I couldn't help but remember my father's tale of the afterlife and wonder if, somehow, I'd just been granted access.

I ripped Rival's Curtain off my head and gasped. The space where the man had been standing was empty. Nothing but dead air. I wobbled a little. Inhaled and exhaled. Either I'd actually glimpsed another dimension or I'd had one too many energy drinks.

Somebody said something, but I was too busy trying to gather my senses. The entire room returned to normal—pale, lifeless.

The exotic colors and surreal luminescence were gone. It was so incredibly bland it was depressing. And the transition hit me with all the shock of a hand grenade.

Matisse followed my gaze to that empty spot. Then he looked back at me, his eyes wide with anticipation. "You saw something. What is it? See? I told you!"

I opened my mouth, but couldn't find the words. A rush of nausea followed. I'd gone from the fast lane into reverse in approximately 0.9 seconds. It was metaphysical whiplash.

"Someone's here," I finally said. My voice sounded so lifeless. "Who... What's happening?"

Kanya stepped sideways, staring at the empty space the burnished man had just occupied. "Something's right here?"

"A person?" Matisse said defensively. "No! No one's here, Kanya! Not in the Asylum. He's just getting used to the glasses. Can't you see? He doesn't understand yet."

"I think he understands just fine." Kanya's gaze roamed about the room. "There's someone here, father. I knew it. He brought something with him." Her tone was accusatory.

Matisse shook his head. "That's not possible, Kanya. You know that."

But there was someone else in this room. Although trying to explain the experience seemed impossible. I extended the goggles in front of me, staring at the strange device. Then I looked at Matisse and his daughter. "What the hell is this thing?"

"You need to tell us what you saw," Kanya said firmly.

"Please," Matisse objected. "There's no one else here. There can't be. Give him time. He's upside-down. Look at him."

"Father, I told you this was gonna happen. We're being watched. The Black Council. The Summu Nura. Someone'll find a way in eventually. You can't just go traipsing all over the world and not draw attention. I told you! This's what they want. It's all theirs anyway!" Then she looked at me, her tone dead sober. "And they'll use anyone they can to get it back."

If it were any other time, I'd have defended myself. I was not working for the Black Council or the Summu Nura, whoever they were. And I couldn't imagine anyone, or anything, piggybacking their way into the Asylum on my sorry ass. But being that my head was spinning and my understanding of reality had just been t-boned by an invisible trapeze artist, I kept my mouth shut.

And peered at the crystalline lenses.

"Look again." It was Kanya. Her tone had softened. "Tell us what you saw."

"Kanya," Matisse objected. "Let him rest."

"No," she said. "He saw someone, father. More than just sprites. Or all the crazy colors. He saw someone."

I looked at her. She was right—I knew what I'd seen. No amount of sarcasm or rationalization could erase it from my brain. I had the evidence right in front of me. Objective evidence. All I needed to do was surrender to it.

"Reagan Moon." She took a step toward me. A thin, hard smile creased her lips. "The world's bigger than you think."

Was she channeling my dead girlfriend, or what?

I could feel my heartbeat thrumming through my body. This was crazy. But I couldn't go back. Not now. There was too much riding on it. I'd never met a story I couldn't tackle, and I'd be damned if this was it. Besides, this had the making of the biggest story in history... at least, my own personal history. If Rival's Curtain was for real, it could change everything. Science. Physics. Religion. Sports betting. Okay, maybe not that last one. But lots of things.

I swallowed hard. Then I glanced at Matisse. He dabbed the sweat from his face with the sleeve of his shirt. His eyes were glued to me as I put the goggles back on.

This time, I wanted to give myself a few seconds to let things compute. So I closed my eyes and stood there with the glasses on. Breathing. Breathing. When I finally opened my eyes and refocused, the entire room was glowing with a newfound vibrancy. Every particle, every molecule, had blossomed with life. I was trapped inside a Jackson Pollock painting, for God's sake!

Suddenly the burnished man was up in my face.

I stumbled back, frantically swiping my hands in front of me to drive him off. But I touched nothing. Instead, I backed into a stack of wooden crates and sent them crashing to the floor.

"Someone's there!" Kanya shouted. "He sees something. Father!"

"Wait!" I quickly steadied myself. "Wait."

Matisse and his daughter were little more than shadows through the lens of Rival's Curtain. Dense and cumbersome blocks of matter. A thin penumbra of light flared along their skulls, like a partial eclipse on the horizon of some dark globe. Brain waves maybe. But the rest of their bodies were dark.

The burnished man had stopped. He was looking at me, studying me, and appearing somewhat humored as he did so. I compensated. Only without the humor. I straightened and turned to face him squarely.

He straightened too, standing at attention like some daft soldier.

I raised my hand in a semi-salute.

He did the same.

"I am not seeing this," I muttered. "Am I?"

He nodded enthusiastically.

This was no trick of light. Good Lord, this was real! I was seeing someone who existed in another dimension. Someone who was responding to me. Is this what Columbus felt like when he saw his first Native American? No. This was more like finding out that the Human Torch was real and living next door to you.

His skin and clothing were all the same color, a soft golden hue. He radiated a faint energy; slight tendrils of heat seemed to follow his motions.

"Who are you?" My voice was feeble.

"In here?" Matisse said. "It can't be!"

"Matisse," I said firmly. "Someone is in here."

The burnished man had stepped back, and looked at Matisse

with a smirk.

"In fact, he thinks you're funny," I said.

The man looked at me and issued two thumbs up, smiling broadly.

"Me?" Matisse objected. "How am I funny?"

I looked at the burnished man for a response. He twirled his index finger around his temple, indicating that the wine-drinking Spaniard was cuckoo. Then the burnished man crept toward me, peering at me, perhaps studying the strange goggles I was seeing him through.

"What does he look like?" Kanya asked.

But I was too enthralled with him to answer. We continued looking at each other. I think he knew I was preparing to describe him because he stepped back toward the center of the room and spread his arms, as if putting himself on display.

"He's a man," I said. "I mean, he looks male. I think. But his features are fair. Almost boyish."

He stroked his cheek proudly as I said this.

"He's young. 20-ish, maybe."

The burnished man furrowed his brow in playful approbation.

"Okay." I said. "I guess not. Younger."

He shook his head, now in obvious frustration.

"Older?"

He nodded vigorously and stretched his arms out wide.

"A lot older, I guess."

"A dead man." Matisse wondered aloud. "Impossible! How could a disembodied spirit get into the Asylum?"

The burnished man shook his head emphatically.

I was caught up in what I was seeing and mimicked the man's gesture, shaking my head also.

"Of course not," Matisse said. "The dead can't enter here. This is a holy place. Then what is he? Something of another order maybe. A genie? A mixed-up wraith perhaps."

The burnished man signaled 1-2-3 on his fingers and then

signaled Yer out! with his thumb.

I laughed at the gesture. I had to admit, this guy was kind of funny.

"Sorry, Matisse," I said. "You struck out."

"The Asylum's holy ground." Matisse's tone was defensive. "Only a good spirit or a holy being can enter here."

"Well, maybe you got a leak."

"Then he must've come in with you," Kanya said. "Followed you here. Or maybe he's... assigned to you."

"Assigned? Yeah, right."

"An angel," Matisse said, almost breathless.

"For me?" I said.

"For him?" Kanya echoed.

"It has to be!" Matisse proclaimed.

"Wait a second," I objected.

The burnished man nodded happily and pretended to strum invisible suspenders.

An angel? How could this possibly be? Angels had feathery wings and flowing robes, didn't they? And haloes. They had haloes. They did not look like an airbrushed street mime. Besides, why would an angel be following me? I didn't even believe they existed! At least, before today.

"Does he have a name?" Matisse asked.

"I don't wanna know."

"Of course he has a name," Kanya responded. "Angels always have names. Gabriel, Michael. Go on, ask him."

I cleared my throat and looked at the man. "You heard them. Do you have a name?"

The burnished man opened his mouth, then shrugged and spread out his arms again. Wide.

"Bernard," I said indifferently. It was the closest name I could come up with that sounded similar to burnished.

"Bernard?" Kanya wondered "That's a weird name for an angel."

The burnished man shook his head.

"Yeah, that's it," I said. "Bernard."

If I was going to be seeing invisible people, I might as well have a little fun with it.

Bernard put his hands on his hips and glared at me.

Matisse said, "I don't believe we've had an angel here before. Fantastic!" He clapped his hands together in celebration. "What does he want? Ask him what he wants, will you?"

But I didn't have to. Bernard was right in my face. More precisely, he was staring at my chest and a strange bluish glow that emanated from there. I backed up, trying to locate what he was looking at, and I suddenly realized.

It was the Tau.

# CHAPTER 13

I REACHED UNDER MY SHIRT and drew out the Tau. The bluish light filled the room.

"I think he wants this."

"*Ohhh.*" Matisse came closer. "What is it? Where'd you get that, my boy?"

He passed through Bernard, who scowled and stumbled out of Matisse's way. Matisse reached forward, took the Tau, and started to remove it from me. I instinctively snatched his wrist and held it there.

"It's all right," Matisse said, relaxing his hand. "I just want to look."

Bernard was peering at me, the corner of his lip curling in the faintest smile.

I'd been commissioned to protect the Tau, whatever that meant. Despite being mortally conflicted about ghosts and psychics, protecting the Tau was the one thing I felt, with reasonable assurance, that I could do. However, I also knew Matisse posed no threat. So I released his hand.

"Good," he said. Then he lifted the cross over my head and studied it. I watched the proceedings through Rival's Curtain, captivated by the newly lit surroundings. Matisse's cranium flared as he hunched over the Tau. But the light cast by the cross illumined his face even more. In its glow, Matisse was no longer just a dense block of matter. His features came to life. He was like a kid marveling over a hidden treasure, his synapses pulsating with an electromagnetic halo. His eyes etched with kinetic vibrancy.

"How did you acquire this, Mr. Moon? It's quite... peculiar."

"My girlfriend." I was watching Bernard, who stood on tiptoes looking over Matisse's shoulder at the Tau. The angel seemed equally spellbound by the cross.

"Your girlfriend?" Kanya asked.

"Well, she used to be my girlfriend. Until she was vaporized."

Matisse said, "And where did *she* get it?"

"I don't know. She just told me it was special and that I should protect it. Well, I should say *a medium* told me Ellie wanted me to protect it. He's one of the mediums who was murdered. That's why I came here. It's confusing, I know. But she—I mean, *he*—was emphatic about that. He said *she* said I should protect it. And then someone killed him."

They were speechless, no doubt wondering what kind of drugs I was on.

Finally, Matisse said, "It's a Tau."

"Yeah. That's what she called it."

"The symbol of the cross of Christ," Matisse said. "Predates the early Christians by centuries. Some used it as a charm. A talisman. The Franciscans adopted it as their emblem. *Incredible!*"

Matisse continued studying the Tau, turning it over and back. Bernard watched over his shoulder appearing equally fascinated, their contours illumined in the blue glow.

"And Bernard wants *this*?" Matisse said.

As he asked that, Bernard jerked his head up and motioned for me to follow him. He pranced out of the room and into the hallway, leaving trails of color swirling in his wake.

I followed, mystified.

"Where're you going?" Matisse called after me. "Mr. Moon! What is it?"

"I don't know," I said over my shoulder. "He just left."

"Follow him!" Matisse barked. "Hurry! Don't let him leave."

But I'd already started after the angel.

Walking while wearing Rival's Curtain proved difficult. I banged my thigh into the table and clipped the doorway on the way out. It didn't help that Matisse was behind me, huffing and babbling, nudging me forward anxiously. And smelling like a vat of wine. My vision and sense of perspective had not yet adjusted to this strange new world. Bernard waited in the front office. He bounced excitedly upon seeing me and then ran to another part of the room. Another wash of color rippled behind him. I carefully navigated my way through a growing palette of rich hues and irradiation. In the front office, Bernard stood at the map boards, tapping a certain point on the maps. His eyes beamed with excitement.

I stopped. Matisse bumped into me.

"What is it?" he said. "Is he there?"

"Yeah."

"What's he doing?"

"It's the map," I said. "He's pointing to something on your map."

I carefully picked my way through this wonderful world of luminosity. In this world—the world of Rival's Curtain—the map was but a skeleton of Matisse's. Yet I could tell that the angel was indicating a point in the center of Matisse's marking. I approached the map, stopped, and drew my fingers along the paper to that single glowing index finger which rested there. I planted my finger right next to the tip of Bernard's. He smiled proudly, removed his finger, and backed up, his hands folded across his chest.

I removed the goggles and the world suddenly returned to normal. I'd gone from high-def living color to low-res black-and-white. It was like a sledgehammer to my brain. I groaned.

"It's downtown," Matisse said, almost disappointed. "What does that have to do with the Tau? Or Bernard?"

"Whatever it is, those murders all triangulate this area." I removed my finger, tracing the crude circumference demarcating the psychic murders.

"Father," Kanya said from behind me. "The ghost currents have been intensifying in that same region."

"But why?" Matisse's gaze dropped to the floor. "What's the connection?"

I massaged my temples to fend off the dizziness. My skin was turning clammy, as if my body was undergoing some sort of low-grade shock.

Kanya watched me wrestling against the rising nausea. "Your body just needs to adjust to what your mind is seeing."

"Oh, that's all?"

Matisse began pacing, thinking aloud to himself. "Downtown. Downtown. Let's see... There's Merlin's. But they've been there for years. Just a five and dime occultist. The Cauldron's downtown too. Trinkets, talismans, that sort of thing. Nothing on this scale. Downtown, let's see..."

He kept pacing, scratching at his beard, his lips moving wordlessly.

Finally, Kanya said with a note of surprise, "It's Spiraplex."

Matisse stopped in his tracks.

"It has to be," she said."

Matisse looked at me, his eyes crimped in thought. "Yes. Of course! How could I have missed it?"

"Volden's one of the foremost esotericists in the world," Kanya explained to me. "And, coincidentally—"

I finished her thought. "—Volden is also behind Spiraplex."

She nodded. "The currents have been intensifying in that area for the last few weeks. Before that, it was random. But lately, the activity has been concentrated downtown. We knew Volden's arrival would result in an up-tick of  paranormal activity. But something on this scale...?"

"*So stupid!*" Matisse slapped his palm on his forehead. "Spiraplex. The spirits are being summoned to Spiraplex."

"Time out," I said. "Summoned? How do you know that? Spiraplex has been one big secret from the get-go."

"They are drawn to Volden's madness," Matisse said, undeterred by my line of query. "Spiraplex is a beacon of some sort, a magnet drawing the undead, the lost, to itself. In the very center of the City of Angels."

"That *would* explain the ghost currents," Kanya said. "Spiraplex is the epicenter. Everything's converging there."

It was difficult not to concede. If there really was a world of Invisibles, of other exotic entities like Bernard roaming the streets of Los Angeles, it was hard to imagine them not wanting to have a peek at Soren Volden's technological funhouse.

I shrugged and said offhandedly, "Sort of like one big ghost box, I guess."

They glanced at each other.

"What did you say?" Matisse asked.

"I, uh—a ghost box. You know, those gizmos that are supposed to channel the dead."

"Yes, yes. But why would you say that?"

"I... My friend Jimmy with the LAPD found one. A ghost box. A homemade contraption made from a jukebox and a bunch of other scrap parts. Some drug addict believed that someone, or some *thing*, wanted to get in touch with him and was hoping that a ghost box would do the trick. You know, help him communicate with the dead. Poor guy cracked before he had a chance to get the message. Apparently, it wasn't the only one."

"There were more?" Matisse asked.

"Jimmy said they'd confiscated half a dozen similar devices, amateur ghost boxes."

"That would explain a lot," Kanya said.

"Explain what?" I asked.

"If anyone could do it, Volden could."

"Do what?"

"Yes," Matisse mused. "A ghost box would have that effect. Especially one that big. That would also explain his research with electromagnetism. If he could create a massive field of electromagnetic radiation, there's no telling what would come out of the woodwork. Or what evil he could channel."

"Wait a second," I said. "You're suggesting that Spiraplex is—"

"A massive ghost box, Mr. Moon. A conductor to the spirit

world."

"That would explain why other people are building ghost boxes," Kanya said. "It's precognition or something. They're all foreshadowing the big one. The manifestation."

I pointed at the Tau. "So what does *that* have to do with Spiraplex?"

Matisse held the cross out and looked at the Tau. Somewhere in that other dimension, his face probably glowed from the luminescence of the cross. He set it on the table and pulled out a phone which he used to snap several pictures. He puzzled particularly over the letters on the back. "Some form of Latin, it appears. But I'm not sure." Matisse looked up at me. "Maybe your friend can help us again."

I shook my head. "If you guys are *that* interested, maybe you should have a look yourselves." I extended Rival's Curtain.

Neither of them made a move.

"We use it sparingly," Matisse said. "Often at great cost."

"Gee, thanks for the heads-up."

"You have a knack for it," Kanya said. "I've never seen someone take to it that fast. You're a... a natural."

I glanced at her. She wasn't saying this to butter me up. In fact, it sounded more like a guilty admission on her part.

I brought the strange device back to myself and studied it.

Finally, I said, "Promise me, if I put these on again, you won't let me get stuck over there."

"Ha-ha!" Matisse slapped his knees. "That's the spirit!" Then he said matter-of-factly, "We can make no such promise."

"You won't be 'over there' anyway," Kanya said. "You'll be right here. And, of course, we'll keep an eye on you and make sure nothing happens."

I nodded. "Okay then. I'll ask Bernard about the Tau and what those letters mean. After that... I'm done." It was somewhat disingenuous. The possibilities of the Curtain seemed endless now. What kind of power could someone wield who possessed such a thing? What secret knowledge could someone gather about our world that was heretofore unknown? All that bullshit about us being germs, about coming from Nothing and returning to Nothing. And here I stood salivating over some inter-dimensional X-ray specs. Yeah, I wanted more shots at this. So I added, "At least, for *now* I'm done."

"Fair enough," she said.

I raised the goggles, exhaled a great puff of air, and slipped them on again.

This time, I didn't need to give myself a chance to calibrate. Everything was right there. The world in front of me exploded into life; we were swimming in an ocean of hues. Only now, things looked different, really different, as if we'd been submerged in iodine or a solar flare had erupted inside the room. Maybe we had gone from heaven to hell since my last visit. The atmosphere rippled with heat tentacles whipping upward from some invisible cosmic kiln. Everything was tinged in rust and blazing crimsons, like the embers from a nuclear winter. Ash or fallout dappled the air, forming pale eddies here and there. This bleak world was quite unlike the one previously inhabited by my guardian angel.

I murmured something, fighting the urge to rip the goggles from my face. But that wouldn't change anything. The landscape in this dimension had changed. I couldn't pretend it hadn't.

The next several seconds were a blur. I quickly scanned the area for Bernard. The once colorful anemones had withdrawn, leaving only faint, particulate sparkles. Something large and bulky occupied the spot where the angel had been. It possessed a vague humanoid shape, angular, like some monolithic Easter Island giant staring skyward. Nevertheless, it seemed to undulate; a block of knuckles and elbows writhed under an opaque leathery film. As I tried to make sense of what I was seeing, the entire thing turned, rotated, pivoted on some invisible axis, bringing a smoldering wedge into view.

It was disconcerting and completely disrupted any sense of perspective I'd managed.

I stood petrified. If my heart didn't go out any second, I was sure my bowels would.

It was as if a cube of space—not just an atmospheric distortion, but something in between perceptual depth, another layer to what my mind intuited—had been carved out and rotated in front of me. Only this wasn't just space, but a living chunk of something quite animate. It tumbled toward me with a sort of a visual *thwomp* and sat (or stood) perhaps six or seven feet away, throbbing. *What the—?* I couldn't believe my eyes.

Something else was in the Asylum! Something dark and living and very, very nasty.

The seething wedge of light opened. It wasn't just a crack, but an orifice, yawning, looking very much like a volcanic crevice. Or a mouth. A molten glow radiated from deep inside, growing, spreading like a radioactive sinkhole. As it did, spidery appendages blossomed from within it, sucking out from its torso in hideous spasms. These long knuckled limbs spread wide, doubling the thing's size instantly. It rose. Higher. Until it towered above me like a monstrous tree, teetering on spindly arms and branches. The mouth widened, becoming a smoldering sneer.

I stumbled back, shielding my face.

"They're here!" I cried weakly, swinging blindly at the air. "Bernard!"

And that's when I heard it. On another frequency, to be sure. But I heard it. Not in my head, in my mind, but with my own ears. A susurration of many voices.

They were calling me.

*Moon. Moooonnnn!*

It was the first time I actually heard the Invisibles. And it wouldn't be the last. However, at that moment, I didn't have time to appreciate the occasion. The spidery monolith pounced on me, its mouth now a gaping infernal gorge. And I fell helplessly into it.

# CHAPTER 14

JAMES BURNS IVORY FROZE TO DEATH in heavy snow in the Angeles National Forest several years ago. He became separated from his party during a hike, stumbled into a snowy ravine, and wandered for several days. Search parties were assembled and eventually, in growing desperation, the man's girlfriend hired a psychic. Psychics are of interest to the Blue Crescent, even when they're not being murdered. I was assigned to the story. However, before the psychic could even adjust her antennas, Mr. Ivory was discovered by authorities. Reportedly, he was completely nude except for a pair of thick wool socks.

The story was salvageable for the Crescent because of this. Dead naked frozen people are right up our alley.

Survivalists call it being "cold stupid." A slightly more clinical term is "paradoxical undressing." It's a state of paralysis of the nerves brought on by extreme cold, giving the victim a feeling of warmth. Apparently, this hypothermic condition confuses the nervous system, causing someone who is freezing the sensation of extreme heat. Which is why it is not uncommon for someone who is freezing to death to remove their clothes in the hopes of cooling down. James Burns Ivory simply speeded up the inevitable by doing so.

That particular story was bouncing around in my head when I gasped and woke up. Kanya stood over me. Her hand was on my forehead. I sat straight up and a sheet dropped from my bare chest.

"Oh," she said. "You're awake."

It'd been so long since I'd felt the touch of a woman that the realization almost made me forget that my hands were freezing.

Almost.

I clenched my hands, opening and closing them, trying to chase the ice out of my joints.

"I was just tryin' to cool you down." Kanya lifted a sopping washrag as if to prove it. "You're burning up."

I cupped my hands together and puffed into them in an attempt to get my feeling back. She was right; the rest of me was feverish. Rivulets of sweat coursed my chest and glistened on my forearms. At least I hadn't gone cold stupid. Or had I?

"What happened?" I said woozily.

"You passed out."

I thought about that for a second. But my brain had been replaced by a bowling ball. I fought to focus my eyes, to ground myself, but the space in front of me did not want to comply. I kept working my hands, wringing them together to get the feeling back. My shoulder throbbed and my nasal passages felt like I'd snorted a gallon of hydrochloric acid.

"Where am I?"

"The same place you were."

She wasn't being difficult. So where had I been?

"Matisse's," she said, in answer to my thoughts. "The Asylum. You were using the goggles. Don't you remember?"

The feeling was returning to my hands now. I looked around and recognized the rumpled bed. It was Matisse's bedroom. I was on the couch. A small refrigerator and table sat across from me. Then I winced and massaged my temples.

"So who Roto-Rootered my head?"

"It's Rival's Curtain." She set the washrag down on the table next to my shirt and some bloody cotton balls, and approached, gazing intently at me. "You really took to it. Fast. I've never seen anything like it."

A faint floral scent came with her. Not overly-sweet. I recognized the smell and my mind combed through the possibilities. *Rose?* No. *Hibiscus?* No. Her eyes sparkled with wonder, as if I was her latest lab specimen and she couldn't wait to test her new scalpel on me. She bent slightly, the neckline of her blouse opening just enough to expose a choker with a small Jade-like stone. It dangled over an expanse of smooth olive skin. I was acutely aware of her presence: the warmth of her body near me, the shimmer of light in her silky black hair, the smooth curve of her breasts. Someone had ratcheted up my senses for the entire room seemed to be buzzing. And then it struck me. *Dahlia.* That was it. She smelled like dahlia.

Kanya straightened. She knew something about me had changed. Suddenly, I felt self-conscious. Exposed. What was happening to me? Why was I noticing these things? I looked away.

"Why's my shirt off?" I asked, swinging my legs off the sofa.

"Be careful." She extended her hand. "You cracked your shoulder on the table. You were bleeding. We carried you in here."

I reached over my right shoulder and winced as I felt the tender spot. There was no blood on my fingertips.

"You have a big scar back there," she said. Her eyes were the color of pennies, newly minted copper.

"One of many." I swallowed and then leaned forward with my elbows on my knees. Dark things were dancing on the periphery of my brain, like a bad dream waiting to pounce on you the second you doze off.

*Moon. Moooonnnn!*

"So what happened?" she asked.

"When?"

"When you passed out."

I massaged my knuckles, working out the residual chill, and stared off into space. It started to return to me. The hellish landscape. The disembodied voices calling my name. The cube creature preparing to eat or abduct me. *God, what's happening to me?* My heart quickened at the thought.

"What's wrong?"

"Nothing," I said sharply.

She watched me. Finally, she put her hands on her hips. "Well? What happened?"

I wasn't sure where to begin. Finally, I said, "I'm not sure. There was... something else."

"The angel?"

"No. Something different."

She straightened. "Like what?"

The memory of that pulsating block thumping toward me and blossoming limbs and legs and pincers made my mouth go sour.

"I'm not sure," I said. "It... it came out of the air. Out of space. That's the only way I can put it. Sort of lifted away from everything else. A block. Or a cube. I wasn't sure it was alive at first. Then it started moving. It had these legs or arms. Like a spider or a crab. But the size of a flippin' refrigerator. And a mouth. It had this huge mouth full of... fire. God, this is nuts! I can't believe I'm even saying this."

I pressed my palms against my temples, hoping to force some sanity back into my brain.

"You're not nuts," she said. "Go on."

But I couldn't go on. I slumped back on the couch, shaking my head in incomprehension. At this rate, drinking myself into a stupor was sounding more and more like a reasonable solution.

She watched me struggling in my mind. Finally, Kanya pursed her lips and approached. She stood directly in front of me. The black leggings hugged her thighs, accentuating every muscle, every curve. With legs this muscular, she was either in training to be an Olympic cyclist or preparing to put me in a leg lock until I begged for mercy.

"I don't think you understand how serious this is, Reagan."

I glanced up at her. "And I don't think you understand that I just got knocked on my ass by some *thing* from the fifth dimension."

She kept watching, waiting. Then the cork popped. "Listen, this is not another one of your *tabloid stories*. Do you realize that?" There was disdain in her tone. "I don't know exactly who you are, but this is serious. People's lives are at stake. More than you realize. You're in danger. This city's in danger."

"Let me guess—the whole planet's in danger."

Kanya bristled. "You have no idea what this is about, do you? You come barging in here and... If the Summu Nura have breached the Asylum, then we're in big trouble. And if you're the one who saw them, then you're in even bigger trouble."

"Summu Nura. Black Council. I think the Asylum is getting to your guys' heads."

"Yeah? You're the one who passed out. You're the one seeing angels. Whatever you saw got to *your* head. Listen to me. My father's committed his life to this. I know you think he's crazy. I can tell by the way you talk to him. You think he's just some whacko who enjoys giving you stories whenever you ask. Then what? He crawls back into his hole until your next visit? Is that what you think? You're just using him. That's all you're doing. Admit it."

She burned the words in with a caustic stare.

"You should be ashamed of yourself, Reagan Moon. You and that screwy paper you work for. He's a good man. A *great* man. He's risked everything for this. Everything!" Her fists were clenched, her breathing heavy. She seemed to catch herself. Then she backed down and her demeanor softened.

It was the first real sign of vulnerability she'd shown. She walked to the center of the room and turned her back to me. She was trying to compose herself. After a moment, Kanya turned to face me. Her eyes glinted with moisture, but her voice did not quaver. "I don't know what my father sees in you. But if you can help us, if you can use Rival's Curtain, then you have to. You have to help us."

I wasn't about to mount a defensive. I was being a stubborn jackass. I debated apologizing for my attitude. Instead, I yanked the sheet aside, pushed myself up off the couch, and stood there wobbling.

"Careful." She stepped toward me with her hands extended.

"The goggles. Where are they?"

"Wait. What? You're still—"

"I thought you wanted me to use them?"

"Well, yeah. But..."

"Then lemme see them."

I scanned the room for Rival's Curtain. My body awakened at the thought of putting the goggles on again. The synapses and neural sensors of my brain started bubbling with anticipation. Is this what a lerium addict felt like craving his next fix?

She said, "You saw what happened last time. You blacked out. We should wait. Give yourself a chance to recover. Besides, we need a plan or something. Next time, who knows—"

"Where is it?"

"I don't think that's a good idea. Not right now. You need to rest."

"No!" I shouted. My skull reverberated from the outburst. I grimaced, staggered back, and then steadied myself. "No. You guys wanted my help. Well, here it is. If it's that serious, then let's go."

"Listen, you need to sit back down." She approached, but this time the smell of dahlia was not on my mind. She opened her hand just inches away from my chest, as if she were about to nudge me back onto the sofa. She had rings on her index and middle finger. Both plain. Both pewter. One was fatter than the other and had a name or phrase inscribed in script across it. I didn't attempt to decipher it. My adrenaline was spiking.

I brushed her hand away.

She took a step back and raised both hands, palms open toward me. I couldn't tell if it was a show of surrender or if Kanya was getting ready to drive my nose back up into my cranium.

"Reagan," she said with exceptional calm. "Listen to me. You need to sit back down."

"What about the world?" I said mockingly. "I thought I was supposed to save it."

"Sit down."

"And if I don't?"

"She's right," Matisse growled from the doorway. "You need to sit down, Mr. Moon."

He stood there scowling, rolling the sleeve of his shirt back down his forearm. Then he walked in, glaring at me. My bravado deflated like a tire on a spike strip. The Mad Spaniard was old enough to be my father, but senior citizenship had yet to catch up to him. I felt like a child under his stern, dead serious gaze. I was making an ass out of myself. The goggles had left me on edge, intoxicated me to the point of stupidity. The vision of that hideous creature coupled with Kanya's warnings about others being in danger caused me to feel like I was being pushed inexorably toward something I deeply feared.

I plopped back down on the sofa.

"Good." Matisse relaxed. "You wouldn't want to tangle with Kanya anyway. She has a purple belt in Kajukenbo."

"Kaju—what?"

"It means she can kill you with any part of her body. Or just paralyze you, if she's in a good mood."

Kanya looked away. She was pissed.

An object wrapped in tan cloth lay on the table next to the washrag and bloody cotton balls. Matisse went to the table, grabbed my wadded up shirt, and tossed it to me.

"Why do you think I keep Rival's Curtain locked up?" he asked. "For this very reason. It'll do more than just open your eyes to the Invisibles. It'll intoxicate you with power. Perhaps that's why its previous owner took a power drill to his temple. Some things are better left unseen, Mr. Moon."

I slipped my shirt on. "You were the ones who gave me that stupid thing."

"Yes. And I'm glad we did, as you'll see in a moment. Now," Matisse approached. "You saw something. I need to know what it was."

"I dunno," I said exhaustedly. "I don't know anything anymore."

Kanya glanced at me with a note of disgust. "It was an outrider, a *cytomorph*."

"The Summu Nura." Matisse shook his head in dismay. "In the Asylum? How?"

"What's a cytomorph?" I asked.

"It was only a matter of time," Kanya said to Matisse. "I told you that. Holy water and rosaries can't stop them."

"But they haven't crossed," Matisse countered. "It can't be. Not yet."

"Why not yet? You've been careless. I told you that. And then you let people like him down here..."

I said, "Can someone explain what the hell's going on?"

"Watch your language," Kanya snapped. Then she shook her head, as if she had no other choice but to talk to me again. "You saw a cytomorph. They do the dirty work for the Black Council. They're sorta drones; synthetic organisms developed to adapt to different spheres, environments. They eat their way into the fringes, into dimensional membranes between worlds, calibrate, camp out, and bring back details to the Summu Nura. They've been trying to infiltrate us forever."

"Fortune's found us, Mr. Moon." Matisse had a kick in his step. "Your arrival's been timely. Now we know the reason for the ghost currents. Volden's building more than just a high-tech pleasure palace. He's in league with the Summu Nura. Why else would they be on the prowl? Summoning ghosts and banshees is the least of their aims. They want to build a bridge, a dimensional transport. Which is exactly what a ghost box would be.

"The Black Council's powers are greatly limited on earth. They've sought to expand their influence here for ages. But we're a privileged planet, Mr. Moon. There are those who," he cast a long, penetrating look at me, "watch out for us. Were the Summu Nura to cross over, they would rule with an iron fist. The world as we know it would fundamentally change. We'd be little more than a cattle farm, a fill-up station for their trek across time and space. The only thing they're missing is a power source big enough to propel a conductor that size."

And just when I thought things couldn't get any weirder, they did.

Matisse said, "But I'm afraid we have an even bigger mystery on our hands."

"Bigger than *that*?"

"The Tau."

I touched my chest as he said that, suddenly realizing that I no longer had the cross. I'd shown it to Matisse shortly before I passed out. How long had it been out of my possession? My heart leapt inside me. *Ellie!* I jumped to my feet again.

"Where is it?"

"Calm down. It's right here." Matisse walked to the table and unwrapped the Tau from the leather cloth.

I snatched it from him and put the cross on, relieved to have the relic back in my possession. "I'm supposed to protect it," I said awkwardly. "Just don't ask me why."

"I think I know why, Mr. Moon," Matisse said.

I stared at him.

Matisse said, "The letters on the back of the Tau. Do you know what they say?"

I shook my head, sensing that the answer I was about to hear would make my life a lot more difficult.

"It's Latin, basically," he said. "Early Latin. It reads *Imperia*." His eyes glinted mischievously. "My boy, you are protecting one of the seals of the Seven Guardians."

# CHAPTER 15

SEVEN GUARDIANS. Why was it always seven?

Matisse walked around me in a slow circle, scratching his beard. "Tell me again—where'd you get that, Mr. Moon?"

"My girlfriend," I said numbly.

"And where did she get it?"

"I have no idea. She said it was special. That's all. The next day, she was dead."

Matisse stopped and looked at Kanya.

"I'm tired," I said. "I want to go home."

Kanya put her hands on her hips. "I don't think that would be a good idea."

"I'd completely forgotten about it," I said. "Until this morning. Some guy showed up at my apartment. Big Swedish guy. Probably bench-pressed tour buses on his free time. He took me to see Felix Klammer. Klammer hired me to investigate Ellie's death."

"The accident?"

"Right. Only, he thinks it wasn't an accident. He thinks it was murder."

"Felix Klammer" A thin smile curled the edges of Matisse's lips. "Why am I not surprised?"

"He could help us," Kanya said.

"Seems he already has." Then Matisse turned to me. "But go on.".

"Hold on a second," I said. "You guys know Klammer?"

"Know him? Who do you think pays the bills here?"

I stared in amazement.

"It's a very long story, Mr. Moon."

"Apparently like a lot of things around here." I glanced at Kanya. "So what does Klammer want with us?"

"Klammer's motives are inscrutable," Matisse said. "But his intentions are becoming clearer: to stop Soren Volden.

"And how're we supposed to do that?"

"I'm not sure. But it may explain why someone's murdering mediums. Apparently, Klammer and Volden both want the Tau. And they'll do anything to keep you from finding it."

"Keep me from finding it? Klammer basically led me right to it. That doesn't make sense," I said. "Besides, they're too late."

"So where did she get it?" Kanya finally said. "Your girlfriend. How'd she get the Tau?"

"I told you—I don't know. Ellie had all kinds of religious stuff. Old Bibles. Crosses and curios. She was really into those kind of things. You know—sacred things."

Kanya folded her arms. "So how'd she get hooked up with *you*?"

"Pity. Or penance. Take your pick."

"Would you two stop it!" Matisse glared at us. "This isn't a game."

"She gave it to me the day before she died. That's all I know. It's been stored away for the better part of a year. Until today."

Then I straightened. "Okay. Your turn. You guys obviously know a lot more than you're saying. What's all this stuff about cytomorphs and Black Councils and these Seven Guardians?"

"Yes," he drawled. "Quite a lot, isn't it?"

He began pacing, his brow furrowed in thought. Finally, he stopped and said, "I may've been wrong about you, Mr. Moon."

"I've always been misunderstood."

"Ha! And deservedly so." Matisse snorted. "So what do you know about the Imperia?"

The mention of that name made me wince. "My father told me about the Imperia when I was a kid," I began. "He was never quite clear what it was. Celestial guardians. Planetary protectors. A cosmic crime fighting ring, more or less. It was kids' stuff. At least, at first it was kids' stuff. The older I got, the more serious he got. I could tell it was something he really believed in. It was more than just a fairy tale or comic book story. In fact, he said he'd talked to them once."

"To the Imperia?" Matisse gasped.

"Yeah. During an NDE, no less. He said one day..." I sighed from deep within. But here it came. "He said one day I'd be a part of them."

It felt like a great confession. Like I was finally exposing some horrible deformity that I'd spent years concealing.

They were fixated upon me.

"When he was killed," I said, "it pulled the rug right out from under me. Any hope I had about being something special disappeared that day. Any beliefs he had about me went with him."

A deep silence passed between us, as if some sacred moment had descended.

"Young man," Matisse said, "what you saw through Rival's Curtain is just the surface. There's... *others*. Great watchers. Cold minds always plotting, conspiring against beauty and all that is holy. Seeking power. Like the Summu Nura."

He continued pacing, as was his custom when he was embroiled in thought, walking back and forth before the cluttered whiteboard.

"The Summu Nura. Sumerian for *those deprived of light*. The Lightless Ones. Some see them as evolutionary flotsam, minds without shape, pure thought or energy. Others believe they may be astral vampires or some form of complex quantum parasite. It's all speculation, of course. Whatever they are, they have great interest in us. In earth. In our species.

"No one knows when they first appeared. Through Cain, perhaps. Amenhotep. Nero. Vlad the Impaler. It's hard to say. They lay their seeds in madness, constantly seeking to perpetuate their lineage. To cultivate. To harvest. To feed. To advance their kind.

Always looking for new life forms. But without vessels, bodies to occupy, they are powerless, little more than ghosts. It's why their sways never lasted. Whether through chance or Providence, their attempts to control and populate the earth have failed.

"It was after the Black Plague, when Man was at his weakest, that they finally staked a claim. That's when the real war started."

"War. As in..."

"Good vs. Evil. God vs. Satan."

"Gee, how original."

"You expected something else? It's all part of the great schism at the heart of the universe, a bitter struggle between the agents of the Invisible. Ellie knew this, yes?"

I just stared at him.

"So a child was born," Matisse continued. "A gifted one, in a small village in the remote English countryside. Newtonia, they called it. Nothing but accursed ruins now, a decrepit plot of land. A sacred site for Druids and amateur occultists. But the child... Some claimed it was a virgin birth, others believed it to be witchery. Sidney DeFelius was his name."

"DeFelius," I said, searching the archives of my mind.

"I doubt you've heard of him. History has not been kind to old Sidney. He was a child of enchantment, gifted with strange powers, abilities of persuasion and ingenuity. And the dark arts. As he grew, he gathered darklings around him. Chimera. Revenants. All manner of devil's spawn came to him. Summoned, God only knows how. Through alchemy or magic. Human sacrifice, perhaps. Soon the entire village came under his sway, lifeless zombies nourished and harvested for DeFelius' army. An entire village! Great feats of magic followed him, and those who challenged him vanished or were silenced. He could smite herds of livestock, the legends said. Dry up wells, shrivel limbs with only a word. No one dared challenge him. The Summu Nura had finally taken root!"

I glanced at Kanya, who seemed equally enthralled by her father's tale and his accompanying theatrics.

"Darkness fell over the land," Matisse intoned. "The countryside became wild with fear and superstition. The first phase had begun. Eventually, if they weren't stopped, the entire realm would've come under their power. But then a man arrived. A holy man, they say. An emissary from on high. A lone knight. Who knows? He was an enigma who came and went, as do all great men. He spoke of the wrath that was to follow. A coming apocalypse. From which they could save themselves.

"Seven men—that's what he was seeking."

"Seven," I said. "The number of heaven."

"Yes. A coalition who'd pledge to fight the Summu Nura. With their pledge, the stranger promised, would come power. Blessing from on high. Angelic assistance! Strength to overcome the Lightless Ones in all their guises. Yet the call wasn't without cost, as are all great callings. Their lives for the land. Eternal vigilance! Seven men were chosen. Men of honor. Fearless. Contrite. They called themselves the Imperia and chose the Tau as their symbol, forging seven amulets.

"A great battle ensued. DeFelius' army and its zombie horde fought against the Imperia. But God was with them, just as the stranger had promised. Fire and brimstone eventually consumed the hordes. Newtonia was leveled and remains cursed ground to this day. The Summu Nura fled, leaving their earthly shells, disembodied once more. DeFelius was never seen again.

"But the war had just begun. The Black Council was formed, a consort of Summu Nurian powers, ever plotting to take us captive. They would return. To this day, the Seven Guardians of the Imperia are said to walk among us secretly, communing with the angels, ever vigilant, crushing the serpent wherever he should appear."

Matisse stopped and his head slumped forward, as if telling the tale had exhausted him. Finally, he drew a deep breath and looked at me.

I jabbed my thumb at the Tau. "You're telling me that this..."

"Is one of the seven icons. Yes."

"So let me get this straight, the Imperia is a coalition of celestial beings and humans trying to keep things from going to pot."

"Basically."

"And I've got one of their pendants."

"It seems likely."

"And I'm supposed to protect it."

He tilted his head. "Or use it."

I raised my hands. "Easy, cowboy. Protecting it's one thing. Using it? I wouldn't know the first thing about that. Sorry."

"But your father's dream."

"Look. Both of you. I'm not part of this... this Imperia. My membership expired a long time ago. And I sure ain't looking for a fight with some celestial mafia."

"If Volden's in league with the Summu Nura," Matisse said, "and his ghost box becomes operable, life forms unlike any we've ever seen could cross over. A dimensional door of some sort could be opened, Spiraplex being the conduit."

"And so what am I supposed to do about that?"

"I'm not sure. But if the Tau's resurfaced, not to mention a guardian angel along with it, and they're both connected to you..."

"Would you stop calling him my guardian angel."

"...and the cross is blessed with power..."

"If it's blessed with power, it's not working."

"...you'd be the obvious candidate to use it."

"You're outta your mind! Both of you."

"Me?" Kanya protested. "I didn't say anything. Until we can prove Volden's in league with the Summu Nura, or that he's actually building a ghost box, we can't be totally sure of the connection."

"Finally, some sanity," I quipped.

"And even if we were sure, what could we do to stop him?"

"Exactly."

"Besides," she said to Matisse, "what could the Imperia possibly do with *him*?"

"Ri—Hey, wait a second."

"There's only one solution," Matisse said. "We get into

Spiraplex. See for ourselves."

I guffawed rudely. "Have you seen that place? It has more security than the Kremlin."

"Yeah," Kanya said, "But we do have someone who can use Rival's Curtain."

"And?"

"There's no other way," Matisse said. "We can't march in and request an interview with Soren Volden. And if we wait until Spiraplex opens, it could be too late. We have to find a way in. A way to gather some information. It's our only chance!"

I clucked my tongue. This was crazy. Sneak into Spiraplex? I'd already run from the cops today. Breaking into Volden's high-tech amusement park had all the makings of a TMZ headline. And a jail term. No. There had to be another way.

That's when I suddenly remembered. As I did, the pit of my stomach spiraled.

Kanya was watching me. "What?"

"Uh..."

"What's wrong?"

"I can get us in," I mumbled.

They looked at me.

"Mr. Moon?" It was Matisse.

"I can get us into Spiraplex. I think."

"How?"

"They invited me."

Kanya and Matisse exchanged puzzled looks.

"I have a press pass," I said. "Someone came to our offices today. I almost forgot. They want to give the Blue Crescent an interview."

"Ha-ha!" Matisse clapped his hands. "Then it's true."

"Please don't," I said.

Matisse leaned in and whispered, "The Imperia are with you."

# CHAPTER 16

KANYA DEMANDED TO GO WITH ME to Spiraplex. I put up little resistance, and suddenly we were a team.

"I can pretend to be your assistant," she said. "Reporters have assistants, right?"

My first impulse had been to talk her out of it. But that would've been insincere. My gut told me she could handle herself just fine. And I wouldn't mind having her around. Especially if she knew Kuji-whatever. But there was something else about her that piqued my interest. Maybe it was the way she stood up to me. She wasn't afraid to call my bluff or call me a fool. I respected that. More likely, it was the sense that we both shared some immense secret, which neither of us were quite ready to admit.

She changed into something more professional looking. Not that professionalism was a trademark of mine. But when she emerged from Matisse's room with her hair in a pony, wearing slacks and a pressed button-up shirt, I couldn't help but do a double-take.

She frowned. "What?"

"Nothing. You just..." I shrugged and offered an embarrassed smile. "You look great."

"Thanks," she said almost begrudgingly, turning away to finish buttoning her shirt. She was genuinely embarrassed. I couldn't imagine that Kanya had experienced a shortage of flattery in her life. Still, I was slightly aghast at my brashness. If someone was keeping track, I was on the downside of gaining points.

Matisse watched our exchange. Then he proclaimed, "You need strength. You must eat!"

At the mention of food, a wave of exhaustion rose up inside me. This had been a long day, and it was only going to get longer. He hustled into his little kitchen, started a pot of coffee, and made us something to eat. Bean and rice burritos. Like me, the Mad Spaniard knew how to eat on the cheap. Despite the nausea I'd experienced wearing Rival's Curtain, I was starving. The food was plain, but homemade local tortillas and killer salsa salvaged the meal. Kanya seemed to revel in the food, and I wondered if maybe I could show her my Mexican omelet recipe sometime. That is, if we didn't get eaten by cytomorphs along the way.

But I tried not to think about those things. And the grandiose expectations everyone suddenly had of me. I had the Tau. It was safe. That's all I needed to know right now. And whatever those things were on the other side, they couldn't touch me here, on this side. At least, as far as I knew. Still, the implications about my possible involvement with the Imperia just hung there, unspoken, the proverbial elephant in a very small room.

I finished my cup of coffee as Matisse gathered up our plates and lectured us. "You're just going in to have a look around. Remember that. No fancy business." He peered at Kanya.

"You're assuming we can get in," I said.

Kanya said, "I thought you had a pass?"

"I do. I'll have to go back to my apartment to get it. And my gear. But who knows. They've got security up the whazoo. The guy might not even be in. Who knows. It's a gamble."

Matisse grunted.

"Besides," I said, "if we get inside, what're we looking for?"

"For one, you're looking for any evidence of Volden's involvement with the Summu Nura," Matisse said. "Kanya will help with that. Their presence is easy to discern if you know what to look for. And if the angel was right, Spiraplex is far more than just a high-tech arcade. A ghost box of that size would require a massive conductor. Something to transmit an impossible amount of energy. We won't know until you get inside. And you have a camera, yes? Try to take some pictures."

"Don't get your hopes up. No one's leaking any pictures from Spirapex until Volden says so. Trust me. Reporters have been crawling that place since they broke ground. If we do get in, they're confiscating all electronics. I'll guarantee you that."

"You're probably right." Matisse pursed his lips and grew quiet. Then he jabbed his finger into the air. "But we have an angel! If we're being guided, if the Tau is yours, then—ha!—trust your instincts, Mr. Moon." He leaned closer and whispered. "And trust Bernard."

I stared at him dully. "Let's get going before I call the whole thing off."

Matisse hurried into the other room and emerged.

"And you must take this," he said, and extended Rival's Curtain to me.

I straightened. My mind's eye seemed to snap open. The burnished man, the spidery outriders, the vivid dreamscape all around us. A chill whisked up the back of my neck. Could I handle it again? And what would downtown Los Angeles look like through these magical lenses? My stomach flip-flopped at the thought.

I said, "You sure you can trust me with those?"

"We don't have a choice," Matisse said soberly and passed the visors to Kanya. "If you're able to get inside, one glimpse through Rival's Curtain should tell us all we need to know. Just use them sparingly. If the visors fall into the wrong hands..."

Kanya wrapped the specs in a soft suede cloth and placed it in her handbag. It was a large, rather funky crocheted purse with a colorful Chinese dragon stitched across it. The only unprofessional looking thing about her.

We walked together to the freight elevator.

"Be careful." Matisse summoned our attention. Then he wagged his finger at me and said to Kanya, "And watch out for him."

"For me?"

Kanya glanced at me. "I'll keep a good eye on him, Father."

She kissed him on the cheek. We got into the elevator, stepped over the salt line and closed the heavy metal doors. The elevator lurched and began its ascent.

In that confined space, the fragrance of dahlia mixed with the smell of rust and oil. She had her back to me, and I sensed a little tension in the air. Was she nervous about pretending to be my journalistic intern? I doubted it. Then what? I couldn't imagine someone with her type of confidence being intimidated by someone as harmless as me. The elevator rattled to a stop. As we stepped out, the stink of the alley and the nearby river basin struck me. Despite the smell, it was great to be outside again. Kanya yanked the doors shut.

"It locks automatically," she said. "It can only be unlocked from inside the command post, or by key. And there's only one of those."

"Let me guess. You don't have it."

"We live and die with my father."

The air had thickened from a cover of clouds that now blanketed L.A. Rain was coming. Lots of it. I'd agreed to drive, but as we walked through the alley and approached the Cammy, I remembered the funky clothes smell in the cab. Damn.

She stopped and stared at the vehicle.

"It's my work car," I said defensively.

"I don't think I've ever driven in a car with racing flames."

"It's... *vintage*."

She just kept staring.

I opened the passenger door, quickly collected the empty soda cans, the bag of pretzels, and fast food wrappers, and brushed off the seat for her. Okay. This looked bad. Arlette always said I was a pig and this was my payback. So much for first impressions.

As we drove to my apartment, the world seemed different to me, alive in a new way. The smells of the city, the glaring neon lights, the hookers with their vacant eyes, the dark alleys full of whispers and hunched forms.

My mind kept drifting back to the vision of that invisible world. I watched the parking structures and storefronts pass by with a newfound interest. What did they look like in that other dimension? Were they teeming with cytomorphs and exotic flora like the Asylum? I fought the urge to rip the goggles out of Kanya's handbag, pull over, and study my surroundings through the magical lenses. And Bernard—was he somewhere nearby? He couldn't fit in the cab with both of us, could he? I let my eyes wander across the dash, the column, the console, from Kanya's loafer-clad feet to her lap, where her hands were folded. She stared out the window. Streetlights splashed across her face, weaving her features in and out of detail. The tension I felt in the elevator was still there. Yet I couldn't tell if she was mad at me or just nervous.

I cleared my throat and tried to ease into conversation. "He's a pretty remarkable guy."

"Hm?"

"Your father."

She kept staring out the window. "Yeah. He is."

Somewhere in the distance, the wailing of a siren sounded. The light turned red and we stopped. The Cammy's engine rumbled like a tiger. I aimlessly watched the traffic cross the intersection.

"Look," I said. "You're right about us using him. But it's not what you think. I like him. And he likes to talk about that stuff."

She adjusted her bag on the seat next to her, but she didn't respond.

"Of course," I said, "Some of his ideas are kind of wild, but—"

Kanya turned to me. "So why don't you believe?"

"Huh?"

"You're a paranormal reporter, right? Why don't you believe?"

The light changed.

I glanced at her and wrung the steering wheel. It felt like I was being cornered. How does one explain years of regret and emotional sandbagging in a few sentences? As I prepared to offer a lame response, the car behind us laid on its horn and I accidentally punched the gas and lurched the Cammy forward.

I apologized, but Kanya was locked into her thoughts. "People are different, Reagan. They have different experiences. They see things. Know things. Things happen that you can't always explain. I just... I don't understand how someone can go through life dismissing everything. Forcing everything into a box. The world's too darned big."

She was starting to sound like Matisse. And Ellie.

"Listen." I cleared my throat. "I think you guys are mistaken about me."

"I hope we are. All that stuff about the Imperia and your father. And your girlfriend giving you the Tau. I don't understand how you *couldn't* believe. It's like you've been moving toward this your whole life."

I thought about that and said, without any sort of defensiveness, "I guess that's one way to look at it."

"How else could you look at it? All my life..." She settled back into her seat and turned toward the window. "All my life I've wished I could be someone else. I'd give a lot for a second chance."

She went silent again.

It wasn't the right time to press her. But it seemed to validate my hunches. She was harboring some secret. I knew it. Her tough persona was a façade. Perhaps it had to do with her father. Or her sister. Or another man. Whatever it was, the show of vulnerability was enlightening. She might be a kick-ass martial arts expert. But deep inside Kanya was broken up. It was obvious. Yet something else seemed to come out of that brief interaction. For her words buoyed something in me. Maybe this little adventure of mine wasn't some cross to bear at all. Maybe I *had* been moving toward this my whole life.

Maybe.

I turned east on 7th, and then onto San Pedro. There was a spot across the street from my apartment which I pulled into. I turned off the engine.

"I'm just going to run in," I said. "You don't mind waiting here?"

She didn't. It was bad enough having her ride in the Cammy.

Having her see my apartment would throw her into shock. I was sure of it.

I hustled across the street and entered the apartment. It was dark inside and for the briefest second, the thickness of the shadows made me stiffen. I cursed my cowardice and threw the light switch. My backpack was next to the bed. I dumped the contents. I was sure a camera would be confiscated; nevertheless, I grabbed one and stuffed it in the pack, along with a notepad and a couple fresh pens. A telescopic tripod was in the other compartment, along with another lens and some extra memory cards. I was good to go. Then I went into the kitchen and retrieved the press pass. I dug the exotic flower, still wrapped in plastic, out of my jean pocket. Its faint licorice-like scent filled the air. Perhaps later I could do an image search online and see if I could identify what sort of plants Matisse was cultivating. I set the flower on the countertop. As I prepared to leave, I glimpsed the key to Mrs. Richardson's apartment.

Chelsea!

My first thought was to let her skip her evening snack. It was already way past dinner. Besides, her owner said she needed to lose weight. But thinking that way only made me feel bad. What was happening to me? I couldn't even renege on my duties as a cat-sitter without feeling guilty.

I locked my door and went across the hall to Mrs. Richardson's place. Her apartment smelled like cheap perfume and was way too clean. Perhaps when I retired I too would spend endless hours worrying over the sanitization of my apartment. Hopefully, I'd live long enough to experience such worries. I retrieved the cat food from the top of the refrigerator and proceeded to fill Chelsea's bowl. As I did so, the Persian puffball ambled into the kitchen, plopped down, and watched me with cool disinterest.

"I'm doing this for your owner, not you." I set the bowl on the floor. "And she's right—you need to lose some weight. Look at you."

Chelsea started licking her paw, ignoring me. I scowled at the cat.

My cell phone rang, startling me. I returned the box of cat food to the top of the refrigerator and dug the phone out of my pocket. It was Jimmy Pastorelli. He could only want one thing.

"Jimmy. Whatcha got?"

"Hello to you, too."

"Sorry. *Hello.* Now whatcha got?"

"So against my better judgment, I opened the Bastion Sails case file again."

"And?"

"I'm afraid, you'll be hard pressed to find anything resembling homicide there. Sorry."

"Figures."

"But those two techs who were on the job that day—the ones that took the fall for Bastion Sails—well, they're both, how should I say this, out of the loop."

"What do you mean?"

"One William Brower was shot during an apparent robbery a couple months later. Random. No suspects. The case is cold, buried. His partner the day of the incident, Kuroki Yukio, is a missing person. Disappeared several months after Brower's death. Wife said he had a history of depression. No leads. Either way, both are out of the picture. One less lead to anything tangible."

"Damn."

"So if you were planning a shakedown, you'll have to reschedule."

"And if they were the only witnesses..." My mind was assembling the pieces. "You're suggesting there's a connection?"

"I'm not suggesting anything, Moon. Until someone can uncover tangible proof of something nefarious, this isn't going anywhere. And my guess is, you have no tangible proof."

He was right. And unless I could get someone at VM to incriminate Volden, the chances of getting tangible evidence was slim.

"There's somethin' else," Jimmy said, interrupting my train of thought. "But you didn't hear it from me."

"Cross my heart."

"You're a person of interest in the Medium Massacre."

It shouldn't have hit me as hard as it did. They'd probably found my card. Hopefully somebody hadn't seen me fleeing the scene. That would require a little more explaining. Either way, hearing it from Jimmy was unnerving.

"Moon? Did you hear me?"

"So that's what they're calling it?" I said. "The Medium Massacre?"

"Yeah. We have a few questions."

"I'll bet you do."

"You don't sound surprised."

"I'm not. It's a long story."

Silence.

Finally, Jimmy said, "Listen, if you have something you're hiding, I suggest you don't. There's a couple guys down here that'd like nothin' better than to rid the world of another wannabe PI. Especially the kind that visits psychics and writes about spooks."

"They're just jealous."

Another long pause.

"Better watch yourself, Reagan."

"Thanks Jimmy. When this all blows over, remind me I owe you one."

"*If* it all blows over, I will."

I hung up and watched Chelsea meander to the food.

So the two techs who'd been in the tower that day at Bastion Sails not only took the heat, they were conveniently quashed. If this didn't reek of corruption, I don't know what did. Somebody didn't want them talking. That was obvious. Perhaps Selwyn Brook, community liaison, could fill me in when we got to Spiraplex.

I opened the door and glanced back into Mrs. Richardson's apartment. My eyes burned. The perfume was killing me. Chelsea looked up smugly. I wrinkled my nose at her and turned the light out. When I turned back, preparing to leave, I noticed my apartment door was slightly ajar.

What the—?

I was certain I'd locked it. Klammer's warning about danger rang in my ears. I slipped back into the shadows of Mrs. Richardson's apartment and closed the door slightly. Then I peered through the crack, staring at my place and contemplating my next action.

Soft thumps emerged from inside my apartment. Someone was inside! Mind you, I hate thieves. Next to criminal lawyers and DMV clerks, thieves were at the top of my "most hated professions" list. But the way things were going, I knew this was no petty thief trying to jack my DVR or video game console. So should I storm in and surprise the intruder? The memory of Gollo's punctured body was answer enough.

I slunk back into the shadows and waited.

Something brushed past my leg and I yelped.

Stumbling back, I struck the counter and a saucer clattered from the edge before shattering on the floor. Chelsea skidded into the other room, having scared the bejesus out of me. When I returned to the door and peered out, a figure was backing out of my apartment. I had to fight the impulse to lunge into the hallway and make a scene. Discretion got the better part of me. I crept forward, angling myself so as to peer through the slightly open door, crunching glass under my shoe and hissing at the sound.

It looked like a woman. Her hair was butched and bleached. She was wearing a black windbreaker, but the hood was drawn back, partly revealing her face. It was pale and oddly misshapen. High cheekbones. Narrow. As she pulled my door shut, with the other hand she reached to her side and slipped a long thin blade into one of the pockets in her cargo pants and buttoned it. She wore black gloves. Across the back of that hand peeked a tattoo: a serpentine torso from which rose multiple heads. The tattoo climbed up her wrist and disappeared under the elastic sleeve of the windbreaker. It appeared to be the image of a hydra.

She didn't seem to have taken anything. She tinkered with the lock, slipped something small into her waistband, turned, and loped to the stairwell making nary a sound.

I was torn between needing to protect the Tau and wanting answers. The latter won out.

If there was to be an altercation, it would be better off happening in the street, anyway. Although, by the looks of her blade, any altercation that put me within arm's length of this sweetie would be a losing proposition. Making a mental note to return to clean up the broken glass before Mrs. Richardson returned, I grabbed my backpack and quickly exited, locked the door, and stuffed the key into my jeans pocket. Then I jammed down the hallway. I stopped before turning down the steps and listened, just to make sure she wasn't waiting. The soft clang of the security door sounded below. I hurried down the steps—all 12 of them, but taking two at a time—and lunged into the night, not six seconds after the intruder.

I skidded to a stop and looked both ways. But the sidewalk was vacant. No one. Not for blocks.

Fog swirled past, twining my ankles before evaporating. I looked up and Kanya was leaning against the Cammy across the street, watching me.

# CHAPTER 17

I DIDN'T SEE ANYONE," Kanya protested.

I was facing her, amping on anger and out of control endorphins. "She couldn't have just disappeared."

Kanya glared at me and said crisply, "I didn't see anyone."

A car approached, cruising slowly, its headlights peeling back swaths of pitch black shadow.

Kanya took my arm and gently pulled me out of its path.

My heart was racing. "How could you not see her?"

Okay, so now I was being burgled by phantoms with bleached hair and hydra tattoos. I scanned the street again. But it was a ploy to ratchet down my nerves. She was long gone, whether through magic or A-grade diversion.

I hoisted my pack over my shoulder and returned to my apartment. This time Kanya came with me. She waited while I went to my bedroom. I went straight to the lamppost, but it was unmoved. The closet had been ransacked and several of the dresser drawers were overturned and lying on the floor. The thief had been looking for the Tau. I was sure of it. That's what this was all about. The knife was... I didn't know what the knife was for. Would she have slit my throat to get the cross? I had to admit, it was a possibility. I scanned the rest of the apartment, but knew I wouldn't uncover anything.

I found Kanya at my desk, studying the oddities there. She set down the bronze mechanical cube that she'd been looking at. A sort of Rubik's Cube for Sufis. Supposedly, the cube would release a genie when someone managed the right combination of numbers and alphabet. Of course, how to find the right combination was a whole other story. But maybe the way things were going, I should try. Having a genie and an angel as a bodyguard would definitely not suck.

"Lemme guess," she said, scanning the clutter.

"They're after the Tau."

She nodded. "And if they killed the medium..."

I stared at the cushions and drawers strewn about the living room.

"If they killed the medium, then I'm in the middle of the best story the Crescent's ever seen."

She arched an eyebrow.

We hustled downstairs and drove straight to Spiraplex. As we went, Kanya tried to rehearse possible scenarios for when we arrived. But I was too busy mulling everything that had happened that day and glancing in the rearview mirrors. If I was a person of interest in the Medium Massacre, like Jimmy had said, the LAPD would not be far behind. The question now was whether or not someone would beat them to the punch.

Spiraplex had been the talk of the town for the last couple of years. They'd demoed an entire city block to make way for the project. Of course, there were stories about the crews uncovering ancient burial grounds or catacombs. The reports couldn't be substantiated. It was all part of the growing urban legend about Spiraplex, no doubt contrived by Volden to create interest. The perimeter of the building was surrounded by black-tarped fencing, scaffolding, and barriers. Posters announcing the future opening of Spiraplex blanketed the area, on facades and benches, promising it would be the Eighth Wonder of the Modern World. The entire structure was made to simulate huge limestone blocks etched with hieroglyphics. Intricate parapets and ornate columns decked the building, winding up its exterior like an immense stairway to the sky. It rose perhaps twenty stories. Several large spotlights blazed upward along the tower, illuminating winged, gargoyle-like figures at the peak. On the rooftop, bright lights revealed a crane and more scaffolding.

Volden had promised the unveiling to be unlike anything the world had ever witnessed. And after hearing about the ghost box and the Summu Nura, I could only imagine what that might involve.

As we approached, traffic slowed. Gawkers and tourists milled about the sidewalk snapping photos and gazing up at the structure. Two large sphinx-like statues could be seen overtop a plywood catwalk with a gated entryway. Several black clad security manned this station. I began searching for a place to park. The nearby parking structure was for hotel residents only, and the street was jammed, so I drove around the block until I managed to find a spot in a residential area just off the main drag, about a block away. We parked under an overgrown ficus tree in front of a gated house with a Beamer in its driveway. I turned off the ignition and we sat there, listening to the engine cool.

Kanya removed her seatbelt and lifted her handbag onto her lap. She stared forward.

Surprisingly, I was not nervous. I'd calmed down and focused my energies on the task at hand. Call me weird, but the chance to help Ellie (if that was really possible), the chance at some sort of redemption, had burrowed into my psyche. Even if my father wasn't around to see it, making a go at something grand, something out of this world crazy, stirred a sort of abandon inside me. I'd always gotten a rush from my quirky adventures. But this was different; it's what he would have wanted. Hell, it's something he would have done! Of course, it could all end disastrously. But at least I was trying.

Kanya cleared her throat. "So did you love her?"

"Excuse me?"

"Your girlfriend."

The way she said it didn't seem forward or nosey. I nodded. "Yeah. I loved her. I mean, I was getting there. I'm not the type of guy who falls in love every other relationship, if you get my drift. Maybe I'm just too heartless. But Ellie was the first. We really clicked. She always believed the best about me. It was weird. I'd be doubting myself and being cynical, but she seemed to see past it. Like she knew something about me I didn't even know. She had a way of... lifting me up. Making me feel like I meant something. Why she saw anything in me was a mystery. So yeah, I loved her." I shrugged. "Why do you ask?"

She stared out the windshield. "Because this is about her, isn't it?"

"Yeah. Pretty much."

She nodded to herself. "I know what you mean. About losing someone you love, I mean."

I looked at her and she met my gaze. I didn't feel like I needed to probe. We understood each other. It was an odd little moment that I'd revisit more than once in the following days. If the timing had been better, maybe we could've shared our mutual losses over beer and sliders at Lucille's. But cytomorphs and ghost currents have a way of gumming up the works.

Kanya inhaled, then exhaled a great gust. "Are you ready?"

"Probably not."

"Okay, then. We play it by ear. If we can use your pass and get in, we just keep our eyes open. That's it. We don't force anything. The more information we can bring back to my father, the better. And if we *can't* get in... well, we play that by ear too."

It confirmed everything I'd sensed about her—she was cool.

I nodded, grabbed my backpack, and we got out of the Cammy. Spiraplex rose before us into the night sky framed against the clouds like some Mesopotamian monstrosity. We crossed the street and followed the fenced barrier. Typical construction fencing, it was linked tightly, no sagging panels that might allow for vagrants or thrill seekers to get a peek inside. Security cameras were mounted at driveways and in between scaffolding. Welding sparks showered off a ledge high above, and jack-hammering rumbled away somewhere inside.

Suddenly, Kanya extended her arm and stopped me. Up ahead, at the street corner, a man in security garb was on a walkie-talkie. Then she tilted her head, motioning behind us. I turned to see a second man on the opposite corner also holding a walkie-talkie and watching us. Well, that didn't take them long.

"I guess sneaking in is out of the picture," I said softly.

"Just keep walking."

We did. We approached the security guard at the corner, who made a point of making eye contact with us as we passed him. The entrance came into view further down the block. The crowd pressed in there, laughing and flashing pictures on their phones. One of the spotlights stood nearby, sending its blazing spire into the sky. Our pace slowed as Kanya rehearsed her plan again.

"Okay." She adjusted her handbag over her shoulder. "You show them your press pass. Hopefully they don't quiz us too much. If they do, we work for your newspaper. I'm your assistant. If they ask my name, I'm, uh..."

"Lois."

She scrunched her nose. "Why Lois?"

"You know, like Clark Kent's girlfriend."

She scowled. "Lois Lane?"

"She was a secretary or something, right?"

"She was also kinda nerdy."

I smiled and nodded. "Exactly. Lois."

Suddenly, something swept past me. A bristling cataract in the atmosphere that put my senses on high alert. I immediately stopped. Goosebumps skittered up my spine. It was as if we'd passed through a translucent barrier. Or bumped into something neither of us could see.

"What is it?" she asked.

"I'm not sure."

The shadows seemed alive, full of whispers and slithering horrors and hate-filled eyes. I found myself wringing my hands, for a chill had gripped my knuckles. Deep inside my marrow the icy sensation pulsated. The same chill I'd woken with after wearing the goggles.

"Psst." Kanya got my attention, and pointed back the way we'd come. The corner was vacant. The security guard was gone.

"Where'd he—?"

"Shhh!" She nudged me into silence.

I kept wringing my hands. Something was happening. I could feel it unfolding. In my gut. In my very joints. In the atmosphere. Something was playing out. But what was it?

I glanced back to the crowded entry of Spiraplex. Laughter. Jostling. Camera flashes. No one was interested in us. We were just spectators, lost in the shadows. I quickly scanned the area. Plywood sheeting formed a barrier, running the remaining length of the sidewalk. Behind it was a fenced catwalk drawn with black tarp.

That's when I noticed the image of Anubis, spray painted on the plywood in front of us, in between posters and gang graffiti.

Kanya caught me staring at the effigy of the Egyptian god of the dead.

"That's odd," she said.

"Isn't it, though."

We both gazed at the crude, spray-painted likeness of this ancient symbol.

"Give me the goggles," I said.

"Here?" She stared back down to the corner, but it was still empty.

"Why not here? It's not against the law to wear weird aviator glasses. This is L.A., baby."

Kanya stepped further into the shadows with her back against the plywood barrier, and rummaged through her bag.

As she did, I opened and closed my hands, trying to break the strange chill from my bones. My heart was racing now. I concentrated on taking slow, steady breaths. All that stuff about the Imperia and the Tau made the moment seem fraught with tension. Could I really be on the receiving end of some cosmic commission? If so, what was I supposed to do about it? *Play it by ear*, that's what

Kanya had said. It seemed like reasonable advice.

She handed me Rival's Curtain. "Be careful, Reagan. You remember what happened last time."

"I remember." I took the goggles.

I didn't give myself a chance to reevaluate the decision or to worry about the weird sensation in my hands. I put Rival's Curtain on.

It was not what I expected.

Neither the abstract color wash of the Asylum, nor the fiery din of the outrider's world was present. The surrounding cityscape was nothing but vast dull blocks of umber in a void of glacial black. Here and there, odd luminescent colors flared and faded. Apertures seemed to open in nearby buildings, corridors that revealed oddly shifting masses of color, before folding back in upon themselves. A maze of ink black interrupted by bolts of roiling chrome. As my eyes adjusted, I could make out a bluish sheen illuminating our immediate area. The sidewalk and the cars lining the street took shape, returning a sense of perspective to my surroundings. The nearby structures were little more than dense blocks of dead matter as seen through Rival's Curtain. Inside, humanoid prisms came and went. Further down, a mass of conflicting color pulsated like some huge glowing amoeba. I knew it was the crowd gathered in front of Spiraplex.

"Reagan," she whispered. "You okay?"

"Yeah," I said, turning to look at Kanya. It was the first time I'd really studied her through these fantastic lenses. While her form was dark, a penumbra of warm yellows seemed to halo her head.

"You're glowing," I said. "In a good way."

She stifled a little laugh.

I continued surveying the area, turning to look at Spiraplex. As I did, I stopped abruptly. A sickly green haze emanated from the structure, churning skyward in an immense plume.

"Good Lord," I muttered.

"What is it?"

"Spiraplex. It's, like, reeking. Oozing slime. Or smoke.

Something."

A thick pea green shroud coiled about the structure, a slow rolling fog that folded and refolded into itself. It had a strange quality, both liquid and living. A blob of protoplasm the height of the Queen Mary. Tendrils of vapor swept out from Spiraplex like an invisible current spun out from some noxious spring. There were voices in it. Minds, aware of us. Eyes, watching us. I could sense them. The sky seemed toxic from the rising haze, as if the atmosphere of this dimension had been tainted by the very presence of this structure. I stood dumbfounded, looking up at the hideous slime.

I was about to describe what I was seeing when something blazed into my peripheral vision and I lurched sideways.

"What is it?" Kanya turned into me, nearly knocking the goggles off my face.

The image of the spidery cytomorph flashed through my mind. However, it wasn't one of the dimensional outriders. Bernard stood on the sidewalk, not six feet away. He was waving his arms trying to get my attention, practically doing jumping jacks.

"Hey," I said. "It's Bernard."

"So *that's* what you felt."

Bernard nodded emphatically when she said this.

"What's he doing?" Kanya asked.

As she said this, Bernard stepped closer, until he was directly behind her. The angel looked past her shoulder and pointed to something beside me. I turned, trying to spot the object of his interest, but saw nothing. When I looked back at him, he shook his head. Then he raised one hand, spread his fingers, and with the other hand pointed at those fingers.

Huh?

I held my hands up and, as I did, gasped.

Faint blue currents danced atop my fingertips, electric tentacles that crackled and dissipated into the darkness. My hands were electrified.

# CHAPTER 18

MY GOD."

"What is it?" Kanya whispered. Then she said, "Your hands?"

She was watching me staring at my hands. I had them raised in front of my face. Through Rival's Curtain, I could see silvery blue currents twining from my fingertips. In that other dimension, the world of the Invisibles, Bernard stood at Kanya's shoulder, his eyes wide with wonder. Surely, an angel had seen such things before. Electrified hands couldn't be *that* unusual to a 1000-year-old celestial ragamuffin. Nevertheless, Bernard appeared enthralled. We both gaped at my energized hands. Veins of electricity snaked through my fingers and wove into the darkness. Yet my joints felt cold. What was happening to me? My world had been turned upside down—*with me in the middle of it!* Rival's Curtain had awakened something in me. Either that or I was, indeed, cold stupid.

"Can you see this?" I asked Kanya.

"See what?"

*No, of course she couldn't.*

I turned my hands over and back, watching the soft crackle of blue swirl away into the night. Then I lifted them skyward, twirling them like a child and reveling in the neon swirls.

Suddenly, Bernard started waving frantically, jumping up and down trying to get my attention again.

"What is it?" I said.

"What's what?"

"No. It's Bernard. He's pointing to something."

As I turned my attention to the fence, where he was motioning, Bernard stepped through the barrier. He disappeared behind the plywood. Then his glowing fingers poked from under one of the panels and wiggled wildly.

"The fence," I said, going to the spot where Bernard was. I slipped my fingers under the plywood. As I pulled back on it, a large metal nut clanked to the sidewalk and the board opened, separating from the post, leaving a wedge through which I could see the burnished man. I let the section close, and stood up.

"He wants us to follow him."

"Well then," Kanya said, "Let's go."

"W-wait a second."

"What? You've never trespassed before? He's an angel, Reagan. How much trouble can he get us in?"

Her question didn't make me feel any better.

To slip behind this barrier was to cross some line. We'd be officially breaking laws. But Klammer had paid me to cross this line. At least, straddle it. *I want you to investigate your girlfriend's murder,* he'd said. And this is where it had led me. If Ellie'd really been murdered, it deserved investigation. However, if I got caught sneaking into Spiraplex, Arlette would have my head on a platter. It would totally ruin any future chances for the Blue Crescent. Not to mention *my* chances for keeping a job with the paranormal tabloid.

Spiraplex's hideous green glow churned skyward like steam from some massive engine.

"Listen," Kanya said. "The security guard's still gone. If we're gonna make a move, we need to do it now. The worst they can do is arrest us for trespassing."

"You sure about that?"

I stooped down and peered through the fence. Bernard was pointing and jabbing his finger at the opening in the plywood barrier.

I've done a lot of crazy things, but this had to be the craziest—sneaking into Soren Volden's technological Elysian when I had a pass to go through the front door. Go figger.

I rose and quickly scanned the area. The closest camera was near some dead flood lamps and a stack of pallets behind the barriers, angled away from us.

"Okay," I said. "Stay close. If we bump into anyone, we... we have a meeting with Mr. Brook, community liaison guy. That's it. We'll say we... we got lost or something."

"They'll never believe us."

"I know."

I looked down the street. The bustle of dark energy still roiled at the entrance. The other way, where the security guard had been, was dark. I removed my backpack, pulled the fence back, and held it as Kanya slipped through. I handed her my backpack and followed. It was a small opening and I caused more noise than I would have liked when my shoelace became entangled in the fencing and I was forced to wrestle free.

We found ourselves in a dark tunnel. I readjusted the goggles and stood studying our surroundings. It was the catwalk. I could make out bare bulbs illumining a route that sloped down into the bowels of Spiraplex. Bernard leapt into my field of view and nodded enthusiastically. Then he bolted forward.

"This way," I said, motioning us downward.

Walking with the visor was still difficult. I imagined it was kind of like driving in one of those Euro cars with the steering wheel on the opposite side, where everything would seem turned around. I moved slowly, occasionally reaching out to steady myself or keep from bumping into something. Bernard kept stopping along the way to accommodate me, and then waving us forward. We descended and the catwalk intersected at a T, both routes following the base of the building in opposite directions. Now we were thick in the green soup. It made my skin itch, seeped into my pores and labored my thoughts. Even the blue glow from the

Tau appeared deadened by this noxious haze. I wondered if I should caution Kanya, but my guess was that she was well aware of the weird invisible world around us. And if she wasn't, maybe it was best she didn't know.

Bernard turned right at the T and I followed. Voices of men in conversation rose nearby. Kanya was at my side and, when I stopped, she hissed and grabbed my arm. The smell of plaster and grease was in the air. If we were caught, it'd be impossible to explain ourselves. But Bernard didn't seem too concerned. He was up ahead, casting a golden glow about the crude tunnel. He turned and waved us on.

"C'mon," I said to Kanya, and continued forward.

As we went, the voices grew distant. Thick jumbled shapes rose and fell. Planters or trees. It was hard to tell. But the eerie green luminescence thickened like a fog around us.

Nearby, more voices came and went. The sound of electric tools and the smell of sawdust filled the air. Suddenly, we emerged from the catwalk. The cool night air struck us. I looked up and the stars shone like nuclear pinholes in a canopy of black. This wonder was drowned out by Spiraplex. The structure towered overhead. The thick haze appeared to be oozing from its very joints. It encased the entire building, an ectoplasmic sheath. Like a monstrous undersea anemone, tentacles of the ghastly slime opened and then recoiled as we passed.

We descended a walkway and entered a densely dark cavern. I could hear our footsteps echoing in this place.

"Be careful," Kanya whispered from behind me. "Can you still see him?"

"Yeah. Where are we?"

"It's a parking structure," she said. "Underground."

That made sense. Hundreds of thousands of tons of thick concrete. No wonder it looked so lifeless in here. The decline steepened and I was forced to slow down to navigate safely. Bernard's form seemed brighter in this pitch black. Golden warmth radiated from his lithe form, illuminating the path as he went. The walkway curved, winding along a block wall that was to our immediate left. Suddenly, Bernard stopped and extended his hand for me to do the same.

"What is it?" Kanya asked.

"I don't know. He sees something."

Bernard tilted forward and then tiptoed around the corner.

Don't ask me why an angel had to tiptoe.

We waited. I took the chance to study the subterranean structure through Rival's Curtain, but it was nothing but dense black. Faint notes of color flared here and there before disappearing. Somewhere inside the structure, the sound of a car engine revved to life.

Bernard had better hurry up.

After a nervous minute, in which the engine shifted into a low idle, Kanya asked, "What's going on?"

"I'm not sure. He went around the corner. He wanted us to wait."

"If we just stand here, someone's gonna see us."

"What do you want me to do? We're following an angel. What trouble can he get us in, right?"

Behind Kanya, a blob of ghastly green drifted. The haze was seeping into the structure, following us, tracing the path we'd traveled. Silent fingers ebbed forward, lapping at her ankles before folding back in upon themselves. And now I could see eyes. And faces. Spectral images churning inside the hideous brew. I pulled Kanya toward me, away from phantasmal slime.

"What is it?" she asked.

*Moon. Mooonnnn!*

This shit was alive! A sense of dread welled up deep inside me. I had as much chance fighting ghosts, devils, and haunted green gas, as a can of kerosene does putting out a grease fire. I looked down at my hands, but the electrical charge had left them. I pulled Kanya further down, the way Bernard had gone.

"What is it?" she protested. "Reagan." She yanked free.

That's when I noticed that the ground nearby was glowing.

Bernard burst from around the corner, panting, and frantically motioning us forward.

"It's him!" I hissed. "C'mon."

Bernard was jogging now. Deeper, deeper into the structure. Leading us. We passed a tunnel, our footsteps echoing into what now sounded like a vast subterranean complex. I could only imagine how many catacombs, ducts, and secret corridors a billion dollars could buy someone.

"Where's he going?" Kanya asked between breaths of air.

"I don't know."

Bernard skidded to a stop and pointed both index fingers at a single door, smiling broadly. He looked like some demented game show host proudly declaring 'Door Number One' for the studio audience. There was a card scanner near the handle of the door. But we wouldn't need it; the door stood slightly open.

"Hey," I said. "Thanks."

He gave me the "OK" sign with his fingers.

"Where's it go?" I asked. "And what do we do when we get there?"

He furrowed his brow and touched his finger to his lips, signaling for me to be quiet. Then he gestured for us to get going.

"Shh!" I mimicked his gesture. "He said to be quiet."

I lifted the goggles and perched them on my head.

"What's wrong?" Kanya asked.

"I need to see where the heck I'm going, that's all."

I steadied myself against a rush of dizziness. Bernard's burnished glow against the dense black disappeared and gave way to the dull, dimly lit subterranean environs. The engine revved again somewhere in the structure. It was getting closer. The squealing of tires sounded.

"Hurry up!" Kanya said. "Someone's coming."

I opened the door and we slipped inside. The door clicked shut behind us.

I stood with my back to the door, massaging my eyes and trying to recalibrate my senses. We were in a rather large concrete foyer. A metal bin sat beside the door, the sleeve of a surgical gown draping from under the shiny lid. The room opened upon a flight of concrete steps, beside which ran a ramp. A gurney sat cockeyed at the bottom of the ramp, with a sheet draped off its edge. Tread marks suggested considerable gurney traffic had moved up and down this ramp. What was going on down here?

Like me, Kanya stood pondering the presence of the gurney and the ramp. It was cold in here, almost to the point of refrigeration. A slight chemical taint was in the air. I gazed up the steps, not bothering to count them, for on the landing above us I could make out retracted mechanical doors and behind them an oval tunnel with a stretch of bright lights running down its overhead spine. We looked at each other. Then she started up the steps.

"Wait a second!" I said.

"He said this way, right?" Kanya looked down at me, frowning. "I thought you were supposed to be a daredevil, or somethin'."

"Who said that?"

She snorted in derision, turned, and started up the steps.

"At least I've managed to stay alive," I called after her.

She whipped around and angrily pressed her finger to her lips.

I did not possess the ego to worry about being upstaged by a woman. So I hurried up the steps and caught up to her. We stopped on the platform and stood side-by-side staring down a long brightly lit tubular tunnel. In a corner, off to the side, was a well-worn office desk and swivel chair. An old model landline phone sat on the desk and next to it, some manila files and ink pens. A few plastic surgical gloves hung limp over the rim of a wastebasket nearby.

Kanya nudged me and then pointed to a security camera in the corner. It was aimed straight at us. I froze. Until I noticed a single wire dangling at its side. The lens looked dead.

"It's been disconnected," I said.

"Bernard?"

Was that what the angel had been doing? But how? And if so, in what other ways could an invisible being interact with the physical world? Had he distracted the security guards outside? Or one in here? Had he loosened the fence or opened the door? The possibilities made my head hurt. Even worse, I'd started the morning as a skeptic and was now debating possible ways that guardian angels protect their clients.

I returned my attention to the tunnel before us. Pneumatic, hospital-style doors stood open on either side of the brightly lit tunnel. At the far end, some 30 to 40 feet away, the tunnel appeared to open into another corridor.

"It almost looks like a decontamination chamber."

"It does." Kanya hunched forward. Then she pointed to black tread marks woven along the surface of a smooth floor. "Lots of traffic. They're running gurneys through here, or something."

"Yeah. But why?"

She rose and stood with her hands on her hips, staring down the long tubular runway. Debating. As I was. We both recognized the gravity of what we were about to do. And we both seemed to share the same conclusion.

"Do we have a choice?" I asked, anticipating her thoughts.

"Not really. This is the way he wants us to go."

She was right. And since I was supposed to be a daredevil, I stepped in front of her, through the doors, and into the corridor. I held my breath, half-expecting to be doused with chemicals or trigger an alarm. But nothing happened. Kanya joined me and we hurried through the tunnel until we came to the second set of pneumatic doors. They opened as we approached, bringing us to an immediate halt.

A long, dimly lit corridor now stretched before us. Neither of us dared move. A few more steps and we would be officially inside Soren Volden's Spiraplex.

The walls were surprisingly drab. Plain fixtures cast fluted beams of light upward. It reminded me of the lobby of a cheap hotel, the kind Arlette didn't mind putting me up in when I was on the road. Several sets of double doors, perhaps 50 feet apart, staggered the corridor on opposite sides. These doors were tall and unusually ornate. Large black vases containing what appeared to be stalks of pussy willows stood against plain, almost shabby, wallpaper. Perhaps even more unusual, dark narrow walkways intersected this corridor, disappearing at odd angles into deeper bowels of the structure. This place had all the charm of the Mummy's Crypt.

I cautiously stepped out of the tunnel. Kanya followed and the pneumatic doors hissed closed behind us. After the bright light from the tunnel, my eyes were struggling to adjust to this dingy corridor. I thought about putting on the goggles but was fearful of what I might see. Besides, I had to be prepared to move quickly in the event we were found out.

Other than the gentle hiss of air through some overhead ducts, it was quiet. Morgue-like quiet. Death-on-your-heels quiet. I crept down the hallway, studying the place. Along with the trace of chemicals, a scent of smoke laced the air. It was an odd combination. This had to be some sort of medical facility. Either that, or they were reviving the Egyptian custom of embalming. I was not having a good feeling about this. Not at all.

"Now what?" Kanya whispered.

"We play it by ear."

"Funny."

I approached the nearest corridor intersecting ours. It was considerably smaller than the one we were in, narrow to the point of claustrophobic. I poked my head inside. The walls looked like fake sandstone blocks, the floor descended at a slight angle, disappearing into pitch black. Was this some sort of ventilation shaft? I leaned into the tunnel. Not only could I detect fresh air emerging, but the echo of water pattered somewhere down below.

I withdrew my head and stepped back. There were maybe a half dozen other similar shafts intersecting this corridor.

"What is it?" Kanya asked.

"You got me. Some sort of subterranean maze."

I stared down the hallway, trying to get a sense of my next move.

"The goggles," she said. "You should put 'em on."

She was right. Bernard would help us. After all, he'd brought us down here. Now he could show us what he wanted. The goggles were still propped on my forehead. I reached up, prepared to slip Rival's Curtain on again, when voices sounded somewhere nearby. In one of the other rooms there was also a shuffle of movement. If we didn't move, we'd be caught dead to rights.

"Ahhh!" I turned to run, but the decontamination tunnel we'd entered through was too far behind us. And wandering into one of these dark shafts would be inadvisable. The voices were too close.

"Over here!" Kanya pointed to the closest set of double doors across the hall. She padded across the carpet and I followed. The doors looked to be made of dark wood like mahogany, and inset with various Egyptian symbols. The semblance of a hieroglyphic scroll formed the wooden frame. A green neon glow emanated from under these doors. Being there was no exterior handle, Kanya spread her hand on the doors, prepared to push. As she did, they retracted.

But neither of us moved.

"Good Lord," I said, staring into this place.

The voices rose. The doors on the opposite side retracted in similar fashion and someone started into the hallway.

"C'mon." She yanked me in and the doors closed behind us.

We stood in a dark cool amphitheater looking down on some sort of pagan temple.

We glanced at each other, for the moment oblivious to any danger we might be in. A long walkway descended toward two large bronze stands, perhaps eight to ten feet high. Flames blazed in these basins, casting shadows dancing about the perimeter of the room. Between these immense torches, at the center of this room, sat a squat, dark structure. Pictorial frescoes lined its walls: carvings of winged creatures, scarab beetles, and palms. Apparently, Soren Volden had a fetish for all things Egyptian. It was chilly in here, refrigerated. Yet the most amazing thing about this subterranean temple, the one that had both me and Kanya gaping, was rows of capsules filled with green liquid standing on end, facing the temple in silent witness. Dozens and dozens of glowing cryogenic tubes surrounded this shrine.

They were not empty. They appeared to contain humanoid forms.

Kanya mumbled something.

"What the...?" I repositioned my backpack over my shoulder. "What is that? What are those things?"

I wandered down the aisle, peering at milky forms floating gently in strange liquid. From here, they looked like the type of oddities you'd find in sideshow specimen jars—a two-headed pig or a horned human fetus. As I approached, trying to get a better look, I could see a thick blanket of condensation covering the glassy surface of the tubes, making it impossible to verify exactly what was being held inside. Were they experimenting on simians down here? Even worse, humans? Then there was the possibility that something alien was pickling in these jars.

This was quickly becoming the worst of all possible scenarios. Is this what Bernard wanted us to see? If so, and if I'd had my wits about me, I would have taken my camera out right there and started clicking and posting pics to the internet, turning this subterranean scene into a viral phenomenon. However, I didn't have a chance.

"Hey!" a voice cried from behind us. "Hey you!"

I spun around. As I did, the goggles slipped from my forehead, falling perfectly in place on the bridge of my nose.

The space turned red. Ghost flames whipped the air. A dark humanoid shape stood at the entrance to the amphitheater, the doors we'd just passed through, looking down on us. It was a human, I could tell by its density. But draping this person's back was something else, something sickly gray. Two leathery-like manta wings folded over each shoulder, giving the appearance of a cape. Yet these wings weren't for flying but seemed to be embedded or inserted into the person's body near the pectoral region. It was an immense invisible parasite. As I watched, terrified by the vision, something rose from behind this person's neck. Large bloated eyes rolled listlessly, as if awakened from slumber.

"You gotta be kidding," I said to myself.

"Who are you?" the man, not the parasite, said. "How'd you—? What're you doing in here?"

But I didn't say anything because the little gray creature had awakened. It unburied its head from its host. Apparently, I'd disrupted its nap, or its dinner, because at the moment it appeared very angry.

# CHAPTER 19

I SNATCHED THE GOGGLES OFF MY FACE.

It was a man in a lab coat standing at the double doors, gawking at us. A clean-cut 30-something with wire rim glasses. A real nerd. Did he realize an invisible parasitic manta was attached to him? If so, he wasn't showing it.

"What are you doing in there?" he exclaimed. "How'd you get down here?"

He probably wouldn't believe me if I told him my guardian angel breached the security fencing, distracted the guards, disabled the cameras, and led us to this cryo-crypt for God knows what. Which left me stumbling for a response.

"We, uh..." I fumbled the goggles and gave them to Kanya. She quickly stuffed them in her handbag. "Come again?"

Apparently, my inability to answer was enough for him.

"Nettles!" Lab Guy yelled back down the hall. "Nettles, tell Bruce we need someone down here. In Khepri. Axis Hall. Now!"

"Wait a second!" I shrugged off my backpack, zipped it open, and scrounged for my press pass.

"Whoa!" He held up his hands and backed away as if I was about to produce a grenade and pull the pin. Obviously the squiggly gray monstrosity strapped to his spine hadn't actually given him a spine, for a look of absolute terror filled his face.

"No." I whipped the pass out and shoved it at him. "I'm a reporter."

He continued backing away, refusing to even look at the pass. "Nettles!" he shouted over his shoulder again. "Nettles, Khepri room. Hurry!"

I could only imagine what kind of commotion that thing on his shoulder was making. Kanya had stepped sideways and I thought for a second she might try to make a run for it or overpower the man. Thankfully, she did neither.

An elderly blonde woman, also wearing a lab coat, ran up and stood next to Lab Guy. Her eyes were fierce, her lips pursed tightly. The first thought that crossed my mind was whether or not she had an invisible leech strapped to her as well.

"Who are you?" she said flintily, looking at me, then Kanya.

"I'm a reporter. Reagan Moon. With the Blue Crescent."

"A reporter? Sonofabitch." She glanced down the hall.

"I'm here to see Selwyn Brook," I said, stepping toward them with the pass extended.

"You're only ten floors off."

"Who?" the man said.

"Brook. With PR," Nettles growled. She snatched the pass from me, looked at it, and seemed to get even madder. She gestured for us to get out of there, pronto. I slipped my backpack on and as I did, I glanced back at the strange layout behind us. Humanoid forms of some kind floating in green liquid tubes. Dozens and dozens of them. What in God's name was happening down here? Was this what Bernard had wanted me to see?

"Hurry it up!" Nettles spat.

As we hustled out of the room and back into the corridor, two men jogged up. For a moment, I thought they might be twins. Both above average height, olive-skinned, long drawn faces, heads shaved nearly bald. They were dressed in open collared shirts and jackets. Security goons. One had a firearm drawn and at his side. Great! I hoped Bernard was watching this, because he was the one who'd gotten us into this mess.

The doors closed behind us.

Nettles handed my pass to one of the two, the one without the gun. She said, "Caught'em snooping around down here. Don't know how they got in. Reporters, apparently."

"That's right," I said. "I'm—we're reporters. That's all."

He glared at me. Then he flashed the card to his partner.

"How'd you get down here?"

I shrugged. "A couple wrong turns?"

Apparently, this was the wrong time for sarcasm. The man with the gun wrung his fingers on the grip while the other ground his teeth, drawing out cords of sinew along his neck. They obviously did not have a sense of humor. Either that, or they were debating who would rip my head off and who would shit down my neck.

"Look," I said. "We have a pass. Selwyn Brook. He's giving us a feature on Spiraplex. It's right there! Check it out if you don't believe me. You don't think we'd be stupid enough to sneak in when we were invited? C'mon. I just figured we'd have a look around. That's all. We're reporters, man. Looking for a scoop. That's what we do. Like I said, we got lost, took the wrong turn. We ended up here. Go on. Check it out if you don't believe me." I gestured in appeal to the pass.

Yet my impassioned plea only seemed to make them grow more irate.

I was about ready to fall on my knees and beg for mercy when one of them pulled a digital device from his pocket and pecked away at the touch screen. He scanned the bar code on the pass. He shot a glance up at me, pecked away at the device again, and then said, "The sensors are disarmed." He pointed back the way we'd come. Then he said to the two technicians. "Where's Briggs? Who disarmed the sensors?"

Nettles shook her head and looked at Lab Guy.

"It wasn't me!" he whined.

I was sure Bernard was dancing a jig around these brutes.

The goon held my pass up. "How'd you two get in?" he demanded.

"Look," I said, trying to ratchet the tension down and walk back my earlier idiocy. "We're here to see Mr. Brook. That's all. We don't mean any trouble, okay? If we've caused any, we apologize."

As if *we* posed any real trouble to these armed hulking thugs.

Some unspoken dialog seemed to pass between them. They were contemplating whether to off us right here, dismember our torsos, and put us out with the trash, or just submerge us in one of those green tubes.

Finally, Nettles said, "Eleventh floor."

Eleven. A Master Number. Double digit of the same number. When that happened, the vibrational frequency of the prime number supposedly doubled in power. So, because the number one was that of purity and new beginnings, 11 was, like, perfect balance.

Whatever.

The guard who was holding the pass returned to his device. While he spoke softly to someone on the other end, the man with the gun leaned in. His pupils were an odd turquoise. Almost luminescent at their core. An unusual pungent aroma came with him, like wet animal hide. Or curdled cologne. The atmosphere seemed to thicken as he bent toward me.

As if I was entering the space of something full of malice and not quite human.

"You know," he said, "You're in no position to be a smartass. Especially down here. If not for her," he glanced at Kanya, "you might just get lost and never be found again."

Her? I was about to follow-up when something flared in his eye, an unmistakable spark deep within his pupil. Shades of Frankenstein's monster! Even more disturbing was that he knew I saw it. Because he smirked.

My lips parted. I swallowed hard and nodded. "You're right. So I'll just..." I brushed my hands atop my thighs. "I'll just stop talking."

He nodded very slowly. "That's a fantastic idea, hotshot."

Kanya gazed straight ahead. No doubt, she was calculating a possible escape route or a plan of attack. I wondered if a purple belt in Kuji-wawa could actually take these two water buffaloes. I was pretty sure I could handle the lab geeks. Provided I did not have to wrestle any invisible parasites in the process. Hopefully, it wouldn't come to that.

Lab Guy was staring at me, starting to lean forward in scrutiny, his eyes creased into slits. I could see the machinations of his brain working. Maybe that creature on his neck was feeding him a line. He was going to ask about the goggles. I knew it. He'd seen me wearing them. He saw me hand them off to Kanya. Now he was remembering.

"He checks out." The other guard got off the phone. "Brook's expecting him."

"See?" I stretched out my arms in appeal. "I told you."

They did not share my enthusiasm. The guard begrudgingly handed me the pass back. Then he extended his hand. "Your bags. Both of you."

I quickly shrugged my backpack off, hoping to mask any concern I had about them confiscating Rival's Curtain. The man took my pack, rummaged through it, and pulled out my camera.

"You can pick this up at the front when you leave. Cell phones or recording devices, I need those too."

The thought of Volden's hacks scanning my emails and phone records made me hesitate.

"It's policy," the guard said. "Until we open, no cell phones or recording devices are allowed on site. If you don't wish to comply, we can escort you out. Which I'd be delighted to do."

I handed over my cell phone. Then he motioned me forward. His partner holstered his sidearm and patted me down, intentionally stuffing his fist up my crotch with enough force to seriously jeopardize future generations of little Moons and make me gasp for breath. He rose, sneering, and then signaled Kanya over.

When she passed her bag to the guy, I cringed, partly because if I opened my mouth I feared I'd sound like Freddie Mercury in a falsetto competition. To her credit, Kanya did not make eye contact with me or betray anxiety. Even when he removed the goggles and stared at them. At this point, Lab Guy leaned in and they examined Rival's Curtain together.

I cleared my throat. "Just some old machinist goggles." I sounded like I'd inhaled a tank of helium. "She's an antique dealer on the side."

Kanya blinked.

Lab Guy tapped the amber lenses. Then he took the goggles from the security guy and raised them to the light. *Oh shit!* He held them with both hands, at arms length, angling them at the fluted wall lights. But apparently, Rival's Curtain had no effect on him. Either that, or the glasses looked harmless enough to actually pass for some old machinist goggles. He returned them to the security guy, who returned them to Kanya's purse without incident.

I fought to refrain from breaking out in applause right there.

After patting Kanya down, the main security guy said to the lab workers, "Reset those sensors. Check that door. And find Briggs. You two," he pointed at me and Kanya, "follow us."

In the end, it had been Selwyn Brook's invitation that had saved our hides. Funny how fate works. Or was it the Imperia? Either way, I'd have to thank someone other than me for getting us out of there.

They led us down the hall to a set of doors at its end. The man with the gun dropped behind and trailed us, probably hoping we would run so he could send a hot projectile into our brain matter. As we went, I found myself wondering at what other strange experiments Soren Volden might be conducting down here. If my intuition was correct, we'd just glimpsed the tip of an Everest-sized iceberg.

The doors opened upon a brightly lit corridor. Far behind us, the two technicians watched while engaging in whispered conversation. The doors slid shut, taking the medical smell and the chill with them. The VM symbol marked these doors. Next to them was an eye scan device for entry.

So much for getting back down here.

Two sets of elevators stood on opposite ends. They escorted us to the far end, which proved to be an extremely spacious elevator.

The guards stood such that we were forced to stand between them. The door slid shut. "Floor 11," said a delectably digitized female voice from the console, and the elevator launched smoothly toward its destination.

The air was thick with fury. I could feel it. I was pretty sure if we hadn't had that pass our destinies would have included being ground into dog food for some hungry canines. Yet right now, there was more than just a couple of angry bouncers jammed in that elevator with us. I knew it. Could *feel* it.

There were Invisibles.

My sense of perception had been so tweaked since wearing Rival's Curtain that I found myself drifting in and out of conscious awareness of that other world. It was as if the two had been intertwined. What was happening to me? What was happening all *around* me? Were there smoldering cytomorphs towering over us as we stood there? Were parasitic mantas suctioned to these creeps? Was Bernard standing nearby enjoying my ruminations? It was as if the two worlds were overlapping inside me. But by the feel of it, something other than harp-playing cherubim were crowded next to us inside the elevator. I glanced at the man next to me. The guy had to be 50 pounds my superior, not an ounce of it fat. But there was something other than the size of these men that was deeply disturbing. These Bobbsey Twins were not human.

We reached the 11th floor and the door slid open on a curved, well-lit corridor and a series of executive suites. An information desk sat vacant in front of us. On top of its dark wood counter lay a tool belt and some wood shavings. Tall Egyptian statues with headdresses and staffs rose between exotic palms. A woman was vacuuming further down and a smell of paint and new carpeting was in the air.

"This's your floor," the guard said. "Brook's office is to your right. A couple doors down. Just look for the nameplate."

"Thanks." My normal voice had finally returned to me.

We hurried out.

The second man said, "And I suggest you don't go wandering off again."

"On my best behavior," I said. "Promise. And be careful with my camera, okay?"

If looks could liquefy, his would have turned me to gelatin.

We stood there for a second listening to the elevator descend to its destination.

"Is there a reason..." Kanya queried, looking straight ahead, arms at her side. "Is there a reason you have to get under everyone's skin?"

"It's a bad habit of mine. I'm sorry."

"Ya think? If we get outta here alive, it's really something you should try to work on, Reagan."

"You're right." I sighed. "What's another item on my self-improvement list. But what's this about getting out of here alive? Of course we're going to get out of here alive."

"I sure hope so." She glanced at a security camera. Then she motioned in the direction of Selwyn Brook's office and we walked that way. "This place is crawling. I can feel it. I'm not sure what it is, but something's wrong."

"Well, if you're talking about the thing attached to that lab guy..."

"What kind of thing?"

"Oh, I dunno. Gray. Wings. Big eyes. Buried in the base of the guy's skull. That kind of thing."

"That's just a grub."

I looked aslant at her.

"Your basic demon," she explained, appearing annoyed at having to do so. "You know, the little devil that stands on your shoulder and whispers in your ear? Only these guys can actually attach themselves to our brains. They're pretty low-level, fairly common. Can't do much beyond drain the life out of their host and dull them to everything that's good and beautiful. Occasionally, they're behind a mass murder or a celebrity overdose. But mostly it's smaller, mundane stuff like plagiarism and road rage."

"*Your basic demon.* I'll have to remember that."

"Lemme guess," Kanya said. "You don't believe in demons."

"Well, I didn't this morning."

"And if I'm not mistaken," she said, "those were cryogenic tubes down there."

"Yeah. But what was inside them?"

"I dunno. VM *does* traffic in high end research. But I doubt they were specimens for show-and-tell."

We padded across the carpet, passed a large vase inscribed with the eye of Isis, and found the office of Selwyn Brook.

Kanya straightened her shirt collar and looked at me. "You okay?"

"I'll survive."

"All right. Then let's get what we need and get out of here. And, if you don't mind, try being a good boy."

"Yes, ma'am."

I knocked on Selwyn Brook's office door. Before my hand even returned to my side, the intercom buzzed.

"Mr. Moon!" a cheery voice sounded. "Please, come in."

The lock disengaged. We entered a large spacious office with a desk the size of the Rock of Gibraltar. Huge plate glass windows rose behind his desk. They looked down upon a vast atrium area inside Spiraplex, perhaps several football fields in length. It was breathtaking. At the far end of this vista rose level upon level of floors and suites. Apparently, the center of Spiraplex was an immense terrace with flats and offices lining the interior of the walls, looking down upon this courtyard as if it were some vast hive. It was hard to imagine that something this fantastic, this magnificent, was being erected only miles from Skid Row.

But I didn't allow my gaze to linger just yet. I turned my attention to Selwyn Brook. He had shoulder-length wavy hair, slicked back, and a tan that wouldn't quit. He wore a perfectly tailored black blazer over a gray turtleneck, quite dapper, and an earbud was implanted in one ear. And he smiled a lot. If they'd cloned Joel Osteen, this guy was definitely one of the prime models.

"What a surprise!" Brook loped toward us with his hand extended. "You should've told me you were coming tonight." His grasp was strong and confident. And his smile? I was almost blinded by those teeth of his.

"I'm sorry," I said. "I've been busy on another story."

"Not one as promising as this." He winked. "Believe me, it isn't every day that a personal invitation to Volden Megacorp's latest project goes out. Your employer—what was her name?—Arlette! Yes. Arlette seemed quite excited about the possibilities of a feature. Hopefully, we can work out those details. Some of which I'd like to discuss this evening."

Brook was obnoxiously peppy. Working for an outfit like this, with charm to burn, dude had to be a lerium user. From the looks of it, he was also probably one of those health freaks who moisturized and received weekly manicures. He punctuated his statements with flamboyant hand gestures, winks, and that pearly white smile. A perfect fit for Hollyweird.

I said, "I'm sure we can work out details for a feature."

Brook nodded and then looked at Kanya. His eyes seemed to sparkle wolfishly. "And I take it this is an assistant?"

"That's right," I said. "This is, um..."

"Lois," Kanya blurted. She winced as she did.

"Lois." Brook practically drooled the name. He took her hand and lightly lifted it, as if she were the Queen of England. I thought he might kiss her pewter ring for a second, at which point I'm sure she would compensate by kicking his balls into orbit. Instead, he squeezed her hand affectionately. "Lovely to meet you. Lois."

"She's an intern," I said. "Journalistic assistant."

"And I'm sure she's a fine one." Brook paused for another smarmy second, then released her hand and walked back to his desk.

Kanya glanced at me and curled her lip in disgust.

"Got caught sightseeing, I hear." Brook turned. While his smile remained, his eyes were frosty. "They found you in the Lower Chamber."

"I apologize. My investigative impulse got the best of me. It won't happen again."

"Mm. You're lucky. You could've got lost. It's easy down there, I hear. Mr. Volden is fond of the Pharaoh's Labyrinth. Never been there, myself. They say, during construction, a tradesman was lost in one of the chambers. He was never found again. Shame."

"Yeah." I cleared my throat. "I could see how that might happen."

"The Cosmagon are another story."

"The Cosmagon?"

"They are under strict orders, Mr. Moon. Trust me—they're very efficient. If you hadn't had an invite, I'd hate to think what could have happened to you and... *Lois.*"

"So..." I swallowed. "Who are the Cosmagon?"

Brook wandered to a bookshelf, caught his reflection in a picture, and raked his fingers through his hair until a lock dangled perfectly at his forehead. "Mr. Volden's personally trained security staff. He uses them around the world. You can imagine what kind of scrapes one might get themselves into with undertakings such as his. We like to think of them as twenty-first century Mongols. With death rays. Hard to keep up with the weaponry VM develops. It's even rumored the Cosmagon can... teleport." He turned around and smiled. "Rumor, of course. Forgive the mess. We're still unpacking. Our Grand Opening is approaching and Mr. Volden has us burning the candle at both ends."

I forced a polite laugh. "Of course."

"And please," he added, "this is all off the record, I'm afraid. In due time you'll be free to introduce Spiraplex to the world. But if we see any of this in print or online before our approval, we'll take legal action. Something I'm sure the Blue Crescent—that's the name of your paper, right?—something the Blue Crescent could sorely afford. I'm sure you understand. Nevertheless, we want to give the Blue Crescent an exclusive, inside story. It's quite an honor. No date has been specified. We're waiting on one crucial architectural element. Mr. Volden is particular like that."

"So when do we get to meet him?" Kanya asked.

"Volden?" Brook tipped his head back and issued a canned laugh. "Like God, Mr. Volden is a mystery. *I've* never met him. And I've been with VM for... I've lost track. You should feel privileged to have come this far. It's not every day that a paparazzi and his assistant gets an invitation from one of the most important men on the planet."

I furrowed my brow. "I am *not* a paparazzi."

He smiled dryly. "Of course you're not."

"And you mean Volden was the one...?"

"You didn't think *I* invited you, did you? Apparently, he considers your reportage above average. Me? I'm just an appendage, a servant to a much greater cause. Him—" He raised his hands into the air and then said reverently, "Soren Voldon is the sun of our system."

I wasn't sure if he was hamming it up or this guy was a genuine douche.

He shook himself from his momentary euphoria. "How rude of me. You've come here to see Volden's work." Selwyn Brook marched proudly to the plate glass window and looked down into the vast courtyard below. "Then let us do that."

He motioned us over.

As we approached, he stepped back, making a slow regal gesture with his hand. "Welcome to Spiraplex! The Eighth Wonder of the Modern World."

Despite the sideshow intro, Kanya and I stood next to each other, gaping, as the entirety of Spiraplex came into view. It was, indeed, a sight to behold.

The interior of the building was conical, rising toward a peak. Something with the appearance of a massive Tesla coil spiraled down from this pyramidal apex. The walls twinkled with the lights from offices and suites looking down upon the inverted terrace. From here, it was a rather disorienting visual feature. Lush gardens hung from the walls, planters trailing vegetation. Similar to the exterior, the walls were embellished with hieroglyphics and Egyptian motifs. Escalators moved seamlessly along the sides, weaving between floors. One entire level near the bottom was lined with columns and inset with shadowy, tomb-like quarters. A miniature Nile bordered by palm trees in ornate planters flowed through the courtyard, a ribbon of aqua blue.

This place made the Hanging Gardens of Babylon look like my grandmother's patio garden.

Yet despite all this beauty, what stood in the center of Spiraplex left me breathless.

A statue of Anubis, partially surrounded by scaffolding and tarps, rose perhaps six or seven stories. It was black with bronze and gold highlights, and sat like a proud sphinx in the middle of Spiraplex. Feet extended. Curved neck rising smoothly. Ears erect. Snout staring forward. The monstrous guardian of this modern-day ziggurat. At its base, a passage followed the perimeter from which several doors were visible.

I was speechless. It was the first thing Klammer had shown me. The pictures of Anubis were all over the city. *They Live!* But who lived? Demons? Angels? God, I was going insane! If Spiraplex was top secret, how did word get on the street about the Egyptian death god anyway? And what did this ancient icon have to do with anything?

"Anubis," Brook said. "The Egyptian god of the dead."

"Your boss obviously has a thing for Egypt." I inserted a hint of sarcasm in my tone, to see if he would bite.

"The cradle of life, Mr. Moon. Perhaps the most advanced civilization of its time. Mathematics. Medicine. Astronomy. Agriculture. Alchemy. Magic. Everything finds its root there." He stepped between us, staring down at the lush environs. "It's been decades in the making. The City of Angels will never be the same. Tropic gardens. Restaurants of the finest international cuisine. Shops curating trinkets, ointments, and memorabilia from around the world. Two dance clubs, for those who enjoy the nightlife. And an arcade unlike anything ever experienced."

"That's all?"

He chuckled. "Oh, there's more."

"It's incredible," I said. "Really, I'm... speechless."

"Yes. But it's just the surface," Brook said. "The greatest of all his accomplishments, and the pinnacle of the Volden dynasty, is the one we have yet to reveal. The one you've been brought here to witness."

This made me step back from the window and disengage from the fantastic architectural vista. I blinked. "What do you mean?"

"The *Dreamchamber*," he whispered.

"I thought that was just a rumor."

"It once was. But now, it's the next step in human evolution. Dreamchamber technology will reshape the world, open frontiers that man has never dreamed of. Alzheimer's. Mental illness. Insanity. These will be a thing of the past. The brain—*this* is the last and greatest mystery. Which explains our motto: *To the stars, through the mind!*" He tapped his temple. "And now Mr. Volden holds the key."

Geez. At this point, I was convinced Brook wasn't a person as much as a collection of homilies.

The Dreamchamber. Supposedly it was the project Klammer had joined Volden to develop. Their Magnum Opus. A line of prosthetics that could map the brain, manipulate thinking, transmit and encode memories, ultimately creating the potential for Mind Uploads. Freaky stuff, for sure. Yet the possibilities were limitless. Guilt, depression, psychosis could all be cured. Artificially adjusted. Humans could be reprogrammed. Bad men could be fixed. No more need for the death penalty. Or pharmaceuticals. But word along the grapevine was that their research had drifted into the metaphysical. The un-scientific. Apparently, they bumped into something along the way that gave Klammer second thoughts. They conjured something bad. Which made Brook's mention of the Dreamchamber all the more interesting.

I was about to dig a little deeper when Brook held up his hand to stop me. He pressed his finger to the ear device. "Yes?" He listened. "Be right there." Then he turned to us. "Excuse me for a minute, will you?"

He loped to the door, stopped with his hand on the handle, and turned. "Help yourself. There's drinks in the refrigerator. Adult beverages, if you like." He pointed to a small bar in the far corner. "Or if you'd just like to enjoy the view. Be my guest. I'll be right back."

As soon as the door closed behind him, Kanya started digging through her bag. She pulled out Rival's Curtain and handed the goggles to me. "Quick! Put'em on."

I took them. "What?"

"Hurry!" She bolted to the door and stood with her back to it, head tilted, listening for any sound of Brook's return.

"But—" I glanced over my shoulder at the looming Egyptian statue. "I don't know if I want to see this."

"What are you talking about? This is what we need to see!" She pointed out to the atrium. "If something is going on here, then it'll show up. Trust me. Now hurry!"

I'm unsure why I was so hesitant. Maybe the dull gray demon clinging to Lab Guy had spooked me. Or the cytomorph tumbling through the dimensional skin at the Asylum. Whatever it was, this place had to look like a three ring circus through Rival's Curtain. The nausea, the disorientation, was reaching a boil inside me. God, did I have to do this?

I reached up and touched the Tau underneath my shirt. I think I said something—a sort of... *prayer*. Then I turned to the courtyard of Spiraplex. Drawing a deep breath, I put on Rival's Curtain.

It was like a backhand to the brain.

And then the voices started.

# CHAPTER 20

*MOON. MOOONNNN!*

Swirling, battering my mind.

I grew rigid at the sound of the ghastly voices. Now I knew where they were coming from. As much as I'd like to have curled up in a ball and played dead, I couldn't surrender. I had to witness this thing. I readjusted Rival's Curtain. Whoever was calling my name could see me. They were watching me. And now I could hear them. Whatever these visors were, they had dislodged something inside me that could never be repaired.

I think Kanya said something to me. If so, it was lost in the shuffle. She had her back to the door, anticipating Selwyn Brook's return. But I was fixated on the grand event unfurling before my new eyes.

With the voices came a blur of motion. Green. Toxic green. A Niagara of sewage. I stretched forth my hand in order to get a sense of perspective, touched the glass, and steadied. It was a column of liquid fog rising in the center of Spiraplex. As if the earth was vomiting its bile. A geyser of pain and malevolence. This was the same slime that blanketed the exterior of the building. But this was huge. A towering, inverted cyclone that cocooned the statue of Anubis and coiled upward, whirling and twining its way to the shimmering Tesla coil. It was breathlessly immense.

I was definitely going to cop a migraine after this.

"Oh. My. God."

I staggered numbly from the window as I peered at this vision. The surreal landscape of the Asylum was no match for the horrific grandeur of this thing. Its sickly glow illumined the walls of Spiraplex and everywhere—on columns, porches, and planters—hieroglyphic symbols refracted an eerie phosphorescence. Resonating the evil. The walls of the structure sparkled like the night sky, reflecting the vile pillar of Anubis.

I could hear Kanya calling my name now. But I was too enthralled to respond. For inside the green spire were living things; limbs and eyes, charred torsos, monstrous tentacles, entities in torment, faces twisted in agony. This was worse than an H.R. Giger nightmare. Holy shit! It was a torrent of souls rising from the bowels of the earth. Like someone had uncapped hell and I was the witness.

*Moon. Mooonnnn!*

"Reagan," Kanya hissed. "He's coming!"

I staggered back, staring at this cyclone of torment rising from the god Anubis.

"No," I muttered. "He's already here."

They Live! Of course they do. They live and they're just stretching their legs—angels and outriders and every demented monstrosity in the Lovecraftian bestiary. And now there was a death spire impaling the globe through the heart of Los Angeles, California. A world unlike anything my pea brain had ever entertained. A Luciferian pyre. And I was witness to it. Reagan Moon, guardian of the Tau. Scared witless.

"Reagan! He's coming!"

I numbly removed the goggles, held them to my side, and stood dumbfounded as the real world caved in on me.

This wasn't a ghost box. No. It was so much more.

Soren Volden had opened hell.

Kanya rushed across the room, snatched Rival's Curtain from me, and stuffed it in her handbag as the door opened.

"You're in luck." Brook strode in and then stopped in his

tracks when he saw me. "Mr. Moon. Are you all right?"

"I'm..." I swallowed hard. "I'm fine."

"You didn't drink the amber vial, did you? The one in behind the absinthe?"

When I didn't answer, Kanya chimed in. "No. We didn't drink anything."

Brook peered at me for a moment and then relaxed. "Well, I have a special treat for you. A foretaste, you could say, of our main course."

"I can't imagine," I said numbly.

"The Dreamchamber." His eyes sparkled. "We've scheduled a tour just for the two of you."

The vision of that swirling mass of hellish protoplasm at the core of Spiraplex did more than just weaken my knees. It left me emotionally gutted.

"The Dreamchamber." I mimicked his words. But I was unprepared for another round. In truth, I was spent. If someone offered me a hammock and a Mai Tai, I'd be fine just chilling, staring at the ceiling and losing myself for the remainder of the decade.

Kanya gathered up her handbag and watched me intently. She knew I was out of sorts. Still, I managed to agree and stumble behind the two of them as they left the office of Selwyn Brook.

We entered the elevator. I was feeling wobbly and stepped to the back where I leaned into the corner. The door slid closed and we descended. Brook was too busy fawning over Kanya, going on about quantum consciousness or some nonsense, to notice me. I could smell him, not just the exquisite cologne and minty fresh breath, but the stench of something else. He probably had one of those gray buggers glued to his cerebral cortex. Figures. I couldn't imagine his charm and articulation attributable to anything other than your basic demons.

I drew my fingers through my hair. Paranoia had begun uncoiling inside me. And fear. Everything that Ellie had said was true. Hell, she'd been prepping me for this! Guardian of the Tau?

Shit! Kanya was right—at this stage, the best that I could hope for would be to make it out of here alive.

We stopped on the sixth floor. Six, the number of...

...it didn't matter! Nothing mattered right now except getting out of here. Surviving. Getting away from that hellish spire rising at the center of this infernal structure.

The elevator door opened upon a pristine seascape.

What the—? I straightened, staring forward.

Waves lapped the shoreline of a pure white sand beach. Palms overhung soft rock outcroppings, creating pools of shade. Gulls drifted by, buoyed by a warm breeze. Turquoise crystal water revealed glinting fish and kaleidoscopic reefs. It was as if we'd been transported from Los Angeles to the Caribbean in less than thirty seconds.

Brook stepped out with Kanya. They were standing in front of a huge screen, a super-high def, semi-circular panorama that filled the entire wall behind them. I followed them into a cool corridor that was illuminated only by the enormous LCD image and its churning, ever-changing, picture-scape.

Other than the movie screen, the decor was almost plain here. There were no Egyptian symbols, planters, or vases. A series of windowless rooms traced the opposite walls. At least we didn't have to look out upon Anubis.

Brook's tone was hushed. "We're still working out the bugs. But this—" he motioned to the corridor of rooms stretching before us, "this will change our world forever. Follow me."

As he loped ahead, Kanya dropped back, came alongside me and scrunched her brow as if to say, "Are you all right?"

Even though I wasn't all right and would probably never be all right again, I nodded. She could tell I was fudging.

The beach scene morphed into a tropical forest, flushing the entire corridor from warm yellow to deep green. Brook stopped at a numberless door.

"A session's in progress," he said. "What you're about to see has been witnessed only by a few." He typed something into a keypad panel next to the door before looking up into what I realized was some sort of micro camera device. The door clicked. He pressed his finger to his lips and opened the door.

I hesitated. This was all going down so fast. So fast. We entered a dimly lit passage, which was bordered by a studio or booth. Brook entered this room. He closed the door gently after us. A technician sat before a computerized flat panel, his face glowing in greens and whites. He wore a headset. A large plate glass window separated us from another area. We were in an observation room.

My head was throbbing now. Apparently, seeing the Invisibles was not conducive to keeping brain cells.

The tech glanced at us, then at Brook, and returned to his work. The booth looked out upon a dimly lit office or exam room. At its center rested an oval platform and facing it was a reclining padded chair, similar to the kind one might encounter in a dentist's office. A column of blue light glowed upward from the platform and within it, soft waves rippled and undulated. An elderly man reclined in the chair, facing this blue column of light. He appeared relaxed, not quite asleep, his hands folded across his waist. Electrodes draped from his forehead and temple, and trailed to another panel in the corner where a second technician stood.

Either this was the ultimate video gamer's fantasy console or something fantastically weird was happening inside Spiraplex.

"We call it an M-graph," Brook said. "Holographic mnemonics, to be exact. M-graph technology is an immersive experience, as you'll see. Through neuroscience and imaging technology, we're now able to pinpoint where emotions and personality resides. For instance." He pointed to a digital map of what I assumed was the old man's brain glowing on a nearby monitor. Swaths of colors—greens, reds, and yellows—swelled and then dimmed on the image. "Resilience, the capacity to recover from adversity, resides in the prefrontal cortex, the amygdala. One's outlook on life is located in the ventral striatum. And then there's memory formation and storage. Through Volden's research, we're now able to chart the complex processes of memory formation, which involved changes to the molecular structures and synaptic transmissions of the brain. VM has been at the forefront of this research. By stimulating selective neurons, we can reenact and selectively activate protein synthesis, almost perfectly emulating how memories are made. Volden's research has allowed us to do much more than just map the brain."

Brook's tone had become almost rapturous. This guy was all in. I don't know what VM was paying him, but he'd probably practiced this spiel a hundred times over, and enjoyed doing it every time. He circled to the opposite side of the tech, gazing out at Dreamchamber.

"Just as the contours of the brain harbor emotional states," he continued, "manipulating certain areas of the brain can summon those emotions. As well as memories. The M-graph can restructure that raw data into an actual image. A holographic recreation of the memory!"

I pointed to the blue column of light rising before the elderly man in the chair. "So... so that's a holographic projector?"

"Of a sort, yes."

"And you're able to decipher what that guy's feeling or thinking, and... *turn it into an image?*"

"A full-immersion virtual-reality environment. Just watch."

Brook nodded to the technician in our booth who then spoke into his headset. The tech in the Dreamchamber responded by turning to a computer panel next to him. Suddenly, a gentle wave rolled through the blue holographic cylinder, from bottom to top, leaving a foamy, static-like discharge in its wake. That digital residue hovered inside the holographic cylinder like a cloud, or a phantom seeking shape.

I half-expected Captain Kirk to appear any minute.

"He recently lost his wife," Brook said. "They'd been married for over forty years. Imagine that. But now, through the power of Mnemography, he can visit with her again. Literally."

The old man peered at the smoky column. The technician nearby spoke into his headset, and the one inside our room responded, quickly adjusting several controls. The holographic image roiled, and then crystallized.

The phantom form became cloudier, more dense, losing its translucence. Slowly it began to take on the appearance of a person. I watched in amazement. It was a middle-aged woman wearing a nightgown. A life-size representation. She started as a ghostly figure and then her features hardened, became more concrete and defined. A wave passed through the holographic column, a blip, and her form continued to take shape. Her motions were fluid, not at all like that of a projected image. This was real! She smiled at the man and extended her hand to him. She was reacting to his gestures. Or was he simply creating her responses in his mind? The old man rose on his elbows, leaning closer to the hologram of his deceased wife. His eyes were now glistening with tears. He stretched his hand forth as if to touch her. However, the electrodes on his head prevented him from much movement. Nevertheless, he smiled. And wept.

The Dreamchamber had allowed him to contact his dead wife.

Brook smiled. "She's just like he remembers. And why not? She's an amalgam of his own memories. She *is* what's in his brain. Now, he can talk to her again. Look upon her. Communicate with her."

"But... it's not real," I objected.

Brook tapped his temple. "If it's in here, it's real to you. Look!"

They were speaking now, the old man and his holographic wife. Now, the tears were streaming down his cheeks.

"Just think of it," Brook exclaimed. "Think of the possibilities. Psychologists can use the M-graph to unearth painful memories and lead their patients to healing. Care to revisit a pleasant time in your childhood? Mnemography makes that possible. Those 'glory days' when we were young, adventurous, carefree—they're all at our fingertips. Or perhaps you just want to," he issued a low, almost sinister chuckle, "...experience that one night fling again. And again. The Dreamchamber will revolutionize how we interact with reality."

A lot of things were stewing inside me. But despite what you might think, the foremost question on my mind was not how fantastical this technology was. It was *Why me?* Why was he showing *me* this? Why had they specifically requested *me*? When the Dreamchamber technology was first floated, government and religious groups had expressed *ethical concerns.* It was no wonder. Technology that could dig into someone's psyche and make memories real—especially memories of the prurient or criminal variety—was bound to open a Pandora's Box of legalities. And ethicalities. Not to mention the power it afforded those who controlled such technology. So how could the government not want to get their grubby hands on something like that? But apparently, something had transpired to ease the Feds' concerns, or else I would not be witnessing this in the middle of Los Angeles.

Unless VM was operating completely under the government's radar.

"It's incredible," I said.

Brook folded his hands at his waist. "We believe M-graph technology will be that next step, provide a scientific basis for an unprecedented spiritual awakening. As Mr. Volden likes to say, *Paranormal is the new normal.* We'd like to think that the Dreamchamber will make normal what Humankind has only dreamed of."

I watched the old man wiping his eyes, laughing, as he conversed with the holographic image of his dead wife. It was the 21st century version of a séance. I found myself thinking about my new employer, Felix Klammer, and wondering if this was why he split.

If so, I couldn't blame him.

Brook thanked the technician and quietly escorted us back into the hallway. "Tomorrow we'd like to give you the complete tour. Photographs, interviews. An unprecedented first glimpse into Spiraplex. We've made all the proper arrangements. You'll be using the same pass, so hang on to that. Above all, be prepared to have your socks blown off." He issued a hearty laugh. "And please, do bring your lovely assistant again."

I nodded numbly.

"I'll cover more of the specifics tomorrow. There *are* a few technicalities we'll need to agree on, but I don't foresee a problem. I'll be in most of the day. But let's just say seven-ish, shall we?"

Selwyn Brook escorted us from the Dreamchamber to the ground floor. As we left the elevator, I stared back up at the towering statue of Anubis. From here it was the size of an apartment building. With ears. According to legend, the dog god guarded the abode of souls. Somewhere in the world of the Invisibles, that abode was now wide open; a spire of hellish delight was rising from the statue and permeating the structure known as Spiraplex, oozing its way into the City of Angels. No wonder the freaks were coming out of the woodwork. Gollo was right—the *manifestation* was just around the corner. If this place wasn't the biggest ghost box in existence, it was at least the very doorstep of hell.

They returned my camera and our cell phones when we left, just like they'd said. Breathing the chill night air had never felt better. I was glad to leave that godawful place.

Even though I knew I'd have to return.

# CHAPTER 21

I THINK IT WAS TIMOTHY LEARY WHO SAID that once the mind is stretched, it never returns back to its original shape. Okay, it probably wasn't Leary. Although he knew a lot about stretching minds, I'm not sure that the little mind he had left should even be trusted. Nevertheless, it was good to know that minds were not beyond stretching.

We arrived at the Asylum after 11 p.m. I was running on fumes but nevertheless thrilled to be leaving the 18th behind. If not for the adrenaline coursing my body, I could have curled up in the bed of the Cammy and slept till morning. It wouldn't have been the first time. Of course, Kanya had asked what I'd seen when I put on Rival's Curtain in Brook's office. This time, I didn't skimp on details. The ghastly green column. The tortured images. The voices. It was everything she and Matisse had feared. And more.

She called Matisse on her cell phone to let him know we were all right and on our way. I hunched over the steering wheel, watching the city lights blur by, wondering at the strange invisible denizens that flitted about this city. *Paranormal is the new normal.* Damn straight.

I parked in the alley behind the Asylum. Matisse must have been watching us from down below because the freight elevator buzzed as we approached. When we reached the lower level, Matisse was waiting anxiously.

"*Mi chica!*" He hugged Kanya. "I lit a candle for you. Both of you!"

I said, "I think we're going to need a lot of candles before this is over."

"I heard it on the radio," he said. "Another medium was murdered."

Kanya and I looked at each other. We were no closer to uncovering a motive for the Medium Massacre than when we had left.

"Well, then," Matisse said anxiously. "Let's have it. What'd you see? Is it true?"

Kanya repeated the question to me, as if prodding a confession. "So? Is it true?"

I shuffled into the control room, slung my backpack on the table, and dropped into a chair.

"Honestly?" I said. "I don't see how it can't be."

My admission was probably the scariest thing that had happened all day.

Matisse dropped into the chair across from me. "A ghost box. A bridge to the realm of spirit. Good Lord! The Gleaning is upon us." Matisse leaned forward. "I need to know everything. Everything!"

He listened enthralled as I told him about Bernard leading us into Spiraplex, discovering the strange subterranean cryotubes, meeting the scientist with the invisible parasite, the mysterious Cosmagon. The massive statue of Anubis, oozing its invisible blight. And then the Dreamchamber. Reliving the story a second time left me even more exhausted.

"How could I have been so blind?" Matisse slammed his fist on the table. "Volden's far more powerful than we imagined."

"Well, as powerful as he is, he's still missing something."

"Yes?" Matisse asked.

"He's right," Kanya said. "Brook said there's one more thing that must happen, one more element Volden needed before Spiraplex goes public."

"Then we still have time," Matisse said.

I instinctively touched the Tau. If they'd been after the relic to complete their project and thought I had it, why wouldn't they have made a move? It'd been right under their noses. Then again, did they know I even had it? Maybe they assumed no one would ever be dumb enough to waltz in there wearing the cross. But this assumed it was the Tau they were after.

"Perhaps this is to our advantage." Matisse rose from his chair and began pacing. "Whatever he's looking for, it means we still have time."

I watched him hunched in thought, walking back and forth, scratching his beard.

"Well," I said. "Who knows what he's looking for? And besides, what can we do to stop him anyway? Something that big... I mean, we can't just march in there and blow the place up."

Kanya looked sideways at me.

"Ohhh, no," I raised my hands in protestation. "Don't even. I don't do explosives. I'd like to keep my day job, and my limbs, thank you very much."

"If Volden finishes that thing," she countered, "you might not have a day job to go back to."

"This's foolishness." Matisse dismissed us with a brush of his hand. "Blowing up buildings won't solve anything."

"But if it's *that* serious..." Kanya spread her hands.

"You can't fight the Invisibles with bombs, Kanya. You're talking nonsense!"

"But isn't that what you're doing here, father?" Kanya motioned to the warehouse of occult paraphernalia. "Taking *things* out of circulation? You're disarming something *invisible* by removing something *physical.* Maybe taking a building out can do the same thing."

Matisse peered at her. "We are *not* blowing anything up. *My God!* What is wrong with you?"

I got the sense they'd had this discussion before.

Matisse kept pacing. Finally, he said, "Klammer was the one who started your little investigation, is that right?"

"Yeah."

"Then right now, he's the only person who ties everything together."

"Well, good luck finding Klammer. He's not just under the radar, I think he probably invented it."

"Think back," Kanya said. "Was there something else he said? Something that could help us?"

"We've already been through this." I exhaled in exhaustion. Then I raked my fingers through my hair. "He said he had reason to believe the Bastion Sails incident wasn't an accident. What reason? I don't know. He suggested that those people were intentionally killed. But who knows? My sources told me that the two technicians who were on duty—the only two actual witnesses—are both out of the picture. One was murdered, a burglary supposedly, the other went missing."

"How convenient," Kanya said.

"Yeah. But there's just not enough evidence one way or the other."

"Volden's covering it up," Matisse said. "That much is obvious. He wouldn't leave tracks. But why would he want to kill them—all 13 of them? It was just a college group, right? They had no connection to Volden, did they?"

"Not that I know of. They were with Windsum, an alternative energy group made up of college professors and corporate types. And up-and-coming private sector people like Ellie. She was always trying to save the world. Geez. But as far as details of my conversation with Klammer..." I shook my head and continued trying to reenact my meeting with the hooded billionaire. "He said some mumbo-jumbo about her spirit living on. That I could help her. I thought it was crazy. I *still* think it's crazy. How do you help someone who's dead? He sent me to the old seer and... that was all. Said the guy might be able to contact her spirit. And I guess, the guy did. Course, it was the last job he ever had."

I exhaled, slumped forward, and buried my face in my hands.

Matisse muttered something and I could hear him walk over and plop into the chair again.

I prided myself in my resilience, but this was too much. I was officially tanking. I pressed my hands against my skull as if I might squeeze the memory right back into it. As I did, the image of my electrified hands popped into my brain. I could see myself standing before Spiraplex earlier that evening, gaping through Rival's Curtain, joyously watching neon blue tendrils twine from my fingertips into the sky. Yeah, that was fun. And even though they felt just fine, I spread my hands in front of me and stared at them. My own hands. Conductors of invisible energy. Who knew?

And then it came to me.

"What?" Kanya said. "You remember something."

"He said their bodies were being harvested."

Matisse and Kanya looked at each other.

"The cryochamber," Kanya said.

"Yeah."

"Good Lord," Matisse exclaimed. "Why didn't you say so?"

"I just did."

"Then those *were* people down there," Kanya said. "The gurneys. That's what they were for. And all that traffic. He's harvesting bodies."

"Yeah," I said. "But harvesting them for what?"

Matisse bolted out of his chair and went to a chalkboard where he drew a crude sketch of a human body.

"The human body is like a generator." He drew wavy lines of energy along the cranium of his sketch. "The human brain alone can generate enough electricity to power a light bulb. Organic energy. The average adult has as much energy stored in fat as a one-ton battery. In theory, if one could accumulate enough bodies and tap into the material and immaterial elements, a vast farm of organic energy could be harnessed." He drew a second figure and connected them with a line. And another. "At one time, it was postulated that clones could be bred simply for the purpose of fueling massive generators, a farm of synthetic humans could provide unlimited energies."

"That's a morbid thought."

"Of course, we're decades away from such technology. If it's ever possible. But Volden is ahead of the curve. He'd suggested something bigger and far more grandiose. He called it *soul harvesting*. Not only could the organic and metaphysical components of one's being be tapped, the mind itself could be uploaded. Thoughts, knowledge, experiences could be transferred between minds. Similar to a computer upload. In theory, someone could become exponentially more intelligent by uploading the knowledge of others."

"I think you've watched *The Matrix* one too many times. Besides," I said. "Where would he get enough bodies? *Living* bodies?"

"Hospitals? Human trafficking? Runaways? I don't know. A man of his stature would have a lot at his disposal." Matisse shook his head. Suddenly, he said, "Wait a second. Her body—Ellie. What happened to Ellie's body?"

"They never found it." I stood up. "They never found any of them!"

We looked between ourselves. My heart was pounding, my mind racing.

"It was Bernard that led you down there," Matisse said. "Is that right?"

I nodded dumbly.

Kanya said, "He wanted us to see that. Reagan, he led us there on purpose."

"Then they weren't vaporized," I said. "They were kidnapped. And the only two people who could spill the beans were offed."

"Dear God in heaven." Matisse crossed himself.

"If she's down there, I'm going back."

"Are you crazy?" Kanya said. "Those Cosmagon creeps didn't like you the first time. I'm sure they won't like you any better the second."

"Bernard got me in the first time. He can do it again."

"He's an angel, not a magician. Look," Kanya said. "Brook wants us back there tomorrow, right?"

"Yeah, but if she's down there—"

"If she's down there, what do you propose to do, Reagan? Fight off Volden's entire team of henchmen, get past all their security cams, and carry her out over your shoulder with guns blazing? C'mon. Besides, we don't even know if she's down there." She paused. "Or, if she is, what condition she's in."

"Kanya's right," Matisse said. "Things are falling in our favor. We must move with caution."

"Well, I'm going to do something," I said. "If Ellie's in that place, jammed in one of those tubes, I am not sitting around and waiting for her to become a human battery. Whatever the hell that place is, and whatever's going on there, she's having no part of it."

My hands had flushed cold. I clenched and re-clenched my fists, trying to eliminate the feeling. In that invisible world all around us, I knew my hands were flaring blue electricity. Anger burned hot inside me. It was hard enough coming to grips with the fact that Ellie was murdered. The thought that she'd been kidnapped and might be used by some mad scientist in his chamber of horrors was making me insane. Still, Kanya and Matisse were right—moving irrationally, recklessly, was the wrong thing to do.

"Reagan." Kanya stepped closer. She spoke softly, but there was resolve in her tone. "This has to be hard for you. But my father's right. Things are coming together—the murders, you coming here, Rival's Curtain, Bernard. We didn't make it through there by chance. We're being helped."

I looked at her. Her black hair framed her copper eyes, a picture of flinty confidence.

"Ellie's down there." The words came out stony, almost shorn of emotion. The helplessness of my plight, the reality of everything I had been moving toward, cauterized into a single molten aim." And I'm going to save her."

Kanya nodded. "But this time we go in the front door. Okay? And from there... we play it by ear."

A smile nudged the corner of her lips.

"Besides," she said. "You need to sleep. You look awful."

I didn't need to look in a mirror to confirm her observation.

# CHAPTER 22

MATISSE OFFERED TO LET ME SLEEP in the Asylum that night. I'd confessed to them that I was a person of interest in the Medium Massacre, which meant sleeping at my apartment would not be very smart. And who knew whether the chick with the bleached hair and the tat would be back. Nevertheless, I declined the Mad Spaniard's offer. Frankly, I was reeling from the possibility that Ellie's body could be imprisoned in Spiraplex, a virtual guinea pig for some psychotic prodigy. I needed to get some space, get away from the subterranean crypt for a while. Clear my head. I still had the key to Mrs. Richardson's and knew a trick for accessing the fire escape in the alley behind my apartment. I could crash on her couch. Sure, that would irritate Chelsea. Which made the idea even more enticing.

Matisse, Kanya, and I agreed to meet in the morning and devise some plan of attack. Whatever it would be, I was pretty sure it wouldn't work. Just because I had an angel on my side did not stop me from being a pessimist. Not only that, but knowing Ellie might be down there made the chances of me actually sleeping impossible. So I was already on the losing end of things.

Matisse took Rival's Curtain, wrapped it in its cloth, and locked it back in the safe. After what I'd seen, I couldn't blame him. No wonder the last guy who wore it took a power drill to his temple. To my surprise, as I left, Kanya followed me into the elevator.

A thick blanket of clouds had draped the sky. Their underbellies reflected the eerie neon glow of the city lights. I could taste the rain in the air. I dug a sweat jacket out of the back and put it on. Kanya watched as I got into the Cammy and fired it up. The engine rumbled fiercely in that enclosed area. Man, I loved this car. Hot rod flames and all.

"Hey." She had let her hair down. The breeze whipped her hair about her face. Her eyes sparkled in the vapor lamp. This girl was alive in the night. She brushed the hair out of her face and looked up into the cloudy sky. Her lips were pursed ever so slightly. When she did this, it drew a dimple on her cheek. I could tell she was fighting to say something.

"Yeah?" I asked.

"I was kinda hard on you today. I apologize."

This surprised me a little.

"I didn't notice," I said.

She frowned.

"Okay," I said. "Apology accepted."

She looked at me and then her gaze flicked away. She wanted to say something else. I waited, and gave her the chance.

She didn't take it.

"You said you had a hunch about me earlier," I said, trying to lead her.

She shifted her weight. "Yeah, I did."

She didn't offer to fill in the blanks, so I left it at that.

"Okay." I lightly tapped the gas pedal and the engine growled. "Just thought I'd ask."

"It's getting late. We'll talk tomorrow. Go get some sleep." She started back to the open freight elevator, and then turned. "And be careful."

I gave her a thumbs up.

I love L.A. at night. It can be an exhilarating place, probably for all the wrong reasons. Of course, the Warehouse District is not the best place to appreciate the nocturnal sights. So I made a quick exit.

It was nearing 1 a.m. Even though it was cold, I rolled down the window. Cold air in your face does wonders for sleep deprivation. The damp, quiet night seemed to awaken my senses. I thought back upon yesterday—the infernal 18th—as I drove to my apartment. Was Bernard with me now, fighting off cytomorphs, Summu Nura, and your basic demons? I could only hope so.

I reached under my shirt and removed the Tau as I drove, letting it hang loosely over my chest. I angled the rearview mirror down and peered at the strange icon.

*There's a reason you haven't died,* Ellie had said. But for this? This was why I hadn't died? And if there really was something like the Seven Guardians of the Imperia, how'd I become part of their loopy narrative? And what was I expected to do about it?

I slipped the cross back under my shirt. Then I pulled my phone out. The battery was almost drained. There was a missed call from Arlette. She'd be awake and would be thrilled to hear about the Dreamchambers and my invitation to return to Spiraplex tomorrow. Instead, I speed dialed Jimmy Pastorelli and put him on speaker phone.

"Do you know what time it is, Moon?"

"Please, don't act like you're sleeping."

"You're right. I was just getting ready to hit Langer's and run over a case file before calling it a night. What's up?"

"The Bastion Sails accident."

"Here we go again."

"Jimmy, this is important."

"Go ahead," he said with feigned exhaustion.

"Those folks disappeared, right? No traces of the bodies."

"Yeah," he drawled suspiciously.

"And there's no record of foul play."

"None."

"Has that happened before?"

"No. What do you mean?"

"You know, that kind of accident. Where lots of bodies just go missing, are, I don't know, disintegrated or destroyed, and there's no remains. No evidence."

"Hm. Missing bodies are a weekly occurrence in L.A."

"Sure. But I'm not talking about one here or there. I'm thinking, like, a bunch of them. All at once. And they're just gone. Poof. Vanish."

He paused. "I dunno what you're gettin' at, Moon."

"Think, Jimmy. Another accident, maybe. Or... something. People just gone, can't be accounted for."

The line went quiet.

"Jimmy?"

A wave of static, as if the phone was being moved.

"Well, I'll be damned," he muttered.

"What is it? Jimmy?"

"Shanghai. Last year."

"Go on."

He spoke slowly, as if a thread of understanding was unspooling in his brain. "Chinese businessman. Jumped from the Ritz-Carlton and went splat on a cab. Apparent suicide. Only this guy had some magic roots and talismans on him. And I'm the official 'magic roots and talismans' guy around here. So they called me in. It was Asian folkloric bullshit. He was trying to fend off a curse, or something. Guess it didn't work.

"Anyway, he ran a firm in Shanghai, experimental nuclear facility. It'd recently been shut down because of an... accident."

"Lemme guess."

"You got it. Reactor accidentally discharged. Fifteen, twenty people were vaporized. Bodies were never recovered. Barely a blip on the international news. Funny. They fingered the techs for criminal negligence and they disappeared into the prison system never to be seen again. The plant got shut down and then Don Ho makes his way to the U.S. with herbs and spices, only to throw himself from the balcony of a luxury hotel."

"Or be thrown."

"Heh."

"And his connection to the States?"

"Volden Megacorps," Jimmy said thoughtfully.

"Surprise."

"Ain't it."

"So a group of bodies disappear, and no one's there to verify actual death."

"Yeah." Jimmy's tone was but a whisper. That detective brain of his was probably in high gear.

"And a similar accident happens here less than a year later."

"Yeah."

"So if Soren Volden needed bodies, living bodies—for whatever reason—he could possibly have a few at his disposal. And no one's bothered to ask the right questions."

"You missed your calling as a PI. But why would he need a buncha bodies? Not very becoming for one of the world's wealthiest men."

"That's another story. But if my hunch is right, some of those bodies might be down in the basement of Spiraplex."

A long pause followed.

"Moon, I dunno where you're going with this. Or what you really know. But do yourself a favor and put the brakes on it."

"I'm in way too deep for that, boss."

"That's not a suggestion, Reagan. Remember what I told you about being a suspect in these medium murders?"

"Unfortunately."

"Well, word coming out of homicide isn't that you're a suspect. I think you're fast becoming the *prime* suspect."

"Huh?"

"I dunno what the hell happened, what you may or may not have done, but you're officially in over you're head, Kolchak."

"I guess so," I said dully.

"And in case you're thinking otherwise, I will *not* cut corners on an investigation just because we share an interest in ghosts and vampires."

I knew this to be true about Jimmy Pastorelli. He took his job very seriously. Even if he did traffic in conspiracy theories.

"Jimmy?" I said.

"Yeah?"

"Don't forget werewolves. We like them, too."

A long pause. Then he said, "You'll be hearing from us. Watch your back, Reagan. And remember, you didn't hear anything from me."

He clicked off.

Wow. So the Bastion Sails meltdown wasn't the only one. And the way things were going, I'd probably get fingered for those too. Did I mention that the 18th was a special day for me?

I decided to cruise my street first, just to make sure there was no one casing the place. Other than a beat up old Honda that looked to have been through the street racing wars, I recognized all the cars. Still, I wasn't taking a chance. The best way to reach the fire escape was through the parking lot in the back of my apartment. That lot was full, but it wouldn't be smart to park there anyway, so I found a spot around the corner near M&M Pawn. An Indian guy owned the store. I'd swapped him an old Underwood typewriter for cash last year. Supposedly, the typewriter was haunted and could channel spirit communiqué. Sort of mechanized automatic writing. Course, I didn't share that little detail with the owner. Nor would it have upped the selling price on the Underwood. I got the bad end of the deal, but I was desperate for money at the time.

I got out of the Cammy and as I prepared to lock the door, remembered the gun under the seat. I couldn't take any chances. Whoever was playing with me was serious. I reached back in, retrieved the gun, and shut the door.

I just hoped I didn't have to use it.

I looked up and down the street. Then I circled the Cammy. Several drops of rain pattered the sidewalk. The storm had arrived. As I reached behind me to stuff the pistol in the back of my pants, I caught a blur of motion out of the corner of my eye. A large shape rushed from the shadows with barely a footfall. I tried to spin around and raise the gun. But before the thought had even completed itself, the attacker had seized my gun hand, spun me back around, planted my face against the passenger side window, and pinned my wrist awkwardly against my tailbone.

"Aww!" I cried through gritted teeth. "Watchit! Watchit!"

The gun was loaded and all I could think about was it going off and rendering me a paraplegic for the rest of my days. But I'd be a dead duck if I let go of it. Damn. I should've been more careful.

"Drop it!" the person rasped.

Muggings were common around here. Just last month some punks busted a guy's nose before swiping his high-tech phone and a to-go order of Thai food. Petty crime by L.A. standards. But this wasn't a mugging. I was sure of it. Not with everything going on.

I was leaning precariously over the gutter now, one arm pinned against my back, my face pressed against the Cammy window. I caught the stench of sewage trickling below. I'd gotten out of some tight spots before, more from quick instincts or smooth talking rather than primo self-defense skills. Yeah. I knew a few tricks, and could jab with the best of them. But in this position, my options had been significantly reduced. And by the feel of it, this person could break my arm with relative ease if they chose.

"Drop it!" my assailant demanded again.

If I surrendered the gun, I'd be in trouble. So I tried to locate the attacker's foot, thinking perhaps I could stomp a few toes. As I did, they tightened their hold, twisting my arm a fraction from breaking.

"Awww! Okay! Okay!"

I let the pistol slip from my fingers. The gun didn't have time to hit the ground before they'd leveraged their weight against the back of my legs, buckling them. I fell backwards. Using my own motion, they flung me onto the sidewalk, forcing me onto my back, and straddled me with the pistol at my throat.

"Where is it?"

Several raindrops struck my face. A soft shower had begun. I choked out some incoherent words, but was unable to speak with the gun jammed in my larynx.

My attacker ripped back their hoody. It was her—the woman who'd broken into my apartment. The bleached bangs were a dead giveaway. One pale blue eye glinted mercilessly in the streetlight. The other was just a scarred empty socket. Her black windbreaker shimmered with raindrops. She had her knees dug into both sides of my rib cage. I was sure that with the slightest move this vixen could puncture both my lungs.

She nudged the barrel up into my Adam's apple, nearly shutting off my air flow completely.

"Where is it?"

"What—?" I gasped. "Where's w-what?"

"Don't act stupid!" She loosened her thigh clamps just slightly. "Give it up, and you can go back to your shitty loser life."

A metallic shimmer shone in her mouth. Either she was wearing a tongue stud or she was the latest Terminator model.

I hedged, fearful even to repeat the question. My hands were free, but I was fairly sure that any attempt to snatch my pistol would end badly. Especially being it was halfway inside my gullet.

In response to my silence, she bent forward, nudging the pistol ever closer to the back of my throat. "The cross, dickhead. We want it back."

*The Tau!*

Had she known it was under my shirt, probably six inches from the gun, she might have shot me on the spot. What the hell was so special about that thing? And who was this chick working for? But I didn't have time for that. I'd been pledged to protect the Tau. Even if the pledge was issued by an over-the-hill medium who possibly contacted my dead girlfriend and was stabbed to death with a magic wand.

I raised my hands in surrender.

"Easy, easy," I gasped.

She re-tightened her grip around my torso.

"Upstairs." I pointed in the direction of my apartment. "It's. Upstairs."

It was the only way I could think to buy time.

But it didn't work. She drew back her opposite hand, made a fist, and landed a solid blow to my jaw, holding my body in place with her lower torso just to make the punch more effective. And—God—did she pack a punch.

I went black for a second, watched the streetlight wink on and off. For a moment, it was all warm, and empty, and delightfully painless. Nirvana via fist. But it didn't last. Reality came crashing back in on me. I blinked rapidly, tears welling in my eyes from the blow. This one-eyed witch wasn't fooling around.

"—already been upstairs, shit-for-brains!" she hissed. "Stop lyin'!"

I waved my hands, signaling that I was tapping out. But the words that left my mouth were gibberish.

"You have it!" She leaned in, her face dreadfully close to mine. "Don't you...?"

She smelled of demons and death. And her body odor was off the chart. Her single eye darted back and forth, studying me. I thought for a second she might plant a big wet kiss on my lips. Instead, with her opposite hand, she patted my chest, reached under my shirt, and snapped the Tau off my neck. She lifted it up. Her eye widened. And she almost smiled.

The decision to react was instantaneous.

Yet as I prepared to swat the pistol away, somewhere in the distance, tires squealed. Then a wash of light struck the Cammy and bleached the wet sidewalk brilliant white. A car thumped over the curb, just missing a fire hydrant, aimed straight at us. It was like something straight out of Grand Theft Auto. Except my head was the one that would splatter.

I didn't have time to worry about being run over. I had my opening. My attacker turned in reaction to the careening automobile and I punched her hand away using the ball of my fist. The gun went flying. As it did, it discharged and the bullet glanced off the sidewalk, then a nearby apartment. Someone screamed out of a window above.

Seizing her wrist, I spun away from the onrushing car, dragging her with me. The car skidded to a stop and I heard a door pop open. Three more feet and we'd be under the chassis. It was so close I could smell oil and radiator fluid. There was no time to locate the gun, or identify who'd driven over the sidewalk to join our tussle. I pinned her wrist to the sidewalk with both hands and straddled her. As I did, I glimpsed the hydra tattoo on her wrist and forearm. She grasped the Tau with this hand. I jammed her hand into the sidewalk, releasing a primal yell, and kept crushing it down on the concrete until she was forced to release the Tau. Turnabout was fair play. However, before I could recover the Tau, with her opposite arm she drove her fist into my ribcage, right where her knees had seconds ago threatened to collapse my lungs. Pain exploded in my side.

"Moon!" someone barked.

But I recoiled from her blow and, as I did, she kicked off of me and jumped into a standing position. She stood silhouetted against the high beams of the automobile, exhaust fumes glowing about her, the light rain creating silvery haloes on either side. She faced a massive, muscular figure that stood squared against her.

It was Blondie.

"You," she hissed at him.

My pistol lay at his feet and he kicked it away from her.

"Sidra," he said thickly.

"This's between us." She turned slightly and gestured back at me. "They stole the Tau."

The cross! It lay nearby. I scrambled on my hands and knees, pain lancing my ribcage, and rolled onto my back with the Tau clutched to my chest with both hands.

I could see her face clearly now. A pale web-like scar inside a puckered eyehole was the only apparent defect of a rather beautiful, if rugged, face.

"Not anymore," Blondie said. "Your boss isn't playing fair."

His hands were open. He stood poised. This guy was a tank.

The rain had increased, matting her hair. "Since when does fairness matter to you?"

If I hadn't experienced her wrath firsthand, I would have believed this to be an uneven match. Apparently, battling the Swede would have to wait. The assassin named Sidra pulled her hood on and tightened it. She glanced back at me as I clutched the Tau, shivering in the rain. Then she hissed something and bolted into the shadows. Blondie made no effort to follow. He picked up the pistol, stuffed it into his jacket pocket, and approached me as I lay writhing on the asphalt.

"You should be more careful," he said.

"Thanks for that advice." I rolled onto my hands and knees, groaning as I did so. I held tightly to the Tau. If this thing had protective powers, they'd expired. "So what the hell's goin' on?" I struggled to my feet and swayed. Every breath hurt and I was sure she'd bored a hole into my throat with my own gun. "The old man's dead. The cops are after me. And there's a ghost box the size of Mount Rushmore that's going to go live if we don't stop it."

Blondie watched me without emotion.

"Klammer," I groaned. "I need to see him. What am I involved in? What does he know?"

"You must come with me."

This was a relief. Maybe now I'd finally get some answers. However, Blondie must not have gotten the message that I was willing to comply. He approached, stepped behind me, and wrapped his thick forearm under my throat as quick as a cobra strike. I was not ready for this. The chokehold was so swift, so efficient, that I had no time to fight back. He was much stronger than I anticipated, which is saying a lot. I dropped the Tau as the Swedish bodyguard choked me out.

It was an ideal end to the worst day of my life.

# CHAPTER 23

THEY WERE WATCHING ME. All of them. Some with eyes creased in concern, some in awe. Others in rapt anticipation. I was surrounded by a gallery of onlookers. An outdoor amphitheater. Columns and porticos of white stone rose to meet a powder blue sky. The scent of blossoms laced the air and with it, a surreal tranquility. Was this heaven? No. I didn't deserve heaven. Through finely hewn archways, I glimpsed lush gardens, freshly tilled earth, and joyful streams tumbling over smooth boulders. Yet the pristine surroundings seemed not to concern the onlookers. They were fixated on me.

My gaze wandered the crowd. Old and young looked on, a craftwork of faces. Some of them seemed strangely familiar. All of them were attuned to my presence. I tried to speak, but couldn't. Why were they watching me? And what evoked such fear and astonishment in their eyes?

Suddenly, their gazes were torn from me and moved upward, upward, not to the steely blue sky, but to a vast shadow encroaching upon the land. A shadow eating up the terrain like an approaching eclipse. Storm-like in its intensity. Raging. Roiling. A tsunami of blackness churning toward us, ripping up huge swaths of earth and tossing it aside like pebbles.

I turned and stumbled back at the sight of this monstrous shadow.

Then it was on us. A plodding gargantuan figure towered over me, blocking out the sun. At first, it seemed to have no shape. A mountain of mass tottering toward me. Then the angular shoulders and headdress became clear.

It was the great Egyptian deity, Anubis.

Through the swirling clouds, the eyes of blazing green peered down at me, full of malice and hate. When it located me, its feral canine snout peeled back revealing razor sharp teeth. It raised its head to bellow. But instead of a roar, laughter issued from its gaping jaws. Laughter that seemed both to mock the crowd and me. A godless cackle that thundered across the land. The Edenic hills echoed with this beastly cry.

That's when I noticed that the shadow was not a shadow at all, but living things; hordes of dark creatures rushing forth, scuttling, clawing, and chewing up the virgin sod as they raced toward us.

I was pinned to the ground, on my back, gripping the earth in helpless abandon. I knew I must do something, but what? What could I do against such a confluence of evil?

"Reagan!"

It was a voice I knew. And hearing it seemed to silence everything around me. The imps and monsters, the giant death god, all of it became mute.

Except for that lone voice.

"Reagan!"

I sat up, trying to identify where it came from.

He was just as I remembered. Standing between me and the shadows. My father approached. I recognized his gait. It was unmistakable. I suppose you could call it a limp. He'd had his heel crushed. One of the many stories he liked to tell me. The injury ended his military career and left him permanently gimpy. It was, in fact, what caused him to leave the service. But that limp was, to him, like a badge of honor.

He approached me. He always seemed so confident. I knew enough about him to know it wasn't confidence, at least, not in the way one becomes full of themselves and deluded by machismo. He'd just come to believe that the Universe was on his side because he was on the side of Good.

And he believed he'd been sent back to accomplish something.

I struggled to my feet as he approached. Now, the chaos of evil around us had become but a fog. A distant maelstrom. Fading. Fading. Anubis and his army of darkness were little more than a blur on the periphery of my mind's eye. Inconsequential. My father was here! And that—*that!*—was more important than anything.

He stopped in front of me and smiled.

"How are you?" he asked.

"I'm hanging in there. It's been hard since you left."

"I didn't have a choice."

"I figured."

"It's your time," he said. "It's your time, Reagan."

He hadn't aged a bit. In fact, he seemed... younger. More alive.

I tried to speak again, but couldn't. *My time for what? I can't fill your shoes, I never could.* Yet I'd become mute.

He smiled knowingly, "You haven't let me down. I know that's what you believe. But it's not true. I couldn't be prouder."

He wasn't lying. Nevertheless, this confused me. How could I *not* have been a disappointment to him? I was a cynical paranormal reporter barely making ends meet.

A great longing welled in me. A sorrow that could not be quantified. A yearning that could not be compressed into any one single emotion, word, or action. I so wanted to be with him. To stay in these Elysian Fields under the shadow of Darkness with my father. Where I knew I'd be safe.

I tried to speak again. To no avail.

He stood there and I reached out to him. Just like I had as a child. Just like when he'd stepped out to take that bullet for me. I reached out to him. Reached across this dream void.

My hands were glowing. Electric blue.

Icy hot veins sparked the air, trailing from my fingers like neon. The atmosphere crackled with the charge. Heat raced up my arms, filling my torso with liquid fire. I raised my hands to the sky in wonder and watched those tendrils of electricity flare into the hideous darkness like some vast highway, racing through clouds and winds. And twine their way into the shadow that was upon us.

My father laughed. It was full, exuberant.

"It's your time," I heard him say.

I woke with a start.

Sitting straight up, rigid as a beam.

Where was I? It was cool in here. Moist. Drab. Then I stared at my hands. There was nothing unusual about them. No heat. No cold. Nothing. It was a dream, a trippy, emotionally-loaded dream.

My jaw ached. And my ribs. Either I'd been used as a crash test dummy or someone had beat the crap out of me and dumped me here. I tried to remember what had happened but felt groggy, as if I'd been drugged. What was going on?

I dragged my fingers through my hair and refocused on my surroundings. I was indoors, a tiny, windowless room. Low ceiling with popcorn texture hanging in clumps, revealing wooden paneling underneath. Classy. The air was thick with must. And mold. I'd been lying on an old mattress and box spring. It smelled of chemicals. A nightstand sat nearby with a pitcher of water and, next to it, an empty syringe. A small flat panel TV hung cockeyed above a cheap dresser, its wiring dangling haphazardly down the wall to an outlet. I turned. The ache in my ribs and then my jaw forced the memory into my head. I'd been jumped. Sidra. She was after the Tau.

*The Tau!*

I immediately reached up and touched my chest. The cross was in place. But how? I remember she'd snapped it off during our scuffle. I removed it and studied the piece to make sure it was undamaged. The cross looked fine. However, the original leather strap was gone. In its place, a length of knotted twine or hemp had been improvised. I massaged the area on the back of my neck where the coarse twine had lain. Someone had made sure to return the Tau to me. But who? Either way, I had the cross back. I issued a sigh of relief, and slipped the icon back over my head.

Now it was coming back to me. Sidra wanted the Tau. In fact, she said she wanted it *back*. If it wasn't for Blondie, she would have gotten it back and probably taken one of my ribs home as a trophy. After that, Blondie choked me out. So who was I fighting here? Apparently, friends and enemies were starting to blur. What's new?

I slung my legs over the side of the bed with a great groan. How long had I been out? I had to get out of here. Meet up with Kanya and Matisse. Get back to Spiraplex somehow. Figure out a way to get back down there and look for Ellie, back to the Lower Chamber. That is, if I wasn't being held prisoner here.

I patted my pants pockets in search of my cell phone. But my pockets were empty—no phone, no keys. No gun. I groaned again as I tried to stand, but my head throbbed. I thudded back onto the bed.

As I did, the TV flicked on.

"Greetings, Mr. Moon."

Having been recently assaulted by a one-eyed ninja and choked out by a Swedish bouncer, I froze, thinking some new menace was upon me. But the raspy voice was coming from the television. And the voice was familiar. A digital picture fragmented into pixels and then assembled, bringing with it the image of Felix Klammer.

"You're awake."

"Where am I?"

"You've done quite well, Mr. Moon. Things are moving swiftly."

The box device over his head was almost completely in shadow, the wall behind him a soft white. He appeared to be broadcasting from a small room or a studio.

"Where am I?" I massaged my jaw. "And why'd Blondie

knock me out?"

"My apologies. My assistant can, at times, be rather heavy handed."

"Ya think?"

"We needed to speak and I couldn't count on your cooperation. Not with the way things are going. Not to mention, your... *instability*. Going rogue seemed highly within the realm of possibility for someone undergoing events like yours."

"*Instability*? I'm just trying to figure out what the hell you got me involved in. Anyway, you're just the fella I wanted to see."

I attempted to stand and this time was successful. I swayed, collecting my thoughts. I noticed my keys, cell phone, and press pass on the table. I moved that way, my head feeling like a medicine ball.

"It was a mild sedative," Klammer assured. "We couldn't have you running off. Or running into the police. Your incarceration would not help matters. Not when we're this close. Apparently, you needed the sleep."

How could he see me? I scanned the room for a camera, but couldn't locate one.

"How long was I out?" I massaged the back of my neck. "And where am I?"

"You're in safekeeping. And sufficiently rested, I hope, for your next assignment."

"Can I opt out?"

"I'm afraid that will be impossible," Klammer said. "You're all in, Mr. Moon."

"Ain't that the truth." I gathered my belongings and jammed them in my pockets. "Where's my gun?"

"You won't need it. It'll only complicate matters."

"As if things aren't complicated enough." I shook my head. "Did anyone tell you that the old man—Gollo, the guy you sent me to see—that he got stabbed to death?"

He did not answer.

"No?" I said mockingly. "Course not. Or that now I'm a suspect? Did Blondie happen to pass that info along to you? That the LAPD has fingered me for the murder of the guy you sent me to see? Or maybe that this cross, whatever the hell it is, that someone's looking for it and they're serious about getting it?" I shook my head. "I don't know what the hell's going on, or what you got me into, Klammer. Or what those... those *Invisibles* really are. But I need some answers."

I'd worked myself into an angry mess; I caught myself trembling.

Finally, he said, "So now you're a believer?"

"Stop toying with me!" I snapped.

Klammer sat there until I dialed it down.

I stared dully at his image on the screen. "Ellie's down there, isn't she?"

"Yes."

"You said she was dead. Is she?"

He paused, and then readjusted himself in his seat. The motion seemed difficult for him. He wheezed and the box on his head passed momentarily into the light, before he leaned back into shadow. Why was he wearing that device? For the first time, I wondered whether he was seeking to hide his identity from me. A veil draped the contraption. I could detect movement, like breath, underneath.

He folded his hands on his lap. "I joined Soren Volden with the best of intentions. Together, I believed we could benefit humankind. Advance the species. Brain research was growing exponentially. The possibilities, likewise, were endless. We would eliminate Alzheimer's, repair brain injuries, reanimate dead limbs. Quadruple human intelligence. The technology was there. I joined with that promise. But the brain—it's a great mystery. Our research revealed as much. Dark places in the imagination. Bridges to the prurient and evil. A gateway, as it were, to other dimensions."

"Other dimensions? We're talking about the brain, right?"

"Quantum consciousness, Mr. Moon. The brain is that one

organ which connects us uniquely to the metaphysical, an intersection of the material and the immaterial."

"Okay, this is getting deep."

"Exactly. The mind. Where does consciousness come from? Is the mind subject to the law of physics, as everything else must be? Or does it transcend physics? For instance, what space does a thought occupy? Does it just reside in the frontal lobe or the cortex? Or a memory? Is it just inside your head, the hippocampus, a random collision of synapses and neurons? Or does it, perhaps, connect us with something *other*? Something equally real, but of another order. Could those non-physical components be gateways to other... dimensions?"

I shook my head, more lost than disbelieving. I'd done minor research into evolutionary neuroscience, but this quantum nonsense was way out of my league. However, with a whole new layer of reality having been peeled back, I was not in a place to play the skeptic much longer.

"The Dreamchamber," I said. "That was part of it?"

"*Part* of it, yes. M-graph technology was the tool which brought it all to life. Then Volden's methods turned... *unsound.* I should have known from the start. We learned that the Dreamchamber could bring *other* things to life. Dark parts of the psyche could be manifest." He grew still. "Entities could be channeled."

I thought about the old man in the Dreamchamber, communicating with the holographic recreation of his wife. A chill coursed my body. Could it be it wasn't a re-creation at all, but an actual spirit? The Dreamchamber was nothing more than a neuroscientific séance.

Klammer said, "It isn't humankind's advance that Soren Volden cares about. It's *his* advance. His survival, I should say. The survival of his species. We've become his Guinea pigs, fodder for a new empire. He used me. And now the technologies I provided will pave the way for something abominable."

"So this *is* between you and him. We're just pawns, aren't

we?"

"Trust me, Mr. Moon, you're more than just a pawn."

"And that complex under Spiraplex," I said. "There's bodies down there, aren't there? Lots of them."

"Cryopreservation. Impossible to say how many poor souls he has in stasis by now."

"Then why don't the police know?" I demanded. "Why'd you come to me instead of them?"

"Because the police can't stop Soren Volden. Only you can."

I stared at him and then snorted in disgust. "This's a joke. This whole damned thing is one big joke."

"Soren Volden is not of this world, Mr. Moon."

I squinted at him.

"Pfhh!" I brushed my hand through the air.

Klammer continued: "To survive, Soren Volden must drain sentient beings of life. You could call him a vampire, of sorts. Nothing like the crude pale parasites of cinema. He is quite old. I learned this strictly on accident, or else I would've acted sooner. At first, it was the homeless, travelers, those off the grid. Those who would never be missed. He abducted them. Used them. Then he found he could take large groups. Young, healthy, brilliant ones. Without suspicion. To... *feed upon.*"

"Then Ellie's group was never atomized like the police said."

"A brilliant ploy, especially since they possessed the technology to do as much. Which is why the accident was never questioned."

Though the possibilities had nagged at me for the last 24 hours, the finality of his words opened emotions that I hadn't expected. Part of me wanted to storm into Spiraplex with guns blazing, broadcast this wacky tale far and wide. And snatch Ellie's body from this madman. But the other part of me swooned at the possibility of seeing her face once again.

And then there was that part about Soren Volden being inhuman.

"So why the game?" I said. "If you've known this all along,

why not just say so? Spill the beans up front? What's the point of dragging me through all this crap?"

"Because this isn't about what I know. It's about you. It's about what *you* know. It's about what you *must* know. Some things must be discovered to be believed."

I wandered to the bed and plopped on to it.

After a long minute, I asked, "Is she dead?"

"Not in the sense you mean it. No."

"Then how'd she contact me?"

"Until she's released from his grip, Ellie Wells cannot move on. She's in a limbo of sorts, a dimensional netherworld. She needs your help."

I swallowed hard. "The Tau. Why do they want it?"

"Because of what it can do for you."

"What it can—? It hasn't done anything for me except cause problems. And where did Ellie get it?"

"Perhaps you didn't know as much about your girlfriend as you thought."

"Yeah. Well I know I'm going to get her out of there if it's the last thing I do." I stood up.

"Matisse is correct. Volden's grown strong. And now he draws closer to an event, a Singularity, which will change your world forever. He seeks to bridge the gulf between the living and the dead—that which is forbidden. To join the here and now with the hereafter. And to prepare the way for... *the Summu Nura*."

My head was spinning. The thought of Ellie in some hellish limbo, being tormented, had thrown me for a loop. I stood there forlorn.

"So how do I stop him? Volden. I mean, if he isn't human..."

"I don't know."

"Huh?"

"Some fates await writing."

"Whatever."

"This is your time, Mr. Moon."

I looked up at him.

"So I hear."

Klammer said, "If you need more money, you'll find some in the top drawer."

"I don't need any more money. I need answers. And a company of Navy Seals wouldn't hurt."

"Stay the course, Mr. Moon, and you'll have your answers."

"And the Seals?"

Klammer chuckled.

I shook my head, turned to leave, and then stopped. "By the way," I said, "what's wrong with your head? I mean, the box get-up."

Did I mention that, on occasion, I can be rather untactful?

"I like you, Mr. Moon. I hope we can continue our relationship."

Then the TV clicked off.

My ribs hurt, as did my jaw. I hobbled to the door, tried the handle, and a second room opened before me. Dull light fingered its way under another door. I was inside cramped musty quarters. I opened the second door upon gloomy, wet daylight. I was inside a trailer park. It was morning. A wet morning. I'd slept the night. I had to hurry.

Under an awning on the trailer across from me, an old woman in a bathrobe smoked a cigarette and squinted at me.

"Where am I?" I asked.

She looked me up and down and rasped, "Earth."

Then she dropped her cigarette, ground it under her slipper, and let the screen door slam shut behind her.

Funny.

From the looks of it, I'd need a cab. As I dialed cab service on my cell I went back inside and found a wad of money in the top drawer, just like he'd said.

Oh, well. If I had to travel by cab, I'd need all the money I could get. In fact, maybe I could use it to rent a company of Navy Seals.

# CHAPTER 24

TURNED OUT I WAS IN SIMI VALLEY. The cab picked me up and I wedged my aching body into the corner of the backseat. I'd been shot at once before. It was actually quite exhilarating. After the fact, of course. Not long ago, some local cultists also had me on their hit list because I'd done an interview with one of their defectors and let her air all their dirty laundry. They threatened to insert hungry black scorpions into every orifice of my body and sell tickets to the event online. Good times. But this wasn't like any other story I'd ever covered. It was turning into *my* story. And I was growing fearful that it wouldn't turn out so well.

The windshield wipers slapped the rain like some watery timepiece, ticking down to Armageddon.

I removed the Tau as we drove, and studied it. What was so special about this thing? And where'd Ellie gotten it? In the back of my mind was a thought I did not want to entertain. That Ellie *was* actually a part of something—something she'd never told me about. Could she have been living a double life? That was nonsense! But the more I thought about it—her trips to Europe, her little circle of hipster academic friends, her dabbling in weird sciences—I couldn't shake the possibilities.

Down deep was the worst thought of all: *she'd been using me.*

I sloughed off the thought with a cluck of my tongue, and continued studying the piece. I tilted the Tau attempting to catch the light off its surface. I'd never been big on religious iconography. Ankhs. Jewish stars. Oms. I'd seen them all. If someone had to reduce their beliefs to amulets and anklets, how meaningful could their beliefs be? Ellie, on the other hand, wore her crosses with pride. I turned it over and traced my fingers across the Latin letters on the back. *Imperia.* When I looked up, the cabbie was watching me in the rearview mirror. He quickly looked away. I sank further into the corner, out of his field of view, and slipped the Tau back on, tucking it under my shirt.

We turned off the 405 heading east on the 10. I had four missed messages, one from an unknown number, 310 area code. Los Angeles. The rest were from Arlette. I almost dreaded to call her. My battery was on its last leg, but I went for it.

"Moon!" she answered. "Where've you been?"

"Let's see—hell and back?"

"I said I'd cover for you, but this's ridiculous."

"Now what?"

"You're officially a suspect."

"I know."

"Some detectives dropped by the office last night, asking questions. I told them we were planning on doing a piece on local seers, just like we talked about. Everything went great, I thought. Your ass was covered. Then we learn this morning... *you're a suspect in the Medium Massacre.*"

Even though I knew this, hearing it from my boss left me momentarily numbed. Man, I was in the shit.

"I spoke to someone at the precinct," Arlette continued. "All off the record, of course. But your prints were everywhere."

"I *was* there," I said tiredly. "I told you that."

"Yeah. And how about the murder weapon."

My heart sank. "Oh crap."

"That's right."

"I picked up the wand. Dammit!"

"And the lerium?"

"What?"

"Lerium, the poppy. They found that in your apartment, too."

"What are you talking about?"

"Please don't play dumb. You're in serious trouble, Reagan."

"Oh my God." My stomach dropped. "You mean the flower..."

"The lerium poppy. The one they found in your apartment."

"Matisse..."

"What?" she asked.

Why would Matisse be growing lerium poppies in the Asylum? An entire greenhouse of them. There had to be an explanation. He was probably just doing some type of whacky research. But as much as I wanted to believe the best, I couldn't. Something was going on down there, now I was convinced of it. Kanya. Cricket. And twenty-thousand square feet all to yourself. If I made it back the Asylum, the first thing I was going to do was get some answers.

"Look," I said. "I can explain everything. *Most* everything."

"Well, unless you plan on being a fugitive, I suggest you get over there pronto and explain yourself to the police. They've already got you for fleeing a crime scene. And now they got other stuff. I'll stand by my story. But the rest of it's on you. Understood? I won't allow you to bring the Crescent down. Do you hear me?"

"Arlette. I'm innocent. I swear, I'm innocent. You have to trust me on this."

The line was quiet. It wasn't like her to equivocate. It was usually yea or nay. Rarely did you have to ask Arlette to explain what she really felt.

I said, "Remember that guy in West Hollywood that thought he was a werewolf and preyed on gay men?"

"Yeah?" she said suspiciously.

"Lured them into his S&M dungeon and made them sex slaves before eating their organs?"

"Yeah?"

"Remember how the networks picked that story up and our circulation doubled."

"Yeah?"

"This is bigger than that, Arlette. A *lot* bigger. A thousand times bigger. You have to trust me on this." I was practically pleading.

There was a long pause that was punctuated by a sigh of exasperation. "I do. Just don't come here. Not until this gets worked out. Okay?"

It was her soft side. Like I said, Arlette has a soft side. It's just trudging through her Iron Maiden persona that you have to deal with to get there.

"Thanks," I said. "But I'm not coming there. I'm going to Matisse's to get some cool 3D specs before heading back to Spiraplex, hopefully with an angel named Bernard."

"Are you losin' it?"

"Kind of. And now I've got a couple more questions for the Mad Spaniard."

There was a long uncomfortable pause. I thought about her at my front door yesterday. Her excitement at the VM connection. And her not-so-veiled concerns about me. She was a good woman. Even though it was hard to imagine anyone could dent this woman of steel, her ex had done her wrong. Damn him.

After a moment of pause, she said, "Be careful, Moon."

"Will do, boss."

I hung up. We exited the 10 on San Pedro. I'd given the cabbie general directions to my place. But if I was a suspect, they'd be casing my apartment. Going to get the Cammy and my backpack with my writing stuff would be a bad idea. So I told him there was a change of plans and directed him to the Warehouse District. Kanya and Matisse would have some sort of plan by now. They had to. Besides, I needed the goggles. Bernard had helped us get in. He'd have to do it again.

I told the cabbie to park around the corner from the Asylum. The steady drizzle continued, leaving the asphalt glistening. I craned my neck for any sign that we'd been followed. Other than a trash truck noisily emptying dumpsters, and a semi truck being unloaded at a recycling plant, the street was empty.

I removed the wad of money from my coat pocket and peeled off two one-hundred dollar bills. I handed them to the cabbie.

"Wait here."

He raised an eyebrow.

"It might take a while," I added.

"As long as it ain't all day," he snatched the bills, "I'll wait right here."

I got out and hurried through the wet alleyway. As I turned the corner into the Asylum, I stopped in my tracks. Splinters of broken glass littered the ground. Windshield glass. This was not here last night. Not that I could remember. I approached, quickly studying the area. If there had been tire tracks, they'd been washed away by the rain. Something had gone on here. This was the last place I'd spoken to Kanya. Had someone been waiting for me to leave? Dammit to hell!

I raced to the intercom near the elevator and crunched the button with my fist. It faintly sounded from down below. But there was no response. I punched the button again and again. But still, it went unanswered.

My hair was starting to drip moisture and I could feel the dampness penetrating my jacket. There was no way to break into the Asylum. But were they even down there? I moved into view of the surveillance camera and waved my hands, jumping up and down like a nut. Then I punched the button again. And again. Still no answer. This was futile. Maybe they'd gone to Spiraplex. But without me? No. Something had happened. Blast it! I looked up into the gray sky.

Suddenly, the elevator door buzzed. I lurched at the sound. Yet I didn't move right away. Instead, I allowed my instincts to roam. Perhaps I could tune in to that other dimension and get a sense of what was playing out in the ether. But my adrenaline was overriding everything. I took the handle and yanked the doors open.

And I stood there, taking it in. Studying my environment. Something didn't feel right about this. Maybe it was a trap. I could disappear down there and never be seen again. No one knew I was coming here except Arlette. And, like I said, she was vowed to secrecy about the place. I stared at the freight elevator. Then I noticed that the line of salt had been trampled, scattered about the inside of the unit. A struggle had gone on here. Someone had entered, or exited, and put up a struggle to do so.

I leapt into the elevator, yanked the doors closed, and held my fist over the button.

"Bernard," I said. "If you're still here, you better have my back."

That's how far I'd tumbled in one day—*I was talking to invisible men.* Sheesh!

I punched the button and the elevator engaged and began its descent. I felt like Dante being led into the ninth circle of hell. *Abandon hope all ye that enter here.* What madness awaited me inside the Asylum? For some reason, I reached back and touched the corrugated cross welded to the wall. I needed power any way I could get it. The elevator groaned to a stop. Before I opened the door, I scanned the interior for anything I could use as a weapon. There was nothing. Well, if I'd been kept alive for a purpose, as Ellie always said, I'd have to trust I hadn't lost my mojo.

I braced myself and yanked the doors open. They issued a thunderous hollow clang throughout the warehouse. But there was no one waiting for me. I took two steps out of the elevator and gazed out across the vast floor space. There was no signs of struggle. Or signs of life. What was going on here?

"Matisse!" I shouted. "Kanya!"

My voice echoed, then died in the concrete cavern.

Someone had opened the door, so they had to be nearby. The cameras and controls were in the command post. And the forklift was parked outside it. Bingo. But before I went there, I'd need a weapon.

I hurried around the corner where Matisse kept the flamethrower and the javelin that he'd nicknamed the *Finger of God.* He kept them in a large wooden crate with black heavy hinges that was topped with two herbal branches lying in the form of a cross. Hopefully, I wasn't disrupting Matisse's counter-spell too much. I brushed the herbs aside and lifted the lid.

A musty cloud rose and I started coughing. I glanced at the

command post to make sure I wasn't attracting the wrong attention. I removed the javelin and measured it up. It was much heavier than I would have liked, not to mention awkward. I'd wielded a few weapons in my day, just never a javelin. But unless I wanted to fire up that flamethrower, this would have to suffice.

I crossed the floor holding the Finger of God at my waist, leading with it like a spear. My heart was in my throat. I ducked under the camouflage netting and the rosary. The command post was in shambles. Books were toppled, the table lay overturned. I stepped inside, leading with my new version of Sting.

"Matisse? You in here?"

No answer. A couple steps further allowed me to see down the hallway. My senses were on high alert. If I tried hard enough, I felt like I could recreate the world of the Invisibles and discern the colors and phantasms that, no doubt, swirled all around me. As I prepared to call out a second time, I noticed blood streaks across the floor, into the hallway. It was still fresh. Someone had crawled or been dragged this way. I gripped the javelin and followed the crimson smears.

"Kanya?" I said. "Matisse?"

I reached the first room, the one with the safe and library of books, and froze. Matisse lay propped against the wall near the safe, bloodied and lifeless.

# CHAPTER 25

I LUNGED INTO THE ROOM, swiping the javelin in front of me. But there was no one else. I dropped the weapon and hurried to Matisse.

His left eye was nearly swollen shut and seeped liquid. Welts and bruises lashed his arms. Blood soaked his side, leaving his shirt nearly black, and formed a thick pool on the floor. I leaned over him, taking his wrist to feel for a pulse. As I did, he groaned.

"Matisse! God, who... It's Moon!"

His good eye opened and he fought to focus on me. When he did, a thin frail smile creased his lips. "*Mi amigo*. It's true."

"Wh—what's true?"

"I am... a fool."

I gently lifted the shirt from his belly, revealing a single four-inch wound oozing thick blood and fluid.

"What happened?" I said. "God! Who did this?"

I bunched the shirt up and applied pressure to the wound.

He winced. His skin was ashen gray. He'd lost too much blood. He gazed up at me, and then his eye drifted shut.

"Matisse! Dammit! You are not dying! Do you hear me?"

That's when I noticed the tracks along the crook of his arm. I leaned closer to make sure I was seeing this right. Then I lay the bloody shirt aside and rolled his sleeve up until it was unmistakeable. Slight bruises and discolorations marred the interior of his arm, a lot of them. Matisse wasn't diabetic that I knew of. He wasn't taking medication. Besides, this looked more like the careless, haphazard work of a junkie.

It couldn't be.

I quickly scanned the mess scattered across the floor. A bookend. Splinters of ceramic. A vile of holy water, unbroken. Then I saw it—a used hypodermic needle. I scrabbled to it, rummaged through the debris, and carefully lifted the needle. Then I put it to my nostrils. The smell of licorice was faint, but unmistakable. The smell of the flower. Lerium.

I returned to the Mad Spaniard. "Matisse?" I held the needle up. "Why?"

His hand fumbled forward for me. I tossed the needle aside and took his hand. His grip was still strong. As he did, a tear tumbled out of his eye and down his cheek.

"Lerium," I said. "Why?"

He nodded. "It was... the only way. To see... To carry on..." He winced and grappled for his side. Fresh blood was spilling from the wound now.

"Hang on!"

He brushed my hand aside. "Kanya," he slurred. "He... they took her."

"Volden," I murmured.

"Yes."

Bastards! They must have followed us here. But how'd they manage to get in? And why would they want her? Details would have to wait.

"Anu..." Matisse moaned. "Anu..."

I peered at him. What was he babbling?

Then he reached out, grabbed my shirt and drew me closer. "The Star of Anu! They... they've taken it. It's what... they wanted." And he slumped back against the wall.

"The lightning rod?" I turned and looked out into the warehouse. "They wanted that crazy lightning rod?"

My disregard for the Sumerian relic yesterday seemed ages away. If Volden was willing to kill for it, I might have to rethink my position about the Tower of Babel being just a stupid myth.

"Come on," I said, positioning myself over him and preparing to scoop him up in my arms. "We're getting you out of here."

"No." He shook his head.

"Then I'm calling the cops."

"No! No one c-can know about the Asylum."

"Somebody already *does* know about it."

"Spiraplex..." He swallowed hard and licked his dry lips. "You must stop them."

"I know, I know. I talked to Klammer. Volden's not... he's not human. He's shipping bodies in and feeding on them or something. Needs them to survive. He's in league with the Summu Nura, like you said. But why would he want that lightning rod?"

He grit his teeth and trembled. "*Babel.*"

I stared at him. *What?*

"Spiraplex," he said. "It's... Babel."

I squinted at him. Suddenly it seemed to make sense. The Tesla coil. The subterranean mausoleum draining energy from human hosts. The hideous disembodied spirits twining about the pagan god. And now the original lightning rod from that mythical edifice. Volden was building more than just a video arcade. He was erecting a 21st century conductor to the spirit world. A Sumerian ghost box. A modern day Tower of Babel.

These rich guys had way too much time on their hands.

"Come on," I said. "We've got to get you to a doctor."

As I approached, he shook his head limply. "It's too late."

"We're going."

"The safe," Matisse said. "Take it..."

I peered at him in incomprehension.

"...the Curtain," he gasped. "Take it!"

Life seemed to be draining from him as we spoke.

"Matisse! Dammit, you are not dying on me!"

"It's yours." He grimaced. "It was meant for you. Go on."

"No."

He clenched his fists and barked, "Take it!"

In that momentary outburst, I glimpsed the stout old Spaniard. It quickly passed, however, and his body drooped limply.

I looked at the safe. A bloody streak smeared its surface. I navigated through the clutter of books and went to it. I yanked open the huge door. He must have unlocked the combination after his attackers had left, for nothing had been disturbed. Rival's Curtain lay in the same cloth, on the same shelf. I took it, set my shoulder into the door of the vault, and it clanged shut. Then I scrambled the tumbler.

Matisse hunched forward, his breathing growing more labored. I stooped down and took his hand. He turned his eyes up to me, the same frail smile creasing his lips.

"The Asylum,"he said between shallow wheezes. "Watch it. Finish the work. Promise m-me."

"Matisse. No, I..."

He gripped my hand in his. I leaned closer. Sweat glistened on his brow. The once tanned complexion was now deathly pale. He patted the collar of my shirt, grabbed the twine cord, and yanked the Tau out. Then he spread his large hand over it, simultaneously covering my heart.

Tears welled in his eyes again.

*Please, Matisse, don't do this.*

"Forgive me," he said.

I nodded.

"You..." His chest heaved in erratic spasms. "You're n-not alone. Reagan."

Then he released his grip on the Tau. He drew several gasps, his body shuddered, and became calm.

"Tell her I love her," he said. His hand drooped to his side and he folded forward. And the Mad Spaniard breathed his last.

I remained there for a moment, too stunned to believe it all. It was the second dead man I'd seen in 24 hours. But this one hurt. God, this hurt impossibly. I hung my head and listened to my own breathing.

How had it come to this? What could I have done to stop it? But there were no answers, only emptiness.

Finally, I rose and stood staring down at his body. Too numb to feel rage, but knowing the rage would surely come.

"Farewell, my friend," I said.

Suddenly, I tensed.

Something passed through the atmosphere, leaving it charged. Not a draft. More like a ripple of static electricity. My skin bristled. Something was here, in this room! I instinctively moved to the javelin, quickly scanning the place as I did. And then it struck me. Whatever else was in here, it didn't occupy *this space.*

I looked at the goggles in my hand.

*No...*

I lifted Rival's Curtain, and then stared at Matisse's corpse.

*It couldn't be.*

Slowly, tremulously, I slipped the goggles on.

It was a moment I would never forget.

Looking through the lenses, the room was awash in radiance. Not the hellish pall of the cytomorph, but a brilliance that spoke to warmth. To life. To invitation. The confines of that subterranean warehouse were long gone. I had no visual sense of walls or ceiling or girders in the least. Before me stretched what I could only describe as a landscape. A vast invisible country next door to mine. Rolling fields of color blending seamlessly one into the other, joining a distant canopy of cobalt. It was as if I'd been transported to another world. My sense of distance was confounded. Yet my immediate field of vision was taken by a torrent of motion flowing before me.

Being a journalist, I've learned to ply words. But I could find no adequate metaphors for what I was seeing. If I were forced to undertake a description, I'd have said it was a river—a golden river, perhaps not of liquid at all, but of fierce current whose closest edge was serene and inviting, but whose opposite side was turbulent and of immeasurable distance.

And as I gazed out to the opposite shore of this dimensional river, I saw a figure. It wasn't Bernard. This person was of another nature altogether. An unusually luminescent figure whose body seemed to be one with the landscape, absorbing the ruddy colors of this place but of a whole other quality. They were trudging uphill in great strides with their back to me, arms chugging, loins thrusting them upward toward the radiant blue skyline.

Between us was froth and foam. The river, I knew, was impassible. Of course, if someone would have seen me, I would have been staring at a wall, the lifeless body of my friend before me. There was no danger of tumbling into these golden cataracts. Nevertheless, before me stretched a barrier, a veil. As real as the walls that surrounded me. Perhaps, even more real.

And I knew that one day I must cross this river.

Suddenly, the figure turned. Even from here, I knew it was Matisse. Taller. Leaner. Face glowing with the youth of a thousand summers. He looked across the river, spotted me, and smiled. There was sadness in his smile, not for what he was leaving, but for us. Then he spread his arms wide, motioning to this land, and he laughed. He threw his head back and laughed. No, I couldn't hear a thing. But I could feel his joy. Then he clapped his hands on his knees, rose, and looked at me. I felt miles—no!—light years away. Yet distance was not a proper descriptor of what now separated us. He waved and I raised my hand to him in goodbye. Then he turned and bounded toward that skyline on his last great journey.

I watched him go.

The landscape slowly faded, the golden river disappeared, replaced by the thick dark lifeless shapes of concrete and steel. The blue glow of the Tau was the only light left.

I removed Rival's Curtain and just stood there at the foot of Matisse's crumpled body.

At that moment, I knew—although the word *know* seemed so feeble in describing the certainty I felt—that everything Ellie had said was true. My father had seen it too, this land just beyond the great river. I was here because of them. And others.

Surrounded now by a great cloud of witnesses.

A single tear coursed my cheek. In later days, I would describe it as a baptism of sorts. That tear, washing me of my unbelief.

I stood there for longer than I should have. What with Kanya kidnapped, Matisse murdered, and some otherworldly billionaire setting to fire up the lightning rod to the Tower of Babel, I should have been out of there. But seeing Matisse go—both here and there—somehow made the world seem right.

Now I owed it to more than one person to see this through to the end. And I'd do everything in my power to, this time, not let them down.

# CHAPTER 26

I SAT IN THE BACK OF THE CAB with Rival's Curtain on my lap.

The vision of Matisse's glorious departure had quickly faded, like most visions do. I did not have the time or the emotional energy to ponder an explanation for Matisse's apparent use of lerium. Was he an addict? And if so, how can one battle the unholy while possessed of such evils? If people were judged on the basis of the absence of vices, I had a feeling we'd all be screwed.

Yet these questions would have to wait. The task that lay ahead absorbed me. Even with an angel on my side, I was walking into a den of cold-blooded killers and multi-dimensional miscreants. The vision of the Mad Spaniard's march to glory gave way to a growing fear. My ribs ached again, as did my jaw. It was a nagging testament to my very-much human vulnerability.

"You okay, bud?" The cabbie glanced at me in the rearview mirror.

He had his directions; we were heading downtown. But apparently, I wasn't looking so hot. I was hungry. I'd just witnessed another death. And the sedatives Klammer had administered still lingered in my bloodstream.

"Yeah," I said. "I'm okay."

Above the buildings and high rises, Spiraplex became visible. Now I knew it for what it was: a monument to something ancient, something purely pagan. I could make out a crane on the roof and some scaffolding. Were they already in the process of erecting the lightning rod? And what exactly would happen when they did? All I knew, all I could think about, was that I had to stop them.

It was mid-afternoon, yet the sky was pocked with thick black clouds. The showers had broken, but by the looks of it, the reprieve would only be temporary. The dank sky turned the mood dull and gray.

"They say it'll be the storm of the decade." The cabbie tried to start a conversation. "Headed straight our way."

"Yeah?"

"Yeah. Better find somewhere dry."

I nodded. But my mind wasn't on storms. Although this one appeared perfectly timed. Hell, for all I knew, Volden had summoned the damned thing himself.

Construction upon Spiraplex had turned the surrounding blocks into a maze of detours and congestion. So I had the cabbie drop me off about a block and a half away. I'd walk the rest of the way. I handed him another 100 dollar bill. His eyes widened.

"Ya need me to wait again?" he said, hoping for another payday.

"Sorry. This is it."

"Okay. Thanks, bud."

"No problem."

Hey, I could get used to this over-tipping thing.

I stood on the sidewalk, watching him drive off. The bustle of traffic and pedestrians was all around me. The rain had left the streets ripe with the smells of moldering sewage and the hiss of tires across the asphalt. Angelinos don't do well with weather. It's the downside of a great climate that rain becomes more a nuisance than a respite.

I found shelter under the canopy of a nearby souvenir shop, out of the flow of sidewalk traffic. T-shirts emblazoned with palms, sunny skies, and busty beach babes plastered the storefront display. I extended the goggles away from my body.

There was no other way to do this. Of course, I'd look slightly odd walking around the city with a funky pair of aviator's goggles on. But this was Los Angeles, which meant I'd probably fit right in.

"Okay, Bernie," I said to myself. "Don't let me down."

Then I put on Rival's Curtain.

It was like a plunge into a dark ocean. A veil of moonless midnight. The surrounding buildings created a backdrop of dense black. The sidewalk, however, teemed with odd shapes and colors. Thunder sounded overhead. I looked up to see the sky fuming, not with clouds, but phantasmal forms. Ghostly green currents spiraled their way to Volden's tower like the fingers of some massive spectral storm system being sucked toward the eye of a cyclone.

Someone bumped into me, knocking the goggles cockeyed across my face.

"Whatchit!" the stranger said.

I readjusted the glasses. The passerby glared back at me. His shadowy form was illumined by a sickly gray manta embedded across his shoulder. The blur of pedestrians became a convolution of color. Some were unencumbered by the demonic parasites and strode by with their craniums glowing. Some carried hideous flora or fauna, twisted organisms and leeches attached to them like barnacles across a shipwreck.

I always knew L.A. was a freak show.

As they passed, these creatures turned to take notice of me, extracting their heads and craning their necks to peer my way. Angry eyes and reptilian faces pinched in hatred or surprise. I was an intruder into their once private domain.

As I stood gaping at the menagerie of beings, Bernard raced into my field of vision, gripping his head and spreading his arms to the sky in dismay.

"I've been busy," I said, uncaring who was watching. "Sorry."

He shook his head in frustration.

We couldn't talk here. I crept to a nearby alley and backed inside.

Bernard followed and stood, bobbing excitedly on his toes. Thunder rumbled again and we both looked up past the building into the green swirling mist.

"Look," I whispered. "If you're supposed to be helping me, you're not doing a very good job."

He scowled and pointed an accusatory finger at me.

"I can't wear these stupid things all day. How am I supposed to follow you if I can't see you?"

He pursed his lips and tapped his forehead.

"Okay. I'll try to do a better job. I need your help again. We need to get in there."

He nodded and pranced back onto the sidewalk, waving me forward.

"*Safely* this time. Is that possible?"

He opened one hand and then the other, as if to say, Maybe, maybe not.

I followed as Bernard wove his way through the foot traffic. To do this, I had to keep the goggles on and navigate through the crowd. It took all I had not to stop and ogle the parasite people. Hosts, that's what we were. Hosts for invisible entities. Some possessed numerous eyes, others had tentacles rather than wings and buried them deep inside the host's cranium. Some were so deeply attached as to have fused with their carrier and appeared as blobs of organic culture, growths. Perhaps, at some stage, they would simply *become* their host. Or their host, them.

And here I thought my view of the human race couldn't get any worse.

We turned the corner and Spiraplex came into full view. I froze. For the ghost currents had become a raging miasma. A vast tower of green spiraling energy rising from Spiraplex, filling the sky.

The ghost box.

*Moon. Mooonnnnn!*

I could see them. And apparently they could see me. Hundreds of thousands of them. Souls in torment summoned from their personal hells to once again walk the earth. I thought about Matisse trudging upward to splendor. But these poor souls did not have such a luxury. What kind of power could summon such things?

Whatever it was, I didn't stand a chance.

I stood, staring dumbfounded into the sky. Faint wisps of rain spattered my face. Then Bernard rushed into view, doing jumping jacks to get my attention. I looked at him. He waved for me to hurry.

The crowd was still there gathered in front of Spiraplex, fawning for a glimpse inside the next Wonder of the World. Only now, I saw them for what they were. A hellish clan of parasites. A menagerie of gills, claws, antennae, mandibles, and webbed digits gathered under the toxic sky, carried there by unwitting humans. I'd been in some bad crowds in my time but this was, hands down, the sickest.

I diverted my attention away from this mob. The strange mist that enshrouded this complex cast an eerie sheen upon everything, a noxious incandescence that tainted this parallel world. And here they thought L.A. had a *smog* problem. As we approached, I could make out a group of unusual entities at the entryway of Spiraplex. From their proximity, they stood apart from the crowd, perhaps members of the security staff. However, the parasites attached to them were unlike any I'd yet seen. If the others were grubs, as Kanya had called them, then these had graduated to the larval stage and advanced to full blown incubi. I could only describe them as walking oil slicks. Yes, they were bipedal. I could make out arms and legs. But where the man ended and the parasite began was impossible to discern. Was there even a *man* there? It left me to wonder whether I was, in fact, looking at humans or something of another order entirely. A spectral sludge seemed to ooze from these person's arteries and rise into tendrils that twined themselves around limbs and torso, flaring into a head of rippling currents. They swayed as they moved, like seaweed in some undersea garden. Only these were sinewy black things with flat elongated eyes, portals of the blackest night. Watching them walk was almost comical, their oily tendrils sweeping gracefully through the toxic air. Liquid men. As we approached, their heads whipped toward me, in unison, flat black eyes fuming with arctic hatred.

I stopped dead in my tracks. This was too much. Even worse, my guardian angel was leading me straight toward them.

"Bernard," I hissed. "Hey!"

He turned and I fought my way out of the foot traffic, found the construction fencing, and pressed my back into it. Silhouettes passed with angry eyes watching me. But having something solid against my back gave me a sense, however brief, of being grounded in reality.

"The front door?" I said. "Really? You want me to go in the front door?"

Bernard nodded vigorously.

"Did you see those guys?"

The angel brushed his hand dismissively their way.

"Yeah, maybe to you. Look, I need to find Kanya. And... Ellie."

He nodded, soberly.

"She's down there, then?"

He nodded again. His expression was as grim as an angel's expression could probably get.

"Okay. I'm trusting you."

Bernard clicked his heels and saluted me proudly.

"I can't let them down, Bernard. I can't let them down again."

His features softened and he smiled lightly. Then he straightened and motioned me to follow.

As we pushed deeper into the crowd, a visible reaction swept through the demonic parasites. They squirmed and plucked themselves free of their carriers to watch our approach. Eyes cold and full of malice, teeth gnashing. The Invisibles were having a fit! They didn't like being seen. Which made me wonder if perhaps our ignorance of them was their most powerful weapon. Yet despite their agitation, I pressed through.

The crowd grew more raucous the closer we got to the entrance. Cameras flashed and revelry ensued. We passed into the congested, bustling courtyard. Three of the walking oil slicks stood in the entryway to Spiraplex, watching my approach.

I gasped and put on the brakes, because behind them rose cytomorphs. An entire platoon was patrolling the base of Spiraplex, moving in and out of dimensions. They would thwump into view, pivot and open, and rise swaying on gangly legs. As they did, their block bodies and fiery mouths turned and focused my way. Despite all the commotion surrounding the facility, apparently I was the center of their attention.

I stepped sideways and scrabbled to the barrier, jostling people as I went. Someone cursed at my rudeness as I tripped and slammed into the fencing.

"They saw me," I panted. "They know I'm here."

Bernard squeezed past a couple of humans who'd been hooded by pale corpuscular-looking entities. He curled his lip at them and then looked at me with his brow creased, as if pondering my overreaction.

"Okay," I whispered to Bernard. "Let me guess—they knew I was coming."

He nodded mockingly and arched his eyebrows comically. *Ya think?*

"All right. I've had enough. I'm taking these glasses off. I can't go any farther. Just stay close. When I get inside, the first chance I get, I'm putting them back on. So be ready."

He nodded.

"Just, whatever you do, you need to help me find them. Ellie and Kanya. And get them back."

He curled his lips in frustration and jabbed his finger to the sky.

"Oh," I said. "Right. And keep them from firing up the lightning rod."

He smiled and then bowed reverently at the waist.

This guy was a card.

I perched the goggles on my head and the pall of real life slapped me in the face. Bleak sky. Monochrome colors. Major buzzkill.

A couple standing next to me was staring. They had 50's doo-wop hairdos and donned more ink than an office supply store.

"Who were you talkin' to?" the guy asked.

"Me? I..." I shrugged.

"Hey," the girl said. "Where'd you get the bitchin' goggles?"

"The Sumerian Dynasty, I believe."

I stuffed the goggles into the pocket of my sweat jacket and left them looking at each other. I trudged through the crowd for the entrance. There was no sign of the cytomorphs, of course, just the security guys. These were the things I'd seen through Rival's Curtain. In this dimension, they had the same appearance as the other Cosmagon. Heads nearly shaved bald. Elongated faces. Black turtlenecks under blazers. All of them had pieces. The construction fencing funneled everything toward a wooden barrier stenciled with the words *No Trespassing*. The men stood there, watching the crowd mill about and preventing prying eyes from too long a look at Spiraplex. Just past this barrier I could make out a walkway winding through tropical flora to the interior entryway, which was flanked by two massive sphinxes. I approached the barrier but didn't need to get the guards' attention. They were already looking at me.

"You have business?" one of the men said.

My head had started to throb from removing the goggles. I focused on the man and tried not to think about the oily entity twined about his being.

"I'm here for Mr. Brook."

"Your name?"

"Reagan Moon, with the Blue Crescent. I have a press pass if you need it."

He took the pass and offered it to one of his partners who starting scrolling through a digital device.

"Wait right here," the first man said.

He entered a makeshift guard shack nearby, while the other man/thing stood watching. The first man returned and handed me the pass. He moved the barrier enough for me to slip through. This started a newfound bustling within the crowd; pushing and shoving, cameras flashed, and a water bottle catapulted from behind us, emptying the remainder of its contents as it struck the barricade.

The security men cursed, stepped forward, allowing me to pass through them, and demanding the crowd to back up. I left them there and followed the first man as he led me through the manicured walkway.

We arrived at the front entrance. Sphinxes rose in statuesque splendor, perhaps 15 to 20 feet in height, on each side of a bank of gleaming glass doors and body scanners. Two individuals manned the scanners, and I was passed off to them. Apparently, the scuffle at the barricade had increased, as the security guy hustled back to assist the others. It was somewhat a relief to know that oily devil-thing had left us.

"The content of your pockets here." The attendant shoved a tray toward me. "Belts. Watches. Jewelry. Cell phones."

My heart leapt. *Here we go again.* Provided they weren't actually weaponized, neither the Tau or Rival's Curtain appeared to contain anything that would trigger the alarms or elicit suspicion. But if these were sought-after items and the cytomorphs had already spied me, I was dangling on a wing and a prayer. My backpack had gotten lost in the shuffle, probably still back in the Cammy at my apartment. All my interview and camera equipment were in it. Dammit! This did not look good. Showing up for the most important interview of my professional life like a complete amateur. Like so many things recently, I'd have to trust that, whatever happened, things would work out for the good. Not quite the outlook of a pessimist, I know. But when forced into a corner, even the most cynical of us can muster hope.

I removed my wallet, car keys, and cell phone. A second attendant behind the body scan device watched as I dug the goggles out of my jacket and placed them in the tray.

I held my breath as they motioned me into the scanner, yet I passed through without incident. Apparently, they were satisfied that I did not have explosives in my underwear or that the Tau really posed that much of a threat.

As I gathered my belongings from the tray, one of the attendants said, "Mr. Brook will meet you in the lobby," and directed me to a marble stairway that descended into a lush garden of giant tropical plants.

The doors whispered back as I left the security checkpoint. As I descended the steps, a spacious domed canopy stretched overhead. It was made of a black, marble-like substance, elegantly lit and engraved with intricate celestial patterns. Just past this lobby, I could see the feet of the massive statue of Anubis at the center of Spiraplex. I shuddered thinking of that spiritual vortex curling its way into the sky.

I had to force myself not to over-think this predicament. Nevertheless, the reality of my plight had sunk like an anvil in my gut. I was sure that every one of my moves was being watched. If I was the only one who could stop Soren Volden, then here I was, as helpless as a puppy facing a meat grinder.

I didn't have to wait long. Selwyn Brook came strolling into the foyer with his signature smile.

"Mr. Moon! So glad you returned."

"Wouldn't miss it for the world."

"I don't blame you. This is all you brought? No camera, tape recorder?"

"You'd be amazed at what I can do with my phone."

"Really. And your lovely assistant?"

"I'm afraid she was detained."

"I understand. Well then." He wrung his hands together. "As I mentioned, we'd like the Blue Crescent to carry the exclusive feature. As you saw yesterday, there're many wonders associated with Spiraplex. It'll be impossible to show you all of them in one sitting."

"Understood."

He left the lobby, walking toward the main mall, speaking as we went. "As you can imagine, decades of research, huge amounts of blood and treasure have gone into the creation of this masterpiece. We really are on the cusp, you know. The human species will finally reach its appointed apex."

I nodded, but inside I was thinking about how human evolution could possibly involve murdering each other to get to where we need to go.

We left the lobby into the vast open area. The Anubis structure seemed mountainous. Last night's dream flashed into my mind, and the dense shadow that had passed over the land. And I thought of my father.

*It's your time, Reagan.*

But my time for what?

"Feel free to take notes," Brook offered, as we strolled across the vast intricately tiled expanse. "Take pictures. Ask questions. But remember—nothing will be published without our approval. As I promised, we want you to experience the fullness of what Spiraplex will offer. Trust me," he turned and smiled, "You'll never forget."

We entered the elevators and he pressed a button. "Floor six," said the female voice. *The Dreamchamber.* As the doors closed, I noticed an archway at the base of the Anubian statue. A white-coated figure passed through it into darkness. *The god of the dead.* That's when I realized: The cryogenic chamber was directly below the great statue of Anubis. What better place to stash corpses than beneath the mummy king?

The door slid open on the sixth floor. A desert oasis was on the panoramic wall screen. Warm yellows, tropical trees laden with fruit, surrounding a turquoise pool. Nothing like simulated paradise.

But something wasn't right.

Brook stepped out and the second he did, two Cosmagon rushed in from opposite sides. I didn't have time to resist. Nor would I have. They took me by each elbow and pulled me from the elevator.

"Easy, fellas. Easy."

They ignored my advice, nearly yanking my arms from their sockets.

Sidra was standing there. Waiting.

She swaggered up and stopped a foot away from me, so close I could see the blood vessels under her dead eyelid. I attempted to step back, but the Cosmagon had me in a virtual straightjacket.

I could smell her. It wasn't just the stink of a woman whose cheap deodorant had stopped working earlier that morning. It was the same stench I'd noticed on Brook. The smell of some *thing*. She was a carrier.

She reached up to my throat with her tattooed hand. I flinched.

"This—" she reached into my shirt, found the twine, and ripped the Tau over my head, "—is for me."

She turned and tossed the Tau to Brook who was standing to the side, smiling.

"And this—" Sidra stepped back, raised her fist, and slung it like a sledge at my jaw— "is for you."

# CHAPTER 27

KANYA MEANS *POISINOUS FLOWER*, did you know that?"

A small man stood looking down at me. I would have thought him an adolescent at first, if it weren't for the thin goatee that traced his stark features. He was rather pale, dark hair slicked tight revealing a spacious forehead and wonderfully large eyes. I blinked. Then the pain came crashing in on me. My jaw. My neck. My skull.

Sidra!

I lunged for the man only to find I was strapped into the Mneumonics chair, in the Dreamchamber, reclining before the holographic device.

"Of course, she wouldn't tell you that, would she, Reagan Moon?" The man puzzled at me. His large eyes explored the length of my torso. "How do you prefer to be addressed? *Mr. Moon?* Or may I call you *Reagan?*"

I didn't answer. In fact, I wasn't sure if my jaw still worked.

He made an odd, feminine gesture with his hand. "Well, then. *Reagan* it is. You see? I prefer congeniality, especially with those whose essence I require."

I was bare-chested. I must have blacked out and been dragged into the Dreamchamber by the Cosmagon. I glanced down to see thick leather straps across my wrists and ankles. This was worse than a tight squeeze. In fact, *hopeless* was probably the more accurate descriptor for my current plight.

"I had to oblige Sidra," the man said, watching me with his large dark eyes "It's the price for keeping good help. You must throw them a bone once in a while lest they drift to greener pastures. Or plant their own. I will say, however, that Sidra may want you for more than just a punching bag. Her tastes tend to the, how should I say it, exotic. Nasty girl." He put his fingertip to his lips and smiled. "For the moment, I wanted you alive. Besides, brawling around such expensive equipment cannot be tolerated." He motioned to the Dreamchamber, its control panel, and holographic mechanisms.

Then he rested his hand on my arm. A strange mirth seemed to possess him. "Matisse and his daughter have hidden many things from you, Reagan. The least of which was how a Spaniard received a French name. You realize that now, don't you? Their secrets, I mean. One best fights devils who knows his own. Despite that holier-than-thou persona of his, Matisse had his devils. Lerium was just one of them. A pesky habit to quit. Or so I hear. It was to our advantage that he didn't. But that's another story. Sadly, it was the world of devils that consumed him. Poetic justice, don't you think?"

I remained mute. I was quietly calculating how I could get free of these straps to slap this overly chatty munchkin. Apart from biting his nose off when he came close enough, my options were limited.

"Yes," he purred. "Poor Matisse. I liked him. We're the same, you know. Both believing in the import of our mission. From opposite sides, of course. Felix, however—" his features darkened. "Felix can rot, I'm afraid. He didn't have the courage to do this on his own. He couldn't stand against me. Most of those old boys can't. Why, Felix can barely walk. Did you know that? Too much teleportation does that to your species. Instead, he goes tooling around, looking for pawns and puppets to do his work, to build gizmos to keep him from losing his head. Literally. That's what you are, Reagan. Did you know that?" He stroked my cheek with the back of his fingertips. "You're a pawn."

I recoiled from his touch.

He continued. "If Felix hadn't interjected himself, you'd be ignorantly blissful of all this. There'd have been no need to murder those oracles, no need to open old wounds. Even Matisse might have been spared. And you would have remained quite in the dark about that comedy troupe, the Imperia. But now the cat is out of the bag, and you're all so much worse off for it."

I finally swallowed and said, "Soren Volden."

"How astute." He applauded lightly. "And you're the latest superhero who's supposed to stop me."

I tugged against the restraints. "I'm not a superhero."

"No? Then how do you explain that?"

My eyes followed as he pointed toward a nearby console. The Tau lay next to Rival's Curtain.

He smiled. "It's back in our possession. Where it belongs."

"I don't know a damn thing about that."

"Really? Your father just thought it looked cool, or something? Another piece of hardware for his trophy case? And Ellie Wells—she didn't steal that from us?"

I hesitated. "I don't know what you're talking about."

"Please Reagan. You can't be that dense."

I felt a little shamed by his observation. He was right—how could I be that dense? The signs had probably been all around me. I'd never seen any of this coming.

"What do you think they were doing at Bastion Sails?" Volden continued. "It was her little community of do-gooders. Always seeking to undermine our progress. Ever since Newtonia when they fashioned those infernal icons, formed their paltry legionnaires, and propped themselves as earth guardians. Quite the reach for a species that cannibalizes itself with regularity."

"So that was you back then," I said. "Sidney DeFelius."

He arched an eyebrow. "So you *are* paying attention. One of many aliases. When you've been around as long as we have, you tend to change aliases like you change clothes. Alas, I believe the

Modern Era and its disbelief in devils was when the Imperia lost steam. Hard to fight monsters when they're mythologized. A wonderful tact on our part, wouldn't you say? No need for angels if the devil can be denuded. Your problems started, I'm afraid, when they tried to resurrect the old guard. Your father was of that bloodline, did you know that? Fancied himself as being a descendant of Saint George, or something. A real dragonslayer. He should have known better than to assume a mantle he could not defend. Bestowing it upon *you* was even a worse idea. Nothing like high expectations to drive one to... mediocrity—a calling you've excelled quite nicely at, I might add." He patted my shoulder.

"There are other visors, you know." He went to the console and retrieved Rival's Curtain, appearing careful not to touch the Tau. Volden held the goggles out at arm's length, examining them with a humorous grin. "Variations on a theme. All of them designed for a glimpse into the nether. Tragic how you've lost that ability, hm? Second sight used to be secondhand for your species. Somewhere along the way you swapped it for logic and entertainment. Which left the truly inspired to resort to alchemy. Or religion." He examined Rival's Curtain, curling his lip in disdain. "Crude, I know. And ever so fragile."

He dropped the goggles to the floor and stomped on them.

"No!" I blurted.

He stopped. "Already attached? Shame. No different than lerium, I suppose."

Then he continued pulverizing the specs, stomping on them and slowly grinding the lenses under his heel.

That fantastical world of demons and colors and toxic hazes was gone. Bernard, with his nimble ways. I'd never see him again.

"No," I whimpered.

Someone groaned and I craned my neck to see behind me. Two techs were in the control room. And nearby, in the shadows, Sidra leaned against the wall with her hood up and her arms folded. Her single eye glared at me. At her feet lay someone. A small, feminine figure with... *silver-white hair*.

What—?

It looked like...

It was Matisse's *other* daughter. Cricket! What was going on? The heavy eyeliner, the Pixie features. It was her! There was no doubt. This was the giggly girl who'd greeted me yesterday. A large discoloration was on her forehead. She was bound, hand and foot, with black duct tape. But by the looks of her, no tape was required to keep her immobile. She'd been beaten badly.

"A fine specimen." Volden walked to my side and gazed at Cricket. "Either version. I believe her mother was a queen once. Not that royal lineage has benefited our little flower."

I glanced at him, and then back at the girl. Yet the longer I stared, the more she appeared different. Her features were... changing. Her hair flushed from silver-white to raven black, like an inkblot spreading in water, sending out spears and plumes before turning to pitch. As it changed color, it also reshaped itself. In fact, her entire body was reshaping itself. Cheekbones. Nose. Shoulders. This person was morphing before my very eyes!

"Poisonous flower." Volden spread his long thin fingers like the opening of a blossom. "He named her rightly, wouldn't you say?"

I could only gape. I must have been seeing things. I'd received one too many blows to the head in the last 24 hours. Hallucinations were a symptom of multiple concussions, weren't they?

"What?" he said. "You didn't know? Alas, if Matisse hadn't tried to be the hero, I'd have let him explain the dirty details about... *his daughters.*" He chuckled.

The mention of Matisse drew my attention back to this little man. And anger burned in me.

"You're a murderer," I said. "Matisse. Gollo. Those mediums. You killed them all, didn't you?"

"Me? No. I prefer not to waste perfectly good meals. Of course, sometimes you have no choice. However, the sun doesn't agree with me anymore. It's the downside of your planet. So I rarely dirty my hands with such petty operations, much less travel outdoors. For that, I hire others."

He gestured to Sidra.

"Besides," he continued. "Matisse was on his way out anyway. He was hardly even sleeping anymore, did you know that? He'd become quite manic. Careless even. Lerium does that, I'm afraid. However, it also attuned him to... *our world.* Which was his ultimate aim. A lesser man would have given up the ghost, so to speak. The Mad Spaniard? It just made him stronger. More prescient. More aware. But as the wise man warned, 'Battle not with monsters, lest ye become a monster.' Although the term 'monster' is flung about far too carelessly these days, I concur. Matisse was well on the way to becoming a monster."

I shook my head, as much in denial as simple loathing of this creep's reptilian demeanor. "Matisse was a good man."

"Good? Hmph. What is *good*? Is this *good*?" He motioned to the entire Dreamchamber. "Are *you* good? See? The term is quite malleable, especially when looking through the lens of human history, as my species has been so privileged to do."

"That's nonsense. You killed them. Innocent people! You murdered them And that's *not* good."

"The psychics were just collateral damage, I'm afraid. We couldn't have the disembodied warning everyone about a—how would you say it?—an apocalypse. The Gleaning wasn't entirely a figment of Matisse's mind. And with Ellie flitting about, there was no telling what info could get out on the psychic grapevine. The last thing we needed was to have your ex rousing you from your self-induced slumber. So when we learned Felix was sending you to a seer, our only option was to..." he shrugged one shoulder, "silence them."

"If it's any consolation, you were right, Reagan. Most of them *are* hucksters. Con men. Flim-flam artists. It's a sad commentary on your species, actually. The mediators have become frauds, two-bit shysters making a living on gimmickry, exploiting the most vulnerable. Shame on you. You've fallen so far away from any real talent. Nevertheless, there's that small contingent. That unique breed. Gollo was one of them, and the others she killed. They were the real deal, you know? A small percentage, true. But there were those with an ear to the Invisibles. We were forced to keep an eye on them. When the spirits gather, they can't keep their mouths shut. It's a surprising feature of the disembodied—they can be quite loquacious. Couldn't let some freewheeling ghosts out us to some unsuspecting client. When we learned that Felix was involving himself, we guessed he might forgo spilling the beans for piquing your interest, in this case, with someone more... *unorthodox*. We were right. Unfortunately, we didn't reach the old man in time. Hence, the mess."

Images of Gollo darted through my mind. His fluttering eyelids. Telling me to run. To protect the Tau. Warning me of Ellie's predicament. It seemed ages away. *"He's c-coming for m-me. Ray, he's coming! You have to s-stop him. Please!"* And now everything lay in shambles.

"Ellie," I managed to say. "Where is she?"

Volden glanced back at Sidra. "Ellie Wells is where she belongs." Then he smiled wickedly. "She is a live one, Reagan. You don't know what you're missing."

"Bastard!" I fought against the restraints. "I'll have your ass, Volden!"

"Really."

"The police know about your operation. You know that? I told them. Reporters are going to be here. Cops. Creeps like you never win. You might finish us up, but this won't end good for you. Trust me. Whatever's going on here, or *under* here, it's going to stop."

"My. What's gotten into you, Reagan? You're sounding like a bona fide optimist. Been spending too much time around the Mad Spaniard, I see. His faith was, indeed, undying. We'll have to cure you of that."

Volden crossed the room and stood next to Sidra. He was a good twelve inches shorter than she was. Good Lord, I was fighting an extraterrestrial midget.

"What are you?" I said.

He tilted his head, a smile stretching his features comically. "I am unbound, Reagan. That's what I am. I am alive in the fullest sense now. No longer formless. And in case you've not noticed, I can't be stopped. Surely, Felix has told you this. Once Spiraplex is operable, more of my kind will be on the way. It's been a long time coming. And I mean *long* as in eons. Centuries of watching, planning. Seeking the slightest edge. The Imperia's no match for the Black Council. They never were. Seven Guardians. Pah! Despite Newtonia and a few minor skirmishes, we've owned the upper hand.

"We are the old ones, of a higher order. The primitives worshiped us. The ancients plumbed our secrets, coaxed us out of hiding. But our true nature—and glory—was never fully revealed. Being embodied is quite advantageous. A feature your kind has taken for granted. Once we pitch camp in these earthly tents, your species will have no recourse but to surrender to our rule." He raised his head smugly, as if he were some magistrate addressing a knave.

I said, "I think someone's been reading too many of their own press clippings."

Volden scowled.

"The old ones," I repeated. "What's that supposed to mean? Don't tell me you're, like, some creaky old space vampires."

"Please, don't insult me. You've allowed the Blue Crescent to shrink your imagination. Vampires—bah! We're so much more than those dreary parasites. It's not blood we're after. It's the life essence. The spark. *The light.*"

"The Lightless Ones," I said. "The Summu Nura."

"Yes, yes. They called us that once. I do believe it's time for a new moniker. Something more... regal. Don't you think? At least something more catchy."

Sidra approached. She pulled her hood back and shook out her bleached hair. Her single eye glistened in the light. She stood over me, looking even more awful, more menacing, than when she straddled me last night. She drew her fingertips across my bare chest, as if she were drawing an invisible symbol. My entire body tensed at her touch. Finally, her finger came to rest directly on my breastbone, where the Tau had been the last 24 hours.

"You're a little man," she said, her lip curling in disgust. "Without that, you're a little man."

Then she thumped her finger on my chest, strode to the console, and seized the Tau.

My heart quailed inside me, thinking she would dash it as Volden had the goggles. Instead, she carefully draped it over her neck and turned toward Volden, a mischievousness sneer on her face.

"How do I look, darling?"

Volden gnashed his teeth, his face contorting. "Cover it up!"

Sidra rolled her eyes and then tucked the Tau under her jacket. Then she crossed the room and stood before the girl. That's when I realized that Cricket had indeed changed. She'd changed into...

It couldn't be.

Sidra was now standing before Kanya!

Before I had time to make sense of this, Sidra hauled back and kicked Kanya in the face. The impact was so violent that Kanya's head snapped back, slammed the wall, and then hung limply. Fresh blood and saliva drooled out of her mouth.

"Bitch!" Sidra hissed.

My jaw was clamped in anger.

Someone came to my side, startling me. It was one of the technicians.

"A brief sedative is required," Volden said. "With a touch of Sodium Pentothal, I believe. For... compliance. Nothing like resistance to gum up the process. Or fear. But where you're going, there can only be fear. This will just get us there faster."

The technician stood over me. He produced a hypodermic needle.

"Wait—" I fought helplessly against the straps. "You can't!" But I had no chance. He injected me in the arm.

"No! Volden! What're you doing?"

"You wanted to see Spiraplex, did you not? A lead story. Arlette was thrilled, I heard." Volden laughed. "And how better to experience the breadth of my venture than through the M-graph. It's Felix's brainchild, you know? Scared the old boy off. We've learned to tap into your demons, you see. And by the looks of it, you're a magnet for them. Have you ever seen a grown man die from sheer terror? Facing the void like a sniveling baby? Well, this is the power of Mnemonics. Waterboarding is tiddlywinks next to this."

The tech went to the nearby control panel and nodded to the second tech in the room behind me. The console's lights flickered to life.

Volden came to my side. "The rod is being erected as we speak. I'm sorry you won't be able to see it. Perhaps we can reconvene on the other side, hm? Those builders of Babel, they had it right. It was the Promethean fire. The spark of animation. The elemental gods." He gazed upward. His voice rose in exaltation. "Arise, oh mighty ones. Release your fire. Ignite these hallowed halls! Awaken! Awaken, my Anubis! Lead the dead across the threshold!"

He stood with his arms raised, eyes upturned, enthralled in his own rapture.

Had I not been so royally screwed, I would have cracked a joke about psychic smurfs with Napoleonic complexes. But as it stood, I could only whimper.

The control panel pulsed to life. My arm flushed as the injection spread. A wave of euphoria drifted over me. The drugs were already kicking in. Fighting against it would be futile. I glanced at Kanya. She lay limp, her hands bound behind her. The blood formed a crimson streak down the front of her shirt, a growing pool on the floor. If she wasn't dead, without intervention, she'd be awfully close.

The technician removed the nodule strand and placed them on my temple and forehead. The machine glowed and the holography cylinder flicked to life.

Volden returned to himself. He glanced at Kanya and appeared satisfied that she was no threat. Then he cast a look of indifference at me before turning to leave. On his way out, he stopped.

"Eighteen is the number of the moon," Volden said. "Did you know that, Reagan?"

I peered at him, trying helplessly to resist the effects of the medication.

"In the Tarot," he said. "Eighteen is the number of the moon."

I had to think about that for a second. Then the pit of my stomach went spiraling. He was right!

"That's your lucky number," he said. "Isn't it?"

"I don't believe in luck." I fought feebly against the restraints. "Or the Tarot."

He tilted his head. "Well, I don't blame you. We make our own destiny. Which, for me, looks quite promising. It's a bad card, though. An odd coincidence, however, don't you think, Reagan... *Moon*?" Volden smiled. Then he said to the tech, "Whatever's left of them, bring them down to us."

Sidra followed him out of the room, leaving me to struggle against the truth serum in my veins and stare helplessly at the digital palette that was boring a hole into my diseased psyche.

# CHAPTER 28

THE M-GRAPH WAS TICKING AWAY behind me, probably building a chart of my brain. Preparing to dig in. The conductive gel was cool against my skin. By the time the technician had the last electrode in place, I'd reached a dreamy, tranquil state. I can't say there wasn't fear. I knew I was toast. But the adrenaline had given way to detachment, as if I was outside my body watching the events unfold.

The technician worked over the panel until a cone of soft blue light rose inside the hologram platform. They were preparing to probe my psyche. Isn't that how Brook described it? To reassemble my memories and recreate them in living color. Klammer had warned about the dark side, about tapping into our demons. All those morons preaching self-worth and self-esteem didn't have a clue. You can't go poking around in humans and not unearth something awful. Even the most well-educated and courteous of the bunch can be a perv when left to themselves. I could only imagine what kind of monsters lay coiled inside my noggin. And what manner of beasties this infernal machine might awaken.

The drugs were in high gear now. Warmth cascaded through my body, bringing with it euphoria. I had to fight! I couldn't surrender this easily. But after wriggling weakly against the restraints, I realized it was pointless. The straps were tight. Even if I could spontaneously disjoint myself like Harry Houdini, there was no way I was slipping out of this.

"Hey," the technician scolded from behind his console. "Relax."

"Easy fer you to say." My words were slurred. "Look. Let me outta here and I promise I won't come back and kick yer ass."

He snorted in mild amusement. "Buddy, you're not coming back here. Not after this." He looked up from his work, his face glowing eerily in the panel light. "Trust me."

I forced another burst of energy but it fizzled into a weak groan. I felt dreamy. Numb. Any minute, the white rabbit would hop in and escort me to Wonderland. Sweet.

"Kanya," I called weakly. "Kay! Wake up."

She remained unmoving. And the question crossed my mind, was she Cricket or Kanya; or was she both, one or the other, or maybe none of it mattered.

The lights dimmed and the hologram glowed like a spectral pillar. It shone before me and captivated my attention. I lay mesmerized by the holographic beam. Could this device really reconstruct and project memories? If so, what would mine look like? That was both an intriguing and a wildly scary thought. But scary thoughts were probably the very thing I needed to avoid right now.

Kanya groaned.

The tech and I turned simultaneously to look at her.

The other technician muttered something in the booth behind me. He marched out and stood over her. Her eyelids fluttered lightly, but she remained unmoving. A spark of hope flickered inside me. She wasn't dead. At least, not yet. The technician nudged her with his foot, producing another feeble groan from her. Then he bent down and tested the duct tape that bound her hands and feet. Kanya did not awaken. She was in bad shape. Damn them! He turned and glanced at me, and then said to his partner, "She's not going anywhere. If she does wake up, she can watch."

He approached me and checked the straps. I could smell him. That same musky stench of demon like Brook and the rest of them.

"So when I'm through," I said, "you wanna turn?"

He just looked at me. Unemotional. Apparently, going to the dark side had removed his sense of humor. Shame. He pursed his lips and readjusted some of the sensors. I could hear my pulse beeping on the monitor in his control room. He turned and walked away.

"Hey, wait a second!" I called.

He stopped and looked at me, clearly perturbed.

"Hey, I—" I licked my lips. "Listen. He's wrong about me."

He shook his head in disgust and returned to the booth.

"I'm serious!" I shouted. "You think Volden knows everything? Do you? I don't care how old he is. He can be wrong. Anyone can be wrong. It's why we have checks and balances in Congress and... you know, other places. The power can't be vested in any one individual. I tell my boss that all the time. It's the way the system's s'posed to work. Right? It must be a body. Not tyrants. Or monarchs. Ya know? Do you have that here? Checks and balances? I don't think so. You got a tyrant. A tyrant! You like workin' for a tyrant? Bringin' in peons, strappin' them in, and... Hey. Hey! Are you listenin' to me?"

They weren't. They were busy in their stations, ignoring my ramblings.

"You don't get it, do ya?" I directed my appeal to the tech closest me. "What can I do, huh? A big outfit like this? I'm a little man. Didn't you hear Sidra? I'm a nobody, that's what I am. *Nobody*. Of course, she deserves a liver shot or a couple good jabs to her nose. Probably more than that. Anyway, they took my stuff... it didn't work anyway. You know, the cross. I can't do anything. What can I do? I'm, like... I'm a nobody."

God, I sounded like a fool. Even though it was all the truth, he wasn't deterred.

My mouth was dry. I forced back a swallow and glanced at Kanya. No change. She lay limp.

A slight sheen of sweat glistened on my chest and abdomen. If I couldn't loosen the restraints, then I'd have to do something else. Perhaps if I thought only good thoughts, focused my mind on something mundane or distracting, I could keep myself from tumbling into some psychic abyss. But with Sodium Pentothal—truth serum—coursing through my veins, I knew this would be a no-win proposition. Thinking good thoughts meant having only good thoughts. Which meant I was toast.

My mind and everything in it was about to be stripped bare.

A digital wave rolled upward through the blue holographic cylinder in front of me. Static-foam traced its wake. That electronic backwash hovered inside the cylinder, coagulating, a wispy phantom seeking shape. It disappeared. Then another wave rose. Its residue swelled and dissipated, merged again as a foggy silhouette, and ebbed into fragmented pixels.

Something, some semblance or figure, was forming inside the cylinder.

And whatever it was it was coming from me.

I couldn't let this happen. It couldn't end like this. I couldn't die flat on my back. Ellie. My father. Matisse. All their grand hopes and promises. I couldn't let them down again. This would be the worst death ever—freaking out on a dentist's chair. I had to fight it.

I squeezed my eyes shut, hoping to break any connection between the computer and me. But it kept ticking away. Even in the dark of my head, the images seemed to greet me. All the remorse. All the conflict. Closing my eyes couldn't stop this runaway train. Just the thought of having my nightmares sucked into 3D seemed to awaken the images themselves. It was too much.

I opened my eyes and stared helplessly into the blue abyss of the Dreamchamber.

Ghostly specters now roiled inside the digital palette. Like a grainy sideshow, a collage of snapshots, some were recognizable, others little more than abstracts. Images. Images flashed before me. That's all memory is anyway. Image tethered to emotion. I knew these scenes were torn from my own mind, which made them all the more fascinating. I glimpsed my tree house when I was a boy. It swept through the holographic chamber, but a wisp. No sooner had the adolescent joy of that memory exploded than it died. The image faded into the field of poppies outside our house. The same poppies I would lie down in, amongst the bees, dreaming.

Then came the abandoned apartment house where Lacy died, a bleak Gothic vision that would have made Norman Bates jealous. And there were faces taking shape inside the M-graph. Familiar faces. Uncle Arn passed by, before disappearing into the digital mist. Jimbo. Four-eyed Wilson. Simeon, my father's military friend. A melancholy nostalgia accompanied these images. A great sadness welled inside me. Here I was strapped to a chair, helpless, my life literally passing before my eyes. I'd surrendered the Tau and failed to live up to all those lofty predictions. Perhaps Volden was right—I'd been born under a bad sign. Eighteen, the number of losers.

Out of the corner of my eye, I could see the technician manipulating images on a digital screen. As he did, another wave passed through the hologram and then a figure surfaced. It pulsed and then pixelated, becoming clearer. My heart froze. I scooted my body up onto my elbows to make sure I was seeing this right.

It was a woman lying in a large bed. Yes, it was a digital recreation of something in my brain. A fragment or particle of memory. But seeing it here, outside of me, made it all the more real. For it had occupied an important part of my mental make-up.

She was sitting up, her trembling hand extended my way. Her hair was long. White. But her eyes were vacant, as if she'd cried the life out of herself. She looked so lost. So lost. There was no mistaking this person.

It was my mother.

Lying on her deathbed.

"Mom?" I peered at the figure in the hologram before me. "Is that... you?"

I should have known better than to be talking to this thing. But I couldn't resist. Not here. Not now. Not with these emotions churning inside me and truth serum aiding the process. Not with the end of my feeble existence so near.

The image rotated inside the holographic chamber, a 360-degree revolution, which seemed to crystallize as it went. The figure came to rest facing me. The motion made me dizzy. I squeezed my eyes and attempted to refocus. The locket my father had given her was clamped in her opposite hand. She'd worn that nonstop until the day he died, and never put it on again after that. Her eyes remained blank, her mouth moving senselessly. Suddenly, she stopped. Her arm dropped to her side. Then her eyes grew wide and she leaned forward, looking... at me.

Could she see me? How was this possible?

It's hard to explain the emotion of that moment. It wasn't just remorse or regret. It was knowing I could have intervened, I could have prevented her from becoming an emotional basket case. If I'd just been there. Been *all* there. That's the emotion that had cocooned itself in my brainframe these last 12 years. And seeing her now, this clear, this real, only made the knowledge more acute. It didn't matter that this was a digital recreation. It was the stuff of my brain. And that alone made it real. I tilted forward with my jaw agape.

"Mom. It's Reagan."

Her mouth opened. Then closed.

"Mom, it's Reagan. Remember?"

Toward the end, she didn't remember anything except that the love of her life had been gunned down and her son was traumatized by the event. The incident sank her. She was emotionally AWOL for the rest of her life. I was just collateral damage. And I couldn't help but feeling culpable.

"Mom, I tried. But..."

I was speaking to a hologram, a recreation of an image. What a fool! Nevertheless, she was looking at me. I was sure of it!

"I'm sorry," I said. "I should've done something. But I..."

She tilted her head. Her mouth moved again. She was trying to say something.

"What is it?" I demanded. "Mom! Whaddya wanna say?"

She strained to speak. But no words came out.

"I couldn't do it," I said. "I couldn't live up to that. And you... You weren't there. What was I supposed to do? I couldn't even remember. Mom! I couldn't remember."

She looked away, the tears streaming again.

"Don't do that!" I said. "Don't give up! Not again."

Then the image began to fragment. As it did, she turned to me once again, started to say something, but the image disintegrated and swirled into nothing.

"No! Don't go! Bring 'er back," I said to the technician. "Bring her back! I'm not done."

He ignored me, hunching intensely over his work.

I closed my eyes and allowed my head to drop back onto the chair.

I could feel my skin getting clammy; my heart was thudding through my body now. I couldn't surrender to this. I was a survivor, dammit! I couldn't let him crack me. Not this way. I had to train my mind. I could do that. I'd been looking away all my life. I could do it now. I could *look away*. Think positive thoughts. Or, *no* thoughts. Yeah, that was it. A blank slate. You can't draw images from a blank slate. I had to... I had to...

*think no thoughts...*

Then out of the corner of my eye I could see it. Another image rising in the hologram. An image I couldn't turn away from. It was a scene. A scene set against a cityscape. Something strangely familiar.

It was an alley—that much I could see. At night. Like an old black and white clip from a Bogart classic. Surrounded by tenement buildings and trash-lined gutters. A lamppost stood nearby, sort of like the one in my apartment, but not made of Styrofoam and chicken wire. Underneath its foggy halo stood three figures. Tensely facing each other.

I knew this scene. And the people in it. I recognized them, all three of them. Vaguely. But they were all there in the jigsaw of my memory.

The image rocked in the hologram as if on a cantilever, and then settled. Once again, the motion left me spinning. I blinked my eyes in hopes to steady myself and refocus. But this image, this scene—I'd been there. I'd witnessed this.

A man and a woman arguing. A second person stood off in the shadows, watching them. The man's back was turned to me. Tall, strong shoulders. Hands spread in appeal. Or self-defense. He was the good guy. This I knew instinctually. The woman had short-cropped black hair. High cheekbones. A feral look to her gaze. She pointed accusatorily at the man.

What was I witnessing? I'd seen this once. In a dream? No. This had happened. Really happened.

I glanced at the tech who was hunched over the panel, working furiously assembling images. Swiping his fingers across touch screens like some wizard would the ingredients in his cauldron. My breathing had turned erratic. What kind of madness was this?

A blur of motion rose in the hologram as the woman lunged at the man, unleashing a combination of strikes to the head and torso. I instinctively turned away, as if I was resisting the blows. But I was untouched. She danced back with her hands raised. Then I saw it. Something that awakened a memory which had lain dormant for a long time.

A tattoo on the back of her hand.

A tattoo of a hydra.

Sidra!

"Dad!" I shouted, yanking against the restraints so hard the chair rocked. "Dad! Watch it!" The sensors tugged against my flesh, threatening to pop free. The tech looked up from his panel.

I stared back into the M-graph and watched the scene unfold. Helpless. Just like I had when I was a kid.

Only this time, the river of memory came flooding back.

Another parry, and the two of them rolled out of the lamplight. My father tumbled back and leapt into a standing position. He yelled something my direction, but I couldn't hear anything. Just the blood rushing behind my eardrums. Sidra landed in front of him, unleashing a series of kicks, which he dodged before taking hold of her boot and spinning her to the ground.

"Dad! They're gonna kill you! You have to get outta there! Dad!"

They grappled with one another, a flurry of choke holds and close body punches. Until my father managed to take hold of her head with both hands. He gripped her temples, pulling her upward. Sidra rose. Screaming. My father had gripped her head in his large hands and lifted her up. Her screams turned into an animalistic wails. He was gouging her eyes with his thumbs as he dragged her upwards. The holographic image shivered. When it returned to clarity, Sidra had punched free of his grasp. Her left eye was now nothing more than a hollow bloody socket. She stumbled howling into the alley.

My father collapsed and lay panting.

I was spellbound, watching this digital recreation of my own memory peeled from the membrane of my consciousness.

The second person emerged from the shadows. Short. Pale. Meticulously groomed. Large eyes.

It was Soren Volden!

He removed a revolver from under his coat and aimed it at my father.

I turned away. I didn't need to see what happened next. I'd already seen it once. And I couldn't stop it either time. The floodgates of memory were now opened. This is what I'd witnessed, what I'd conveniently blocked out for all these years. But reliving the memory did not bring healing. It only made it worse. The guilt and remorse of that event seemed to choke the breath from my lungs.

I closed my eyes and turned away. But the scene was in my head, playing out like a projector. Volden stood over my father. He put his gun away. He bent down. And then...

I opened my eyes to see Soren Volden remove the Tau from my father's neck.

My father had been the protector of the Tau.

The holographic image scattered and reconstituted. I couldn't take any more. I closed my eyes and concentrated on slow, deep breaths. But it was pointless. This game was over. I opened my eyes to see another form taking shape. Something foul and black rose from the digital soup. An image, limbless but alive. A protean blob, transforming, taking shape. A death angel. Grown in the soil of my malaise. My own personal demon had awoken to devour me.

I was fixated. For the entire Dreamchamber seemed to darken with this evil presence.

I was so tired. Tired of fighting. Tired of trying to be something I could never be. It was over. And the notion that I could do anything about it needed to be jettisoned. I rested my head back in the chair as the holographic image rose, higher and higher, until it looked down upon me. A dark angel. A spawn of my own pain. Its eyes glowed a livid green. Like some monstrous vulture preparing to dine on my emotional entrails. It was inevitable. I would be swallowed by my own failure.

Suddenly, an electrical snap sounded. The lights in the room flickered.

I was slow to react, feeling thick-headed and foggy. Still immersed in my self-pity. Nevertheless, as I looked up, something passed through the holographic field causing a brief rush of static. The technician in the booth behind me said something. There was concern in his voice. Then it happened again. The dark monstrosity that had been taking shape pixelated and fragmented. Only this time, I could see another image, a silhouette, inside the cylinder. It rolled through the blue column, a humanoid torpedo, shattering the dark image. As it did, I glimpsed an arm. A shoulder. Then a torso. They were distinct, slightly burnished in color. And quite fair.

Bernard!

It was like a slap to the face. I straightened and peered at the hologram.

What a fool I was! He'd probably been here all along. But what could he possibly do? He was invisible. Then again, if the demons could see him, who knew what kind of wrestling match was going on in dreamland?

The technician closest to me stepped out from behind his console, trying to figure out what had just happened. The holographic column was now just static. He peered at the projection, his brow knotted in befuddlement. Suddenly, he collapsed. Fell straight to the ground.

I managed to hoist myself onto my elbows in time to see Kanya, who was lying on her side, kick the fallen tech in the face and drive him into the console, causing a shower of sparks.

# CHAPTER 29

KANYA LAY ON HER BACK on the floor of the Dreamchamber. Her hands and feet were still bound. The bruise on her forehead looked worse. A trail of blood traced her jaw and her shirt. The lights were strobing on and off and the technician lay crumbled at the base of the console as it sputtered and smoked.

I blinked hard to adjust my gaze, as if I could force the effects of the drugs out of my system. Part of me was still caught up in the image of my father, Volden and Sidra murdering him. And Volden taking the Tau from him. It stoked my anger. But I couldn't linger. There'd be time for that. I was sure. But not now.

"Kanya!" I leaned over the chair, stretching the sensors taut. "You're alive!"

She groaned. "I know."

The lights flickered and I saw her worming upward. Her slacks were torn at the thigh, revealing another wound. She rolled onto her stomach, got on her knees, straightened, and steadied herself as if she were a supplicant in prayer. Then in a single motion she leapt upright, onto both feet, struggling for balance.

"There's another one," I whispered, as if the man in the booth wouldn't notice that his buddy just had his feet swiped out from under him and his face planted into Volden's high-tech equipment.

Kanya bunny-hopped to me.

"Hurry!" she said. "The tape!"

She spun around, positioning her bindings near my face. For a second, I froze, unsure what she was asking.

The technician in the booth yelled something.

"Use your teeth!" she demanded. "Rip it! Hurry!"

Duct tape is like that. If you could manage a tear, ripping it was a piece of cake. I heaved my body up, mouth wide open, snapped like a dog, and missed the tape on her hands completely.

"Lower!" I said.

The tech in the booth yelled something else. Only this time, I could hear him run into the room, cursing.

Kanya squatted lower, wiggling her fingers in my face now. I heaved my body upward, trying to gnaw at the tape. I nipped her finger in the process. Then I snagged an edge of the tape in my mouth, pulled back, taking a sizeable strip with me.

I spat it into the air as the other technician rushed at her.

Kanya spun away and tumbled onto her back. From there, she thrust her feet at him and glanced the man near the knees. He staggered back and steadied himself. A wicked smile creased his lips. The first real sign of emotion I'd seen from the guy. She remained on her back, watching him. Then he removed his lab jacket and laid it neatly across the back of a nearby chair. He cracked his knuckles. Either he was a genuine bad ass or he figured a woman bound hand and foot was more in his league.

Kanya leapt to her feet again and stood wobbling. The tech lowered his shoulder and drove at her. She steadied herself. Then Kanya snapped the tape off her wrists just in time to drive her open palm up into his face, utilizing his own motion against him. A sickening crunch of bone and teeth sounded. She pivoted out of the way as he spun and dropped to the floor at her feet.

She swooped on him and quickly applied a chokehold. He was out. Maybe dead. Kanya rose and stood panting. Then she bent down and tore at the tape around her ankles. In four seconds, she was free. She wiped her hand across her bloody jaw and winced as she did.

"They followed us," she said. "Used me to get into the Asylum.

I begged him not to open." Kanya hung her head for a brief moment, and then said, "Let's get outta here," as she hurriedly unloosed my bonds.

I sat up, massaging my wrists. I was still woozy, dreamy. Still trying to process everything. The M-gram was now just a dull palette of blue light. I stared into it, as if my father's image would manifest one final time. One final farewell.

"Reagan," she said, a hint of tenderness in her tone. "We gotta leave."

I looked up at her. Had her hair actually changed color before? Or had I been seeing things? Time for questions later. Despite the bruise on her forehead, a fat lip, a bloody shirt and a bloody jaw, she looked great.

"Does your name really mean poisonous flower?" I asked. "And was your mom really a queen?"

She clucked her tongue. Then she hung her head and sighed deeply. Before I could ask what was wrong, she reached across me and slapped me with the back of her hand, nearly toppling me from the chair.

"Hey!" I sputtered. "What was that for?"

"You need to snap out of it."

"All right! I'm awake! Geez!"

I pushed myself off the seat and swayed. It was going to take a few minutes to get my land legs. Not to mention nurse my bruised ego.

She glanced at the technicians. Then she hurried into the booth and scanned the equipment, emerging with only a flathead screwdriver, which she jammed into one of her pants pockets. If she really could kill someone with any part of her body, I could only imagine what carnage she could wreak with a flathead screwdriver.

"They killed my father," she said.

"I know."

"You saw him?" Her eyes widened.

I nodded. "I went there. He was still alive when I got there.

But..."

She hung her head. "They had guns. Tasers. I had no other choice." She shook her head.

"Look," I said. "It's not your fault."

"I shoulda done something." She choked back tears. "He tried to fight back. You know what he was like. He wouldn't give up the Asylum. Not for anyone."

"Yeah. That sounds like Matisse."

"They wanted the lightning rod—that's what they were after all along. We brought them right to it. They loaded it up and dragged me here. And left him there to die."

She squeezed her fists and looked away.

I put my hand on her shoulder. I was so tempted to tell her about the glorious scene I'd witnessed through Rival's Curtain. Her father trudging past the great golden river, into the pristine hills of a far off dimension. But at the moment, it seemed so far away. So impossible. And rather inappropriate. If we survived Volden's chamber of horrors, perhaps I could attempt a description one day.

"If it's any consolation," I said, "they killed my father too."

She looked at me. "Then we both owe them."

She brushed away her tears and quickly composed herself. "They wanted the lightning rod for a reason."

"The ghost box," I said.

Kanya nodded. "It's the power source they needed. That transformer up there shoulda tipped us off. They've probably been watching my father's expeditions for years. Once they knew he'd discovered all the pieces, they made their move. We were playing right into their hands." She pursed her lips in disgust. "I say we find our way to the top of this place and do whatever we have to do to get it back. Or destroy it. Whatever it takes."

"Yeah." I nodded ruefully. "But first I need the Tau."

She looked at me.

"Apparently, it runs in my family," I said. "And I can't beat Volden without it, for some reason. Just don't ask me how or why."

"So, where do we find it?"

"Sidra took it."

Kanya's eyes pinched tight. "I owe her one."

"Well, maybe you'll get your chance. They were going to take us downstairs to the cryochamber. I'm guessing that's where we'll find them."

"So how do we get back down there?" She glanced at the men sprawled on the floor. "They know we're here. It's not like we can walk right past them. Or go sneaking around without being spotted."

"Well, unless these guys tripped an alarm or something, they think we're still up here getting glazed. The elevator's just down the hall. If we can get to it, we go straight down to the basement. That's the way we first came. We just retrace our steps."

"And from there?"

I shrugged. "Look. If that stuff about the Imperia and the Tau is true, if something else is at play like everyone's suggesting, then the best we can do is put one foot in front of the other and hope for the best."

She seemed partly taken aback by my concession. Yeah, I'd come a long way from the cynicism of yesterday.

"Bernard was here," I said. "He's the one who tripped that thing. And whatever kind of monster was manifesting from the M-graph, he stopped it. He's led us this far. And apparently he's still hanging around. All we can do at this point is... trust him. I guess."

She wiped blood off her jaw, put her hands on her hips, and shook her head. "Ya know, everything was going fine until you showed up."

I would have thought it a reprimand until her lip curled slightly on one side.

Huh. I was kind of liking this girl.

She went to the door, cracked it open, and looked out. She closed it. "I don't see anyone. Let's make a dash for the elevator. And hope we don't bump into anyone along the way."

I nodded and started to follow.

"Um," she said. "You leaving like that?" She pointed to my bare chest.

"Oops." My shirt lay on the console where the Tau had been. I put it on. As I returned across the room, glass crunched under my feet. Reflective particles glinted across the floor at the base of the recliner. This is where Volden had crushed Rival's Curtain. The hologram had dimmed to a soft, staticky blue. In its glow, shards of the visor spread along the floor. This is what had started everything. This strange device had turned my world upside down. Now it was just debris.

Suddenly I spotted a larger piece, a pentagonal shard perhaps the size of a quarter dollar, under the chair. I scratched through the fragments and retrieved it. I held it up to the light.

Kanya watched me studying the crystalline shard.

I looked at her. "Might come in handy, huh?"

I stuffed the piece in my pants pocket. Then I joined her.

"Okay." She stood with her back to the door. "Ready?"

The smell of Dahlia was in the air. *Poisonous flower*. Her skin was bristling with adrenaline, her eyes bright with fire. I thought about Cricket and her youthful sass. Could they be one and the same? And if so, were they—or was she—really Matisse's biological daughter? Or royalty?

"Hey," she said. "Are you ready?"

"Other than being really woozy? Sure. Go for it."

She cracked the door open again and peered out. Somewhere down the hall, a power tool ground away. Work was being done on one of the rooms. We exited the Dreamchamber and headed straight for the elevator. The digital walls displayed a moonscape now, a bleak yet tranquil landscape of craters whose curved horizon revealed a serene, beautifully blue earthrise. Who knew what other monstrous experiments would be conducted within these halls. No amount of beach scenes, waterfalls, or moonscapes could make the Dreamchamber any less menacing.

It seemed like an eternity waiting for the elevator doors to open. What would we do if it was occupied? I was aware of every camera in the place. They were watching us, without a doubt. We had to move quickly. I had the strange impulse to call out to Bernard. Nevertheless, I possessed an unusual confidence that he knew that and was watching us with interest.

The elevator hissed open. To our relief, it was empty. We entered quickly, pressed Lower Level, and the door closed. My polite electronic lady friend's voice sounded in the elevator as we started our descent. I found myself anxiously counting the floors, touching the spot on my chest where the Tau had been. Knowing that it was now resting over Sidra's breastbone only made its absence hurt more.

We'd just about reached the lower level when the elevator glided to an abrupt stop in between floors. We were forced to steady ourselves as the elevator jerked, and began climbing.

"Override," said the polite voice.

"Crap," I said. "So much for that."

When the elevator door slid open on the ground floor, three Cosmagon awaited us, looking as sullen as a pack of rhinos with gas.

# CHAPTER 30

"AN ESCORT." I glanced at Kanya. "Isn't that nice."

One of the Cosmagon pulled back his jacket just enough to reveal the butt of a pistol protruding from a shoulder harness.

"Either you come quietly," he said, "or we'll take you piece by piece. You decide."

I glanced at the elevator button. There was no way. We were trapped.

"Those are our only options?" I said. "Okay. We'll come quietly. Because I'm gonna need my hands to strangle that son-of-bitch boss of yours."

The man let his jacket fall back into place while his partners stormed the elevator, one taking hold of me, the other Kanya.

"Easy, easy," I cautioned.

They yanked us out of the elevator and began marching us toward the great statue of Anubis. I looked back across the marbled expanse toward the lobby. Through the foliage and plate glass, I could see that night had descended. Camera flashes illumined a curtain of rain outside. Apparently, the weather had not stopped the crowds. But if some hellacious powers were really being summoned by Volden, there was no telling what exotic beasties were also hoping for a guided tour of the facility. The sidewalks shimmered as rain pelted Los Angeles. The storm of the decade was upon us. Perfect timing.

Our hurried footsteps echoed in this vast empty hall. The first Cosmagon had dropped behind us. He spoke into a handheld device while his partners escorted us toward the base of the death god, apparently unconcerned to deliver us without breaks and bruises. Kanya looked unusually calm as they pushed her forward. She limped noticeably, but was not resisting in the least. Probably just waiting for the right minute to do her thing. I wish I could say the same for myself. The drugs were still messing with my equilibrium, and the adrenaline rose and fell inside me, causing me to alternate between impulsive confidence and utter fear.

Behind the sensation was the thought of seeing Ellie again. Or what was left of her.

We passed several Plexiglas displays containing the remains of mummies and pottery. Large stylistic vases, some as high as a man, were spaced between aqueducts rippling with clear water that triangulated the area. Finally, we passed into the shadow of Anubis.

There was no way we'd be able to overpower these guys, especially if they were all armed. Brook had hinted at the Cosmagon's peculiar abilities and after what I'd seen of them through Rival's Curtain, I had to believe these men were not your average mall cops.

Commotion sounded near the lobby, a metallic clatter followed by raised voices.

I craned my neck to see what was happening. The Cosmagon quickened their pace, practically dragging us along.

"Hey!" someone yelled. "Hey, Moon!"

"Jimmy!" I dug my heels in and turned enough to see Jimmy Pastorelli with two uniformed police officers standing with a security officer at the entrance. "Jimmy, it's me!"

The Cosmagon secured my wrist with one hand, my elbow with the other, applying counter force. He could snap my arm with ease, and I'm pretty sure he would enjoy doing so.

"Reagan!" Jimmy called. "Hey, hey! That man's under arrest!"

The Cosmagon stopped and stood with their backs to the detective.

"L.A.P.D." Jimmy bellowed. "Hold it, right there!"

"You heard the man." I wrestled against their grip. "I'm under arrest. So let us go."

The man who was trailing us joined the group, removed his pistol, and held it against his chest, at the ready. His back was to Jimmy, so the gun was not visible to the policemen. Then the Cosmagon drew us into themselves, and we became a tight bundle.

Kanya glanced sideways at me, her brow furrowed in indecision. Do we try to make a run for it? Or would they? If they did, we'd make great shields. But the police wouldn't fire if civilians were involved. However, if I was a suspect, I was no longer a civilian. Somehow, we'd have to get free of these goons. The base of the statue was half a football field away. And now there were more guns here than a shooting range.

"Jimmy!" I yelled. "Jimmy, they have guns!"

The man holding me drew my arm back and I yelped. I could smell him. But another odor intermingled with him. Something pungent and burning.

Another commotion sounded near the entrance. Yelling. Muffled clatter. Then footsteps echoed and I could hear the officers spreading out behind us.

"Stop right there!" Jimmy ordered again. "Everyone. If you have weapons, drop 'em now!"

The Cosmagon exchanged expletives. The burning smell intensified. I wondered if Kanya could smell this or if it was some new talent that I'd acquired from having worn the sacred visors.

The Cosmagon simultaneously released their grip on us. I stumbled away and turned to face the officers with my hands raised.

Jimmy stood perhaps 25 feet away now. His clothing was soaked. He and his compadres had drawn down on us. Rainwater trickled from their uniforms and formed small puddles at their feet. The crackle of a radio sounded and one of the officers removed it from its holster, summoning backup. They'd found their suspect.

Jimmy's eyes darted back and forth between the Cosmagon and

me. He seemed unsure as to where to aim his pistol. Or who the real enemy was.

"Okay. Drop the weapon," he said to the Cosmagon.

"They were caught trespassing," the Cosmagon said. He glanced slightly at me, but maintained his sights on the officers.

"That's not true!" I shouted.

"There's highly classified information and research being done on these premises, officer. We're an independent firm hired by Volden Megacorps. We have strict orders to—"

"He's lying, Jimmy!" I said. "They tricked me into coming here. Selwyn Brook, on the eleventh floor. Said they wanted to give the Crescent an exclusive interview. He was lying. They wanted me. They killed her father and kidnapped her. Look! They beat the crap out of her. They've already tried to kill me once."

"Okay, okay." Jimmy swallowed. "We'll figger it out, Reagan. For now, just... just hold it right there." He looked at the Cosmagon. "We need you to put away your piece, sir. This man's a suspect and under LAPD jurisdiction now."

I looked at Kanya. She glanced at the large vases nearby, and then issued the slightest wink at me, followed by a slow single step back. I followed suit.

"Reagan!" Jimmy said, moving his gun from the Cosmagon to me. "I warned you about running. Don't do it again. And you—" he aimed his gun back at the Cosmagon. "I need you to drop your weapon. Now."

"Jimmy," I said, continuing my slow retreat. "Remember that thing in Shanghai? All those bodies that disappeared? They're here, Jimmy. And the Bastion Sails accident? They're all downstairs. It's some kinda crazy experiment. They're in suspended animation or something. Trust me. The whole place. It's... it's a conductor of some sort. A giant ghost box."

Jimmy stared for a second. "Reagan, you're rambling."

"It's true!" I said. "All those ghost boxes you found? This is why. Right now, up on the roof, they're setting up a lightning rod. They stole it from her old man and they killed him. Volden wants to open up some kind of door to another dimension, Jimmy. I know it sounds nuts, but it's the truth. I wouldn't lie. You know that!"

I could see it in his eyes. He believed me.

"Remember that cult," I said. "The one downtown? Remember how you thought it wasn't true at first? Jimmy, this is bigger than that. A lot bigger."

It was a good move on my part. The mention of that crime got him thinking. He'd started those investigations as a skeptic. As the story unraveled and the tales of occult madness and ritual murders unfolded, Jimmy Pastorelli was forced to admit that a world of intrigue existed on the fringes. What had looked like your basic network of high-strung Platinum level stockbrokers was a cover for trading of another kind. The one that involves human souls.

"Dammit!" Jimmy shouted. "Don't be pulling that shit on me. You're a suspect in those murders, Reagan."

"Volden." I took another step back, creating more distance between me and the Cosmagon. "He's... He's not what you think. He's a devil, Jimmy. Some kind of freakin' monster. This whole operation is part of some elaborate plan. He's just using us! If we don't stop him, something bad's gonna happen. To all of us."

"All right, Reagan. You'll have a chance to explain."

"He killed my father," I yelled. "*He's killing Ellie!*"

Jimmy gripped his gun. His eyes darted from me to our captors.

"I can't, Jimmy. I've already let too many people down. I need to do something right for once."

"Reagan, I warn you. Not a step further."

"I—I can't." I took a full step backwards and angled my body toward Anubis. I raised my hands. "You're gonna have to shoot me, Jimmy. I've got to find out. If it's really her, I've got to find out. I'm sorry."

I kept backing up, prepared to turn and sprint to the base of Anubis, fully expecting to be shot in the process.

And I was right.

Jimmy shouted, "Watch out!"

In the split second before I flung myself headfirst behind a nearby Egyptian vase, the Cosmagon pivoted and fired at me. I'm sure the shot would have killed me if Jimmy hadn't released two rounds into the man's left shoulder. The impact had minimal effect on him, nudging him sideways just enough that I was spared injury. His compatriots drew their weapons and tumbled to either side. And it was on. The bullets pinged off the marble as I slid across the nicely polished stone and landed in an awkward heap at the base of the vase.

Gunfire erupted as both parties sought shelter behind the stone and tile décor. The vast hall became a riot of sound—gunshots, cursing, radio static, and shattering ceramic. I peeked from behind the vase enough to see the first Cosmagon, the one who'd attempted to kill me, running for cover. Either he was wearing a bulletproof vest or Volden had bred these gorillas to withstand standard ammunition. A dawning bewilderment broke over me. What kind of creatures had built this monument in downtown Los Angeles? What kind of monsters were we fighting? And did normal firepower even have a chance against them?

I got to my knees. The officers had taken cover behind a bank of mummies. Kanya crouched against a marble fountain that was crowned with four archers, standing back to back, from whose arrows gushed crystal clear water. She signaled me to move. I nodded. Then she pressed her hands to the floor, leaned forward like a track star preparing for the starting gun, and darted toward the next series of columns. Even with her bum leg she was already 10 yards ahead of me when I followed suit.

Shots rang out. The whiz of bullets on marble glanced past me. I wove to my right. Then to my left. I saw Kanya tumble, wasn't sure if she was hit, but it was a full on somersault. Then she sprang to her feet with embarrassing ease. Next to her, I was about as agile as a tortoise in mud. The sound of gunfire exploded in Spiraplex, echoing off the lofty ceilings and glass encasements. While the officers fired at the Cosmagon, the Cosmagon were firing at us.

I dove behind a nearby planter, skimming across the marble like a kid on a slip-n-slide. Kanya crouched behind a column 40 feet away. We were directly under the snout of Anubis now. Six or seven stories high! Black as midnight, inlaid with gold panels. Now I could make out intricate carvings and untranslatable ciphers etched along the body. I remembered the ghastly green spire that I'd seen through Rival's Curtain, the spectral cyclone that cocooned this monstrosity. By all estimates, we were standing square in its eye. Kanya caught my attention with a wave of her hand. Then she pointed to the portico which ran under the base of Anubis and the elevators there. She signaled me. On the count of "three," and then ticked it off on her fingertips. One-two-

But as she counted "three," her hair turned silver-white again. Her body seemed to shrink, drawing into the petite body of Cricket. Laughing. Playfully amiss. Like a kid on an empty beach with a very long summer break ahead of her. The transformation was so clear, so obvious, that I missed our count. I just crouched there watching her sprint joyfully to the columns at the base of Anubis, tumbling, zig-zagging past gunfire, her eyes sparkling under those silver-white bangs.

The planter I was behind exploded from gunfire and I flung myself backward, wincing as shards of ceramic burst into the air.

A radio crackled and the Cosmagon and the LAPD exchanged gunfire in the Eighth Wonder of the World. I located Kanya peeking from behind the column near the elevator. But she was fully Cricket now, giggling and clapping, looking as splendidly alive as one could possibly be in the middle of a shootout. She waved me forward.

Oddly, everything seemed right at that moment. I wondered what my father would think of me. He'd seen his share of battles and gunfights. And somehow I'd been drawn into my own unique war. Kanya/Cricket watched me. Her eyes were wide. Sparkling. She was brimming with life and resolve. A regular Wonder Woman in loafers. She gave me confidence. Hell, she'd rescued me from the Dreamchamber. But it was more than that. We were the same. We both had secrets. I could only hope we'd have the chance to explore our similarities someday.

I inhaled and sprang to my feet, making a beeline for the elevator doors, into the shadow of Anubis, as bullets nicked off the marble and the little changeling I'd previously known as Kanya willed me forward.

# CHAPTER 31

I RAN. THE ELEVATOR DOORS were dead in my sights. Images of great Baals lined the portico underneath Anubis. The Canaanite and Phoenician deities were believed to form the seven princes of Hell. It seemed only fitting that the last image we glimpsed before our descent into Spiraplex might be a hellish prince.

Gunshots and shouts continued behind me. It was getting hot and heavy. I caught myself worrying for my friend Jimmy and the mess I'd gotten him into, though it was doubtful that he had any more interest in apprehending me, even if I was the main suspect of the Medium Massacres. In a way, the Cosmagon had done us a favor in their unwillingness to let us go. However, if they survived the firefight with L.A.'s finest, I was sure this was my last chance to try to escape them.

Three sets of elevator doors were divided by two columns. Signs warning against trespassing announced this area off-limits. I dashed to the first column and stood with my back to it. Cricket crouched behind the other column. Sweat glistened on her forehead, but it didn't appear to quell her mirth. She was laughing and coughing, whooping it up like some reckless renegade. My chest was burning from the sprint. If I hadn't taken up jogging again, I'd probably be dying for oxygen about now. Because of my conditioning, it felt like I was just now warming up.

Cricket crouched only 10 feet away. "Hey! 'Member me?"

"How could I forget?"

"Are you okay?" she asked.

I nodded. "And you?"

"Never better. But don't tell her."

"You mean—?"

"Who else would I mean?"

"So she knows?"

Cricket ducked as several rounds tore through the open space between the columns. When it stopped, she peeked at me, laughing and shaking her head. "She pretends not to know. But don't you believe her, K?"

"Why? She hasn't lied to me yet."

She brushed her hand through the air. "You're all the same. Okay. Then let's go. These guys are serious."

"I just hope these work," I said, motioning to the elevators. *Staff Only* was stenciled across their face. However, no eye scan device or card reader accommodated the warning.

"They will," she said. "The guard is currently tied up." She motioned to the firefight and barked out an exaggerated laugh. "Let's just get in there 'fore he does."

Being that I was shielded from the main lobby behind the pillar, I bolted toward the elevator, rapidly pressing the down button before rushing back for cover. Until that moment, I had not considered going up inside the Anubian structure. An entrepreneur like Volden had probably planned guided tours and rides for the kiddies inside the snout of the great monstrosity. I could only imagine what other kinds of surprises one would find inside the body of the death god.

Before I had a chance to return to cover and wait for the doors to open, they did. The elevator was empty. We looked at each other and then hustled inside from our different spots, crashing into each other in a sweating, huffing, heap.

Multiple shots rang out, pinging the columns and sending plumes of dust into the air. I glimpsed one of the Cosmagon running full speed at us. His eyes—I could see them. That odd turquoise. Glowing hot. I got to my knees and rapidly pressed the close-door button. There was no polite female voice that followed. The doors hissed shut.

We both jumped to our feet. And now she was Kanya again, or in the process of morphing, running her hands up and down her limbs, presumably checking for gunshot wounds. Or massaging her changing anatomy back into shape. This time I couldn't control myself and just stood watching her.

Her hair went from white to black before my eyes. Its strands magically reshaped themselves. It wasn't a trick of light. It wasn't my imagination, or some wish fulfillment. I was too close. Too alert. And I had no wish to see such a thing. Nevertheless, there was no mistaking it.

Maintaining the posture of a skeptic is rather difficult when the evidence is right before your eyes. Admittedly, some do. But as much as my unbelief had become a citadel of refuge, I was not so far gone as to remain a bonefide materialist.

She glanced up at me, fully Kanya now, and did a double-take. "What're you looking at?"

"Why didn't you tell me?"

She looked down at her hands and then feet. "What?"

The elevator hissed to the basement level.

"You're a shape shifter," I said. "Aren't you."

She looked at me.

The elevator door opened upon Lab Guy. Before I knew it, Kanya reached for his head, slung one arm around his throat, and with the other, reached back into her pocket, produced the flathead screwdriver, and jabbed it to his throat. He might know something about quarks and cryogenics, but this guy knew nothing about self-defense.

"No!" he cried. "Don't, don't, don't—"

She walked him out into the hallway of the basement, gouging the screwdriver in his gullet. This was the hallway the Cosmagon had first escorted us down. At its far end were the elevators which had taken us up to Selwyn Brook's office.

Kanya navigated the man to the door with the VM symbol on it and the eye scan device nearby.

"Open the door," she said.

"I—I can't." He panted. "I—"

"Either you open it or I'll pluck your eye out and use it myself."

"No!" His glasses were half on his face. He looked at me, as if I'd help him.

I shrugged. "She means it."

A look of terror gripped him. "Okay, okay." He motioned for her to guide him to the doors.

We got there and he placed his eye into the viewer. The double-door hissed open. With it came the smell of smoke and chemicals. The long hallway stretched before us. I remembered walking down that hallway from the opposite direction. Now we were heading straight into trouble.

Kanya refused to move. She held that screwdriver to his throat.

"If you tell anyone, I swear I'll find you and kill you."

He was trembling exceedingly. He nodded.

She pushed him away and he crumbled to the floor whimpering. Then he scrambled to his feet and glared at us. We backed into the hallway, watching him. A sudden flush of boldness seemed to engulf him. His face contorted with rage. I recalled the parasitic creature which occupied his shoulder in some parallel dimension and wondered if it was also having a conniption.

"You'll n-never get outta here!" he spat. Then his eyes grew wild, frenzied. "His gods... they're real. Do you hear me? They're *real*!"

"You mean," I cleared my throat nonchalantly. "*They live?*"

He stopped abruptly and peered at me. Then he started laughing maniacally.

"They live! They live!" he cackled.

Definitely not fitting for a guy in a lab coat.

Kanya jabbed the screwdriver his way, pretending to lunge toward him. He sputtered and stumbled back.

"Shut up, Poindexter," she said, as the door slid shut between him and us. Then she approached the eye scanner and stabbed the screwdriver into it, multiple times, inducing a shower of sparks. She dropped the tool to the ground and the scanner smoldered.

"What're you doing?" I exclaimed. "We'll never get out of here."

"And no one else'll get in. Do you wanna have to face the rest of those guys, too? We need all the time we can get. We can use that decontamination tunnel if we need to. If not, we'll find another way." She motioned to the other shafts that intersected this corridor.

She was right. There were probably a dozen other ways out, in, up, or down this monument of a maze.

We both turned and gazed down the hallway. The greenish glow emanated from the doors of the cryo-chamber.

"They're in there," Kanya said, peering at the door.

I squinted at her. "So you're also telepathic?"

"Funny."

"Okay. Plan of attack." I let the statement hang there.

"Yeah," she said. "Plan of attack. We get the Tau back, keep Volden from firing up the lightning rod, I get revenge for my father, you get revenge for yours, and I kick that chick's butt for not fighting fair. That enough of a plan?"

"Perfect."

Kanya moved with catlike stealth. She was leading the charge now and if something supernatural was in her genes, then I was more than willing to let her be the lead. When she reached the double doors, she stopped. There was no sign of anyone. It was quiet. She reached toward the double doors and looked at me. "Are you ready for this?"

"I'm right behind you," I said.

A little smile crept across her face. She touched the door and it slid open.

Cool air ebbed from this subterranean morgue, as did a faint smell of mold and dampness. The two large lamp stands that stood on either side of the temple blazed, casting shadows helter-skelter about the ornate interior of this large room. Surrounding the temple stood the cryo-tubes. Their soft glow bathed the perimeter in a green misty haze.

I wandered down the walkway that descended to the temple and approached one of the tubes. It rose perhaps seven or eight feet. Condensation dappled its side, clouding its occupant. Before we did anything, we needed to see what was inside these things. I swiped my hand across the surface, revealing a naked man suspended lifeless in the green liquid.

Kanya gasped.

"Then it's true," I said.

I stepped back, studying this person. The man's eyes were closed. Several tubes coiled behind him, probably providing nutrients or chemicals for preservation. His body floated limply, perhaps a foot off the bottom of the tube. There must be two-hundred, maybe two-hundred and fifty of these tubes in this room.

My stomach sank. Ellie was here. I knew it.

I wandered down the aisle, swiping the condensation off the next tube. Another man. Kanya joined me and we stared at this lifeless, nameless, human being floating inside a cylinder in downtown L.A.

"She's in here," I said. "Somewhere."

Kanya nodded.

"Your father was right." My gaze swept the cool amphitheater. "Klammer was right. Volden's harvesting bodies."

The realization swept over me at the horror of this enterprise. I ran to the next tube, wiped away the moisture to peer inside. Not her. The next tube. Not her. How many of them? How many people had he taken? It didn't matter. I'd look at all of them. What would I do if I found her? I'd bring him to justice, that's what I'd do. I ran down the aisle, madly brushing away the moisture to see the face inside each cryogenic chamber.

Seeing my delirium, Kanya called for me. I ignored her.

An immense weight seemed to drape me. This was the culmination of everything Volden was building. Babel. How many bodies had been used to build that empire? Souls just thrown away for the sake of progress. This one would be no different. And Ellie was now just a cog in the hideous mechanism.

I ran through the aisles of the cryo-chamber, wiping moisture off each and every tube, finding only strange, unrecognizable faces. I was oblivious to everything now. Insane with hope and hate. On to the next. And the next.

Someone grabbed me and spun me around.

"Reagan!" It was Kanya.

I stood, sweating, staring at her.

"Reagan, look."

She pointed to a pale hose, soft-looking and milky, that ran along the floor, from the base of one of the cryotubes, before intertwining with the next. These hoses formed large braided cables, perhaps the width of a fire hose, that cordoned each aisle before disappearing underneath the floor. Apparently, each tube, each person, was connected.

I squatted down and touched one of these fat cables.

It was soft, rubbery. Slightly translucent. I removed my hand to see slime clinging to my fingertips.

"Weird," I said. "It's like... an umbilical cord."

I got up.

"They're feeding something," I said, tracing my gaze along this odd cable. I jogged back to the main aisle. The central cord wound its way and dipped toward the center of the amphitheater. Kanya stopped beside me and together we peered at the temple in the middle of this room. Everything was being channeled here.

We hurried together to this ornate structure.

The temple sat in a basin. All of the cryotubes connected here. However, there did not appear to be a door to this structure. It was inlaid with hieroglyphs and etchings, runes and glyphs. It was the culmination of Volden's eccentricities. An amalgamation of occult exotica. Winged creatures, centaurs, and symbols carved into its panels. We walked around the perimeter, looking for a way in, but there was no visible door.

"They're in there," Kanya said.

"Then there's got to be a way in."

I traced my fingers through the etchings, probing lines and punching carvings in hopes of finding a secret switch, something that would reveal an entrance. I pounded on the exterior with my fist, not so much to knock, as to test if it was hollow. But there was no response.

"Maybe there's a lever," she said. "A trapdoor or something."

"You've been watching too many movies."

"Okay. Then maybe there's something you can say. An order. Or command."

"Pfhh!" I shook my head. "Like *open sesame*?"

She stepped back and scanned the panels as if that command would indeed open the temple. It didn't. But something else interesting happened.

"Hey," Kanya said. "Check it out."

She pointed at something small and dark that was scuttling along the aisle toward the temple.

"What is that?" I said, going to see.

It was perhaps the size of a half dollar. Dense black. An insect. A horned insect. We stood over it, watching it chug toward the temple with purpose.

"A beetle," I said.

"Not just any beetle," Kanya clarified. "A *scarab* beetle."

It marched between the two of us, undeterred, and approached the foot of the temple. As it did, a panel along the temple retracted. Then a second. An opening appeared that was triangular in shape.

We both jumped back, startled. Unsure of what might emerge. Nothing did. Except mist. Thick gray mist wafted from this opening within the temple walls, fingering its way along the floor and filling the basin. The scarab beetle disappeared into the mist.

Kanya looked at me.

I shrugged. "I guess it worked."

The fog coiled its way around our ankles and legs. A soft orange glow radiated from within the temple. Neither of us moved. It's as if we both knew this was it. That everything would come to a head here and now. And that there were no guarantees.

"It's been fun," I said.

She smiled. "Just promise me one thing."

"What's that?"

She jabbed her thumb toward the cryogenic tubes. "That you don't let me end up like that."

I nodded. "Ditto."

This time, I led the way. I had to duck to miss hitting my head. I took three steps in and Kanya followed. The fog dissipated around us.

It was a chamber lit only by several wall-mounted torches. Steps rose to a circular platform at whose center sat a massive ornate throne. Soren Volden sat on the throne, dwarfed by its immensity. It was perhaps the worst case of Little Man's Syndrome I'd ever witnessed in my life. He was shirtless, capped with a headdress like some cartoonish pharaoh. Two large hoses or cables trailed behind him, similar to the ones on the cryo-units, and were connected at some point near the base of the throne. Volden appeared to be asleep, oblivious to our entry. A slight sheen covered his flesh, glistening in the torchlight. His head lolled upon his chest, his hands slowly opening and closing upon the armrest in some sort of ecstatic catatonia.

Sidra stood at his side, both of her hands on a short muzzled weapon. The Tau draped her neck.

Behind the throne six cryo-chambers stood in a semi-circle. Six—the number of Man. Why not?

This was the inner sanctum, the holy of holies, the sacred chamber of Spiraplex. Kanya remained unmoving, measuring the situation as I did. Before we could initiate any plan of attack, Volden inhaled deeply and his eyes fluttered open. A satiated smile crept across his face.

He stood and steadied himself before the throne. The braided cords draped from his back. But they did not appear inorganic. They twisted and roiled like the tentacles of some demented cephalopod. Volden turned enough that I could see the thick cables were attached at the base of his spine, near his kidneys, to some sort of orifices. Puckered holes. One on each side.

Reaching back, Volden pulled one of the cords out and it released with a wet suction. What I saw horrified me. Spidery tentacles, perhaps thousands of them, fluttered hungrily at the end of this limb. The conduits were braided, a vast artery of electrical impulses. He carefully laid it aside and released himself from the second cord. Both of these hideous appendages lolled helplessly, like enormous earthworms plucked fresh from their digging.

Until that moment, the idea of Volden being something other than human hadn't really registered. My flesh grew cold. We slowly approached and stood at the base of this platform, staring up at the two of them. Volden watched us gaping at this unearthly scene. He'd seen our brand of dismay before.

"So glad you could make it," he said coolly. "The Awakening is near. I've reserved us some front row seats."

# CHAPTER 32

A DRY RUSTLING, ALMOST BEYOND the range of hearing, filled this temple. Yet my attention remained fixed on Soren Volden.

Sidra brought him a robe and Volden slipped it on. As he did so, I glimpsed his back. The gill-like apertures were closed now. The hideous cords that had been suctioned to his back lay unmoving. They were pale gray now, as if the life had left them. Volden saw me staring at them.

He smiled. "We have a symbiotic relationship, you could say. I keep them alive, and they do the same for me."

"They?"

"Why, my children." He gestured to the cryotubes behind him. "I keep them safe, and they keep me, well, animated. Their knowledge, their experiences, their *joie de vivre*—it's all mine. Imagine that. Oh!" He spotted something and descended the steps to retrieve it. "What have we here?"

Volden scooped up the scarab beetle. He held the beetle in the palm of his hand and brushed it with his fingers as he climbed the steps back to his throne.

"*Scarabaeus sacer.*" He smiled, admiring the beetle. "The symbol of death and rebirth. Transformation! The Egyptians believed they nourished upon their own dung, rose from their dying. A fitting illustration of the cosmos, don't you think? Even if *you* are the ones dying."

But I had looked away from Volden and was staring at the cryotubes behind him. These were larger, more ornate than the ones outside this chamber. The glass was almost black, dappled with moisture.

"You're going to burn for this, Volden," I said. "This's kidnapping. Worse. It's murder."

He frowned and set his pet beetle down near one of the strange cords. The bug hurried there and began scuttling about on the moist sinewy edges. To my surprise, other beetles had congregated there, forming a thick boiling mass of wings and antennae, clambering for leftovers on the end of these odd tentacles. The entire chamber seemed to sparkle with the dark beetles, every seam and crevice housed the scarab army. I shivered with the realization that the dry scratching sound that filled Volden's temple was that of innumerable insects.

"Kidnapping?" Volden brushed his hands together. "Murder? Call it what you want, Reagan. Slaughtering Native Americans was genocide. Or was that just *progress*? That little man in Germany, the one with the camps and the ovens. Now *there* was a forward thinking individual. It's the foundation of your civilization. The survival of the fittest. Well, until your species can learn to survive, I will continue to exercise my *fitness*."

"Those things on your back... What the hell are you, Volden?"

"That depends upon your perspective. If you are forward thinking, unburdened by modernity or science, free of your own fear of finiteness, you would see me for what I am—the progeny of a superior race. A god, you could say. That's what *they* called me. The Incans. The Egyptians. Even the Order of the Rosy Cross considered me ascendant. *Enlightened* is the word they preferred to use. In exchange for a little technology or science, an occasional display of power, they let me help myself. Which I did. The rules can always be tweaked, provided you have backup."

I watched the beetles squirming and scratching as they feasted on whatever detritus remained on the giant umbilical cord.

"So that's why Klammer punted," I said. "Couldn't handle

working with an extraterrestrial monster."

"Felix? Pah! His manners got in the way. And *monster*—that's really not a very nice way to put it. All Felix's claptrap about dignity and ethics. And truth! Now *there's* an outdated concept. Your species is forever trying to rise above the cesspool of its origin. But you—ah!—you've fought tooth and nail against such superstition. Haven't you, Reagan? Flirting with the supernatural, tongue firmly in cheek. I must say, we were a little concerned when you started gravitating toward that hocus-pocus, even if it was to mock it. A skeptic must be oh so careful what he investigates. Nothing like seeing an angel to rock one's world. Wouldn't you agree?"

The mention of an angel stunned me. Did he know about Bernard? It only made sense. If the Invisibles were influencing or controlling these people, then Volden had to be privy to Bernard. If so, it didn't seem to concern him.

Volden studied me, his large eyes sparkling with mischievous delight.

"You just made our job easier, Reagan. And now having survived the M-graph—by the way, you'll have to explain how you accomplished that—it only convinces me that we will make a great team. At least, when my need arises for you." He chuckled sinisterly.

"Sorry to let you down," I said. "But we have other plans. And now I know your dirty little secret." I stepped forward. The rage filled me like salt on a freshly cut wound. "I really don't give a damn what star system you're from or how many Neanderthals you claim to have knocked off along the way. You killed my father, Volden. And I'm gonna take it out of your ass."

He smiled mockingly. "Very nice. Almost inspirational, wouldn't you say?" He glanced at Sidra, who remained steely. Then his countenance fell. "It's just a little too late for theatrics, Reagan. Your time has come and gone. The Imperia are broken down. Obsolete. We have the Tau. We have the lightning rod. And," he cocked his head, "I believe we have lightning."

"You killed my father!"

He raised one eyebrow. "Is that such a revelation? I never tried to hide that fact. It was always right in front of your face. You simply forgot. Conveniently blocked it out of your mind in order to cope. Amazing what the human brain does to survive."

"Well," I swallowed hard. "Now I remember. And what's so special about that damned thing anyway?" I nodded toward the Tau.

"Ah! Isn't that why we're all here?" He said it with a caustic jeer, spreading his arms toward us. "It's the banner of your descendants. The rune of power. The flimsy relic of your resistance. Why such icons hold such fascination, I'll never know." He curled his lip in disgust. Then he stopped and stared at me, appearing puzzled, if not concerned. "Why, you have no idea who you are, do you Reagan Moon?"

Apparently, my dismay at this question humored him. He started laughing and glanced at Sidra who joined him. Their laughter rose inside the chamber in mockery. A great bewilderment draped me. I was the butt of some cosmic joke, a joke that everyone got but me. It was the story of my life. Their derision seemed to batter the little hope I had.

He straightened the robe about him. The color, what little he'd had, had returned to his skin.

"It's a pity," he said. "And rather depressing to have no equal. Nothing reveals one's mettle more than a good opponent. And I'm afraid good opponents are becoming a rarity for me. Which is why men like your father were so curious. I respected him, believe it or not. But he knew full well what he was undertaking when he took up the Tau. Question is, did you?"

"You're either insane or just really bad."

"Those are my only options?" His eyes sparkled at the banter. "We *had* to kill him, Reagan. To snuff out any possibility of interference. He was preparing you, do you realize that? He would soon begin training you, filling your head with all that mush about progeny and history. Had we not stepped in, you might have actually grown to believe that nonsense about the Seven Guardians and their divine conspirators. Matisse, on the other hand, had no idea. Sort of stumbled into it, I'm afraid. He was busy hunting his relics, doing his good deeds for humanity, and—" he looked at Kanya, "adopting illegitimate children."

Kanya's lips tightened. Her hands balled into fists. Sidra re-gripped her weapon and stared Kanya down.

Volden chuckled. "Fume if you must. I speak the truth. Does he know?" Volden gestured to me. "No. Of course not. Things like that one keeps under wraps. Besides, it's not something you lead with on the first date. But take heart, my young changeling. We have no choice as to our origins, only our ends." Volden smiled at her. "You've acted nobly, despite your peculiarities. But, alas, your ends are upon you."

Volden tipped his head in arrogance and meandered along the platform toward the cryo-cylinders.

"She worked for me, you know?" Volden glanced at me.

"What are you talking about?"

"Ellie," he said. "She worked for me."

Was this a trick?

"How do you think she acquired the Tau?" Volden said. "She was quite a prospect. A sneaky one, however. Apparently, she'd done her research. Windsum was just a front for them, you see. Apparently, the Imperia had been busy building coalitions, reviving numerological delicacies, compendiums of arcane knowledge. Reviving old pacts. You didn't think she was exchanging equations with her professor friends, did you? It was a painfully pointless effort, I assure you. Windsum was one such cover. Under the guise of alternative energy research. It was my soft spot. Hmph. Once they learned that one of the Seven Guardians was possibly alive, and that I had, indeed, reacquired the Tau, she made the mistake of befriending you. But all that nonsense about love... It was strictly Platonic, old boy. She just wanted to awaken you to another possible future."

He stopped and looked at me, his brow furrowed in concern.

"Does that hurt you, Reagan?" He straightened. "I hope so. You didn't think it was real love, did you? It wasn't. She was using you."

I glared at him. "You're a liar. Besides, what do you know about love?"

"Yes, well. That's a point. Either way, she stole the Tau. And that, I'm afraid, could not go unpunished."

My breathing had quickened. My mind was going in so many different directions it was hard to think clearly.

"Ellie just took it back," I said, trying to stay calm. Trying to keep my emotions from getting the best of me. "*You* stole it from my father. And you murdered him."

"A dreadful cycle, isn't it?"

"Yeah. And I'm taking them back. Cycle on. The Tau's mine."

Sidra moved her weapon to the opposite shoulder, eying me firmly.

"And so is Ellie." I stepped forward. "Where is she?"

"Why, she's right here." Volden stopped in front of one of the cylinders. "But I'm afraid that getting her back will be impossible."

He brushed his palm across the face of the glass and the tint drew down, unfrosted, to reveal Ellie Wells floating naked inside the cryo-chamber.

I stared, incredulous, trying to make my eyes adjust. Hoping this was an illusion. And at first, I thought I was seeing things. He'd hypnotized me or something. Perhaps there was more than just truth serum in my veins. Maybe I was hallucinating. But, no. This was for real. I wandered up the steps, fixated upon the woman in the chamber.

She was just as I remembered. The light, layered hair, wafting gently in the current. Her diminutive frame. And the tattoo on her left ankle. The blood drained from my head. I was too stunned to be angry. Or think clearly. My mouth dropped open and I went to her.

Volden watched me approach, smiling almost proudly as I did. I could hear the beetles rustling with agitation as I passed. I stopped in front of the cylinder. Ellie was almost eye-level now.

*You're in danger, Ray.* That's what she'd said through Gollo. *He's c-coming for m-me. Ray, he's coming! You have to s-stop him. Please!* She was alive in there. I knew it.

I reached for the glass, lost in my own mind. I think I said her name.

"She's always been one of my favorites," Volden said. "She had so much life! Pity it was concentrated upon such futile aims. I'd wished it not have come to this, Reagan. Believe me. I prefer peace accords to crusades."

His words were distant. I was enthralled with her presence. I'd spent almost a year dreaming about her. Remembering her. Her nuances. Her gestures. The slightest details of her features. Her eyebrows, and the way she'd wrinkle her nose when perturbed. A lock of hair that would finger itself over her left ear. And she loved the beach so much. Her hair always went crazy with the salt water.

I placed my hands upon the glass. Its cold smoothness reminded me of the barrier that actually existed between us. I was still in the land of the living, still infinitely distant. She, however, was gone.

Volden approached and watched me.

I turned and looked down at him. He was pushing dwarf status. A mighty mite if ever there was one. Then I looked back at Ellie. It's hard to explain exactly what went through my mind. But it wasn't good.

"Is she alive?" My own voice sounded distant.

"Oh yes! She'd be of no use to me if she wasn't. Her mind, though, is elsewhere. Drained of essentials. But if you want her back, you'll have to rethink your plan."

"I don't have a plan. I'm better at ad-libbing."

"Well," Volden said. "I might suggest you forgo any violence. Sidra is quite efficient. I once saw her kill seven men. She only had a tire iron, a broken hand, and hadn't eaten in three days."

I glanced at him. "Kanya can take her. Besides, I think she owes her one."

I returned my gaze to Ellie.

"You know, Volden, Ellie always said there was a reason why I haven't died."

He raised an eyebrow, mildly interested in my retort.

"I know, I know." I raised my hand. "You don't believe in that destiny stuff. But Ellie was convinced that all my close calls and escapes weren't just a coincidence. She said something big was in the works for me."

My skin flushed with rage.

I said, "And I'm beginning to think that strangling you with my bare hands is part of that destiny."

I angled my body toward him.

He looked up at me and smiled. "This is where Buddhism could serve you, Reagan. Detachment from passions, you know?"

"But passion is so much fun."

"Yes, but it's not passion that you're feeling now, is it? You want to kill me. To wage your revenge on me. But it's blinded you, dulled your reason. You have no chance here."

"Well, you're right about the revenge part."

I turned to him and clamped my hands around that sinewy little neck of his. His headdress toppled to the ground.

Kanya leapt forward and Sidra aimed her weapon. "Stay there, hon."

Kanya stepped back, her lips pursed in anger.

Interestingly enough, Volden did not resist my attack. In fact, his body almost seemed to yield to my grip. He closed his eyes and retained a creepy smile, as if he enjoyed being strangled to death. Well, I would happily comply. My fingers locked around his throat. My thumbs crushing his larynx. This extraterrestrial leech could go back to the void, or whatever dimensional asshole he'd slithered out of. Hatred fused my fingers around his throat.

Volden's pale skin grew ashen. But he still did not resist. Why wasn't he fighting back? Why was Sidra allowing this to happen? Something was wrong. His eyes fluttered under his lids, his features growing placid. He'd taken the best parts of my life from me! And now he'd just surrender it back?

"Reagan," Kanya said. Then she yelled, "Reagan, stop!"

But I was in too deep. My anger had possessed me. All the emptiness of my existence was in that death grip. I thought of my father. His war wounds, his care for me. Snuffed out without warning. I thought of Matisse, and his passion to stop the flood of evil on earth. And I thought of Ellie.

"Reagan!" Kanya's voice rang with urgency. "It's Ellie! Stop!"

*Ellie?* Her words shocked me. I loosened, but did not release my grip on Soren Volden. I turned and looked at Ellie Wells. Her throat was constricted, as if invisible fingers wrung her neck. Her body writhed in the green liquid. Her arms flailed helplessly in the cryo-chamber.

Somehow I was also strangling Ellie Wells.

# CHAPTER 33

REAGAN!" KANYA CRIED AGAIN, but I'd already released my grip on Volden. He staggered back. Then he drew a long, deep breath. The smile grew across his face and his eyes opened. He straightened his robe. Brushed off his shoulders.

"See?" Volden said, wiping saliva off his face. "You can't kill me, Reagan. If I die, she dies. They all die. We are bound to one another in perfect union. Didn't I say that?"

I stood shell-shocked, staring at Ellie. Her body had grown lax once again. The anguish on her face had left and been replaced by vacancy. She floated lifelessly.

Volden rubbed his neck and winced. Then he composed himself. "It's a natural order. That's the beauty of it. Perfect symbiosis. We were a dying race, Reagan. We needed a home. Your plane, your bodies, are the perfect host."

A deep rumbling sounded somewhere outside. All of Spiraplex seemed to tremble at the sound.

Volden looked up, a devilish glint in his eyes. "They're waiting for us. The Black Council. Waiting to cross over. Boreth and Skai, and Irayna of the Nth Lobe. Why else would I tinker in such primitive methodology? A ghost box. Hah! Such archaic techniques. Little did Matisse know that his intrepid research played into our hands. Spiraplex could be a divining rod, a beacon for the lost ones. *Those Who Live.* Indeed. *They live!* They live on the fringes, in the small places. In the nether. The vagabonds of this universe. Exiles. They will join us here, on this, the day of the great Awakening. And the Succession of the Tau will cease. Here and now!"

Another rumble, and I realized it was thunder. The storm outside was in full force.

Volden listened carefully. His eyes sparkled in the torchlight, while the life seemed to drain from me. My body hunched limply. We were trapped. There was no escaping it. No way out. This was it. Checkmate. *We couldn't kill him without killing them all.* I stumbled to the throne, gripped its back, and steadied myself.

The temple doors opened. I didn't turn to see who it was. I knew by Volden's expression that it wasn't Jimmy, or the LAPD, or anyone who could possibly change this course of events.

Volden nodded toward the doorway and two Cosmagon ducked under the door and stepped into the temple. Sidra aimed her weapon down at Kanya. The Cosmagon hurried up the platform and stepped to either side of me. But I was no threat. Not now. I'd never be able to stop him. Even if I managed to stop Volden, somehow, Ellie would die. She wanted me to help her, but help was impossible.

"Don't look so glum," Volden intoned. "The battle has been hard fought. Ours, I mean. Your battle has been quite... uninspiring. But if your strength is any indicator," he massaged the marks on his neck where I'd choked him, "you still retain some life. Mind you, I would relish the chance to savor your sweetness, and depending on what happens upstairs, I possibly shall. I hear you have substantial knowledge in esoterica and adult beverages. But after what you'll witness, I'd be surprised if you can keep yourself from leaping from the top of Spiraplex and dashing yourself on the pavement below. Either way, I do want to enjoy the culmination of our efforts with you in tow. So, up we go."

The Cosmagon took me roughly by each arm. I did not resist.

"I'm afraid your accomplice must remain. Sidra has her own agenda. I give her that freedom, you know. She's rather territorial, especially when it comes to other females. Although, what we know of Matisse's daughter, she will be a delight to have. In fact, we have a spot for you, dear."

As he said this, one of the cryo-chamber doors hissed open. There was no liquid in it. Tubes dangled from the top as did a long copper coil. It reminded me of a casket, yawning, hungry for its occupant.

Volden struck a contemplative pose, "I don't believe I've ever savored a changeling." He looked at Sidra. "So leave some for me, will you, dear? And I know you find enjoyment wearing that infernal icon," he motioned to the Tau, "but do destroy that thing when you're done." Then Volden straightened and signaled to his bodyguards.

The Cosmagon led me out of the chamber, pushing me through the opening so hard that I stumbled and fell. The amphitheater and its cryogenic tubes glowed an eerie green. The building rumbled again, its girders quaking. Perhaps my surrender had awakened the storm gods. If so, I was their sacrifice. The Cosmagon yanked me upright.

Volden passed through the opening without needing to duck and proudly surveyed the cryo-tubes.

"Reagan!" Kanya yelled from inside. "Don't give up. Do you hear me? Do not let them win!"

Sidra cackled.

If Kanya's words were meant to inspire me, they didn't. The door slid closed on Sidra's laughter, the Tau, and the only girl whom I'd ever really loved.

# CHAPTER 34

IF VOLDEN WANTED TO KEEP ME for dessert, it wasn't showing by the way the Cosmagon handled me. They gripped me, one on each side, forcing me forward when I hesitated. Their hands were like clamps on my biceps. Seeing Ellie writhing inside the cryo-chamber had knocked the wind out of me. How could I defeat Volden if doing so meant killing Ellie Wells? I'd have thought it a ruse if I hadn't seen it with my own eyes. He was right, it was symbiosis... in the worst way.

As much as I knew that Kanya could handle herself, the odds were stacked against her. This wasn't going to end well. And if I ended up in one of those cryo-tubes with my old girlfriend, it would *never* end.

We passed through the amphitheater, back into the hallway. Apparently, Jimmy had been significantly detained, because this area was still empty. The doors that we had entered through remained closed. Smoke twined its way upward from the damaged eye scan mechanism. Volden pointed down an adjoining hallway to a second elevator. He pushed the button and tilted his head, listening for something. A few seconds later, the structure resonated with a thunderous intonation.

"Impeccable timing!" Volden looked up at me. "Have you ever wondered what it means to be in two places at one time, Reagan? When the fire strikes, you'll see it first hand. The fundamental transformation of material, structural reality. Things, objects, intersect the otherworld in ways you've not imagined. Charms. Religious icons. Occult symbols. It's their approximation to something Other, a tangible representation of the Invisible, that does it. This is where their power lies. We learned this in Kabul, on a much smaller scale, of course. They summoned a gorgon, you know. Quite disturbing, I must say. I believe it took up residence with a tribal lord who is now being worshiped. When the Black Council arrives here and Spiraplex becomes their habitat, things will change. Trust me, young man. A new age will undoubtedly be upon us. No amount of negotiations or explosives will compromise our rule. Not when we've been waiting *this* long."

The elevator door opened. They shoved me inside and camped on each side, sandwiching me in their death grip. Both of the Cosmagon were armed. I could see their pistol grips under their jackets. Volden pressed the top button. We were heading to the roof.

"As one who shares your appreciation for numbers," Volden said, "you'll be glad to know we've numbered the 13th floor."

"Great." I watched the digital elevator numbers tick upward. "But I don't believe in luck. Good or bad."

"I don't blame you. It's a silly superstition. Numbers are amoral. Why should one number be better or worse than the next?"

"One shouldn't. But maybe it's not the numbers at all, Volden."

The look of amusement vanished from his face and became one of genuine interest. "What do you mean, Reagan?"

"Maybe we're the ones who are aligned with the numbers, not the other way around. You ever think of that? Maybe the universe is in some type of symmetry, you know? We were just dropped into the program, not produced by it. Someone else is calling the shots. We're just a piece of the mechanism. A perfect piece, for sure. But the key is," I shrugged, "finding the Sequence."

Volden seemed to ponder this as the elevator climbed. Finally he said, "A novel thought. But sequence is of our own making. An arbitrary pattern we choose to invest with significance. Coincidences are just that, random. The only symmetry between us and the universe is the one we make. Being red in tooth and claw has that advantage—it doesn't demand a center. The only center is the one who conceives it. Or has power to create it. Just ask Matisse." He looked at me. "Or Ellie."

I gritted my teeth. God, how I'd love to strangle this freak. But I'd already tried that.

"Detachment," Volden said mockingly. "Detachment."

"How about if I detach your nose from your face?"

The Cosmagon squeezed my arms even harder.

Volden frowned. "Then what would happen to Ellie?" He shook his head. "Either way, Spiraplex has 20 floors. A perfectly round number. Symmetrical, you could say."

"I thought you didn't buy the numerology stuff."

He looked sideways at me. "I didn't say I didn't believe it. I just modify. You see, I respect all religions... insofar as they align with mine."

He returned his gaze to the elevator ticker.

This meant the rooftop was 21. *Twenty-one.* I didn't say anything, but the thought caused a glint of hope to shine inside me. *Twenty-one.* Three sevens. And if seven is the number of perfection, then three of them is only more perfect. Then again, it depended upon who was labeling perfection. Still, no plan of attack blossomed in my brain. There had to be a way out of this, something I was missing. If my father had been involved in some secret society, if Ellie had followed my arc, then I must be missing something. Hell, I'd probably missed a lot of things. Perhaps the only real question was whether or not anything was salvageable.

The door slid open upon a dark, rain-soaked rooftop. The storm clouds were right on top of us, mist racing past the building's spouts and spires. Rain spattered the ground, running in rivulets toward channels on either end of the building. The gargoyle-like figures I'd seen from the street looked more like sphinxes. However, these had horns and nasty claws. Two of the sphinxes were visible here beyond the parapets, water spouting from their jagged teeth. Perhaps Quasimodo would also appear to wreak vengeance upon my enemies. I could only wish.

I glimpsed the city lights through the roiling cloud mass. Los Angeles never looked more ominous. And as I watched, an axe of lightning split the sky, silhouetting the ancient lightning rod. They'd reassembled and erected it, just like Volden had said. The Star of Anu. Carried from the ends of the earth and now raised here in the City of Angels. Our own modern-day Babel. The glint of lightning danced upon its ornate surface. Just yesterday, Matisse had huddled over this piece, enraptured with the supremacy of his find. Now he lay dead, hoofing it into the afterlife with careless abandon. And I was stuck against impossible odds trying to stop a gill-backed parasite with aspirations of world domination.

The lightning rod stood at the center of Spiraplex, perhaps a hundred feet away, on a tiered platform located at the building's pinnacle. Like some pagan altar for the sacrifice of virgins, it climbed into the angry night. The rod stood atop it, shimmering against the clouds, wavering slightly in the gusts of rain. Lightning cracked and veins of neon coursed the sky, illumining the Neolithic figures and etchings on the Star of Anu. It had been assembled, all three pieces, and at its highest point I could see the six-pronged star, the hexagram, its twisted arms like a singular dragon claw grappling for the heavens. A scaffold had been partly disassembled nearby, which I assumed had been used to construct the device. Three large cables stretched taut from the roof, surrounding the lightning rod, and steadying it in place.

Volden stepped into the rain, apparently unconcerned about getting drenched. He removed his robe and stood shirtless. Then he faced the lightning rod, faced the rain, and spread his arms out. And Volden began chanting. Speaking madly into the storm.

Lightning crackled again, so close I could hear the snap and hiss of its passage. A fiery tentacle veined its way dangerously near the rod. The rooftop sprang to life in the white glow and faded to black. I jumped back as thunder followed on its heels, reverberating the rooftop so fiercely I thought it might topple the ancient lightning rod. This was madness! We'd all be incinerated.

Apparently, I was the only one worried about possible electrocution as the Cosmagon dragged me into the rain, closer to Soren Volden and the lightning rod.

Volden looked over his shoulder at me and laughed. His hair was a dripping mat, his face twisted in maniacal glee. This was the culmination of everything he'd planned. How many ages, how much bloodshed, had brought him to this place? He turned back and gazed into the maelstrom.

"The gods have answered!" he proclaimed. "Babel will be reborn. Awaken, Lord Anubis! Summon your legions! Reopen the passage for the Lightless Ones."

He glanced again at me, smiled, and then spoke into the storm, "I have brought you an offering."

Lightning cracked again, torching the sky, charging the air. In those brief seconds, I glimpsed the clouds raging above the rod. Odd shapes seemed to swirl and struggle within them. A confluence of angry shadows joining in this devilish revelry. The sky went black and thunder answered. We were in the eye of the storm.

"Bring him," Volden shouted, and trudged toward the base of the lightning rod. The Cosmagon pulled me forward, practically dragging me. My clothes were drenched. The rain pummeled us now. Yet the atmosphere seemed charged and electric.

Volden stopped at the base of the platform.

"Leave him," he shouted to the Cosmagon.

They paused.

"Leave him!" His eyes blazed. "Sidra needs your help. Now go!"

"As you wish." The Cosmagon said. Then they forced me down and left us.

I fell to the ground and remained there on my hands and knees, beaten. The rain had turned warm, almost monsoonal. It lashed my back like a thousand of the world's softest bullets.

"Come, Reagan." Volden approached and stood before me. "Watch with me. Let us witness the Beginning together."

He extended his hand.

I refused it and climbed to my feet, glaring at him. We were alone, but I had no choice. I was bereft of options. I might as well have had 'dead meat' written across my chest. So much for finding the Sequence. The game was officially over.

He studied my eyes, apparently attuned to my despair. An odd note of compassion seemed to lace his words.

"Just you and me. Soren Volden and the Seventh Guardian. Fitting, isn't it? Sorry it isn't more of a contest. Hand-to-hand combat atop a skyscraper in the midst of the storm of the century—how very dramatic that would be! No, I'm afraid you'll just have to watch. Besides, you have no chance. Bu'idu. Dalkhu. Succubi. Adramalech. They're all here. You've only seen the shadow of my power!"

Lightning snapped overhead, sizzling across the sky. I ducked as massive braids of fire unfurled above us. It seemed to suck the oxygen out of the air. I huddled with my hands over my head, gasping for breath. Volden stood defiantly, his eyes sparkling in the light. It was only a matter of time before the rod caught the lightning and conducted it into this pagan reactor.

Volden cried out in a foreign tongue. I crouched in fear against another strike. What could I do? Killing Volden meant killing Ellie, it meant killing all of them. And even if I could kill him, this storm was aimed straight for the Star of Anu. I was helpless.

The mantle of the black sky cracked again, revealing molten rage within it. Lightning webbed the Los Angeles skyline, capered atop the high rises and smoke stacks like phantom chariots from the gods. An electric arc sprang from the rod. Volden cried out in exultation as sparks exploded and showered the area, sizzling in the rain. The rod rung out with a metallic resonance from the strike.

"Babel!" he cried, with his arms outstretched. "Babel! One tongue! One rule!"

As the brightness faded, images danced before my eyes. It was a peculiar sensation, borne both by the atmospheric optics and intuition. Had I not seen Rival's Curtain dashed to bits, I might have thought I was wearing it. For a series of odd silhouettes, glimpses of amber and sweeping asymmetrical movement, filled the space around the lightning rod. And then disappeared. Something else was in this storm! Or in a dimension *beyond* the storm. But right here. With us.

I stood up and swiped water from my eyes, peering past Volden to this dimensional space. But it was gone. In the distance, a flash of lightning pulsed. It sent shadows skittering across the rooftop. Wind swirled and the rod swayed. Volden was laughing, babbling away about gods and greatness. This creep was all in.

But something else was happening, something that Volden himself did not seem aware of.

My skin bristled. The air seemed to thicken around me, as if energy were gathering. In the split second before the lightning cracked overhead, just when the charge seemed at its cumulative peak, I glimpsed Bernard at the base of the lightning rod. It was a fleeting image. Ghostly. Nevertheless, it was unmistakable. The angel was pulling on the lightning rod, heaving with all his might, trying to topple the pagan beacon. The sky erupted around him. And with the lightning came hellish faces and voices roiling in the storm.

*Moon! Moooonnnn!*

I gasped. The blackness returned, followed by an explosion of thunder. But now I knew what was happening. And what I could do about it. Sure, I was a terrible example of the Seventh Guardian of the Imperia. I couldn't kill Soren Volden. I couldn't revenge my father's murder. I couldn't rescue Ellie. I'd pretty much disappointed anyone who'd ever had faith in me. Nevertheless, I could still do something. Even if I got myself killed in the process.

As I prepared to dash up the platform to the lightning rod, Volden turned and peered back the way we'd come. Then he smiled.

I followed his gaze to see the elevator door standing open. Sidra was walking toward us, her weapon strapped over her shoulder.

The Tau still draped her neck. She looked at me and then Volden.

My heart sank. I should have known. This had been a suicide mission from the get-go.

Lightning blazed overhead, turning the rooftop into a wash of monochrome. But in its light, I glimpsed something that made my heart freeze.

Sidra was not only bleeding profusely from her left shoulder, her hair was changing, turning silver-white. Unfortunately, I noticed this as she raised the rifle and pointed it at me.

# CHAPTER 35

SIDRA STUMBLED FORWARD, keeping me trained in the site of her rifle. The rain hit her, quickly turning the blood-soaked clothing into a burgundy tie-dye, deep red sopping its way down her shirt into her pants.

She staggered toward us, barely able to hold the weapon aloft.

I raised my hands in a show of surrender. But the mystery of it all remained front and center. Was this really Sidra? I studied the person faltering toward us. She was wearing Kanya's clothing, had Cricket's hair, and looked like Sidra. She was even missing her eye! So... who was this? If Kanya really was some sort of changeling, then there was no telling. Maybe Cricket had been imitating Kanya all along. Or was this person all three of them? Color me lost.

Volden appeared to be having the same problem as I was. His smile had faded. He peered forward, fighting the onslaught of rain to discern this person.

She was now 20 feet away. I could see she was trying to say something, looking at me. Her lips moved wordlessly. She stopped and swayed.

"Move," she finally croaked.

"What?" I pressed my hands forward hoping to slow her advance. "Wait."

"Move!" She pressed the rifle into her shoulder.

"Don't shoot him!" I stepped toward Volden. "You'll kill them all."

Lightning blazed, momentarily turning our rooftop showdown into noontime at the O.K. Corral. Thunder followed immediately. It was so loud I thought the reverberations alone might topple the gargoyle-sphinxes. I quickly returned my gaze to the woman.

"He d-deserves to die," she said. Blood had begun pooling at her feet. She was bleeding profusely. "And they..." she swallowed. "They *want* to die."

I must admit, until that moment I had not entertained the thought that I could save Ellie by actually helping her die. Nevertheless, my first reaction to the idea was one of horror. I could never do such a thing! But by *not* doing so, was I keeping her bound to some dimensional no man's land?

The woman raised her weapon, cradling it weakly. However, I could now tell she was staring over my shoulder, looking at some point behind both of us. I pushed Volden out of the way and lunged the opposite direction, almost slipping on the rain-soaked rooftop.

The rifle did not have the tinny metallic burst of traditional rounds. It issued successive automatic charges like a machine gun. But instead of heavy pings, deep thuds sounded, bursts of air or sonar. I couldn't tell. Either way, she wasn't aiming at me, or Volden.

I spun about to see water splashing at the base of the lightning rod. It rung out with each blast. Some of these bullets—if they could be called bullets—tumbled out into the rainy darkness like softball-sized blobs of gel. Others struck home. The Star of Anu rattled and groaned.

"No!" cried Volden, gazing up in horror. "Stop it!"

The strange weapon thudded away. But my attention was drawn toward the woman. As I watched, her features morphed, hair shifting between black and silver-white. Her face was reshaping itself; her cheekbones rose, became more angular. Her empty eye socket stretched, bulged, and a new eye sprung forth. I stood gaping. She leaned into the rifle, her shoulder punching back and forth against the grip as the weapon sent an endless stream of concussions against the lightning rod. The Tau glistened on her breast.

Volden's protestations became louder, until the sky cracked and an explosion of electricity illumined the rooftop, drowning him out and nearly blinding us. The sphinxes seemed to spring to life in the blast of that natural energy. In that flash, I glimpsed a panoply of Invisibles. All around us. The atmosphere was full of them—exotic entities in a fevered, angry mass, writhing and contorting with monstrous appendages, wings and orifices. They'd risen from hell, summoned in this mad attempt to bridge dimensions.

And there was Bernard, wrestling against them. He was dwarfed by the horde of Invisibles. But his brilliance seemed to transcend all of them.

The air tingled as the lightning evaporated. I smelled smoke. And with the passing of the blaze, the sky returned to normal, and the darkness swallowed us.

Suddenly, the woman moaned. It took my eyes a moment to adjust. When they did, I saw her stagger and almost collapse. I was still trying to compute what was happening. But now it was clear. This wasn't Sidra at all.

She grew limp. Her knees folded forward and she twisted to her side, caving under the weight of the rifle. The weapon continued to fire as she fell backwards. The soft bullets arced into the black sky, pelting the falling rain with soft wet thuds. She landed on her back and the rifle sprang from her grasp, firing several errant rounds into the night before stopping. Blood sprayed from her body as she struck the surface.

It was Kanya. Her features had returned and now she lay in a watery pool of red, bleeding out from the wound.

I ran to her and knelt over her. The life was seeping from her eyes. Her hair flushed again, like some odd time-lapse sequence, returning to its black, and the length grew out before my eyes. I was staring, captivated, when she reached up and grabbed me by the collar.

"Reagan," she gasped. "There's... there's a r-reason you haven't died."

Our eyes locked momentarily. Then she patted around her neck, found the Tau, and managed to lift it over her head. She handed it to me, pressing it into my hand. I took it as her head fell back, lifeless. *No!*

But I didn't have time to mourn. Things were happening too fast. I quickly slipped the Tau on. But if I was expecting some burst of power or intuition, I didn't get one. Rather, as I turned to retrieve the gun, I found Volden standing there with it aimed at me.

I rose slowly. "Easy, cowboy."

"Very industrious, that little shifter of yours." He smiled.

"She had the right idea, didn't she?"

"Which one, mirroring Sidra or destroying the lightning rod?"

"Both."

Suddenly, a look of shock crossed his face. He was staring at the Tau, clearly startled by it, and took a step back, his lip curling in derision.

I straightened, suddenly emboldened by Kanya's courageous act and the reacquisition of the Tau. If religious symbols were a tangible representation of something invisible, as Volden had mused, then perhaps the Tau possessed a similar quality. Maybe Anubis, the lightning rod—hell, Spiraplex itself—were nothing more than physical conduits of something invisible. Something *other*. Well, whatever the Tau was representing, Volden didn't seem to like it.

He spat. "You think you can beat us with *that*?"

"I don't know." I shrugged. "But it couldn't hurt."

He looked up as the sky exploded, bathing the rooftop in scalding light. Once again, the Invisibles sprang to life in my seeing. The atmosphere was teeming with them. An orgy of animalistic fury swirled around us. We were at the pinnacle of their hellish inferno. And that's when I saw him. The monstrosity that was Soren Volden.

A bloated black mass—that's all he was. A puncture in space, an amorphous fissure ringed with teeth. A seething bloody aperture that had long ago collapsed. A black hole filled with endless craving. Soren Volden. Summu Nura. The Lightless One.

The vision was so peculiar, so hideous, that for a moment, I just stood enthralled. This little man, this billionaire jet-setting shrimp, was... *that*? I almost wanted to laugh. Until the lightning sizzled and dissipated, and a clear snap sounded, followed by a twanging sound. I turned to see that one of the cables that held the lightning rod in place had sprung free.

*Bernard!*

In that split, chaotic second, while Volden watched the lightning rod teeter slightly from its moorings in the deluge, I lunged toward the platform. Volden yelled from behind me. I slipped and, as I was falling forward, managed to dive behind the base of the lightning rod, skimming head first into the nearby scaffolding. As I did, I felt the passing whoosh of a round of sonar shells.

I flopped around, squirreled under the scaffolding, and came up the opposite side. Volden hustled around the platform, cursing. He seemed to be struggling with the weapon. You'd think a man of his stature would have had his weapons custom fitted. Then again, maybe he figured he'd never have to use them. He heaved the rifle my way and, as he did, I clambered up the scaffolding. But he swung wide and the bullets pounded past, spraying out over the city. If he managed to really aim that thing, I was toast. Or mud.

The lightning rod was 10 feet away, rising opposite the scaffolding. I was perhaps five or six feet off the ground, grappling to hang on to the slippery metal crossbeams. I could see Volden laboring with the rifle. So I quickly scaled another section. For the briefest moment, I glimpsed the lights of the city below through the cloudy veil.

Then Volden cried out. I turned as the rifle sounded. As I leapt toward the lightning rod, the scaffolding exploded in a hail of crossbeams, braces, and pins. Volden shouted something and dodged the raining debris. I struck the lightning rod, but was unable to take hold. I slipped and crashed onto the platform below. If I hadn't separated my shoulder striking the Star of Anu, I'd definitely fractured my ass-bone in the fall. I hoisted myself up, teetered on the platform, and gripped the lightning rod precariously with one hand. The wind whipped by, nearly yanking me from this perch.

As I grappled for footing, Volden skidded into the open and raised his weapon. Yet as he fired, he quickly jerked the gun away and cursed. And I knew exactly why.

He could not shoot me without potentially destroying the lightning rod.

At its base, the Star of Anu was the width of a telephone pole, hardly wide enough to conceal me, but big enough that to shoot me would be to damage the rod itself.

"Damn you, Moon!" Volden glared at me, his hair dripping into his face. "Don't make me go up there to get you."

But I was too busy thinking about Bernard fending off the Invisibles while trying to bring down this Babylonian skywire. The severing of the tension cable had left the rod tilted disproportionately to one side. Maybe I could give it a hand.

I pulled myself up on the lightning rod, leveraged the lower half of my body, and began working the rod my direction, using my weight in an attempt to topple it. It swayed, slowly at first, then with wider and wider gyrations. Volden was babbling something. He was having a hard time ascending the slippery platform and maintaining his grip on the rifle. He stopped down below, at the first tier of the platform. As he aimed the rifle, I swung the opposite way, shielding myself once again from a good shot.

He cursed. This time, I responded with a laugh. The kind of mocking response a schoolboy might issue when missed by the dodgeball. Madness seemed to possess me. What else did I have to lose? I'd lost Ellie. Broken my promises to Matisse. Walked straight into a trap set for me. Led Kanya to her death. And even if I managed to escape, I was still being sought for murder. So I laughed. And shook the rod more violently.

Interestingly enough, the change of angle on the rod seemed to have created a counter rhythm. The rod started to creak and groan.

"C'mon!" I pulled harder and harder. "C'mon, you son-of-a-bitch!"

*Twnng!*

Another line snapped and went zipping through the rain-soaked air. Now only one cable held the fabled lightning rod of the Tower of Babel in place. Volden fired and the sound nodule bore through the rain to my right. He fired a second time, this shot being even further off the mark. He was forced to shoot wide. He could see his beloved game was coming to a close.

I laughed and leaned into the rod with such force that the final line snapped. The rod groaned forward and I pressed myself into it. My entire body lay upon that ancient thing. I let loose a triumphant shout. It was rather foolish of me, seeing that I'd only prevented Volden from succeeding for the moment. As the rod sagged to the ground, tipping over its pedestal, I embraced it with both arms, hugging it as it toppled to the rooftop.

Suddenly, a flash of blue cobalt washed the sky. Before I had time to realize what was happening—and that I was stretched across a lightning rod at the epicenter of the worst electrical storm of the century—the atmosphere exploded around me. White light, dazzling, lit the rooftop like a nuclear detonation. The last thing I remember seeing was Soren Volden, his eyes wide, fighting to keep from falling backwards, gaping in maniacal horror at this explosion.

The rod hummed with energy, an immense conductor of the fire gods' wrath. I didn't have a chance to scream. Sparks exploded around me. My jaw clenched so tightly I could feel my molars on the verge of being pulverized in their sockets. Letting go was impossible. The electric surge fused my flesh to the primeval rod. My body straightened and my back arched in agony. The air sizzled around me, my field of vision reduced to a condensed pinprick of high-voltage agony. My chest burned like molten lava. The smell of burnt flesh filled my nostrils. But I could not retreat. Even if I'd wanted to run, I couldn't. It was as if the fury of that storm was funneled into that single strike.

They say that, at the moment of death, your life flashes before your eyes. I'd written such a thing a dozen times in sensationalistic articles for the Blue Crescent. Perhaps that is true for many. But I hardly had such a panoramic view of my own life. At one time, I'm sure it would have been a singular feeling of regret that my life had been such a waste, so full of disappointment and unopened gifts and promises. However, in that moment, I felt like I'd finally accomplished something. *He was struck by lightning trying to avenge his father's death and prevent some monster from opening Pandora's Box.* That's how the headline would read.

My father would have been proud.

Ellie would have laughed with joy.

Mattisse would have clapped his hands and exclaimed "Bravo, Mr. Moon!"

Even Kanya would have conceded a smile.

But instead of a blissful exit into the afterlife, heat shredded my temples, coursing through my fingertips. My eyeballs seemed to be melting in their sockets. Every cell in my body screamed, wrought with the energy of nature. The crackle of voltage rose all around me, a deafening vibrato. The smell of flesh and smoldering fabric was overwhelming.

The rod continued tipping to the rooftop in slow-motion. Only now it was laced with electric veins. If my jaw wasn't locked tight, I'd have bitten my tongue off. Power surged through me, spiking my body to the ancient structure. I had no choice but to endure its onslaught. The sound roared around me.

I briefly glimpsed Volden, in his human state. His large eyes gaped in terror. And then there were the Invisibles, the horde of hungry denizens. They too witnessed the fiery unfolding. But it wasn't glee in their eyes I saw. It wasn't the triumph of forces that had wrought some great victory. It was horror.

If it wasn't for this awareness, the revelation that Volden and his Summu Nurian pals were shit-faced, the fiery pain in my chest would have consumed me.

Then a great whoosh sounded. The blinding energy seemed to coalesce inside me, draw down into a single condensed heartbeat, and implode. I was catapulted off the ancient lightning rod as it exploded into a million pieces.

I struck something hard, and then everything went black.

I wasn't out for long, maybe only seconds. I awoke with a gasp. Rain pelted my face. I was crumbled against one of the parapets. Lightning flashed, but it seemed more distant. As if the storm was fleeing. Through the wedge of shadows I could make out one of the sphinxes silhouetted against the sky. The rain provided no respite from the pain seething through my body. I tried to move, to gather myself, but I had no control over my limbs.

Though I couldn't see him, I knew Volden was nearby. I also knew he was now no threat. It was more than intuition or deduction that led me to this belief. Something else had happened inside me. An alignment. An odd déjà vu that was less a moment than a haunting realization.

The future had met me here.

And the world as I knew it, would never be the same.

I managed to sit up. From here, I could see Kanya lying still in a pool of blood. My chest was on fire. My shirt hung in tatters on my upper body, smoldering. I reached up, searching for the twine of the crucifix. The Tau was gone. It'd probably been burned up in the strike. I gripped my chest, grimacing at the smell of flesh. The Tau must have grounded the lightning, preventing the electricity from reaching its destination inside Spiraplex.

I staggered to my feet. My limbs were rubberized, my eyes still fighting to adjust. Everything felt weird. My movements. My awareness of the environment. The pattering of the rain, the smoldering embers from the splintered lightning rod. It was as if the atmosphere was alive, kindled with a newfound glory and unfolding in slow motion.

And there was Soren Volden lying at the base of the platform amidst debris from the exploded rod, lifeless. Impaled by the Star of Anu.

# CHAPTER 36

THEY WERE DYING. ALL OF THEM.

Staring at the steaming body of Soren Volden, the hexagram from the lightning rod flaying his chest, I knew that Ellie was now freed. She'd always said she felt out of place, that this world was not her home. It was my selfishness that wanted her to stay. Now I had no choice but to release her. Volden was another story. Did he join the Invisibles in their Danse Macabre? Or go back to the Black Council to plot their next takeover? Either way, by the looks of *this* body, its gaping chest cavity and its smoldering flesh, I guessed he'd have to start shopping for a new model.

With his passing, they were all free—free to move on to their destinies. Despite Volden's grandiosity, they had never been his children. They were his prisoners. And I was glad to have played a part in reversing their fortunes.

Two things happened in that moment that will forever remain connected in my thinking: The strange chill had returned to my hands and I realized that, somehow, it was meant for Kanya.

I turned to locate her body. She lay in a watery pool of blood. Her hair was plastered to one side of her head. A trace of eyeliner bled down each cheek like black tears. I hurried to her, bent over her. She was not breathing. There was no sign of life. *God, no!* I remembered Matisse's final words to me, to tell her he loved her. But now...

My hands were throbbing.

I raised them before me. I hadn't expected my hands to be transparent, but seeing them that way was not a complete shock. Not after everything else I'd seen the last 48 hours. More accurately, my *flesh* was transparent, as if the skin of my hand had been peeled back like a glove revealing the circulatory system, a tight network of veins, and the faint outline of musculature.

And blue electricity.

It was hard to tell whether my eyes were seeing through my flesh, like some kind of built-in X-ray specs, or whether a physical phenomenon was occurring in my body. Whatever the case, I knew that the pain wasn't from this oddity. It was as if the static charge of the lightning was bleeding through my fingertips and I was leaking electrons.

Something was passing through me, some energy. The electric charges that I'd seen through Rival's Curtain were now visible to my naked eye. Fiery blue tentacles danced from my skeletal fingertips, illuminating Kanya's body in its warm glow.

The air seemed to thicken again, as it did before the lightning strikes. Every molecule felt charged.

I stared at my hands, turning them over and back.

Then I looked at Kanya lying there. She had offered her life for me, to bring me the Tau.

And everything came together. Intersected.

I placed one hand over her wound, just above her left breast.

It's difficult to explain what I was feeling at that moment. I'd let so many people down. Begrudgingly descended to the lowest common denominator. Listened way too much to my inner cynic. But something had been awakened in me. *Seventh Guardian of the Imperia.* Could it be? Could it possibly be? My father. Ellie. Always nudging me toward something greater. And there wasn't much greater than being part of some mythical cosmic crime fighting ring.

The electrical charge fluttered, like a neon anemone reacting to an undersea intruder. I pressed my hand to her body.

Perhaps it was my own emotions producing this phenomenon.

Could I be, somehow, generating this bizarre electrical field? If I was, it seemed to find connection in her.

Currents webbed from my fingertips, braiding their way up her shoulder and into her heart. Radiating into her entire being.

The regrets. The anger. I could feel the same things in her. She was not lying when she'd said she wished she could start over.

"Kanya," I said, staring expectantly into her lifeless face. "You said you wanted a second chance. Remember?"

Somewhere in the distance, thunder rumbled.

She did not move.

Words were forming in my mind. Tongues and commands that transcended my logic. Formulas and equations seemed to bubble to life in my brain. I was not a scientific prodigy by any stretch. Yet part of me was acutely aware of air density, chemical interactions between my body and hers, and the loopholes of Newtonian physics. It was as if the curtain of my subconscious mind had been drawn back, accessing a minutia of virgin information. And more. We were more than just a complex switchboard of neurons and secretions. I was an idiot to have ever believed such nonsense. Watching her lying there, lifeless, I knew this was not how it should be. Or, at least, I knew that I had the power to change things.

I brought my opposite hand around and placed it on top of the other.

The electrical current glowed, resonating across her chest, scrabbling into her nerves and muscles. Into her mind.

My chest was burning! My hands were freezing! I wanted to cry out. But somehow the pain was itself healing. Everything seemed to condense in that moment and in that connection between me and Kanya. The patter of the rain, the swirling wind, the distant thunder. It all stopped. And in my mind, we were alone.

Completely.

Alone.

I was studying her face, almost bemused at the spindly blue currents webbing her upper body, when her eyes fluttered and opened. She lurched upright with a great gasp.

I tumbled back and landed on my rear. The glow faded from my hands and, as I watched, so did their translucence. The veins and skeletal joints gave way to flesh. And with it went the chill.

Whatever had happened, we were both returning to normal.

She sat momentarily dumfounded. The rain streaked her face. I sat captivated by her. At that moment, all her guards were down. She had a look of pure innocence. Of peace. I smiled slightly. She focused on me. Then she furrowed her brow, studying my face. As if she were trying to recollect our relationship.

Then it all returned to her.

Kanya struggled to her feet. She clutched at her chest, where the wound was, and wavered. I scrambled upward and took hold of her shoulders to steady her.

She wrestled free of my grip and surveyed the rooftop.

"Volden," she said.

"He's dead." I pointed toward his charred remains. "And the lightning rod, it's... destroyed."

She stared, scanning the debris field littered with the remains of the Star of Anu, and then hung her head. Breathing. Thinking.

"Sidra," Kanya finally said. "She... I had to..." She looked up at me and stopped. Her eyes widened. "What happened?"

She was staring at my chest.

"The Tau," I said. "It stopped the lightning. It kept the ghost box from happening. It burned up."

"No." She peered forward, her eyes wide. "No it didn't. It's..."

I made a face and looked down at my chest. Closer. *It couldn't be!* I tore the shreds of my shirt open to see that the Tau was not gone as I'd thought.

It was... *inside me.*

Under my skin.

Fused in place at my breastbone.

I reached up and touched the scar. It burned. Pale webs formed the silhouette of the cross imprinted on my chest. It sparkled like it had when I'd first studied it in my apartment.

They called them *Lichtenberg figures*. I'd read that somewhere.

The elaborate webbed scar emblazoned upon survivors of lightning strikes. Named after a German physicist. Lightning trees with branches. This one was a great oak that sent arms out across my pectoral muscles and down my stomach.

In the shape of a Tau.

She followed my gaze. Then she looked at me. Her eyes were full of wonder. But I didn't give her a chance to respond.

"C'mon." I took her hand and led her to the elevator. "There's something else I have to do."

I pushed the button for the Lower Level. The lights flicked on and off at the elevator entrance and I worried that the entire building had been short-circuited by the lightning strike. However, the elevator door opened.

Before I stepped in, I turned back to look upon the carnage of the rooftop scene. But the wreckage was not what caught my eye. It was the burnished glow of the angel, standing on one of the parapets looking down upon me. Yet Bernard hardly appeared in concrete material density. He remained another order of being, his torso still possessing a semi-translucent brilliance. It was my *seeing*, my visual acumen, that had changed. I was seeing him—no, I was seeing the whole world—through new eyes.

Bernard folded his arms and smiled down on me rather proudly. I mouthed the words, "Thank you," to which the angel responded by shaking his head and pointing to me. I shrugged sheepishly.

The elevators doors closed and we descended to the bowels of Spiraplex.

It was good to get out of the rain. Pools of water formed at our feet. But my body continued to tingle at the thought of what awaited me. I traced the awful scar now embedded in my chest. As I did, I glanced at Kanya as she pressed her hand over her own wound. It had been healed. There was nothing there.

She was pondering what had just happened.

She wanted to say something.

She had a lot to say.

But not now.

The elevator skidded to a rough stop at the lower level. The lights flickered and the door opened. I steadied myself and then peeked my head out. The lights blinked on and off, but the corridor was empty. I turned back to her. There was no fear or hesitation in her eyes. Apparently, she had come back the same person she always was. Maybe more.

I smiled, waved her on, and turned the corner. We ran down the hallway together.

The doors retracted to the cryo-chamber as we approached. The torches still burned on each side of the temple structure. Yet the green glow that had encased the cryo-tubes was now gone. I did not stop, but ran straight down the center aisle toward the triangular opening. I ducked and entered. Kanya's footsteps were right behind me. The two Cosmagon were lying in a lifeless, bloodless heap, their heads and limbs wrenched into disconcerting angles. I ran to the steps and stopped.

Off to the side, a mass of beetles encased a humanoid form. I could hear their fevered desiccation, chewing away at this delicacy. It was nothing more than curiosity that led me there. Sidra's body lay half eaten. The tattoo on her forearm was the only identifying feature.

I looked back at Kanya, but she was looking at Ellie.

Ellie floated lifelessly, just as she had when I'd first seen her. But now there was a look of peace on her face.

The water inside the cryotube had passed from green to dirty sea foam. Droplets of moisture pattered the floor around the cryo-tubes. The chambers were assuming room temperature. I approached the glass, wiped away the condensation, and looked up at her. She had great hair. Always did. It wafted in the gentle current. Her body was beginning to curl in upon itself, as if she were sleeping. Fetal-like.

I spread my hands on the glass.

There was no electrical charge. No phenomenon to accompany my touch as there had been with Kanya. Ellie was beyond any power I might possess. And I knew this was as it should be.

"Ellie," I said, unconcerned about Kanya. "I took care of it—the

Tau. Just like you said. Kanya helped. And her father. And now—" I reached up and touched the lightning-fused scar. "Now it'll always be with me."

I studied her face. How many times I'd seen it glow with childlike curiosity. To her, the world was full of wonder. Apparently, she was right about that.

"I—I don't know if you loved me. I don't blame you if you didn't. But I loved you. I loved you, Ellie. And nothing can change that." I leaned my forehead against the cryo-tube. "Nothing can change that."

*Who you are isn't all you can be.*

I straightened. I looked up at her serene face. She'd been right about that. I was never all I could be. And now I could be so much more.

I stepped away from the tube. Even though her eyes were closed, I knew she was watching. I knew she was aware of me.

"Ellie," I said. "I... I believe."

In the right setting, that admission would have meant more. But here, now, after everything I'd witnessed, it was just too obvious.

The storm had given me gifts. Kanya was a reminder of that. If I was called to protect the Tau, and it was cauterized inside me, then staying alive was the only way to accomplish my mission. Call it a hard bargain.

The doors to the temple burst open. Jimmy Pastorelli stood there. Half the LAPD was with him. Men in SWAT gear swarmed into the place, leveling guns at us.

Jimmy studied the interior of the temple, the torches, the throne, the dead Cosmagon, the scarabs enjoying their meal, and Ellie floating in the cryo-tube. He stood, mouth agape. Then he lowered his revolver and looked at me.

"Holy shit," was the only thing he could manage to say.

# CHAPTER 37

I KNOCKED ON THE DOOR JAMB. "It's the story you wanted, isn't it?"

Arlette swiveled away from her computer screen. "Oh, yeah."

The latest edition of the Blue Crescent lay on her desk. She picked it up and said, "They're flying off the shelves. Neville's starting a second print. Everybody's buzzing about it. Social media. Press corps. It's gone viral. So, yeah, it's the story I wanted."

If Arlette was satisfied, I knew it had to be good.

"But, one thing." She put the paper down. "Some of it's kinda, hm—far-fetched."

"Just *some* of it?"

"Yeah. It's hard enough believing that lightning actually struck that old rod. But believing that it exploded and the star just happened to stab Volden right in the heart. Now that's just... out there."

I raised an eyebrow. "So the part about him being an astral vampire is *believable*?"

She shook her head, then turned and smiled at me. "You outdid yourself this time, Moon. We got the story every news outlet is dying for. And from an eye witness." She read from the headline: "*Eccentric Billionaire Struck by Lightning Atop Modernday Tower of Babel.* Wow! What can I say? You're the man."

"Ha! Does this mean I don't ever have to go back to the Hollywood Crypt?"

She laughed. "After they tear apart Spiraplex, who knows what other goodies there'll be to report on? They tracked some of his security squad, the... what'd you call them?"

"Cosmagon."

"Yeah. En route from Moscow to Ulaanbaatar. Heading into the Mongolian Hinterlands, apparently. Wouldn't surrender. A big firefight broke out in the terminal. They all died. I guess a couple others took their own lives rather than getting nabbed. Apparently, whatever they know about Volden'll remain a secret. As for the rest of his staff, they're all pleading innocence of malfeasance. He kept them all in the dark... or so they say."

She put the paper down. Her demeanor softened significantly. "I'm sorry I didn't trust you."

I brushed off her apology. Besides, I hadn't told her everything. Rival's Curtain. Bernard. The Tau burned into my chest. Sure, she got a good story. It just wasn't the *whole* story.

As I prepared to leave, she met me at the door. She stood awfully close. I could smell the starch in her shirt. And her almond perfume. Arlette had great lips. Have I said that? She put her hand on my forearm.

"Thanks for putting up with me," she said.

I cast a wry smile. "Ditto, boss."

The Cammy was parked in the alley. I headed back to my apartment, determined to take a much-needed break. I was still aching all over. Now that Volden's ring had been exposed, we'd be burying Ellie again, this time without an empty casket. It was weird, but I had a peace about it this time. No regrets. Somehow I'd come full circle. I'd gotten a reprieve. I'd seen her face, said goodbye. And with everything I knew about Ellie, and the weird new world I inhabited, I was convinced she was not far away.

My cell phone rang, startling me from my thoughts. It was Kanya.

"I saw your story."

"And?" I asked.

"It was a little undercooked."

"What do you mean?"

"Well, for one, you didn't say anything about Bernard."

"I'm saving it for my memoirs."

"And you made it sound like you believe Babel was some ancient myth."

"Now you sound like your father."

"Well do you?" she asked.

"Hm. Sometimes it's better to keep your personal beliefs out of the story, you know?"

"I'll take that as a yes," she said. "So what'll they do with the technology? The M-graph, the cryo-tubes?"

"I don't know. But if the government figures it out, I'm pretty sure Armageddon's not far away. So you're recuperating?"

"Not much to recuperate from. Whatever you did, I'm better."

I thought about that night, my translucent hands, and the blue electricity that had surged through my fingertips. It'd been several days since the event, and I hadn't experienced it again. Nothing close. Apart from acute insomnia, a newfound preoccupation with quantum realities, and a strange scar webbed across my torso, things were back to normal.

Sort of.

"Hey," she said. "You still there?"

"Yeah. I'm just not exactly sure *what* I did."

"Well, maybe I'm not gonna be the only freak around here now."

"You never were."

The line grew quiet on her end this time.

Then Kanya said, "He told me to watch out for you."

"Who?"

"My father. Don't you remember?"

"Oh, yeah. Well, being that I promised him I'd keep an eye on the Asylum, you'll probably have plenty of opportunity to do just that. Besides, I still need an Unnamed Source."

"Well, I'll never be able to fill his shoes."

"This is true," I said. "And, hey."

"Yeah?"

"Sometime you're going to have to tell me how a Jesuit priest got a shapeshifter for a daughter."

It was somewhat forward of me. But seeing we'd saved each other's lives, I figured we were past niceties.

"Yeah," she said. "Maybe sometime I will."

We hung up. But not before I made a mental note to drop by the Asylum and find a way to invite her to sample my Mexican omelet recipe. Followed by a trip to the Santa Monica pier and happy hour at the Chaparral Lounge.

The storm had left the city with sunshine, blue skies, and air as clean and crisp as I could remember in Los Angeles. Burned your nostrils to inhale it. Hard to tell what other things, if any, still occupied the cracks and crevices of the city. Were the Invisibles still lurking nearby? Was the Black Council planning a surprise attack? And what about Bernard? Was he still watching out for me?

My gut told me that the possibilities were now endless.

I'd spent too much time trying to debunk what I couldn't disprove and defend what I wasn't sure of. The only thing I was sure of now was that the world was a hell of a lot bigger place than I once hoped.

Whatever the lightning had done to me I'd have to learn on the fly. There were no manuals, as far as I knew, about what it meant to be the Seventh Guardian of the Imperia. And I was pretty sure that patterning myself after Gandalf would not be a good way to go about this. I'd been imparted with something. But calling it *magic*, well, that didn't seem right.

I kept the shard from Rival's Curtain in a safe place—the artillery box where I'd kept the Tau at the base of the lamppost in my bedroom. Okay. Not the *safest* place. Maybe just the most inconspicuous. Either way, I had a hunch that the crystalline wedge would come in handy some day. I added two more deadbolts to my apartment door. And thanks to Klammer's cash, I was ahead on rent and the pantry was full. Life was good.

Amidst all the recent events, I'd almost forgotten to clean up the mess I'd left at Mrs. Richardson's place. In the interim, Chelsea had missed a couple meals, which probably did her some good. Once I returned, I planned on getting Mrs. Richardson's kitchen back in order. I might be crude and rude and totally asocial when necessary. But may it not be said that Reagan Moon does not fulfill his obligations.

However, when I arrived at my apartment, I found the door

unlocked.

So much for another deadbolt.

I did not enter right away. I stood there for a moment and let my senses calibrate. It was an odd feeling. Part cognition, part precognition, and part street smarts. Between Rival's Curtain, the Tau, and the lightning strike, I'd had a few screws added to the collection, some tightened, some loosened, and some waiting for a matching combo.

The slightest tingle passed through my hands, a fleeting chill that made my heart leap. I looked at my hands, but there was nothing unusual. The feeling subsided.

Then came the sense I wasn't in danger.

I pushed open the door. Blondie stood at the roll top desk, studying the genie's cube.

"Hey," I said, tossing my keys on the desk. "Careful with that."

He grunted and returned it to its spot next to a sketchbook. I'd began chronicling the various forms of Invisibles I'd seen during my brief escapade, from grubs to cytomorphs, and all the exotica in between. Like Lewis and Clark, I too should leave a record of my expedition.

I jabbed my thumb toward the apartment door. "So how did you manage that?"

He tapped his temple with two fingers.

I furrowed my brow. I wasn't about to believe a man his size needed to be telekinetic.

"By the way," I said. "I never thanked you for rescuing me from Sidra."

"Just doing my job," he said without emotion.

"Course, I think you crushed my larynx. But other than that..."

He looked around the apartment. I could sense something in his demeanor. Something much less hostile and impersonal. He looked squarely at me.

"My boss has another job for you."

"Huh? That one wasn't enough?"

He sighed deeply, shifted his weight, and folded his hands at his waist.

*Believe big*. I looked at the picture of Ellie on the desk. *Who you are isn't all you can be.*

I reached up and touched the scar on my chest.

Then I shrugged. "Sure. What do I have to lose?"

THE END